From the Files of the Department of the Arcane:

Summer Sacrifice

As Revealed By:
S.C. Houff

Summer Sacrifice
©2015 Shannon Carroll

Self published edition 2016

Grammar-mancer: Rebekah McGrady
Cover design: S. C. Houff
Cover Art: S.C. Houff
D. O. A. Logo: Oddite Delight Designs

ISBN 0692576452
ISBN-13: 9780692576458

Printed by CreateSpace

THANKS GOES OUT TO....

Evil Bekka who makes me look smarter than I am.

Jeff who laughs at my jokes.

Hal for being Hal

Offered at tribute to the memory of my mother.

Sing to me, Oh Muse.

My Ancestors stand at my back to push me forward.

Thy Angel sits at my side to offer its wisdom

And at my fingers dance my song to live by.

Give me the strength to share thy story.

CONTENTS

DATE: 7/7/1977

FILE #: WJC-4-xxx-Lemon

ORIGIN: Watauga

AGENT ON FILE: M. Shuller

Badge #: CJ-89-7xx3

DOCUMENT TYPE: Field Report

Doctor Duke, Esteemed and wise Burgesses and so on, below you will find the report of what we know so far on the being that you refer to as the She Wolf and the handling of her captivity by Lord Blackmore, Hound to the Prince of Franklin. The Department was contracted to do some work on this subject, as such below you will find our report on the matter.

Reason for Report

As some of you may be more than aware, The Carter County Chamber of Congress as well as the Historical society of Hampton have requested the use of certain lands that belong to Virgil Blackmore as a part of their heritage. While there is some sort of amusement from Byron Crowe with heritage sites (a transcripts of our interview with Mr. Crowe will be attached once we have been able to edit the language to acceptable standards. Agent Schuller informs us that his words are of a "rustic" nature) we understand that there are some financial gains that could not only benefit the Blackmores but also the community at large. It is for this reason we have sent Agent Shuller along with Carter Lewis to investigate the benefits of this and offer recommendations.

Background

Generally, the enterprises of the vampiric world is not the basic concern of the Department of the Arcane. We know that many industries have been headed and founded by vampires but we are in a more perilous situation regarding the Blackmore Estate. Why this matter comes to the Department of the Arcane is because of a concern of a particular resident on the Blackmore Estate. Lord Blackmore has been entrusted with the keeping of the former queen of the Vampires of Gaiman Heights only known as the She Wolf. While we know that the She Wolf has been bound and imprisoned behind a layer of several different types of locks we are hesitating to completely sign off on this matter because of a twofold concern.

First (1) we know that the She Wolf is a very powerful creature which has an amazing pull on various different creatures. She as the ability to control minds and we are concerned that she might use these skills to be used on unsuspecting members of the general population to the disastrous ends that a small area such as Hamptons and Carter County will not be able to handle. Sighted on this is the incident of Sacred Oaks which led to the devastating death of 30 inmates, security guards and the warden. We have yet to completely assess what has been completely lost from this event. Furthermore, despite the locks that have been placed on the She Wolf we are more than aware that Lord Blackmore is one of the She Wolf's offspring. We are concerned with her control on the man who is trusted to guard her cell.

Second (2) we worry that as the vampires would be running this event that there would be a chance that the veil itself would be in danger as well as the fact that there are several different species who would like to see there be some sort of danger to the She Wolf as well as well as the Blackmores. We are concerned for the safety of the mundane visitors but we know that with our involvement that very little will happen. Our concern is the She Wolf herself.

The She Wolf has been housed on the Blackmore estate for quite some time and has been as the House of Burgess. She is currently awaiting a time in which she would be permitted to be put to death without any true concern from opposition from the vampiric peoples. She is currently serving a sentence for her role in the Massacre of the Amber Moon.

The Massacre of the Amber Moon

For many people this is the single most horrible moment in the lives of Gaiman Heights. On June 13, 1919 saw a full moon on a Friday the 13th. While this in itself this is not significant, it does come as often as possible this was something called a Honey Moon. A honey moon is when the color of the moon is a soft yellow and it is full. This is a highly religious time for both Witches and Werewolves. While both groups had been somewhat awkward relationship between both groups. When the covens and the tribes of wolves finally admitted to the alliance they celebrated an opening feast on the full moon. Many people were fine with this except for the She-Wolf. Her inability to trust her enemies believed that this wasn't so much a peaceful gathering but an effort to attempt murder her kind.

At the first Gathering of Luna the soldiers known as the Acadian Guard (the She Wolf's loyal first line of soldiers) set out and executed every man, woman and child who was at the gathering. What was sworn was a single handed blood battle between the Tribes of wolves to see the She Wolf dead. This has not been satisfied due to her imprisonment at the beginning of the

1960s. This led to the Vampiric House of Burgess to distance themselves from the reign of the She Wolf. As such they denounced the She Wolf and backed a second candidate Prudence Goodchild to become queen. What they started was a bloody and violent war in Gaiman Heights.

Who is the She Wolf?

As we are not sure when someone will be reading this report and we suspect that many people within the Department might not be able to be aware of the She Wolf as she might be quite old and we might have working memories of the She Wolf. Below are a few things that we are able to confirm about the She-Wolf.

A. The She Wolf is an Old World Vampire. Whether she was embraced in this country or back in Europe is irrelevant. She is an old world creature. This seems very unusual for those of us who don't deal in dynasties. For vampires, age is very important and origin as well. We know that she is from Europe. This means that she hold on to a few notions that should help you understand where she is coming from. When the New World opened up this created a unique situation for vampires who had no fiefdom but desired to be king so they immigrated to the New World. The She Wolf is one of these creatures which means she doesn't believe in cooperating for a new society and believes in the superiority of her own kind over mundane.

B. Despite the over ruling of her position by the House of Burgess there are people who still believe that she is Queen. No matter what you think of her, the She Wolf does have a loyal group of followers. Many of these served as her personal army which she called the Acadian Guard. The members of this group have long since been hidden from the streets of the city and becomes a mystery. This doesn't mean that there aren't people who will not assist on her being liberated. It is why extreme care must be taken when it comes to the She Wolf. If she were to be able to gain an upper hand and return to the city we would be in the throes of a war that the Department could not even imagine to be able to handle.

C. She has yet to be found guilty. The council of justice is still struggling to figure out what her crimes are. There are many who that agree with her methods. Until they are able to figure that out we will be holding her in a sentence to be brought to her at a future date.

Prison

The She Wolf is currently in a large stone coffin. The relic is made of North Italian marble and built with unusual markings around the edge. We have yet to get out experts to tell us where the language comes from. At this time we consider the runes to in the unspeakable tongue. The origins of this box are difficult to pin point as the origins and historic records do no match. The Lewis Clan have refused to tell us where they acquired this prison. They will simply say that it came to them as a gift from after the War. We can only assume that this comes from less than reputable origins but we cannot confirm nor deny this. As the origins are clouded in mystery we at the Department have chosen to take matters into our own hands. Around this box is blessed iron chain that has been seen by a variety of holy men and women. This locks on these chains cannot be broken without the bloodiest of black magic. She has also been housed in a small cave that sits in the middle of the Blackmore family cemetery which upon inspection has been collected around some of the angriest of spirits. If there is someone is willing to go into this cemetery which we have been informed will be off limits to the mundane visitors then they will have a very difficult time.

Recommendations

At this time we are concerned with what the She Wolf might do but we recommend that the Department maintain contact with the Blackmores and regular investigations on her cell until there is such a time that she will be removed from this plane of existence.

"But the Almighty Lord hath stuck him and delivered him to the hands of a woman."

Judith 16:7

I.   **The She Wolf**

1962

Despite what most Europeans think of American history, there are a great many things that are very old in the United States. In fact, American history itself is quite old when we include the tribes of the first people in this fine country, but that's not what most people think of when they think American history, which is a shame because that history is very important. The United States, as a nation, isn't very old and that's reflected in the opinions of some (not all -- I'm not fond of sweeping generalizations) of our European cousins. These opinions don't mean that there aren't parts of history in the Americas that are not every bit as old as their parallels in European history or even the people who were involved in them. These old things are a part of the very fabric of our country. It is our cousins in the Old World's tendency to use their influence to place blame in this matter on the old things in this country. We are, except for native peoples who were quite happy with their country before we arrived, a nation of immigrants and our culture reflects as such even in the archaic world of the supernatural. This is most evident in the city of Gaiman Heights which is the center of the supernatural world in the modern era. The city had become a refuge point for those who had left their homelands to find a new world and somehow mixed their old traditions with new ones.

While some of these arrivals are quite new to this place, the citizens of the veil have been a part of this changing country since the beginning. The Magi will tell you who, in the fight for independence, was one of their own, the witches will tell you that they were the first abolitionists and two fairies will lay claim to have fired the Shot Heard Around The World. Despite being of different nationalities and species, these new residents all felt strongly in favor of their new homeland. It was a place where they could, for once, not hide in the shadows of nightmares and to breathe (or in some cases, not breathe) a free air. Some of these creatures felt strongly that they had become the cornerstones of America. This is exceedingly true for the ancient, yet forever youthful Queen of the Vampires in Gaiman Heights.

Prudence Goodchild had the unpleasant distinction of being the first vampire to be created in the New World. Her story paralleled that of America and its birth and youth as a country. Prudence had been born into a Puritan community in the Netherlands eight years before her death. She spoke English at home back then, but much preferred the Dutch language which was spoken by the people around them and the children in the commune. This was a shameful thing for her father who had been convinced that God only spoke English. She was reprimanded for it, but even as a child Prudence was a bit of a rebel. She often wondered if she would still be a part of the colony or whether she would have moved somewhere like Rhode Island had she made it to adulthood. She often resolved these musings with the conviction that she would have grown up to become the fat wife of a Flemish banker, which would have made her quite happy. Her biological father would have been displeased. If her biological father had had anything to say about it that would never have happened. He had been busy praying for a miracle to save his child.

Then that miracle had occurred. The stories of the success of their brothers and sisters in Plymouth gave her father hope that they too could build a City on the Hill. His family could be saved from becoming Dutch. Robert Goodchild moved quickly. Within months he had commissioned a vessel and uprooted his wife and child -- along with anyone else from their congregation who could pay to come. Across the unforgiving waves of the Atlantic they had sought their home in the New World. When they finally docked, they settled in the Gaihaim Valley as the natives called it. In the fertile bosom of this strange land they had made their home in Harmony. Her father had felt good about this land. He said he could feel the strength of Christ running through the ground. Prudence would later find out that it wasn't so much Christ as it was the nexus -- a focal point of amazing magical power that had seeped into the ground. It would draw more than her family there eventually, but not in those days. In those days, she enjoyed her childhood. It wasn't always strict and repressive. Prudence had the carefree and pious life that was afforded to someone who was a Puritan. She then fell ill like so many that winter who came to the Boston Colony. She fully expected that she would die that winter. That had been before her other father shared his love with her. She had been granted the gift of immortality out of the Christian compassion and love that one George Trublood had for Prudence's family. The world's first Puritan vampire had wanted to spare her family the pain of burying a child.

Prudence, however, did eat her parents first when she woke up from death's embrace.

The human life of Prudence Goodchild was very far away from where she was now. It was a distant memory that haunted the back of her mind as she sat in the carriage passing quickly through the night down twisting country roads. Prudence Goodchild was not the girl who had shut her eyes in Harmony all those years ago. She was something new and terrifying. Prudence was unusual even for vampires. Many had hoped and expected her to remain nine-years-old. It would be easier to brush her off as a peer if she had remained mentally childlike. It was a false hope as parts of her brain had matured faster than the rest of her even before her death, and afterwards she continued her habits of methodical problem-solving and quick learning until her mind had reached a point where she could retain substantial knowledge and become wiser than her appearance. Prudence had matured and aged mentally into an intelligent young lady while her body had retained the qualities characteristic of a small child from the seventeenth century.

Prudence had a great many skills that she had honed over the years. You don't live long as a freak if you don't learn how to survive. She was also vicious enough when the need came. She had learned how to lead by watching her biological father. Robert Goodchild had become the mayor of Harmony as well as the spiritual leader. He'd been able to keep both his flock and his men under his rule and she knew how to do the same. She had a quick eye for politics and had used that to gain a foothold of support to keep herself alive during her more savage youth. It was how she had caught the eye of Claudius Faustino. Claudius had been given the young Prudence after she had been discovered by the Crone (the oldest and wisest of all the witches). She had been feral then, half mad with hunger. Anyone else would have simply staked her out of compassion, but Claudius hadn't. He had seen the potential of his young ward. More importantly, Claudius saw something that no one else wanted to see. He was older than most of his kind and he'd seen the empires rise and fall and knew very well what it felt like when one was on its way out. Claudius knew that Old World vampires would not survive as the kings in this wild land. He saw the masses who were settling this New World and these colonists were not like their stock in Europe. If this was the population from which vampires had to pick their heirs, they would have the same spirit in their new un-lives as they now possessed in their lives as frontiersmen and women, entrepreneurs, inventors, and explorers. Claudius had been right. Slowly, he saw the change in leadership shift from the high born aristocrats who wanted to carve out kingdoms in this virgin land to the noble rogues who shaped their own country. One by one, most of the leaders of the vampire community changed. The last and most bloody changeover had made Prudence queen. She had done what was needed to be done with the skill that could only be afforded to generals. There had been compassion and there had been death. With her ability to switch suddenly between the two, no one would dispute her throne or crown.

The war for her crown had been long and bloody and she had proven herself well to the high authority of the House of Burgesses. Prudence had shown that she could go to war and win. She executed her usurpers and forgave those who came to her asking forgiveness. She could have used her success and popularity to expand her throne, but that would have been arrogant and foolish. The armies of her neighbors were waiting for her to do so and therefore she chose not to. Her war was over for now and it was time to rebuild and to make her kingdom into that City on the Hill. They would be the example for their world. Her father would be proud of her.

She would rule her society like the heir that she was.

The end finally came last night when spring had become the blistering hot urban summer. The Lewis Clan had walked into the palace with the wretched casket that they had kept the traitor in. Prudence's predecessor had betrayed the confidence of her superiors and murdered people who had treaties with their kind. It was for this reason that Prudence had been able to win the war. She had been the sensible alternative to the dangerously paranoid Old World line. At her command had been the great North American Armies. In the end though, it hadn't been the armies that caught the traitor. It had been a small group of hunters who caught her. The details would stay with her always. The estate had been very hot with the new summer. It had excited Prudence because, like many children, she loved summer. The days were shorter and she felt like she got to stay up later. It was, however, the slow season for the vampires since the days of hunting were short, so there was less to do. Many would hibernate like bears to avoid those days. But for Prudence, it was a time to act like a child. It meant that she would play games with herself that were childish to indulge that part of her mind that had not yet reached adolescence and never would. Her very favorite game was her tea parties. These were a form of entertainment for Prudence and the staff of Trublood Manor knew this. Very few people interrupted her tea parties with her assorted dolls and stuffed animals. It was a sinful game that her biological father would have never permitted her to play. Her biological father was dead now. Perhaps George Trublood, her creator, wouldn't approve either, but he was gone as well. The dead were not allowed to tell her what she could and could not do and no one living told Prudence that she could not be caught with her dolls and tea parties. It was why the Lewis Clan had been cautious to interrupt her that day, but this was very important. They had served their queen well and caught the She Wolf.

The Lewis Clan were hunters by trade and had been for generations now. Prudence had sought them out at the beginning of the war to be her allies when it came to the ultimate goal of survival. Hunters are generally disliked by the supernatural community for the same reason no one likes to have a highly religious person at a frat party -- they have a tendency to judge the underage drinking and often break up the party. The Lewis Clan were more or less judgmental over one specific type of person at this metaphorical frat party. They were what the supernatural world referred to as Van Helsings -- they had dedicated their lives to hunting vampires and *only* vampires, which is as popular a choice among hunters as it is among the vampires. They had made their name off their impressive ability to hunt vampires and that was precisely why Prudence adored them. And their work during this war would not be forgotten anytime soon.

For an instant as she looked at her companion sitting beside her in the car, she saw a fresh-faced young man who was just a boy with a crossbow until the end came. This war had started with Milan Lewis, who she had brought over from England. He'd been supporting his expansive family on a Witchfinder's salary which was utterly laughable these days. Now she had his great-grandson Carter Lewis.

Carter wasn't a boy anymore. Not after the horrors he'd seen. Carter Lewis grew up quickly during the war of Vampiric succession. His family had sacrificed too much and left his clan with wounded and depleted ranks. Because of this, he had been elected patriarch of the clan by his kin. He was the one who had to take down the She Wolf in the name of his family. It did not please him to lead this mission. He hated working for Prudence because it was irritating to be in her presence. To sit in Prudence's company was unsettling for anyone, even if they weren't a third-generation vampire hunter. Her own people were often disturbed to be near Prudence because she was unnatural for their kind. Child vampires were so rare because even the vampires had ghost stories about their kind and none of those stories were good. She looked like an innocent young girl. However, behind that pale face was the heart of a warlord and that knowledge terrified many and definitely scared Carter. He steeled himself with a breath because it could have been worse. The benefit of being in the main car with Prudence was that he didn't have to ride in the armored car driving behind them. In that was Her. No matter how bad Prudence was, She was far worse than anything in heaven or hell.

She had been their mission. The darkly-lit old streets of Gaiman Heights are filled with all sort of creatures that mean harm to the mundane world and She was the worst. Since Her return to the city, the She Wolf and her most loyal subjects, men she called her Acadian Guard, ran the streets of Old Gaiman as their personal hunting ground. She claimed they were seeking vengeance for the betrayal of her long-dead ancestors. The streets had become bleak. Had it not been for the Burgesses raising up some resistance, there would have been no hope left. It was why Prudence had called in the Lewis clan for their assistance. The war had ended now, but the scars would remain. Carter Lewis would always be haunted by the nightmares from his month long hunt of the She Wolf. He closed his eyes and could still see Harmon's mangled corpse lying on the ground with his eyes transfixed in terror. He could feel Garret's snarl as he ripped into the flesh of their older brother, eating meat and blood. Carter Lewis still prayed for forgiveness for dealing the fatal blow to release Garret from his Curse. Carter Lewis jerked away trying to shake the terror of that night. His guilt would remain, but closure would come soon enough.

The She Wolf would see justice.

"The world went forward so fast when we broke free from Mother England." Prudence said into the silence, as if continuing a different conversation from earlier. Carter Lewis wasn't sure if he was privy to it. Prudence sighed mildly as she watched farmland speed by quickly in a blackish blur. "I can remember a time when my kind didn't travel. You stayed where you were born and that was it. Traveling from Arkham to Gaiman Heights was such a chore. This whole motor car revolution is wonderful. I am not bound to Gaiman. With motels and automobiles, this trip to the state of Franklyn is a simple two days. It blows my mind. I don't know how it caught on, but once I understand it the whole world will change. By then there'll be rocket ships and colonies on Mars. My people will be there too. We go where our food is. Could you see it, Carter? Vampires of the Red Planet. It sounds like a Ray Bradbury novel. Coraline reads them to me before I fall into slumber. He is quite popular. I look forward to space travel. Perhaps we can launch Her into space."

"With all due respect, Your Highness," said Carter Lewis, "Why let Her live, so to speak? Her crimes are a capital offense by the standards of your community. Why not execute Her and be done with it?"

Prudence turned her attention towards him with a level of indignation that she could not fully express. Her feline eyes narrowed at him. No one questioned her wisest notions and, more importantly, they never questioned the high wisdom of the Elders. No one ever had and no one ever would.

"The Burgesses have yet to decide her fate. It is not for me to choose for Her. I believe that there are too many concerns to factor in to let Her simply watch the sun rise. There are still some who believe that I am a rebel and She is their rightful queen. Executing Her would make her a martyr right now. We cannot have more bloodshed."

"You mean Her progeny."

"I mean those who thought they should rule the city as Her kingdom as opposed to Her blood. I worry less about that as they are proving to be quite beneficial to our community. I believe one of the hounds assisted you in this matter he found out you were Catholic."

"Who? Doyle?"

"Yes. I'm afraid Doyle Lanagan's loyalty will always be to the Pope first and to the brood second. It is what his kind does. I am hoping he and Carson will bring the warring factions in South Gaiman to peace so we can all move forward. If they are more trouble than they are worth, then you can have your vengeance on those two. 'Til then, this is the best solution I can come up with."

"Seems less severe than She deserves."

"Carter, have you ever been buried alive?"

"I think that your question has an obvious answer, Your Highness."

"Well, I have, Carter." She said finally. "It was rather a terrible experience that I wish to never go through again. There is nothing but anger, fear and screaming when you're in that hell. You can scratch and try to escape, but it's no use. You are stuck in the bottom of a grave with nothing but your racing thoughts. Where your kind would be eventually released by death, we do not have that luxury. One can go mad being buried alive unless you know how to calm yourself down. Perhaps that's why I am considered somewhat off to our people. No one knows how I survived my burial and honestly, neither do I. I am told that sometimes one can fall into a deep slumber during imprisonment, but that might be a pleasant rumor. I suspect you die eventually of self-cannibalism."

"And Her?"

"She will be hallucinating for quite a while on the pint of fairy blood she ingested before she was sealed in. She won't know she's hungry until it's far too late."

The caravan turned down a long dirt road pitted with old gravel towards an ivy-choked antebellum mansion that had been left to rot after Lee's surrender. Each of the five vehicles in this black parade pulled in neatly beside each other on the circular horse drive. Prudence took a moment to steel herself again before reaching into her elegant hand bag. Her small fingers opened a pearl lined compact mirror. This would have to be done quickly, but she had to make sure she looked perfect. Vampires are overly concerned about how they look. The fear of looking monstrous like Max Sherk in <u>Nosferatu</u> lives in the back of their brains. In fact, early photographs of vampires would show nothing but the face of a screaming monster on the print. Vampires were terrified to see this face and firmly believe that others are able to see it, even if they remain composed outwardly. The ultimate goal of vampires is to look as fresh and human as possible. Vampires are no longer human, but they make an effort to maintain as much humanity as they can. As a result of this, the majority of people who consume fashion magazines and the E! Network are in fact vampires trying to keep themselves in step with the latest fashions.

The people who work twice as hard at this are the younger vampires who act more like aging hipsters trying to keep up with the new things.

Prudence saw her own pale, doll-like face slowly making herself feel more uncomfortable. Contrary to popular belief, vampires can look upon their own reflection without any ill effects. The majority of stories regarding vampire's weaknesses are very foolish folk tales started by vampires themselves for their own amusement. However, the grain of truth in this instance is that they are repulsed by their own reflection. They see the horrid monster that they are trying to hide.

As another note, since we are on the subject, being in the presence of a vampire is either very unsettling for the average human being, like sitting beside the weird kid on the bus, or can be very arousing depending on what sort of pheromones one picks up for. Vampires are always unsettled by being around each other, even more so if they share the same creator. It is why so few of them live together. I only mention this because I feel that you, the reader, need to know these things. I'm trying to cut down on this speaking to you and breaking down the literary fourth wall. I did it in the last book...of course I might still anyway. It's not all terrible.

Prudence looked at her reflection nervously waiting for it to attack from the other side of the mirror. She snapped the compact shut. She had the added joy of being a child-vampire and that was just as upsetting to her as it was to everyone else. She let out a growl and sighed as she closed her eyes. She was trying to remain calm.

The driver of the Lincoln walked calmly around to passenger side door and let the girl out quietly. He assisted Prudence out of the vehicle because that's what people did with Prudence. Carter Lewis followed behind her carefully with his cross bow held tight. Part of the job was security for Prudence on this endeavor. No one knew how far Her pull was and quite frankly if the next thing to occur was Prudence's demise, there would be more unrest and war. He could not permit that to happen, no matter what his personal feelings were. He walked three steps behind her, glancing back at his cousins and the armored vehicle. His cousins were exhausted from their journey, but determined to complete this task as they pulled a large stone box from the back of the vehicle. The heavy casket screamed and shook as the eight strong men handled it. He knew that She was attempting to convince them to change their minds.

It had been two days. If She hadn't convinced them by now, then she wasn't going to be able to do it.

Prudence stood upon the grand porch and stared back at Carter Lewis. He followed her between the large Corinthian columns that seemed to be swelling with pretension. She curled her fingers round a large gold rope that was just barely within her reach. She glanced back at Carter Lewis to make sure he was ready for anything as she pulled the rope. An old chime rang out in the late summer night. The wait felt far too long as they heard feet shuffle behind heavy doors within the house. There was a slow creak as the door opened. Prudence smiled at the woman who opened the door at this late hour. Her soft dark hair had been pinned back in loops that formed a fashionable bunt around her round looking head. Carter Lewis idly looked at the woman with a sidelong glance, wondering if the tight antique choker hid bite scars from her transfer over to darkness and thinking what a shame it was that she was no longer human. Even if she wasn't legally bound to someone else, he would have been more than pleased to court with the fine woman at the door. But he knew well enough from the corpse-white skin and the sunken expression on her face that she was undead and that was a line he just could not in good faith cross. She gripped the dark blue petticoat of her hooped skirt as she stared at Prudence and Carter Lewis. Slowly she curtsied demurely at the pair. Prudence returned the crusty politely.

"Good evening to you, Lady Goodchild." She said in a sweet Southern accent that sounded as intoxicatingly soft and elegant as magnolia blossoms. Despite himself, Carter Lewis fell in love with her instantly. "I was not aware that you would be calling on us this evening. You will have to forgive my lack of hospitality. We gave our man, Henry, the evening off. I will say that it is a pleasure to see you."

"Charlotte my dear, you look radiant and your charm is more than enough hospitality," said Prudence politely. This was also a custom in vampire communities -- attempting to out-polite another vampire. "Of course, the pleasure is all mine. May I introduce Carter Lewis? Carter, this is Charlotte Blackmore, the Lady of Watauga."

Charlotte curtsied as Carter Lewis gave her a somber bow. She had hoped to go her whole after life without ever crossing paths with a member of the Lewis clan. She knew what he was. The smell of brimstone and death hung on his freshly pressed clothes. He was a hunter and that made her angry. There was nothing more unsettling to have a hunter in your home. Well, maybe only second to having a child vampire there. She had both on her front step. Despite her dislike, she was going to not breathe a word. They were the Lord of the house's guests and it was not her place to say anything about the company he kept. Charlotte smiled sweetly, letting her fangs glint in the waxing moonlight.

"Charmed, Mr. Lewis." She said through bared fangs. "To what do we owe the honor of this visit?"

"I'm sorry to say that this is not a social call." Said Prudence. "We are here on business. Is the Lord Blackmore in?"

"He is. You'll find him in the study," replied Charlotte. "I will show you to him."

Lord Blackmore was once a noble Southern gentleman from an old, well-respected family. He had excellent manners that he had learned from his father and the kind negress, as he would call her, who had raised him. He was well educated at the finest universities. He had to be as the only male heir to the Blackmore family fortune. He kept himself in the manner that would have satisfied his station. His curly black hair fell stylishly with a smart looking part as it had been worn in the days of his life. He was clean shaven save for a well-manicured mustache. He had even married a well to do debutante from Savannah and his suits were finely tailored to her personal tastes. He wasn't a cruel man in life. Well, not any more than anyone else. There is a common misconception is that there was a level of sadism to owning another person. Perhaps that was true of someone who had one or two. Lord Blackmore was proud to tell you that he had owned more than one or two. He'd had a large herd in his heyday but he never thought of himself as sadistic. What he did was only to maintain a level of decorum so they could continue their work. Perhaps he had a strict hand with his property but that property didn't know better and needed to be taught. He would not apologize for what history would remember as a travesty, but what was simply a way of life for him.

The vampiric life did not suit Lord Blackmore very well. He had been a social creature and now he was very isolated. He'd felt shame for being what he was in his dark un-life. Of course he could not admit to his fall out loud -- not to his wife or anyone else and so he had withdrawn from the world he knew. He lived an hour's drive from-a vampire community. If it hadn't been for his honor he would have let himself see a bright sunshine. Of course, he also had his Beloved at his side and that would have been more than enough to keep going through the dark world. She'd made sure he fed and that they weren't like the hermit vampires in the back side of the world.

She knew that a good Southern man didn't go down without a fight.

He would often sit in his study with a glass of untouched scotch and his shame staring down at what he would call the Farm. He would harken back to a time where there would be work songs humming through the day and that life which was so much better then. Nothing grew there now; in Her assault on his land, the ground had turned sour and black. The dead rock had been tainted with her evil and that was it. That was where he could contemplate how his dark life had become so very dark. That was what he was contemplating that night when the door to his study opened carefully. He turned his head up with a snarl at the unfamiliar smell of visitors in his room. He pursed his lips as he bowed his head curtly to his wife, not acknowledging the guests until they were formally introduced. They all knew that would be the case. Charlotte weakly smiled at him.

"Virgil, Darling," She said. "Prudence Goodchild has come to call."

"With someone who smells like human ash." He said with a low bow. "We are honored by your presence, Lady Goodchild -- especially with your recent victory in Gaiman Heights."

"You above anyone, Lord Blackmore, should know how hard it is to find good help." Prudence said with a polite curtsy. "It is always wonderful to be welcomed into your delightful home whether I am queen or not."

Lord Blackmore led his guests to the formal parlor off of the study. Carter Lewis had expected the house to be in a state of dread and disrepair, but he was pleasantly shocked to see that the rooms used for daily life had been preserved in all their antebellum splendor like the inside of an Egyptian tomb. Prudence climbed on to the fancy couch. Carter Lewis stood behind her keeping his eyes trained on the Lord Blackmore who sat in his sedan chair.

"You'll forgive me if I don't offer you refreshment. We insist that Henry take one day a week off to mingle with his own kind for his own good. He is our eyes and ears in the community and we need him to remain social," said Lord Blackmore. "I could offer your man a drink."

"Carter doesn't abide spirits," Prudence replied. "We are here to discuss business. I assume you have received my correspondences."

"I have. I take it that vile Cajun woman is with your party."

"I believe she is from Acadia. I think she might be offended by the word 'Cajun'."

"I believe I don't give a damn if she is offended by what I might call Her. That woman is a plague sent by God to punish me for my sins. I've told you I'd rather not have her here."

"And I've told you my predicament," said Prudence. "If the Burgesses were the only ones banishing her, it would be one thing, but the college of magi and the union of witches have demanded her banishment. I suppose I should really return her to the city of her origin."

"Will the Cardinal not permit you to send her to Port Royal?

"We both know that she rarely tells the truth," Prudence said. "I strongly doubt that she was really from Port Royal. This is the last place we knew she was before Gaiman Heights."

"I understand that, Lady Goodchild." Lord Blackmore said. "And I formally renew my objection to this intrusion. After the slaughter she visited upon us, I'd rather not have that vile Cajun woman on this land.

"I am asking you to just hold her here until the sentencing has passed. Of course, she has ingested a pint a of fairy blood. I doubt she'll survive to the passing of justice."

Virgil Blackmore leaned back, contemplating Prudence's words carefully. He pressed his fingertips together as a humble smile crossed his lips. It wasn't the justice that he wanted. This was a hell that was so much better. He let out a small chuckle enjoying the pain of the She Wolf.

Maybe he was sadistic after all.

"Lady Goodchild," said Lord Blackmore finally, "Let it never be said that your punishments aren't truly wicked."

"I may have an innocent face, but my unbeating heart is still Puritan," said Prudence sweetly. "We invented state-sponsored punishment."

Lord Blackmore stood up closely eyeing Carter Lewis in the very same way that he had been eyed before by the hunter. He let a nod pass between them.

"Mr. Lewis, I will assume you have a hunting party with you." Said Lord Blackmore. "If you will follow me, I have a place where you can intern that vile Cajun Woman."

A joyous procession walked from the mansion down a long overgrown path. Lord Blackmore snickered as he led the Lewis clan to a wide site in the overgrown forest of weeds that only attempted to grow up where nothing else would. Carter Lewis glanced around the cabins as ghostly figures stood and watched the Lewis clan walk the cold path to the cemetery. The ghosts stood around with their dead eyes watching as Lord Blackmore led them to a stone cave. He smiled very quietly and pointed.

"Bury her here." He told them. "The ghosts have been visiting for a while and now she can have some company. We know she hates being alone without someone to talk to. Don't you, Mistress?"

Lord Blackmore gave a disdainful look at the stone box as it shook with a wave of telepathic swears that invaded his brain. She let out a scream again as her tricks had no effect on her status. *We have peace now,* thought Carter Lewis, *but for how long?* He decided that it was almost certainly not going to be long enough.

II.   Black Friday Rule

Nowish but it'll probably feel like the late nineties.

There are few things that a priest hates more than hearing confessions on an otherwise quiet Friday when he wants to catch up on his summer television. No, let me rephrase that. There are a few things that Father Arthur McCreely hated more than hearing confessions on what would otherwise be a quiet Friday night when he wanted to catch up on his summer television. It wasn't as bad during the summer. He wasn't missing football and unless the Sox were playing he didn't really care about baseball. He just generally hated hearing confession.

He wasn't jealous of the lives and pleasures he chose to give up. He knew many people who felt that way, but he gave up those pleasures up when he became a priest. That wasn't the problem. He didn't partake in the lusting after the sins he was trying absolve because he had to be an impartial viewer of things he wanted no part in having. Something he had never understood was the lust people felt for a life given up. Perhaps it made sense in a time when you were barely a teenager when they shuffled you off for training to be a priest. He couldn't imagine what it was like to give up a life that you had to live to understand your flock. Maybe that was the reason there were so many problems with the sins of the church. You don't know what sort of sickness can be in a man's mind before he becomes a man. It didn't excuse those who perpetrated those crimes. They were still vile hell-worthy trespasses but the church had to take responsibility for them as well. He knew they never would and that disgusted him down to his very core. He hated listening to confession for one very important reason. In his years as a man of the cloth he didn't feel like it was his job was to give forgiveness. He was a priest. His

17

job was to shepherd his flock and guide them to someone who could give salvation. That meant that he was supposed to help them foster a relationship with their Lord and not hand out arbitrary tasks to wash away the sins of the world. It meant they should ask God for forgiveness not him. He blamed his conversion on that thought.

Father McCreely had not started life as a priest. It seemed like a world away when he was minted as Private McCreely. That had all changed one day long ago. His motorized unit had been on patrol in the Green Zone when he found God. His revelation had started when his armored vehicle was hit by an I.E.D. As he sat in the wreckage fighting for his life, he promised to be a better man. The first thing that he knew he had to do was what his mother had always wanted for him. When he got back to the States and recovered, he went into the seminary. Father McCreely was more liberal than some of his associates in the Holy Mother Church. This made him quite popular with the McKean State Newman Center and with the young adults who were a little jaded and bitter from the transgressions committed by the Catholic Church, but still wanted to remain true to their faith. However the diocese of Falls River didn't share his political views. As a punishment for his continual challenging of the traditional ways, Father McCreely was sent to the Church of St. George and the Dragon. It was an awfully English name for a church that was in South Gaiman which happened to be a very Irish neighborhood. He'd rationalized that they added the dragon as their way of fighting back from the St. George part of the name. Then again, he hadn't understood Gaiman Heights for the neighborhood he was living in too terribly well. By the end of his story, he learned that the dragon was more important to this city than St. George would ever be. He might have already known. Early in his tenure at St. George and the Dragon, Arthur McCreely suspected that things in the South weren't what they seemed. It only looked like everywhere else and this felt deceptive. The best exaction of this deception was Doyle Lanigan.

When Father McCreely first came to St. George's, Father Victor Price warned him about Doyle Lanagan. He had told the young priest that there was something very wrong with Doyle, but would not elaborate as to what it was. All he would say was that he was dangerous and had not been human for quite some time. It had sounded like the foolish and paranoid ramblings of an old man who was on his way out. There wasn't anything that scared Father McCreely anymore. He somehow doubted that if Doyle really was less than human that it would be the worst thing he'd ever seen in this town. Five years later he'd found that nothing had changed about his thoughts on Doyle. If anything, Doyle was quite the opposite. The only danger anyone was put into by Doyle Lanagan was the danger that your Friday night was going to be taken up with his personal war with his own guilt. Like clockwork, Doyle Lanagan would be sitting in a wooden box clutching his old world rosary waiting for the priest. Then he would tell him of the transgressions that he committed for the week prior.

This Friday was no different.

"Bless me Father for I have sinned." Doyle started the ritual with no prompting. It did not matter who the priest was. He would start the rote learning of a generation before. He knew it was Doyle. No one else's accent was as thick as an Irish wool sweater. It had almost become purposefully maintained. "it's been seven days since me last confession."

"Doyle Lanagan, have you no home to go to?" blurted out the priest. If he didn't intervene now, he was going to be here for hours. Father McCreely was done with the dance.

"I'm not quite sure I follow, Father," replied Doyle.

Father McCreely leaned back resting his head on the oak wall behind him as he tried to compose himself. That had been an unusual outburst and he'd ask God to forgive him later. He pinched the bridge of his nose to stem the irritation flowing through this conversation.

"It's Friday," The priest said finally. "I am confident that you have better things to be doing than visiting with me, Doyle."

"Well, I…."

"Doyle, I can't do this with you right now."

"But I've lusted in me heart."

"Find me one person living on this planet that hasn't done that. Hell, even Jimmy Carter admitted to it." Said the Priest. "I can't do this with you Doyle. Not if it's going to be the same three things you've done over and over again. What I can do is go have a beer and since it's Friday and no one should be alone I think you need to come with me."

"I don't think that would be…"

"Am I going to have to order you out of the box? Doyle, it's better for both of us if we don't do this dance and we talk like men. If it's easier, think of it as pastoral care. Now, I'm going to go get a beer. Would you care to join me?"

"Yes Father, I would love to have a drink with you."

Doyle didn't want a drink. He knew that when people who started offering drinks meant they wanted to be a friend. Doyle didn't want to be friends with the priest. He was a nice enough guy, sure, but you never wanted to be friends with someone in authority. Churches like St. George and the Dragon were places where paladins and hunters would congregate. Hunters wanted to do him harm in general, but could be reasoned with in specific cases; paladins, however, were bad news for everyone. He knew in theory not to trust if this became a personal relationship and this was a relationship that was shifting dangerously close to being a personal. This was made evident by the fact that Doyle was now sitting on a thrift shop couch that had seen five priests in a large foyer of a double wide that passed for the vicarage. Doyle hated entering the home of a living person. Not because it took extra steps to enter a home since vampires need permission or any of that hogwash. This is generally a lie put out by vampire public relations which often circulate tales to the living to make them feel better. Contrary to popular belief, vampires are more than capable of entering a person's home uninvited, but they just don't do it. Vampires are often very polite creatures that keep themselves to a high standard. One of these standards is to not enter another person's home without permission as it's very rude. Doyle hated being rude almost as much as he hated being in someone else's house because eventually the customs of reciprocity meant that he was going to have to share his home and honestly he never trusted anyone that much.

Doyle cringed quietly. He really knew what he hated about being in other people's homes. He could tell himself it was the vampiric culture all he wanted, but deep down he knew that it wasn't case. Doyle was old enough to still believe in the vampiric superstitions and to hold to those beliefs. He had also been born, so to speak, of an old world vampire. She had always believed in those traditions that hung around from her immigration and that had influenced Doyle. It was like having an old grandmother who raised her descendants with those curses. For Doyle it was something that bothered him about being in other people's homes.

Doyle was old. He came from a time when sitting rooms were where you entertained guests and it was perfectly normal. It was a sign of the prosperity that you had and never showed the deck of cards you were hiding. That was then, but now it felt like these rooms had become less formal and more personal. They were customized with the personal effects of the owner of the home and you could glimpse into the very soul of your host. This made Doyle very uneasy because it got him to thinking about his lair and that made him very self-conscious. There were no pictures in their home because Doyle and Carson never posed for them. They had one photograph, but they would never show it to anyone. It was of a good day back at the end of the Second World War. He hated that picture. He hated how smooth his face looked. The placid skin was that hiding a monster.

Now that Doyle thought about it, he and Carson had no real personal effects around the house that said this was their home. Apart from a few books, there wasn't much to them. Doyle knew they had no soul. These ideas always upset Doyle.

He sat awkwardly on the couch as his foot tapped nervously within the confines of his old brown shoes. He felt old. There was something about sitting in a dated room that made one feel old. He didn't look old. His handsome Gaelic features hadn't faded to yellow in the years since his death. He was paler now than back then but that was to be expected. Vampires paled with age due to a lack of sunlight-stimulated melanin being produced in the skin. Given enough years, their skin tone would revert entirely back to the untouched hue it was when they had been born. Still, his long square face with its unimpressive freckled nose hadn't been marked by the age that would have come with a long life. He felt older than he looked and he hated that feeling. Being old was very tiring because he had to put up with a world that wasn't what he remembered it to be when he was younger or as he could remember. It did not seem fair that he didn't look like the age that he felt. It was a rare incident of a man attempting to make himself look older than he was. He slouched when he walked and wore muted colors that kept him quiet from the world. He thought about doing something with his hair but it never worked. His hair was too thick to dye. He was just pale with thick auburn hair and stuck in his mid-thirties. He felt that his eyes were intensifying with age. He was becoming a monster.

Doyle let out a sigh as he looked up at the wood paneling with quiet apprehension. No matter who lived there, very few things that changed from priest to priest. The chipped wood paneling had been adorned with simple decorations of Catholic Faith. Nothing that said anything about the person who lived there. In many ways that was much like their home. They had nothing too personal and neither did the priest.

Doyle turned his head to one side as his attention was drawn to the Celtic cross in front of him. He found himself recoiling from the cross as if it had a foul odor. It should be noted here that not all vampires are repelled by Christian artifacts. After all, vampires are not just Western creatures. If you take a moment to look through the annals of myth you will find that all societies have vampires and many of them are older than Christianity. It would then, therefore, make no sense for say, a Muslim vampire to be repulsed by a cross, but not a mosque. It was more a psychological condition brought on by religious beliefs that had not been reconciled to his unlife. He was repulsed by these symbols, but he never had a problem being on church grounds or holding on to his rosary. Of course, he didn't notice that either. It had been explained to him once, but Doyle believed that psychology wasn't real.

Father McCreely walked back from the kitchen with the noticeable limp of a man who has a leg that didn't exactly work correctly. It was agitated by the thread bare brown carpet that had been installed by Father Caday three years before he left. Doyle had liked Father Caday and thought he was a priest who didn't deserve being stuck here. He knew that this parish was a punishment for most priests. He'd never known anyone who came to this city on their own accord from the world outside the veil of the supernatural. This place was punishment.

Father McCreely handed Doyle a cold, dark red liquid in a bottle before he slumped into a new looking recliner. Doyle sniffed suspiciously out of habit. You should never take a drink without sniffing it. He knew that vampires had been taken down by hemlock-laced blood (hemlock is a general paralytic for vampires) or worse, fairy blood. A vampire's life was flooded with paranoia. He was safe for now. A familiar coppery smell hit his nose happily without incident. He knew that smell better than he wanted. Doyle glanced back up at the priest who was sucking down a local microbrew.

"It's not fresh or human." Said the priest. "I'm sorry about that. I have a parishioner who is a butcher. He slaughters his pigs on Tuesday. He didn't think it was too odd when I asked for the bottle. That's slightly more common in Gaiman Heights than I was aware. I did what I could to keep it fresh until today. If you'd like I could warm that up in the microwave. I've done some reading that pig's blood is similar to humans but can't be good while cold."

"I drink it bit more than most o' my kind would like. You're right, it's very close to human without it being from a human," replied

Doyle. "It's not as delicious, but it does what it needs to do. You know you don't have to do this. Most of your predecessors didn't even bother. I do come to you as my priest."

"Yea, being a priest is more than giving you forgiveness. I am your pastor and I'm tired of us doing just the forgiving. This dance is boring. You tell me why you are going to hell, I say a few words and you go off and pray. Then we go through it again next week and it's the same shit you did the week before. Doyle, what keeps you doing this? Guilt? Fear that God is going to cut you down? I know that you feel shame because you're an Old Catholic, but Doyle, this is seriously upsetting."

"I'm a monster." Doyle said plainly before he took a swig of the pig's blood. He made a face at the bland taste of the liquid. "I feed on blood. I'm allergic to sunlight and religious items. No good being does that."

"Were you a monster before the Curse?"

"Had to be. I don't know what I did, but I know God's punishing me for something."

"Really. Then why, Doyle Lanagan, were you so evil that God had to punish you?"

Doyle looked down at his shoes. In that moment, Doyle thought about every hell-worthy trespass he'd committed. The things that he'd done before his death. The crimes that he'd had on his soul before he was brought over to the darkness. Then there was Her and things got worse. With his unnaturally long life, it was a very long list. He looked up at Father McCreely preparing to confess to everything he'd ever done. His confessions got stuck as fear and guilt gripped his jaw and throat.

"You can't because you don't know why. You, out of anyone, don't know why you were chosen for this. Despite what you might think, Doyle, none of us know really why we are chosen for our roles. Only God knows that. But I know that God gives us certain gifts and puts us on a path to use those gifts. It's hard to see that as a survivor. I know that but, Doyle, I survived for a purpose and so did you. We have our missions in life ~~Doyle~~ to serve Him. I know it's hard to think about it like this. I know why you feel monstrous."

"Oh?"

"I think you know that I lost my leg when I was in Iraq. I also lost my best friend. Hell, I don't know why I didn't die with the rest of the people in my convoy vehicle. Shit, I get cards from some of the wives and husbands and families from people in my unit and I think I should have died with them. Now, I'm pretty sure that you didn't have the combat experience before your death, but I've seen you in the cemetery at night and trust me when I say I know survivor's guilt when I see it. You feel bad because you survived."

"What do I do about the guilt?"

"I don't know if it'll work for you the same way, but I answered my calling. I became a shepherd of His flock and a fisher of men. Doyle, I believe your calling is higher than mine."

"What is higher than a priest?"

Father McCreely set his beer down on a coffee table as he gave Doyle a practiced calm look. Doyle hated the priestly stare.

"I'm guessing your devotion to the Lord didn't come to you late in life because I know the mark of a true believer. Doyle, when a pious man is given something beyond the normal he must use that gift for a good purpose. Sometimes Doyle, The Lord needs someone to beat the wheat from the chaff. This city has quite a lot of chaff."

Doyle shook his head as he let that uncomfortable thought settle for a moment. He knew what Father McCreely meant by that speech. Doyle just didn't have the feeling of vengeance in his heart and the idea of doling out justice made him feel very uncomfortable. That was not something that he felt like he should have to take on. Sure there were people who were more evil than him. He'd lived long enough to know that was true. Wouldn't that make him as bad as the wicked? He couldn't believe that he was damned for no reason. He had to believe it was because he was evil. But, what if he wasn't evil? What if the priest was right and he was there to do the work of the Lord? Then that would make everything make sense. But that just couldn't be right. Doyle glanced back coldly at the priest as conflicting thoughts swam in his head.

"Regardless of what I believe about you Doyle, I know this: you can't let your life or whatever be held up by your own self-hate. The world is a beautiful place even at night and it is made for you to experience. You can't sit in mourning of your existence. Doyle Lanagan, you are far too important to not share yourself with the world."

Those last words became imbedded in his shoulders as he walked away from the Church of St. George and the Dragon. He turned onto the steamy South Gaiman streets with a dour look. He put a world-worn walking cap on his head and pulled the brim over his eyes. He thought it was a shame that men didn't wear hats anymore. There was something clean and classic about those sorts of things. Perhaps that's why he felt old. That the things he saw fall away were just very classy. That made him a little out of place which was fine by Doyle. There was something peaceful about finding solitude. He didn't have to worry about being a depressant for anyone who would attempt to socialize with him. It gave him more time to brood.

Yes, Doyle Lanagan was a bad stereotype.

He paused as he glanced down the street with a somber scowl. A scruffy blond man glanced back at him while lighting a cigarette and trying hard to be James Dean. What was the point of that? Who was he trying to look cool for? Doyle was pretty confident it was only for his own amusement. Carson's second priority in life, after irritating Doyle, was entertaining himself. Nothing entertained Carson more than pretending to be a matinee idol.

"Shit, forty-five minutes." He said brashly. Doyle hated that New England Irish accent. It felt like sandpaper in his ears. "Usually the padre kicks you out after seven when he can't deal with your whining anymore. I almost thought you'd given up ever getting laid again and joined the order."

"Here I thought you'd be dry humping a co-ed by this time," Doyle replied. "Or did she dump you again for something you did in a dream?"

One of the leaders of the Easter Uprising, James Conelly, had said that when St. Patrick cast out the snakes from Ireland they all came to America and became Irish-Americans. What Old Jem forgot to mention was that when they came to South Gaiman they became the O'Brians. Doyle had no love for Irish-Americans and with each passing generation, he became less grateful or understanding of what his generation went through to bring them here. Carson was everything Doyle hated about Irish-Americans. The ones who felt they were entitled to step on the other immigrants who came after them. They had become thugs just a short time after he arrived. Doyle had spent the last fifty years civilizing Carson and it didn't always take. Sometimes Carson stood on street corners, like he was now, leering like a wild dog looking for a fight.

"The Priest must have gotten to you," said Carson with a rueful laugh. "That wasn't even your best comeback, but no. Norvie ain't with me. She had to work with the suits. Something about a difficult interrogation at the nut house. She'll be meeting us at Pitch's."

Carson had been seeing and then not seeing Norvita Patel for quite some time now. She had a tendency to dump Carson for what seemed like arbitrary reasons. She was also, somehow, an agent with the Department of the Arcane. Then again, what else would a psychic do? Doyle looked at Carson for a moment. The unnatural thoughts that had been with him since he'd spoken to the priest rolled around in his head. He debated sharing these thoughts with Carson and then hesitated. There was no reason to tell him what the priest said. Not yet anyway. He couldn't figure out what he doing about any of these things just yet. He knew that he'd have to have Carson on board though. There was no way he could go hunting by himself. Carson would no doubt want a part of the adventures. That presented a problem to Doyle. Could he keep Carson in check? Doyle knew Carson could get a little out of hand when it came to their exploits. He had to think about this carefully.

"So," Started Carson. "What did the father tell you or is that between you and the Almighty?"

Or he could just have to deal with it right in front of him in that moment. Doyle paused as he reached the end of the street. Carson had a terrible habit of finding out when Doyle was thinking about something and trying to pull it out. He wondered if that was an effect of the blood that they shared. Carson knew better. It was largely due to the fact that Doyle was a terrible liar. Carson could figure out in the span of seconds what was being kept from him. Doyle sighed, looking at Carson as a city bus passed by unceremoniously. Doyle resolved that he'd bring it up to Carson now, rather than brood over it until Carson guessed it anyway. If he didn't like the answer, he'd drop it.

"He says I have survivor's guilt and I need to stop blaming myself for what I've become. It's not my fault."

"You need a priest to tell you that? I could tell you that. Pitch could tell you that. Fuck, Doyle, half the city could tell you that."

"He also said I have a higher calling."

"I knew it! So when do you take your orders?"

"It's not about being a priest. The father seems to think that the curse is a skill to weed out the wicked."

"What the fuck does that mean? Because that still sounds like a priest."

"He says that God wants us to clean out the evil from the flock ."

"Are you saying that a priest wants you to kill bad people?"

"Well, when you say it like that, it sounds like a terrible idea."

"No shit. Killing people sort of defies that whole we need to pretend that we don't exist. I think Prudence would take our heads or nuts or whatever she does to people who do that. 'Sides, do you think a priest would tell us to kill people?"

"Yea, not the same priest who told me I wasn't a monster... unless he was using me." Doyle stopped for a moment and thought. The implications of what the priest had said to him started to make more sense in his head. He blinked for a moment and then turned back to Carson. "Or we could just not kill anyone. Do you remember what it was like doing the street patrols in South Gaiman?"

"No, I try to block out the funnest part of my life. Of course I remember. We found the motherfuckers who fucked up our home and got rid of them."

"I think that the father means for us to do that. Find the people who are making our home a bad place and unsafe and get them out of the neighborhood. We don't have to kill anyone."

"So we hunt them down. Fuck 'em up. Tell em to leave town and then what, snitch to the cops?"

"That's exactly what we do. We lay down the law. I couldn't think of it before. People like that make our home dangerous for keeping our promise to the Department and endanger our brood hunting areas," Doyle said with sudden wild enthusiasm that he hadn't had in ages for much of anything. "I know we can't get the police to come here because of the Department, but if we call Weston Lewis directly he can figure it out."

Carson chuckled at Doyle's wild excitement, which prompted Doyle to scowl at him.

"Do you have a better idea, then?"

"Nah, it ain't that. That idea is tits. It's just hearing you talk like that made me all misty for the old days. Can you even remember the last time you went hunting?"

He could. He had every second of it carved into his memory in vivid detail. The night seemed blood red to him with a haze over everything. Her fingers pointed to a mass of people who moved in a wave of terror. His fangs were drawn with a growl as he crouched into a ball waiting to be sprung forth in bloody vengeance. She rested Her lips against his ear with a seductive growl.

"Good boy." She had whispered. "Now, sic 'em."

Doyle shuddered for a moment as the memory tried to hold on to him.

"Not since we were with Her."

Carson let out a growl as he too relived a memory that wasn't that dissimilar from Doyle's, but with more arousing detail. Doyle didn't say Her name and he didn't need to. Carson knew who he was talking about. She was the wicked giggle in the back of his head that told Carson to slow down. She was the black secret they never spoke about for fear of Her appearing beside them. That was a shared fear: Her returning.

"Okay, its been a while." Said Carson. "So, lets start with something simple."

"I hear that Martin's Park has some new drug dealers we could hit now that the fairy is in Twillingast."

"Naw, that ain't our problem. Parks and safety there belongs to the Grayclaw tribe. Let Adam and Jason handle it. I got something better Doyle. You'll love it."

"Why?"

"Because, Doyle, Charity starts at home."

III. If I Ever Leave This World Alive

1847

The inside of his mouth was so arid that he couldn't swallow the excess saliva without difficulty. Instead, he would let it trickle down his hot throat trying to keep it moist. The wet would only hit his tonsils before it stopped, leaving him trying to choke it out as breathing became difficult. What was left after that dripped off his lips as his back arched in a desperate plea for air to enter his laboring lungs. His fingers clutched the dark green beads on an old rosary. His cracked lips moved noiselessly in prayers to a god who hadn't seen fit to listen to him before and now, in his darkest hour, was still silent. He wasn't going to give up just yet on his Savior. He'd gotten this far. He couldn't assume it was time to give up. God didn't reward those who strayed from His path when the chips were down. That's why there would always be tests. Job had been put through far worse and his faith was firm. Doyle knew that he was going to survive this and, he believed, he'd become a better man for it. Now wasn't the time for him to go home. He pulled the thin, threadbare blanket over his body as he lay on the dirty tenement floor. His skin burned with a fever that covered his body in a hot sweat. It didn't cool him, but left a foul smell. His rich hazel eyes watched the day succumb to the starless urban sky.

He wasn't so much watching the fall of night. He was watching the end of his life.

His mortal thoughts twisted grotesquely as the fever ate into his brain and stole his memories. He licked his lips trying to hold on to what he could remember. He had been born a world away from this squalor. The only boy in a family of seven, born into the life of a modern day serf to the English field bosses. He didn't have many choices in professions. Like his father, he had become a farmer. Even then he was different from the others he knew.

Doyle could read and write. His aunt was a nun and had taught her only nephew how to be literate because that was how the power was going to shift in her mind. The next generation would belong to the Lanigans and they couldn't take that greatness if they couldn't read or write. His father had thought this a waste of time. He'd never learned how to read and they were fine. Doyle hadn't really cared. There was something special about being able to read and that made him feel different. More importantly, it was his escape from a mundane existence even only for a little while. Doyle had wanted out of that life; he had wanted something better.

Doyle was handsome by the standards of the day even if he didn't realize it. His reddish brown hair had a fine wave that was kept neat. He wasn't fat, but thick with farm-toned muscles along his awkward frame. He had deep-set hazel eyes that accented his Gaelic features like mossy gems. What made him most attractive, though was his plain and soft speech. He could have been boorish like his father and his uncles, but Doyle was pleasant and considerate which had made him a hit with his aunts and mother.

He wasn't into politics. Everyone seemed to have a thought about the state of political affairs. His fathers and his uncles were always complaining about this, that and the other. The English wanted this and if they could force a hand, they could get it or the government in Dublin had sold them out. That just wasn't him. Doyle's opinions were his and he didn't have to share them. He knew things weren't great, but what was getting wound up about it going to do? Challenge authority? They hanged the men who did things like that. The old men weren't doing anything to fix the world. They just sat and talked and swore at the government. Doyle knew that things were bad, but he just had to wait. Things would change for the better.

That was before 1847.

In 1840 something happened. The climate on Earth changed slightly, thus causing Europe to have a colder, wetter spring. This was devastating for many of the agricultural systems in Europe as the growing season was shorter. Ireland would have been all right if it had not been for another tragic event that happened.

In the years after the colonization of the New World, the poor of Ireland had become dependent on the solunum tuberssum. It was an easy and cheap food that made people feel full and much later, they would figure out how to turn it into chips. However, this dependence came with a problem. There was a lack of diversity in the potato population of the Irish plants which made them more susceptible to phytopora infetans, or simply, potato blight. The blight took out the primary food supply that had been starting what history would remember as the Gotya Mor or the Great Hunter. At the end of the Potato Famine, over half of Ireland's population was either dead or fled to more hopeful shores.

Doyle Lanagan's story isn't a chapter or even a footnote in this history. His was just a faceless story that was oft-repeated. For our purposes, however, it's the most important story to talk about at this point. In 1845, he was a father of four and had the prettiest wife in the country. In 1847, he was a world away and dying.

His family had dropped like flies. The first to die was his pretty Molly. Molly had been the oldest of Mrs. D'Lacy's daughters. Being Norman, a lineage that his father had spat at despite the fact she was as Irish as he was, meant that she had a small dowry that was more money than Doyle had ever seen. Needless to say, his father overlooked the boy marrying a half-Norman girl with a little more money than himself. Money hadn't been something Doyle had thought about when he married Molly. He'd started courting the girl when she verbally sparred with the neighbor boy and ran circles around him with her quick wits. She could have been born in a barrel for all he cared. Molly was smarter than most, and strong, and if she'd been born in another world and another time, she would have been better off. She could have made something of her short life. Instead she was with Doyle in the life she died in.

The famine didn't kill Molly -- not directly at least. The first sin that Doyle committed was being the father to his son during the time of starvation. The circumstances of Molly's death weren't uncommon in that period of time even without starvation. Her death came in the throes of childbirth. Maybe she could have survived the unsanitary conditions if she hadn't been starving. He hadn't been allowed in when she died. Doyle thought of that whenever he walked into rooms and expected to see the scene of blood and horror. She'd left him in a whirlwind of screams and blood and he would never forgive her for that. What she did leave him with, however, was his only son who he'd held on to for only a short time. His son had suffered the same fate as his mother at the hands of the days of Black 47. Little did he know then that it wouldn't stop there. The trail of death and despair would keep going.

The next to die was his oldest daughter. Watching his children starve was a hell that Doyle hoped to never experience again. Mary Katherine starved to death three months after her mother and little brother. Out of all his children, her death affected him the most. Perhaps it was the short time after the death of Molly and he'd not quite gotten over it. Maybe it was the age of Mary Katherine. He had always been closer to his older child than his younger ones. What Doyle did know was that this was something far worse and something he'd always since considered the reason he was being punished. Mary Katherine's death had affected him more so because he was jealous of it. She was dead and got to go to heaven and be with her mother. He felt spiteful towards God because he had to remain here to watch the suffering. Doyle questioned a great many things in those days and for the first time he started to turn his back on his faith.

His new found atheism had given Doyle a new list of priorities. He could no longer rely on a god who had let a child and his wife die as they had. He had to make it on his own. If not for him then for the remaining children he had. He had to save them from the suffering they were enduring. There was no way he was going to let anyone lay them in graves with mad looks in their eyes and grass stains on their mouths. Like so many who had tried to survive the Famine, Doyle did what he had to do. He sold what he could and collected his daughters to go to the land of milk and honey. Life would be better on the other side of the world. What

Doyle did not foresee was what would become the last hurdle for his life of happiness.

Starvation comes with many side effects that not everyone knows about. For example, your brain starts to work overtime, causing hallucinations. Prolonged malnutrition weakens the immune system to badly that one cannot fight off disease properly. Couple that with the masses of people who were fleeing and you have a recipe for disaster. Fianna was sick before leaving Ireland. Doyle had kept it quiet as they rode to the new world, begging her to hold on just a little longer. His wishes were as useless as his prayers had been. She screamed and wailed through the fever and pain. He wept when she yelled at her hallucinations. Maura followed with the same thing. Doyle watched in grief, wondering which one would die first.

Fianna went first with Maura dying within seconds of docking in America. Both of his girls were buried in nameless graves for the time being. It would be years later that Doyle could have them moved and their memory preserved in a better way. It wasn't just their graves then, but a symbol for all of those who had passed with them. He'd never shaken the guilt of being the one to live. He'd never said it out loud, but some days he felt like he killed his family with his mind.

He'd wanted to lay down and die and yet he didn't. Doyle found that his willpower to survive outranked his desire to die and in time he'd have no choice. Perhaps one day he could put all behind him and have a normal life. He worried at every cough and spike in body temperature relishing this being his final end but never was. Doyle made his way in this new world. It wasn't easy at first for him to find work. Being part of the unwashed masses that flocked to these shores made it harder to find a job or a place to live. That was until Goodchild Textiles opened in the railyards of Old Gaiman. They needed everyone they could get and Doyle was a strong enough man to survive as he was to work. Slowly, he carved out a new life. He lived in the squalor of South Gaiman like the others he knew there, but he had a community. Everything seemed to point to Doyle having a new and interesting life in this world.

He didn't know, at the time, how right that would be.

It first started as a cough he couldn't shake. For all he knew, it was a leftover issue from working in the mills that were not even remotely up to what we could even begin to consider safe. Then it became wheezing and a fever. With little money and the perpetual problem of eating tomorrow, Doyle chose to ignore the sickness in his body until it was too late. He was now lying on the floor of his small one room apartment staring at the cracking ceiling. After all this time, he had to come back to God. He'd kept him so safe 'til now, why on earth would he let him die now? He was sorry for the things he'd done, the curses he leveled against the Almighty, and his lack of faith. Now, he had to believe this was the test that would bring him back.

"Please God," He pleaded. "don't let me die here."

Doyle's prayers were answered by something other than God. It would be this interaction that would make Doyle sometimes wish that he'd just died. He didn't at first, though. She had intervened and she wasn't God. She wasn't in the business of answering other people's prayers, however. She answered Her own.

She was every man's nightmarish fantasy. She had midnight black hair that was pinned perfectly with curls cascading over her pale white skin. Her large, expressive green eyes made Her look like a nonthreatening angel. She was not an angel. She had the lean body of a wolf that stalked in the night and took a human form. She was a fierce and deadly predator. Men, women, and children had been lost in Her wake. She was the hunter of lost souls.

She was the She Wolf.

In the manner that She was accustomed to, She had been tracking Doyle for weeks. The unusual relationship that she had with the men at Goodchild Textiles had become her new hunting ground. So many lost souls looking to make their money in the New World. They had no problem spending the night with the perfect angel she appeared to be and then somehow disappearing. Then there was this quiet factory man who kept to himself. He had something different about him. He wanted to be away from this mortal world. Something he wanted was beyond the shores that he had landed on. There was an undefined strength in his character that would not let go of his life. His quiet devotion to a faith that She, Herself, could no longer stand. She tracked and watched him as he got sicker and sicker. For Her it would be the last toil he'd claim. She'd keep him in that state of guilt for as long as she could for her own amusement.

The She Wolf measured her time wisely. She went in for the kill on the day that Doyle could no longer hold on to his mortality. She walked into his life when he had fallen into a dreamless sleep and watched him quietly. Her cold fingers on his burning forehead woke him up suddenly as he looked at her. She hung over him in a white gown that left nothing to the imagination. His Victorian principles of modesty would have sent up red flags if he wasn't so relieved in his delirium.

"Molly?" He asked weakly.

"No, sweet boy," She said. "I'm not Molly."

"Are you an angel?"

"No, I'm not an angel." Her vaguely French accent wafted into his ears seductively with husky desire. He was instantly too devoted to Her. "I am a lot like you. A stranger forced to face their mortality in a foreign land. I know what it means to come so far and be near death without any hope. I'm here to stop that. I can save you from this."

"I don't want to die here." He said quickly.

"I heard." She said. "And when I'm done with you, you will get to choose where you get to die."

Doyle didn't understand what that meant.

He understood less when She stripped him of his dirty clothes and laid him naked on the sweat-stained mattress. His eyes started to close as She shed Her gown, exposing cold naked flesh to his unimpressed face. This was a sight he would spend the rest of his days paying for. Her bare thighs straddled him uniting their bodies as one. Dominating grunts and moans parted Her lips as She rode him and relished his last moments. His dying gaze looked back up at the woman above him. In those moments he saw her face contorting into dark shadows as fangs were drawn. Her large eyes looked down with iris the size of pinholes. In those dying moments Doyle had found he made a grave mistake. She was no angel or savior. Doyle had given his soul to something most evil.

"Scail an Blair." He whispered in fear. "deamhan fola."

The words sounded like gibberish to Her as much as Doyle's dying accusation was. What she did understand was the look of terror in his eyes. She had seen this hundreds of thousands of times in everyone she'd tortured to this point. Maybe he had declared her a vampire, she thought, but it didn't matter. She drank in the arousal of his terror.

"My sweet boy," She growled like a predator that had found its prey. "You have no idea what I am."

The last thing that Doyle saw in this life was her fangs striking in his throat the second She felt his body convulse with its last breath. He was held there, in his death throes as she drank his warm blood from his veins. With each mounting second of Her pleasure Doyle felt his life going further and further away. The factory, the city, his life here was drifting away. He had hoped that in this final moment that if he looked up he'd see his wife and children greeting him on a distant golden shore and now that was not to be. All Doyle saw as his mortal life faded was black. His fingers curled around his long forgotten relic, hoping for a miracle and praying the prayer of a dying man.

"Holy Mary, Mother of God, pray for us sinners. Now and at the hour of our death. Amen," were the last the words to leave his lips.

IV.   Wheel in the Sky

Nowish

June was too hot to do anything in Susanne's mind -- even in the mountains. The summer had gotten to be too hot, even with the breeze coming down. And it didn't help that it was June. June had always been a bad month for doing the tours. School groups stopped coming at the end of May and the Boy and Girl Scouts didn't start coming until July. Then they would have the Heritage day on the 4th which was nice for the Sons of the Confederacy to dress up and pretend to shoot at each other in a battle that may have never existed. August was the best time though because they would get the book work tourists who were coming down to Old Jonesborough for the Storytelling festival. Northern tourists who thought they were getting in touch with some folksy roots always wanted to tip the half Korean Dulcet who told them about the past. Her favorite time was in October. That was their best time because that's when they would do the haunted tours which were always her favorite. People don't really ever appreciate the grim parts of history. Also, Bernard would be there at the end of the tour with a chainsaw and that always made her smile. She didn't understand why they kept the park open in June. It was the executor of the estate's wishes to keep this place open year round. She'd never met her boss. He only spoke to her through Henry who seemed to do everything on the land. She didn't really care. Money was money and the Blackmores had more than enough. Susanne stopped as she turned to the group with a fake smile to deliver the speech she had perfectly memorized.

"The Blackmore Plantation was the largest plantation in the country and one of three to survive through the Civil War. In its heyday, the Estate was the home of Virgil Blackmore, his elderly mother, his wife, and nine children; plus over two hundred servants

40

and slaves. It remained untouched by Union sympathizers during the war in East Tennessee due to the abandonment of the land before 1849. It remained uninhabited for more than a hundred years until it was handed over to a relative of the Blackmores and turned into the historical site that you saw in the main building and the farm. The family still lives in residence at the Manor House. Despite repeated requests, they wish to keep their privacy and have yet to open their home to the public."

The familiar cloud of doom descended over Susanne as she spoke, trying to sound enthusiastic, but not scared. If you believed the local stories, this land *was* haunted. There were ghosts and strange lights that filtered through the slave quarters and around the graves of the Blackmore family. There were also savage beasts that would eat a man whole and drink their blood. There were wild men who lived in the forest who could turn into dogs. She tried to tell herself that she didn't believe any of those stories. She hadn't when she first came to work for the Blackmores. They had selected her out of thousands of candidates for this job. They were an enigmatic group who kept their secrets very well. The longer she worked there, the more disturbed by the land she became. She would see people dressed in old clothes just in the corner of her eye and then they would be gone. There was no shortage of sounds of screaming and death. Lately, she had noticed she heard singing and someone calling her name. Susanne was starting to be thoroughly creeped out by her job. She didn't, of course, say that it was ghosts. She was a logical woman and those things were not real. Instead, she believed that it was because of her interactions with Henry.

He was an all right looking guy who had been built for mountain life years ago. He spoke with an educated diction. There was just something that felt off about Henry. Perhaps she didn't know how he came to work for the Blackmores, but something was gone from him when he did. There was a hollow part of Henry that had died and he'd never gotten over it. He spoke of the Blackmore Planation with a level of regard that made her feel uncomfortable. It was as if, to her, that Henry had wanted to keep the place protected from the world that came rushing in after they'd agreed to be put on the historic registry. Like he thought the outside world was going to be their ruin. Susanne thought that was stupid. The world was getting smaller each day and eventually he would have to accept that. That didn't put her on any less of an edge. If something violent happened to her or any visitor to the estate it would be because of Henry.

Susanne didn't keep these fears a secret. She knew better than that. It was what she told Desmond every night when she came home. She would prop her feet up and rehash her day. He would tell her to quit. She was better than guiding morbid tourists through the killing fields of a racist murderer. She had a master's degree. She could go off and teach somewhere. She'd stick her tongue out and pull out a thick Korean accent, mocking her mother who would have said the same thing. She would shake her head and tell him that she loved history. She was chosen to tell the story at Blackmore Estate because she was the best at it. If people ignored the black parts of history -- which included the things that the Blackmores had done -- then we, as a people, ran the risk of repeating them.

"I think you just lie to yourself." He'd say to her. "I think you like being miserable."

She never responded to that because she knew he was right.

Today she knew that she would have a ton to complain about when she got home. She'd waited around all day for someone, anyone, to show up for a tour and when they had, she got the group that she could have done without. Maybe it was because if they hadn't arrived she could have gone home early, but she couldn't stand them. There were four in the group. There was a young couple. Surprisingly, she thought they were very polite for a couple in their twenties. She just hated them though. Every time she made eye contact with them, something in the back of her head said that a white boy like him and a pretty black girl shouldn't be together. That was stupid. She was with Desmond who was about as white as she was a monkey. She was half Korean. Whatever was telling her this was a very, very angry old white woman who was extremely displeased. She really disliked them. Apart from that, the only thing that she also extremely disliked was the fact that the boyfriend had started leaning desperately on the girl. He walked closer and closer towards the Farm the sicker he got. And they were not even the worst people in the group. They fell to the other two. They were squat obnoxious men dressed like they were escaping a Quatermaine novel. She hated them not because of that, but the fact that they spoke over her in French. This just made her more and more angry. She felt that someone in the back of her head was telling her to hate them.

That voice was two steps away from convincing her that she should kill them.

Susanne tried very hard to ignore that voice because she knew that she couldn't kill tourists. She was a professional and she was going to work very hard. She smiled at them.

"It was built in 1790 by Cyrus Blackmore, when he was granted land for his service in the American Revolution. He wanted to make his mountain palace." Susanne raised her voice slightly. Even the Frenchmen were quiet. She grinned now at having the power. "Cyrus expanded the land into the woods, which is why it's extremely difficult to arrive here. Some people also believe that its Cyrus's hubris that creates the most lasting story about the Blackmore Estate."

She paused for dramatic effect. This was the money shot, so to speak. She smiled for a moment.

"What is told is that some time ago, a beast wandered through the woods. The first settlers here were plagued by what they call the She Wolf. She had made her lair in the caves that surrounded what would become the Blackmore Estate. They had cornered this beast in the cave and blocked it off so no one could ever enter or leave. When Cyrus built his estate, he allegedly opened her lair against the advice of Roy Crowe and his family. The She Wolf took her time, but eventually she ended the line of the Blackmores. Whether or not that story is true, what is known is that one day every member the Blackmore Estate was gone except for the children and the elderly mother of Virgil Blackmore. It is the largest disappearance in East Tennessee State history."

The girl raised her hand. Susanne blinked as she felt a small vibration in her pants pocket. She hoped that it wasn't Henry. There was no way it could end well.

"Yes?" Susanne asked, ignoring her phone.

"Did anyone ever find out what happened to the men?"

"No one knows." Said Suanne. "Many say that they still live in the house. Others say that it was a mass exodus. There are some indications that this was a massive slave uprising and after murdering the children and hanging them from the porch, they took Virgil and Charlotte Blackmore as hostages, but no one really knows."

Susanne stopped speaking as she looked up. Henry stood at the top of the hill with his hands on his hips. She sighed. She had to speak with Henry. Maybe it was time they shut down for inspection with the Historical society.

"This concludes our tour. Please stop by our gift shop."

She hurriedly ran up the hill towards the Manor House, leaving her group to find their own way out or to the gift shop. The boy in the tour group sat down on the steps of a neglected slave house. His hands shook. Jacob hated the fact that he was sensitive to the spirits and Rachel hated it for him. She sat down beside him with her hands on his back.

"The Ghosts getting to you?' she said quietly.

"Yes," he said, rubbing his temples. "You can guess what they think about us."

"I'm sure it's charming," she said. "Is she here?"

Jacob thought for a moment. He felt his spine twist for an instant as he heard a soft voice start singing to him. He swallowed as he thought about the words swirling in his head. He looked at Rachel with tired eyes.

"Not here specifically," he said finally. "She's in a place somewhere behind a lot of things that I can't get to. If I'm given more time, I think we can find her and be done."

"No, Jacob. We confirmed what they wanted. The Russo brothers can pay us. We're done."

"But there is still a ton of work that we can do. Rene and Pierre don't know what to do," he said. "Charles said…"

"I'm not a witch and you're a psychic. Let's just go home please, Jacob."

Jacob looked up for a moment. He felt his eyes lock with a figure. She was faint and he could have thought she was a shadow. She smiled at him as he furrowed his brow. Any sort of restraint he had was gone. She and him were together. It was who they'd come to find and he found more than he wanted to tell them. She put her finger to her lips. Jacob knew that he couldn't say anything. He smiled before nodding.

"Sure, let's go home."

V.   Take the Skinheads Bowling

Still now

Carson never thought of himself as a city dweller. He wasn't sure he ever wanted to be there. He loved nature and it felt amazing to him. What really fascinated Carson was weather. Things could change from a blistering hot to a cold night in the matter of minutes when the sun went down. Not cold like the winter where it could kill you but comfortable enough to sit outside in your shirt sleeves. He loved the outdoor world and would have been happier to have been born out in the woods. He wasn't going to give up his concrete jungle though. This was where he was from and where he was going to stay. Animals shouldn't leave their natural habitat. This was where he and Francis had lived their lives in the city enjoying the fake nature. used to sit on the roof smoking cigarettes and drinking gin. You could see the stars back then. It was peaceful. The days had been very exciting for them, especially in the summer. He liked running through the neighborhood when everyone was standing still. They'd sip on stolen Cokes. On a very hot day, they would pretend to do yard work at Mrs. McGrady's Boarding House. Mrs. McGrady housed young single girls who would dress in front of the open windows during the hot days.

Oh, the trouble they used to get into back then.

No matter how much he missed daylight, he had always been a creature of the night. Carson had been a night owl before he was turned. In the dark he felt more alive and he could function better than in the daylight. Francis had always thought that maybe Carson was some sort of nocturnal animal. He just didn't belong to the daylight. Maybe that's why he felt like he needed to be a predator. He'd always known he was going to be a fighter. You didn't grow up in South Gaiman without being tough, not when he was a kid. He stopped just short of being a monster. He could have been -- he could have become a vicious terror like Her. He knew that he hadn't gone that far because of Doyle. Carson knew that he needed someone who was calmer to function. He'd had Francis forever and then there was Doyle. When Carson felt like his life was wrong, he would look at Doyle. When Doyle made a choice, then Carson knew what Francis would have done. That was the only way he knew what was right or wrong.

Carson liked this plan. Doyle wanted to go on a hunt. Carson felt so good about it that he worried that maybe it was wrong. Carson had a hard time trusting his own instincts when it came to this sort of thing. He thought about it long and hard. Would Francis be on board? Francis had taught Carson that the best thing he could do was take care of the family and the neighborhood. Carson thought that Francis would have approved of this plan. He wasn't a violent man, but he had known right and wrong. He wouldn't have backed down from this fight. If Francis were alive, he would have been running with them. He would have been the third voice that would have seconded Doyle's plan.

Carson picked up his bat and gave it a hearty swing with his own sick amusement. He loved baseball. If there was anything that if he missed from the days of running around in the sunlight it was seeing baseball games. Had things been different, Carson might have been one of those boys playing. It was a fantasy that he had revisited every time that he swung the large bat into someone's head. It was like enjoying a pickup game back in the neighborhood. He at least felt like he could have a good time. Not like Doyle who was pacing on the roof top's edge with his golf club slung over his shoulder, scowling as he looked down on the street.

"Doyle," He said. "Let me track. I'm better at it than you."

Doyle gave Carson a sneer as he went back to his patrol. Carson swore under his breath. He loved Doyle like a brother but he could be as stubborn as a brain-damaged mule. Carson had been convinced for years that was the reason that She had chosen Doyle. He was too stubborn to die. Carson cringed as he thought about Her. Whether Carson wanted to admit it or not he thought about Her more often than not. With every action he took, he would think about how he would do something and if it would please his Mistress. Most of the time, he didn't care but once in a great while, he'd think about Her and know it was because of the uncertainty of Her fate. He knew that if She came back, he'd be a goner. He shook his head as he looked at Doyle's back. He swung the bat in practice swings. He liked to pretend that he was swinging at the back of Doyle's head. Then, Carson stopped as he sniffed the air. His pupils retracted as a musky scent hit his nose. He grinned as Doyle picked up his head quietly as he too caught the scent.

Vampires are experts on blood and the nuances thereof. They are, as are all creatures who are in touch with their inner beasts, able to track the scent of blood. So, they are familiar with blood and all its flavors. What you might not be familiar with is that blood has no real difference between ethnicities. This does not account for ethnically-related illness, but generally there is nothing different. Blood is just blood when it comes to person A or person B. What varies taste are blood types, but what really mixes it are the chemicals that work through our veins. Hormones and pheromones add different flavors and vampires can smell it. What Carson and Doyle detected was far more pungent than any other smell that night: someone was running on adrenaline.

Carson loved it when his prey ran scared. And someone was scared down there. He was running from the top of St. Mark's and down Broad as if his life depended on it and, at that particular moment, it did. Behind him were four fast moving creatures in hot pursuit. Two of them were excited, one felt prideful and one felt aroused. Doyle crouched down and turned his ear down to the street. His hearing was better than his sense of smell. He heard the calls like wild dogs chasing a wounded deer. Then, he and Carson saw them.

The deer looked small. A thin youth who looked thinner than he should in his tight purple jeans. He had a haircut that Carson had long associated with the stage production of Peter Pan. Behind him were the wolves. In his younger days and before Doyle, Carson had run with a gang. Then he ran by himself. He could lie to everyone and say that he was out to protect the neighborhood. That was incidental. He was there to bust heads. He knew what a sea of bald shaved head meant on another level. This was a gang who was looking for blood and it was going after the deer in the skinny jeans.

He also knew what the elaborate tattoos meant. So did Doyle. They had found their prey.

"So, that's what passes for hard these days?" said Carson. "I'd rather be soft."

"Now, Carson, you can't make judgment calls based on how a person looks. For all you know, they could be Buddhist biker missionaries."

One of the wolves got close enough to hit the deer in the back of the head. This stunned the deer, who stumbled into the side of the building. It was enough of an opening for the wolves. Within seconds, they had the deer down on the ground and were introducing him to the bottom of their Doc Martens.

"Your Buddhist Missionaries are getting ready to curb stomp that faggot," Carson said. "Think you could be wrong."

"Well, I suspect that the swastika tattooed on that fella's head isn't a part of his Tibetan heritage." Said Doyle. "Shall we?"

"Of course." Said Carson. "After you."

Doyle backed up before he started running off towards the ledge. He leapt gracefully off the roof with a certain controlled intensity. Doyle's boot hit the back of the head of one of the skinheads before he leapt back off. Doyle felt bad about that. Of course, one had to consider whether brain damage would make them better? Carson thought so. Then again, Carson was very impressed with Doyle's landing. It was very comic-book-like and a really impressive entrance. Doyle would later tell him it was an accident so that he wouldn't make Carson feel guilty about the fact that he'd been planning that move for weeks ever since he saw it in a movie. Doyle gripped his club and stood up from the downed man. He had no fear. Part of Doyle had always felt partly human but now he was in the den of predators ready to end lives. He was a different kind of predator.

Doyle felt things slow down for him as he eyed the wolves around him. He gripped the handle of his bat. He felt his fangs drop inside his mouth, as the smell of blood began the change. His mouth watered as he realized that someone was scared of him. He stood up slowly, watching them. Carson slipped to the ground like the large hound that he was, watching Doyle and the crowd. He wasn't going to do anything until the deer got safely away. He watched as the boy crawled away and ran off into the night.

Now or never, Doyle thought.

"Good, I have your attention," he began. This seems like a good time as any to mention that vampires have a variety of talents which differ from vampire to vampire. Doyle, for example, could tame the crowds. Right now, the skinheads wanted to break his neck, but somehow, they didn't. They sat enthralled by Doyle's voice, like mice before a snake. "My name is Doyle Lanagan. Somewhere nearby is me associate, Carson O'Brian. We are concerned residents o' this neighborhood. You boys are making an awful lot of noise. We don't think that this is polite. We are asking for you to please leave."

There are a few things that you should never do when dealing with a vampire. You should never make fun of a vampire's shoes, for example. Vampires work hard to look as fashionable as possible. Therefore, to make fun of a vampire's shoes does hurt said vampire's feelings. This social faux pas comes with the nasty side effect of the vampire ripping your throat out. The other thing that you don't want to do is start a fight with a vampire. In addition to being fast, vampires are quite strong. They also don't like getting blood on those very expensive shoes which means that there are few creatures that'll win and even fewer who'll survive. It is generally always in your best interest to not pick a fight with a vampire and to compliment their fashion sense.

Doyle had always been a good sport about brawling. He always sold the first punch. So when Doyle saw the words "white" and "power" coming at him mean and fast, he didn't move. Doyle recoiled from the punch like he was shot in the head. Carson had forgotten this fact about his associate. It was evident from the bone-crunching swing of his bat that took down the second rabid wolf. Doyle shot him a glare.

"What?" Said Carson. "It was a fair fight. Now, it is."

"I had it handled."

"What? By getting your ass handed to you?"

"You have no flair for the dramatic, do you?"

Before Carson could answer, there was concrete rushing towards his face as he was tackled into a trash can. Carson turned with vengeance too look up at the man who had him. Carson wasn't someone who sold punches in a street fight. He was going to give a man a fight in a street and he did. He sprang up violently, bringing fists and hands against the man's neck. Carson had been restrained in his reaction and was proud of himself as he sank his fangs into the man's neck, as opposed to ripping him apart. After he finished, Carson smashed the man's face against the wall and let him drop to the ground.

Doyle, on the other hand, wasn't as physical as Carson – however — he wasn't about to take a second punch. He saw it coming like before except this time he grabbed the wrist. In a fluid action that would have impressed Bruce Lee, Doyle had the man against a wall with his arms pinned behind him. He bit into the back of the man's neck and let out a groan. He had fed on humans before, but they hadn't tasted like this. This blood tasted better than anything he'd ever had before. It was like drinking blood when he first awoke back when the world was new to him and exciting.

Doyle Lanagan finally understood what his purpose was. The priest had been right that this was what he should be doing. He felt righteous in his victory.

He brought his lips to the man's ears.

"Listen, and listen good," he said in a growl. "I saw too many good people die for your freedoms over the years -- many of them in Europe -- just to have some punk kid march down the streets in jackboots singing "Deutschland, Deutschland" in my neighborhood. You and your kind come back to my neighborhood, I'm taking the collar off Carson and you will regret your decisions."

"I'm not scared of you or your boyfriend, you fucking fanged faggot," said the lone skin head. "I will beat your head in like a…"

Doyle sighed. They were having such a pleasant conversation and then he had to ruin their good time by being rude. Doyle felt the need to be rude back. He gripped the skin on the back of the man's head and introduced him to the side of the building. Doyle watched as he fell to the ground. He grinned at Carson. He'd call Weston Lewis later. Now they had to relish this victory.

VI.   An Excerpt From the Journal of Virgil Blackmore

1845

When someone writes the definitive history of the South, I hope they realize that summer time is when the living is easy. The crops have been planted in the spring and all there is to do is watch them grow until fall. The fields will be tended to throughout the summer, but there is little for me to do at this time. It's sort of like a time that I feel myself become lazy and settled in the mountain way of life. I find myself lounging on the porch with a book that I only sometimes pretend to read. I am pleased to announce that Henry has figured out how to sweeten the cold tea properly. I do not imbibe spirits during the work hours and my beloved Charlotte does not drink at all. This is a fine substitute. Joseph, our middle child, has taken to sitting with me on the porch overlooking the fields and pretending his tea is scotch. He will be a fine overseer.

We celebrated Robert's birthday this evening. Isabell, the kitchen girl, slow-roasted a pig for our dinner party. Mother was there, as well as some of our friends from the neighboring towns. I do not think that our two-year-old enjoyed the party as much as his mother did. Of course, she does love to host parties. I know that with her frail demeanor and her lack of understanding of the mountain ways, that she misses Savannah and her socialite days. She will have to find other ways of living. It's why we have so many children. If she cannot be a socialite, then she can be a mother. I even made a joke to that regard which ended exactly as I expected it to. We will be working on that this evening. I wish this life could be her desire, but I am not that different from her. The rearing of the next generation raised up in the Blackmore name, however, is great and important work. I know we will have another child.

Many would worry that with so many children, our wealth would be spread too thin. I have no concerns of that. We have two daughters whom we can marry off to family friends that I know, which will put them and us in good standing. As for the boys, my eldest will inherit the estate as I did from my father. I can hope that dowries and good social status will carry the other boys to a successful place. Charlotte has many friends with girl children their ages. We will spend the Christmas season in Savannah arranging our family's future. We cannot allow our estate to fall into poor hands.

As long as it is well-managed, I do not worry about the future prosperity of the estate. Our harvests in the fall are most abundant. The land will not be exhausted as we have already been practicing crop rotation. The men of the field and I have already started planning. We are discussing the next season's crop planting now. I like to stay three years ahead in case we need to alter our plans. Mr. Cooper -- overseer of the estate since my father's time -- tells me that the harvest looks strong this year. He says that George, the boy who he put in charge of the others, says that the ground is fertile and will be for quite some time. Mr. Cooper, like my father and myself, handles our property with a firm hand. This breeds a healthy fear, which my father said was better than over-familiarity and blurring of the lines between classes. He was fond of Mr. Machiavelli and his literary work. I suspect that Father fancied himself a Medici of the Watauga. While I hold myself to the idea of a firm hand, I fear that George may have told Mr. Cooper what he wanted to hear to avoid a beating. For all I know, that could be a lie and we are doomed. I would hope that George knows that if we go down to poverty then so does he. I will hope for the best, but plan for the worst.

News of that business in Virginia has finally reached my darling Charlotte, much to my dismay. Slave revolts are nothing new, but they are always violent and dangerous. Of course when some bug gets in the craw of a bunch of wild animals what does one expect? I don't need her to know about these things because she worries far too much. I have tried to keep her sheltered from the evils in this world. Her life is better served being unaware of the bad. She didn't need to know about those Negroes slaughtering sixty-five men, women, and children. With her fragile demeanor, I am afraid constant news like this might break her. She barely survived the stress when those Crowe boys threatened to run us out of the county. They did not.

Someone in her sewing circle must have mentioned it. She returned to me in tears as she then related to me the rumors that had been told to her. I assured her that it was purely rumor. Nothing like that could happen here. That was more than enough to calm her this time. At least one crisis has been averted.

I find myself waking up at night shaken by the fear that is occurring here. What bothers me most is what end does this method ultimately serve? I would gladly liberate my property if I thought they could be civilized. With each passing violent act, I know that they cannot be. If you have a vicious dog, you don't let it wander free. You keep it on a leash until it no longer serves a purpose. It seems to me that they are not so far removed from their jungle roots that they can be trusted with their freedom. They are, at the end of the day, still savage creatures. It is the primary reason that I suspect the majority of rebellions will fail. They lack the restraint to survive as a cohesive group. Like pack animals out to destroy, they have no real plan, just chaos. Yet I don't think we can discard them entirely. I believe they can be trained. Henry, our house boy, is proof of that. There is a fair amount of intelligence within him. Henry has learned everything I can teach him. Mae Ella, the mulatto girl we chose for him, even reads a little. If all of them were as smart as Henry and Mae Ella, we'd have to reconsider this whole institution.

They would be nothing without us. We brought them out of the jungles. We brought them God. We clothe them. We are teaching them how to be human beings. We here, at least, take better care of them than Walter Montague does with his property. The things he does, I would not mention in mixed company. There is a reason Mae Ella is more white than most.

In spite of this charity, another pair of my coloreds have run off from the Farm tonight; One of my strongest oxen and a

Melungeon woman. They have taken with them two boys aged twelve and fourteen. It would seem that they have run into the forested hills. I am deeply upset because she had before rejected two young children that she bred. If anything, this reckless rejection of their offspring proves to me that these creatures are in a desperate need of constant guidance. I cannot think of a beast in the wild who would abandon their calves unless the offspring were somehow defective. These little ones are not defective. I should know. I am a master of genetics. I keep my breeding stock strong so there is no chance of frailty. Maybe it's my own fault that I have bred a Melungeon woman with a willful ox. The Red Indian blood might have caused some sort of madness. If that's the case, then Charlotte's plan might be better. She shouldn't be so attached, but she can't bear to see a child without a mother. Mae Ella wasn't able to produce a child with Henry, so Charlotte gave these pups to her. We will see if nurture can outweigh nature.

I find myself consulting often with Henry on these matters. I had hoped that he might have some insight on the actions of these men. Henry straddles two worlds better than I. He tells me that he had none. They don't speak to him in the Farm. They seem to like him less than they like me. I tell him that they are jealous. Henry is an exemplary specimen of his species. My father saw it in him. He pulled Henry out of the field and transferred his ownership to me. If harm comes to him, then there will be hell to pay.

Something dreadful happened today, that I must also record. It was late in the evening when Mr. Cooper returned to our estate. He and a few of his boys departed before supper with one of the bloodhounds to catch the scent of our runaways. He returned at midnight. I was anticipating the return of my property. What I got instead was a man visibly shaken and pale as if he had seen a ghost. I cannot understand why a man of his caliber would be so afraid of an inferior race. I asked Mr. Cooper the question of where they were. He looked at me with a pallid expression. His lips trembled as he tells me where they are hiding. He collapsed to his knees before I can ask him what is the matter.

"In Jessum's Hallow." He whispered. "They're in the hollow. God forgive me. I left them there."

I changed out of my bed clothes and rushed to join the party. Mr. Cooper led me down into the hollow. When I saw the moonlit carnage, I understood why Mr. Cooper is so disturbed.

In the bottom of the hollow, there were seven to ten bodies, some of them stripped of their flesh, bound together in a crude circle. As I step forward, I realize that the rope keeping them together is the lower intestines of my strong field hand. I hesitate before bringing the lantern light closer. Their contorted faces screamed silently and their throats were ripped out. The bottom fell out of my stomach. I know a fear now that I have never known before.

The air is too thick for us to continue our inspection of the scene. Mr. Cooper and I resolved to come back in daylight, bringing a local constable with us. This is something that I suspect was done out of pure, murderous rage for my family. I want to blame it on those Crowe boys who live out in the Cove. They are vicious creatures with no sense of good taste or manners. It would not surprise me if they had become a pack of vicious animals. After the constable's work, we will dispose of them in the daylight when it's safe. Once we have made this choice, however, and were preparing to leave, I heard a song pushing through my ears and my brain.

"One by one, they will fall bleeding and begging like them all.

Caught in the clutches of the She Wolf, they will fight.

She will feed on their baby's blood in the night."

It is a woman's voice that I hear singing to me. She has an accent I cannot quite place. I look to Mr. Cooper, but he has not reacted as I have to the song. My fear is that he is not able to hear it like I have. For an instant in the blackness, I see a pair of green eyes flash at me and then they are gone. I pray that it is the shock of the night and nothing more, but part of me knows that there is something else coming and that chills me to my very core. A wolf has claimed me for her prey and she is waiting to strike.

I will not be sleeping tonight.

VII. Dear Prudence

Nowish

The drive-thru breakfast and cup of coffee he'd eaten threatened to burn his throat with biled vengeance as he hit the curb pulling into the overly long driveway. Carter Lewis hated that taste in the back of his throat but it was less common these days. The acid reflux had gone down when he quit smoking. After thirty years of being a pack a day smoker, he'd finally quit. She had asked him to quit before now and had every day of their long partnership. She didn't want to watch him suffer through lung disease and die. It would be a humiliation for a man who had slugged through countless unnamed battles to finally suffer and die consequential to his own foolish choices. She'd asked him to do a lot of things that he just didn't get around to while she was alive. He'd compiled a list. That seemed to be his life now. He was waiting to die while ticking little things off a list to appease a dead woman. He'd become a reasonable adult in his old age. Margaret would have been proud of him. He pushed that thought away. Her memory tore him apart like nothing else and she would be disappointed in him now as he visited the house at the end of the long driveway. She might have an issue with his choices in companions. Carter Lewis had become a lonely man after her unexpected death so he'd had to find something to fill the role she left vacant. In her sainted place Carter Lewis had adopted a living dead girl to dote over.

It didn't matter what he was doing, Carter Lewis would drop everything to appease Prudence Goodchild. It wasn't much of a surprise to anyone -- except himself -- that Carter Lewis had grown attached to Prudence. His children had accepted this fact even if they were not particularly big fans of it. The reason that the Lewis Clan had immigrated to this country was because they had been contracted to fight a long bloody war. Because of this, much like the relationship between a general and his commander, the head of the clan had always been close to Prudence. The war was over for now and there were no enemies for either of them to fight. He could have shrugged off the council of the child queen and led a life without interaction with vampires. He would not. The last battle wasn't too far behind and they only had each other to remember that fight. Those with whom he'd stood shoulder to shoulder in the trenches were all gone except for Prudence. Carter Lewis would move heaven and earth for Prudence because he had paid a staggering price for their friendship. He held on to the last person who understood.

He'd known Prudence for a long time and, in a sense, they had grown up together during the war. He had been a younger man when they met. No, he wasn't a man then. Carter Lewis was barely man, a mere child, when he became the oldest male of his clan. He'd seen his father murdered by the Acadian Guard. His uncles torn apart by the betrayal of Heller DeWitt when he submitted to the She Wolf. It was a terrible time for all of them and the memories of those bloody times lingered with more trauma than he would ever admit. The War of Vampiric Succession had claimed too many on all the sides. He wasn't the only one to lose friends and family. The war devastated hunter numbers. The Sisters in Saffron lost so many that they disbanded their family. After Heller and then what later happened to Ellis, The DeWitts were all but gone now. They stayed by themselves waiting for the time to redeem themselves. They were the ones who had been spared the true horrors. The so-called family clans (and there were so few) were spared the worst of it. The paladin orders had been decimated by both sides so much that if there were any people left in them afterwards, they had been evacuated from the city. The only one left was the Clan of the Flaming Sword and they had to be on their last legs. Due to their high standards, the average age had to be over fifty now. Even if they had younger members, they were becoming a relic. The world would always change and hunters were the ones who had to evolve the most. The Department could issue a hunting license which took tons of hoops to jump through. If you were lucky, you'd get associated with one of the good guy groups and they paid well, like Prudence, but that was even slowing down. Gaiman Heights couldn't be the base of operation for them anymore. The world was becoming too peaceful. Everyone was leaving except Prudence.

Allies die, enemies mellow and Prudence Goodchild was still nine-years-old.

She never aged. That was a product of the Curse. Her physical growth had been stunted as her youth was eternal. As the world evolved around her, she stayed as young as her dolls. She was wise and a brilliant leader forced into an empire that she was ruling as well as anyone else. Carter Lewis knew that all too well. You didn't succeed the She Wolf without being smarter than everyone else. She wouldn't have survived to being nearly four hundred years old if she wasn't brilliant. Prudence was very old and Carter Lewis knew that her age was becoming a problem. When you remain stagnant, you expect many things to remain stagnant with you and Prudence was beginning to forget that things aged around her even if she didn't. Most recently, Carter Lewis had retired from hunting. It had been a long time coming, but after the second grandchild, it was time. Prudence didn't share this view. Either she didn't understand or didn't care, but Prudence still felt that the only person who could help her was him. Any time that Prudence had a problem, Carter Lewis was on call. He could tell her no. His sons who stayed in the city said to let it go and tell her no. He refused to do so. He preferred to just keep going. He knew that he couldn't say no. Carter Lewis felt like a shark. No breaks, just keep swimming or die.

He couldn't abandon her anyway. True, she was old. Prudence had seen this country forge itself out of the dust and rise. She was a very powerful vampire but Carter Lewis knew of a secret side that she never showed anyone else. At the end of the day, Prudence was still a little girl alone in this world. She had no family to speak of. She was an orphan. If there was one thing that an orphan needed at the end of the day, it was unconditional love. Carter Lewis was a hard man, but he had boundless love to share. She didn't get offered affection in her world. The vampires of Gaiman were scared of her. Her maker was dead. Claudius treated her like his young soldier. Carter Lewis treated her like a grandchild. No one else treated her like that and it had given Prudence a more human side. She fulfilled a role of being desperate for a father's approval which Carter Lewis relished and she had a nurturing parent figure. They needed each other.

This loyalty was why he had driven to Trublood Manor before the rising sun peeked through the thin gray clouds of morning. The voice at the other end of the line had apologized for waking him up. He didn't say anything in response. He had been awake already when the phone rang. The nightmares weren't so bad. At this late stage of his life, Carter Lewis had learned to sleep through them. It was the dreams that were bothering him now. He agreed to arrive and did so very quickly, but not before making a stop. He had, in the blackness, scarfed down a cup of fast food coffee and two biscuits with egg, bacon, and cheese. Carter Lewis knew one thing. You don't see a vampire on an empty stomach.

The sun was peeking through the tops of buildings, painting the sky with the pinks and purples of dawn as he stepped up to the colonial door of Trublood Manor. Not much had remained of the original Trublood house. Most of that estate was burned to the ground during the witch riots of 1609 when the first European vampire to set foot in the New World had been burned at the stake as a witch. Prudence had been the only one who knew George Trublood and had chosen to name the palace after him when she assumed authority of the city in 1919. Her ascension to the throne had created the War for Vampiric Succession. She was coordinated in what became execution square at Trublood Manor. The original manor had been burned to the ground shortly before George's death at the hands of the citizens of Harmony. What remained from the original structure of the Puritan-built cabin was the deeply-built foundation and a well-made back door that had become the trusted person's entrance at the Manor. Carter Lewis was preparing to head to that door when he saw the ageless blonde woman with all the seriousness of Mary Poppins waiting for him. Her maternal face had been wearing a scowl of appreciation and irritation as he stepped towards her. He didn't know how long Coraline had served Prudence, but she was as loyal as they came. It wasn't uncommon or surprising. Vampires are not able to do most of the work they need to be maintained in the mundane world so they will often choose a human to serve them. These humans become fiercely loyal for two reasons. One, there is an unspoken loving bond between the vampire and its human. While this might be related to the human coming into contact with the vampire and becoming obsessed, it can also be less obvious than that. Second is the sharing of a blood bond. Vampires wish to keep their humans with them for all time. As such they are fed a steady diet of the vampire's blood which keeps them moving into immortality but it also comes with a heavy addiction.

Carter Lewis wondered how those two ever crossed paths. He was sure that Coraline had an interesting story, but he never knew it. He hoped that it wasn't because Coraline was a pedophile. Many people become ghouls because they are attracted romantically or sexually to their vampires, yet Prudence had never made it to puberty. The more he thought about it, the more he felt that his other theory was more accurate -- Prudence had hired Coraline to fulfill a role for both of them. Carter Lewis knew that Prudence needed a caregiver who acted like a nanny and Coraline needed to be a mother. Family, he'd learned over the years, was what you make it.

"Thank God you came so quickly," Coraline said with relief. "I can't get her to listen. She is very upset and is refusing to go to sleep until she speaks with you…in person."

"What's going on?" He asked as he marched towards the master bedroom. Rarely would Prudence act like a child. Something was terrible and he had to work fast.

"She said that she was reading Father's prized possession," Coraline explained as she followed hurriedly behind him. She was slightly angry at the man for barging in without waiting for her explanation. "She then said she had to speak to you. I told her it could wait until tomorrow at sun down and she threw a tantrum. I know it's silly, but sometimes even queens need a time out. I thought it would get her to think rationally. Something has scared her and so I'm guessing that it's George Trublood's private work instead of a family Bible."

"She was raised Puritan so you never know what's got her shook."

"I know that she is very upset. Mr. Lewis, please."

"You called. I'm here to help."

The master bedroom was a traditional resting chamber for a vampire. Prudence's bedroom was built into the dugout foundation of the old basement. It was only slightly cold but very dark, or rather it would be had it not been for the care that had been taken to decorate the room for a nine-year-old little girl. The room was decorated as a labor of love from over half a century ago. The cream wallpaper was accented by pinstriped purple flowers. It was made to feel brighter by the pink trim and molding. There was something very English about it. She had painted windows that looked out on old fields of rolling hills with a bright sunny day outside. She watched the fake sky dance with a lovely sun. The bedroom had become a shrine to Prudence's fading humanity which she fought to hold on to. Her furniture had been built by the simple hands of her father. It was the bed she'd died in all those years ago. She laid her head down on the mattress that she had welcomed her into the Curse. Carter Lewis had always thought this to be a trifle bit morbid, but he just didn't understand vampires. She had to remember she had died once. That once there was a little girl named Prudence Goodchild who played out in the sun and walked the earth as a human being. The day she forgot about that little girl was the day she would lose her humanity and if she lost her humanity, she would become a monster.

She unfolded her arms from her protesting scowl when he finally sat down on the edge of the bed. She rarely smiled and this was not one of the days where he was going to get one out of her, but he could tell that she was pleased to see him. Her face and body relaxed as she sat up in her old world bed.

"Coraline tells me you won't go to sleep," he said finally. "Just because you are queen doesn't mean you shouldn't listen to your staff."

"I am able to do what I want and when I want, Carter," Prudence corrected. Her accent had slipped to an informal Dutch sound. She was tired when she sounded less English and more Dutch. "And I assure you I will sleep after I warn you."

"It's an excuse. Go to sleep Prudence."

"I read Father's book," she said quickly. "You know, the one from the German nun."

"George's then. Your real father had no patience for fortune tellers."

"I'm not quite sure if Robert Goodchild can be called my father anymore." She thought for a moment. "We did part on bad terms."

"Do you think your Robert Goodchild would approve of you calling George "father"?"

"I am unsure. When the curtain between worlds is thin again I will see if I can inquire as to his opinion on the matter. "

"So the German nun has got you upset."

"So to speak. Since the emergence of the nexus, I have felt inclined to brush up on what Dagmar has said about the future. It has taken me years to reach enough proficiency in German to be anywhere near where I can read it. Of course I have plenty of free time on my hands. She speaks of the coming of the Lord of the Black Smoke. The wolf queen will fall heralding his return. Carter, war is coming."

"That's not upsetting. It's not surprising either. The Stone kid has changed what has been a pretty normal life up until this moment. Things heating up again doesn't come as a shock. Are you upset about war?"

"Carter, The Nun speaks of us. The forever child queen Living Dead Girl and her most trusted Knight. She speaks of our deaths."

Carter Lewis found his expression easing as he looked down at her. He gave her a weak smile as he realized her fear. The powerful queen with all the immortality that life had thrown at her was just like the rest of humanity -- scared about what awaited her on the other side.

"Oh Prudence," he said finally. "None of us know that Dagmar is even correct on her visions."

"Father believed she was. It's why he permitted his sacrifice on the altar of flame to liberate the Nexus. Carter, I'm scared. I don't want to die."

"You still have humanity in your bones, Prudence," he said. "None of us want to die. There is a blackness that we can't recall and we can't ask people what it's like. Hell, I've tried. My requests have fallen on deaf ears. It's why we have hope that at the end, things will work out all right."

"Is that why you aren't afraid?"

"I'm terrified of death too, Prudence. I just have to believe I'll see Margaret again when I go. I have to hope that my sacrifices were worth it."

"Carter, will you read to me before you go? I would like to hear about Badger and Mole's adventures tonight."

"Of course, Prudence. Anything you ask."

VIII. Children's Story

Also Nowish

The smell of stale blood filled Doyle's nose as the sound of Carson's fists slamming into flesh and bone was punctuated with the pulpy, crackling noises of said flesh and bone being smashed and collapsing. He would have been more interested in helping Carson stomp on this man if it wasn't for another more pressing issue that Doyle was preoccupied with. He had wedged himself between the combatants and a small figure clinging to him like a safety device in a sea of violence. Doyle had forced the child behind him in a desperate attempt to shield the him from the violence that couldn't be ignored. Carson had started grunting with strain from delivering the blows. That was enough to pique anyone's attention. Doyle could feel small eyes peering around his legs to watch with fascinated horror of the display of violence before him. That was when the paternal instinct had cut in for Doyle. He spun, staring at the boy square in the eye in an effort to keep the child distracted from the violence that was happening just a few feet away from him. The wide eyes of the small boy finally looked back at him. This wasn't a situation they had been prepared for in their hunts. This had to be the most righteous of their activities. They'd fought back the Skinheads and now they were saving a child from a pedophile the only way they knew how.

They had to do this one; the pedophile was one of their own.

Feeding on children was a practice that had changed drastically over the years in how it was viewed. It was widely believed that at one time, vampires had ruled most of Central Europe. There is no doubt that Europe's grand nobility had some blood of the beast. During those times they'd had no problem feeding on children. It was a sign of status. The stories of the

67

decadent feasting on orphaned children were the highlights of the vampiric social world. That was when the hunters rose up. Having sworn to protect the innocent they could not, in good faith, permit the murder of children to continue. Those who were smart evolved in their thinking and became aware of how dangerous it was to feed on the blood of children or they were put to death by the hunters. With this subtle shift in those who received the Curse, a sense of humanity returned to the vampiric world. This practice, however, had always been terribly out of fashion in Gaiman Heights since the start of Prudence Goodchild's rule. As queen, and having been placed in the unpleasant position she was at such a young age, the corruption of a child into a monster made her very upset. She disliked pedophiles more than most and demanded a stiff punishment. Carson, who had his own emotional scars and grudges, was eager to enforce the decree when it came out. He hated that the orphans of the world were the ones who always got the brunt of damage. They got swallowed up by the world and spit out. He couldn't just let that keep happening.

This one was special anyway. The child who had gone missing was from St. Nicholas' Home for Children. Carson had grown up there when they still called it an orphanage. It had been the only family he knew, outside of Francis. It was hard enough being without a family in this world, but he wasn't about to let people make his family home a dangerous place. No one ruined Carson's notions of childhood. I mean, you can do what you like, but Carson was somewhat hard to deal with when he was upset.

Doyle had tried to make Carson wait for this one. He knew that if there was a child from St. Nicholas' in danger they would be on call from the nuns. If there was a problem with security, you called Carson. He wasn't going to wait. One child hurt was one too many in Carson's very aggressive opinion. Doyle wasn't going to dissuade him from this hunt. Despite his personal belief that he himself was a monster, there was still a moral right that he had to uphold. As a father, he couldn't let the suffering of a child continue. And as the leader of the South Gaiman Brood, he could not afford to let one of his charges target a child and break the rules. They had a sworn duty to do what needed to be done.

It had taken Carson no time to find them. Like a bloodhound, Carson had picked up on the scent from St. Nicholas and followed it as hard as he could as Doyle followed him with a cold calculation. They knew what they would have to do. Doyle would politely stay out of the way as Carson reaped the vengeance that he'd claim from their prey.

Carson savored the tight grip that he held on to ~~with~~ the collar of the other man as his own shirt was splattered with stale and old blood. The vampire they'd found had to be old world. That didn't excuse his actions, not in this city. The child took one last look before he buried his face in Doyle's shoulder. This was becoming more traumatic by the second and Doyle hated it. No child should have to endure what this one had and Doyle's heart broke for the little one.

"Listen to me because I know it's going to be hard for you to hear, but I want you to remember this." Doyle said in a quiet voice as he hugged the child. "It will take forever for you to understand it but you have to. What happened here isn't your fault. Trust me, God doesn't punish little boys like this. He's a bad man and getting what he deserves, but you did nothing wrong."

"Is he going to kill that man?" Asked the child timidly.

"Is that what you want?" Doyle and victim services were just getting used to each other. Give them a chance. "We can do that if you want."

"I want ice cream," said the boy.

It was a non sequitur for sure but something Doyle was willing to oblige on. Without thinking, he picked up the child and scooted closer to Carson. Carson had become so overly involved in the beating that he'd started to work up what some could consider a sweat. This is a little more horrifying in a vampire largely because it meant there was a thin layer of blood covering his forehead. Carson flexed his hands as they finally grew tired.

"Children," Carson spat. "you sick bastard."

"Carson, the little one would like to get out of here. I was thinking of ice cream. That's a thing children like, right?"

"Yea, of course," Carson said. "Morrison's is down the block. They have ice cream sundaes so big you can ski down them. Why don't you go on and get out of here."

"Are you sure?" asked Doyle. "I can stay."

"I think I can handle this prick." Carson grinned. "You don't want to be here anyway. I'm about to get all Tarantino here."

Sometimes, Carson needed subtitles when he spoke. Doyle barely could understand what was going on. When he saw Carson digging into his jacket, he knew it was time to get out of there. This was about to get really bloody. Doyle held the child to his chest and quietly backed out of the abandoned building. Carson waited for the door to slam shut before he dropped the other vampire. He slammed his foot down on to his throat and narrowed his eyes at the man. He looked down with a slow smirk as his pliers clinked a sickening song.

"You know the rules in this city," Carson said through his grin. "Kids ain't on the fucking menu."

"Please, I'm too old…."

"We don't take excuses and you know it." Carson brought his knee down on the throat as he held the other man's chin. "Now, open wide."

It was so quiet that the only sound that could be heard was the hum of the neon sign at Morrison's. His eyes looked around at the yellow walls and the nonthreatening pictures of candy and ice cream. He finally looked over to the young boy who was enjoying what the man behind the counter described as the Amaya. Doyle knew who Amaya was and was only mildly concerned that the small nymph had a sundae named after her, but the boy liked it. That was more important. He carefully watched the boy whose feet kicked over the edge of the chair, missing the floor with bare feet. The only time that he stopped shoveling in thick blobs of ice cream covered in sprinkles, candy, whipped cream, and double chocolate hot fudge was to push up the sleeves of his two-sizes-too-big t-shirt to help him get the ice cream in his mouth without swallowing any fabric. Things almost felt normal for Doyle. Then, there he saw the child stop and stare at him. He gave the boy a warm smile trying to calm things. Something had crossed the child's mind and he was disturbed by his thought.

"Are you fattening me up so you can eat me?" He asked finally.

"What?" Doyle was horrified at first. Then he had to realize what the child had been through. Of course he would think that after dealing with the other vampire. That horrified Doyle even more, but he knew that he would have to make things better. "No. I would never eat a boy. That would make me a bad man. We're friends of Sister Jack who runs the orphanage. Carson knew you were in trouble and she is very worried."

"Oh," Said the boy as he looked back down at the ice cream. "I didn't mean to run away. He said he was going to be my new dad. Is she mad at me?"

"No, she's not mad at you. It wasn't your fault."

The child nodded as he twisted his spoon into the cooling fudge. He scrunched his nose as he thought. His eyes drifted back up to Doyle.

"Mr. Lanagan," asked the child. "How did you know I was in trouble?"

There are lies that we tell children. Many of them are to spare the innocence we are only allowed to have for such a short time. Doyle knew that it just wouldn't be smart to tell the boy what really happened. He could hear screams of pain and scared tears. He had heard the pleas to go home that he'd made. He couldn't tell him that Carson had kept his head down to the ground and hunted the smell of the boy through the streets to lead them to where the child was. He was going to be traumatized for a long time already. There was no point in telling him that there were monsters who were tracking his scared body.

"We're friends with Santa Claus," Doyle explained almost too naturally. "He told us where to find you. He cares a lot about the kids at St. Nick's and he told us you were in trouble."

"He does? Wow. Is that why he comes to St. Nick's first every year?"

"Of course he does." What Doyle didn't mention was that Santa Claus was very real (did you expect him not to be in Gaiman Heights?) but that Santa came twice. The first time was Carson who dressed up as Santa Claus every Christmas to give them the gifts that he and Doyle had bought. "He knew you were in trouble but he couldn't leave the North Pole just now, so he asked us to find you and take you home."

The child slowly nodded. It was obviously a lie, but that was the best explanation he'd heard.

Once the child had his fill, he and Doyle left Morrison's and started to look for Carson. It wasn't that terribly difficult to find him. They had only gone a couple of blocks before they found him standing on a street corner puffing on a cigarette. The brown-black hues of blood were splashed over his shirt, jeans, and face. Doyle worried as he looked at Carson as he slumped against the light post. The he looked again at Carson leaning against the light post with his head back as he took long draws from the cigarette. Doyle felt disgust work through his shoulder blades. That kind of pleasure came from sexual gratification. On some level, Carson was as bad as Her. Doyle was terrified of this sort thing. There were parts of Carson that were much like Her and that made Doyle sick. Carson cast a hazed look over at Doyle and the child and nodded as a grin crossed his face again.

"I take it he's been taken care of." Doyle said flatly.

"Oh yea, I totally Madsened that guy's face." Carson laughed as he opened his left hand. In the center of his hand were four elongated canines. A moment of illness pulsed throughout his body. Even Carson felt uneasy. Four fangs meant that you would die a horrible death. Starvation was the worst way to go. He smiled at the child. "You ready to go home?"

The child nodded, still slightly awake.

It was well after midnight when they made it to the drawing room of St. Nicholas' Home for Children. It was nothing when Carson had first passed through these doors. It had been a small house where three nuns permitted the homeless children to live with them to keep them out of the mills that would have been their deaths at that time. Sister Alma Regina tried to take in as many as they could handle. They were given money by the bishop and that's when it became an orphanage. Sister Alma Regina was gone now. In her place was was a succession of women who shared her same world view. The most recent was Sister Jaqueline "Jack" Slattery. Carson had long fantasized about her being more than a nun. Sister Jack wasn't an unattractive girl and was far too young to be throwing her life away at St. Nick's. He never understood it until he and Doyle began their campaign. All people have callings and sometimes you have to take the consequences to work for a higher law. Sister Jack walked back into the drawing room wrapped in a terry cloth robe covering what looked like standard pajama pants and a t-shirt from a marathon she did in her college days. She smiled at the two of them with relief on her face. The wayward lamb had been returned home. There was no greater joy.

"You have no idea how much it means to me that you got Dylan home." She said quietly. "I don't know why the police weren't working harder to find a ward of the state, but thank you. Do I want to know where you found him?"

"He was with a real baddie," Carson said. "But he ain't going to bother you or St. Nick's anymore. Even monsters got rules, Sister. I piked him myself. That's when we…"

"I can guess what that means and I don't need to know anymore. Carson, you and your…"

"Brother," Doyle said quickly. "I'm his brother."

"...do a lot for us, I don't know what else to say."

"It ain't nothin'. If you ever need anything else…"

"I know," Sister Jack said. "My predecessor left me with a note. You're the worst kept secret with the nuns in Gaiman Heights. Carson, we couldn't do this without you. Thank you so much."

They were still working out the kinks of their post hunt routine then. The buzzing feeling of feasting on blood and then doing something for the community would have them running down the street like a teenager on an energy drink sugar rush that would be swiftly followed by a harsh crash. Things felt different tonight. There was a quiet that had been over them that neither one of them could shake. Carson didn't want to admit to it, but the fact that this was his first family had been circling in his head. There was something sobering about that even to him, and tonight brought it home for him.

"Do you ever regret not being able to be a father anymore?" Carson finally asked. "In the traditional sort of way?"

"Do you?" Asked Doyle.

"Not really, but it wasn't a priority of mine when I was alive, but you…"

"Why would you assume I would regret that?"

"Because of a lot reasons. One, you're a regret filled mopey bastard. Two, you were a father. Do you regret not being able to have a conventional family?"

"We're monsters," Doyle stated. "I don't think a conventional family would be wise."

"That ain't what I asked and you know it," said Carson. "I should have figured that you'd say some horse shit like that. Is every part of your life about you punishing yourself for something I ain't sure you even did?"

"No, and no I don't." Doyle finally said. "I had it once and it wasn't meant to be. I'm not planning on going through it ever again. Are you? You've got Norvita. What are you going to do if she wants to have more and there are things you can't give her?"

Carson shrugged.

"I don't think about it, honestly." He said finally. "At some point she is either going to die or she's going to grow up and want a family, but I ain't worried about it. That's not the point of being with Norvita. You can't plan for something you can't control. Just enjoy. Besides, who wants to marry a vampire?"

"Bellas." Doyle said flatly.

Carson sighed with a wave of hatred. For as long as vampires have existed, there have been girls who wanted to be a part of their life. These are vampire groupies or Bellas. This was a segment of the populace that had been welcomed as source of food until it became evident that they weren't there for the abuse. Bellas had romantic notions of being able to save their vampire from his inhumanity or of falling into blood-sucking love with them. While most vampires like having some contact with human beings, they are typically solitary creatures outside of those settings. Bellas often do not see that and are obsessively involved in the lives of the vampires they are stalking. This is not well received by many vampires.

"Yea and fuck that noise," said Carson. "I ain't putting a ring on my finger so I can have crazy hot sex with a psycho chick who thinks cutting and offering her blood is a deeply religious moment and treats the Condition like it's a punishment to either share or relieve. I don't need another you in my fucking life."

"Thanks."

"Doyle, monogamy is overrated. You find someone who you want to spend all your time with cool, but we suck blood. That means it's pretty fucking hard to stay loyal to one chick. It would be like eating the same sandwich every day for the rest of your life.

Meatloaf is great, but sometimes you want a hamburger or a steak. It's why Norvie and I fight all the time."

"I thought you fought because she's really pretty when she's angry."

"Yea, the makeup sex is pretty bangin'... look, but I'm also not down with eating one thing all the time. Alls I'm sayin' is that girl seeking one of us out is going to do it because they read some romance novel or some shit and think they can be the hero of our story. No one is meant to be saved from this life. I'm sure we ain't meant to find long term partners."

"What if someone wants a more personality based relationship instead of well…"

"Then, then you are as fucking dumb now as the day you fell off the potato truck into the fields of harps and shamrocks."

"Why do I even bother talking to you?"

"Because I'm the only one you ever talk to about this kind of shit. Maybe you talk to the priest about it too, but quite frankly Doyle, it's just me. 'Sides, you ain't never brought this up before. There someone you looking at?"

"No."

"You don't even jerk off? I don't believe you. I've seen those girlie pictures on your computer. The dark haired chick. She's pretty cute, Doyle. She'd be worth the complex ways of getting a hard on just to rub one out to her."

"It's not like that."

"Then what is it like…are you gay?"

"No, I'm Catholic."

"Doyle, that ain't mutually exclusive. It's cool if you're a homo. After all the shit we've gone through, I can't judge you."

"It's not like that. I made a commitment and a vow years ago to my Molly. I have no intention of breaking that vow now."

"You're the worst goddamn liar I've ever met. There was someone you've been mooning over and I ain't seen her. So, I know you are just too much of a fucking chicken to even ask her out."

Doyle turned his head towards Carson with a cold sneer. They were moving into territory that Carson had no business being in. If Carson were somewhere near normal socially, he would have backed off by this point. However, Carson never really backed down from anything, so he leaned forward, looking Doyle in the eye.

"Who is she?" Asked Carson.

"Drop it." Doyle commanded.

"No, I ain't gonna do that. Who is she?"

"No one."

"I knew it, it's the girl on your computer."

"I said leave it alone."

"Nope."

"Fine, I need to go pray."

IX. Warrior's Code

1922

Where Doyle Lanagan left this world begging for mercy, Carson O'Brian left it swearing like a sailor. He had ended with his fists balled and struggle still working through his body but he did not go gentle into that good night. His last night had started like most nights started. It had started with some sort of panicked chaos that he had caused. Now, Carson was running away from angry men. His toes stung with the shock of being banged against thin shoes as he ran down a street of burning concrete. His breath pushed out raggedly as the men yelled curses at him in street Italian. Carson laughed loudly as he panted for air. He'd learned tonight that if you wanted to live much longer, then you shouldn't pick a fight at the gin joint run by the Italians on the corner. Of course, Carson had never been one to pass up an opportunity to show what kind of hard ass he was. Something about tonight felt like it was the end of everything for him. He was standing on the end of his life and he was going to make the most of it.

Tonight, Carson O'Brian was going to die.

He'd been waiting for something like this for years. Carson had begun his life fighting for everything he could get. He fought when he came screaming from his mother as she died in labor. He didn't know how many there were like him, but from what he could figure out from living in his father's shadow, he had been prolific. The runt of the litter only ever knew his only full-blooded brother, Francis. They were the two who found their way into the caring arms of Sister Alma Regina and her fledgling orphanage. Carson and Francis would call this their home for the next sixteen years. Carson would also tell you that stories you heard about being raised in an orphanage were total bullshit. He had a great time with his expanded family. His mother was the aggressive nun, his fellow cast-off children his siblings. His favorite, of course, was Francis. Francis had the task of handling Carson and in many ways became his father. He had to. They were the only family they had so they clung to each other. They were each other's best friends.

Francis and Carson were so very different people even as children. Carson was small for his age and Francis was a tall broad-looking boy. Francis also lacked the temper of the runt of the litter. He wouldn't back down from a fight but he would never start one. By the time Carson was eight, his aggression had made enough of an impact on his character to the point that he became vicious enough to attack anyone who was ready to test him. Carson also spent a great deal of time in trouble, much to his own chagrin and the beatings he'd gotten from the Sister. He wanted to be like Francis who had never gotten into trouble for fighting and seemed liked by the nuns. Carson had tried very hard to not be the impulsive one. Controlling himself that tightly just made him more irritated and then he was more aggressive. That wasn't good for anyone. That was why one day Francis pulled the younger O'Brian brother over to the side to speak to him.

"We ain't the same, Carson," Francis began. "No one wants us to be the same, neither. I ain't as good as you when it comes to fighting and you are good at it. Your talents will go elsewhere. What is that the sister says? Be who God has meant you to be and you will set the world on fire. You just ain't found who you supposed to be yet."

Carson thought that meant that he was supposed to be some sort of lackey to the genius mastermind. He was plenty smart, but he was much happier intimidating people with his own personality. Who knows what he would have become if Francis hadn't kept him on a short moral leash. He had known even then that Carson was never going to be a gentle soul, but you could at least aim a mad man in a chosen direction. He taught Carson to be the better man that he should have been. You took care of family first and foremost in life. That meant if you had extra, you kicked it back to the orphanage. Even later in life, Carson made sure he gave what he could to those kids. You never started a fight you couldn't finish and you keep people who don't belong out of your house. They went looking for trouble on that front and people feared the O'Brian boys. No one went to South Gaiman unless they had to. When they weren't a couple of street hooligans, the O'Brians did odd jobs. Life was good for the two young men.

Or it was until a world went to war.

The United States didn't enter the gas-filled fray of the First World War until 1916. In that time, men volunteered for the war that they thought would be over by Christmas, but the numbers could not keep up. By the time Francis turned eighteen, he fell victim to the Selective Services Act of 1917. He became a soldier and marched off to France. Carson almost wouldn't let him go alone. He'd faked his age to enlist or planned to, until Francis told him no. He was meant for something else. Carson could still remember the parting words of wisdom handed down to him by Francis.

"Carson, be good," Francis told him. "I'll be back in six months. Don't lose your temper and keep your head down."

He didn't come back in six months. He didn't come back at all. Carson never learned where he was buried, but he always figured it was somewhere in France. He hadn't cared much to think about it out loud but at night it would bother him. Where did he go to die? What did he die from? Carson was never sure what killed Francis. He wanted to believe it was a German's bullet but it could have been the flu or syphilis for all he knew.

Carson had been on his own then. His moral compass was gone from this world and now Carson had no direction or map. Well, that wasn't true. He had the direction that he'd come up with when Francis was still around. Carson kept his campaign of saving the neighborhood going. It was different now. Francis was gone and he had been the one who could keep things from going overly violent. Without restraint, Carson had become a terror of the neighborhood. Nothing bad happened yet, but that was because no one wanted to step across Carson.

He'd look back at those times with a bit of shame at how he acted. Carson had started to target people who were like his forefathers a generation before. He would be repentant when he became a more civilized man, but until then he was no better than the rest of the people in his world. There were people who came over who didn't speak his language and were taking his spot. He believed they were making his home unsafe and it was time to get them out of his neighborhood. He learned later this was wrong. His afterlife was saved by Doyle being Doyle, but in that moment, he was going to start being violent towards the new invaders.

Tonight was the night his crusade had drawn first blood. He'd shoved glass in the face of some punk at the gin joint. That got the blood up of the two men who were now chasing him down the street. Carson was having a great time with it. He was testing his fate. This felt like the end, but if he could escape consequences yet again, then things were getting better.

This is where he made his first mistake.

Confident in his victory, Carson looked back to see where his attackers were. If he hadn't done this, then he would have seen the couple walking in the opposite direction. It was inevitable really, the pale woman with the uncomfortable-looking man on her arm had been out later than most in South Gaiman. They were clearly looking for some kind of trouble. Carson would have had a better time with them than with the Italians. However, he wasn't looking for them. Instead, Carson ran head first into them, accidentally grabbing a bit of a gem-covered bodice as he recovered his balance. The male of the couple let out a small growl as he was shoved to the side.

"Geeze Nancy, don't get your knickers in a twist," Carson called as he ran away. "Ain't my fault cow is givin' a squeeze for free."

Before She could utter a word to the man who had just called her a cow, the pair of Italian gentlemen ran past them screaming obscenities at Carson. She blinked softly as She watched. Something had piqued her interest and now She had to intervene.

"Doyle, that man sassed me," said the woman. "We won't let those men kill him before I do."

Doyle quietly nodded as he eased his protruding fangs back into his mouth. She gladly took his arm as they casually changed direction on their walk. Hunting was over, whatever she smelled in Carson, if for no other reason than he was rude to her, She wanted to see what She could get out of him. Arm in arm, they followed the party down the narrow street that ended into a blocked alley.

Carson hunched forward like a cornered animal attempting to figure out his next move. He was terrified but he was alive. His breath came out raggedly as he watched his pursuers pace forward, looking at him like he was a mongrel who had to be put down. Good, thought Carson. Something primal and feral took over. He was starting to feel rabid. He spat for good measure as he balanced his weight evenly on sore feet. One of them yelled at him in Italian. Carson didn't speak a word of their language, but he understood intent. Carson picked up a long metal pipe while looking at them.

"Yea?" he yelled back. "So does your mom."

Carson watched as the men he had egged into chasing him came at him with one last charge. With all of the strength that he had (which was quite a bit), Carson swung the pipe as hard as he possibly could at them. He heard a skull crack under the metal pipe and then he heard the sound of a body dropping as he whirled towards the second attacker. The second man was able to pull Carson down with a strong clothesline. He'd gotten on top of Carson and started into a punch. That lasted until Carson threw a fist into his throat and a kick into his groin. He rolled off of Carson with a groan. Carson leaned over and punched the man two more times for good measure before banging his head down on the concrete.

In the alley entrance, Doyle felt himself stiffen as her dark-painted nails gripped his bicep. She let out a soft moan as She watched. There was something exciting going on before them. In a moment something had changed; She let out a soft pant as her breasts rose eagerly while she watched. She licked her lips. She had found what She wanted and it was going to be bloodier than what she saw now. Doyle knew what was coming. Someone was going to die by her hand tonight.

Carson stood up with a rough laugh as he wiped spatters of blood from his face. He popped his neck as he turned to leave the alley. He stopped as he noticed the couple. She let go of Doyle's arm and walked quietly towards him. Carson stopped with a soft swallow. She was stunning and given the chance to, he would do whatever she asked of him. He nodded for a moment looking at them.

"The fuck do you two want?" He growled at them. He had to still act tough.

"In a word, you." She said. Carson felt his heart leap. "That was quite a fight that you had with those men. It was not a challenge and beneath you. How about your take on a real man?"

"What? That stuffed shirt right there?" Carson laughed. "Yea, you're on."

She smiled at Carson as Doyle leaned down. Gently she whispered something in his ear.

"Don't pull punches," She said softly. "Hurt him, but his last breath is mine."

Doyle nodded as he slid off his suit jacket and handed it to Her. She smiled quietly as she watched Doyle roll up his sleeves. This wasn't going to be a fair fight, Carson thought and he was going to get the first hit in. Doyle heard Carson run at him and sensed the whoosh of his fist coming towards his face. He turned with not a single word and stared Carson coldly in the eye. Carson stopped for a moment, with a heartbeat of unusual hesitation. He had slowed his punch before he felt Doyle's cold, hard hands grip his wrist. He tried swinging with the other fist only to be stopped by a hard swat. Carson felt his wrist throbbing as his fingers went numb. Without warning there was a sudden counter punch that exploded blood across Carson's face, followed by a fast kick.

Carson stumbled back with each rapid strike. And they were just so fast he realized as he watched those cold brown eyes. He again tried hitting with his better hand to no avail. Eventually, Carson stumbled back into the trash. He found his hand landing on a conveniently splintered piece of wood. Carson gripped it as best he could. It was a long shot, but he had to try. He couldn't just let this guy beat him to death. With all of Carson's strength, he shoved the piece of wood into Doyle, piercing the soft meat of his torso. For a moment, Doyle stumbled back weakly. Carson thought that he was safe. This was mistake number two.

All sound from the city was gone in a heartbeat. Carson could hear nothing as he stared up at Doyle who stood crouched over him like a beast preparing for the kill. He was hunched forward as a scream tore from his mouth that was like no sound that Carson had heard before. His eyes drifted over to the woman who had been watching the fight raptly. Her skirt was hiked up and her fingers danced slowly along skin excited by the violence before her.

Doyle hands gripped the wood lodged in his torso and pulled it out slowly before dropping it to the ground. He leaned back with another growl that shook the buildings. As he stared back at Carson, his pupils became furious pinholes burning in a hazel flame. Carson backed up as quickly as Doyle moved in. She followed behind him with a smug grin, gripping the back of Doyle's shirt like a leash.

"What…what the hell are you?" Carson whispered.

"He is my pet and he'll be ushering you out of this life." She answered.

She released Doyle's shirt, letting him fly at Carson. Doyle lunged quickly. His fangs ripped into Carson's collarbone, instantly tearing hot red blood out of his body. Carson dropped as Doyle stood up. He breathed quietly as he drifted further away from his body. She sat upon his lap and looked down with a soft smile. She couldn't let him go. After all, he had fought so hard and now he was looking at her with all the love and loyalty she expected from the dog he was. She leaned down against his neck and bit down into his already torn flesh. Carson wasn't the screaming type, but somewhere inside of him that was all he wanted to do. Her body rocked against his as it stiffened and shook with shock. She worked slowly until he was barely breathing at all. Without looking away from Her newest prize, She offered her wrist up for Doyle who bit open a vein, allowing blood to flow freely. At first Carson found this act repugnant and confusing, but the smell of Her blood was somehow too intoxicating to him to resist it. He brought his lips to Her proffered wrist and finally drank greedily. He felt Her influence begin to work through his body as his eyes slowly shut. She smiled with vicious pleasure, looking down at him as his vision went to black.

"Fuck you," were the last words that left Carson's mouth.

X.   The Courtship of MurderDoll_Marcie

Nowish

For those of you who were wondering, Carson was right. If you weren't wondering, I'll tell you all the same. Doyle did fancy someone special. The problem was that Doyle hadn't met her in person in the real world. This sounds awkward, but I can explain.

Vampires work very hard to stay on the cutting edge of trends. You know this because I told you earlier to never make fun of a vampire's shoes. Vampires like to keep themselves in vogue and in the latest fashion, if not even a little ahead. Most vampires are not fond of this practice and would much rather let themselves go, living in castles while watching television and playing to stereotypes. But of course they cannot. They keep up with the latest trends so that they can blend in with their food sources. For a vampire, their whole un-life is like being the thirty year olds who are at the frat party. They are only awkward-looking to the other people their age. There is really nothing more pathetic than being behind the curve when it comes to your food. If you were attempting to figure out who on Earth would actually buy those items from Sky Mall or the Sharper Image...vampires would -- except for Doyle. Doyle was less interested in staying in front of the curve than most. This was largely due to what could be described as crippling depression. This is not generally a part of the vampiric condition, but more about his own personal trauma. Most vampires enjoy being vampires, because what's done is done and immortality is fun. Doyle had yet to learn how to enjoy it because he spent most of his time lamenting his own loss. That was, until his favorite place went digital. In 2004, Goodchild Memorial Library put their works online. He was not quite sure why he chose to join the library then, but at first it was simply to be able to ask for help from the head librarian. He wouldn't admit it, but Doyle was smitten with the librarian. Because of this obsession, Doyle had installed wifi and bought himself a laptop. Instantly, he was given a new world where he could interact with others and somehow become a more social creature. In this cyberspace, Doyle had found a way of getting over being Doyle. This connection brought a brand new world to his fingertips.

Doyle had always been something of a naïve explorer when it came to New Worlds. He thought that it was going to be the same when it came to the internet. He charted with his own wondrous amusement this grand world. He started simply enough. He opened with an e-mail address because he assumed everyone had e-mail. He didn't understood the purpose of e-mail except that it would send him things like penis enlargement and transcripts from Nigerian princes. He'd never taken anyone up on those offers. Snake oil was snake oil, whether you presented it as bottled or as digital letters of hopeful dreams.

Doyle became bolder as his confidence grew and started looking at websites. He found that the place where he got his e-mail had news on a regular basis as well. This was great for Doyle. Doyle had learned how to read at an early age. That had done him no good until he'd arrived in the United States. That's when he could find himself reading anything that he could get his hands on. With the internet, he could find news all over the place. This was amazing for Doyle since he could obsessively read and keep to a minimum the amount of waste, which was great for Carson. He was never happy with the number of papers that Doyle would leave scattered around the kitchen table. Carson wasn't a reader, no matter how hard they worked at it. Carson knew how to read and was really good at it -- he was just happier not being a reader. Doyle finally had a place to enjoy his news from anywhere he wanted on the globe and more importantly, he found people to share it with. This had become confusing to Doyle since there was no real point in his life that he would have ever considered talking to someone about politics. It was something he'd seen family members do in times past and it was always rather boring to him.

Of course that was a different time.

It was always very jarring for Doyle when he thought about where he was in the world and where he came from and that was a lot of his problem. He wasn't a struggling farmer and now he was living a life that he knew his father would have called decadent. He felt guilty because he hadn't shared his prosperity with the poor people of his homeland. What Doyle discovered online was that there weren't any poor people left in Ireland. That gave him some pride. That meant he could relax and enjoy the internet. That was how Doyle was dealing with his new life -- he was staying informed. In his advanced old age, he had become his father.

Doyle could have told you that his online interactions had started innocently enough. A comment or two on a blog post, and so on, but it wasn't that same old story at all. He read the articles and then got into the comments and found that news was very upsetting. He couldn't understand why people would even argue over whether or not there was truth in reporting. As he matured on the internet, he learned about such things as trolls and that you shouldn't always feed them, but until those lessons came, Doyle was a soldier in the flame wars. As time passed, he started to get a feel for what was true and what was not of everything the internet told him. As he went through it all, he realized that that the anger came from people who he noticed had some very similar background stories. Doyle saw something in those angry words that he understood better than most. Behind the bluster, he knew that they all had something very much in common with each other and with him. All of them were so lonely.

Doyle understood that feeling no better than on a lonely Saturday night after a week of good hunting. He sat in the kitchen of their lair. He knew that it seemed too weird to have a kitchen when neither of them ate in the conventional sense. Of course, Norvita ate constantly. The downside of having something that ate was that it seemed to do it all the time. But really, Doyle liked having a kitchen that had evolved into some sort of classic 1950s retro styles. It was a cleaner kitchen than he'd ever had and perhaps he was oddly obsessed with the cleanliness of his home. Doyle liked the kitchen for two main reasons. One, it was closer to the signal for the router. For those of you who have never played this game, I am very, very jealous of you, but where the signal is stronger, the speeds are faster -- or so Doyle believed.

I'm not quite sure how true it was, but this bolstered his excuse to not be upstairs in his bedroom that shared a wall with Carson. And that was the second reason he preferred to be in the kitchen. By this time on a Saturday, Carson was engrossed with other activities. He knew that those activities involved to Carson swearing seductively at his barely legal girlfriend while she made sounds that Doyle would have normally associated with a wounded donkey during their inarticulate sexual play. The kitchen wasn't next door which meant he didn't hear the headboard banging repeatedly against the wall -- however, with Doyle's very sensitive hearing, he could not quite block out the squeak of aged old springs forcibly compressed by a mini-hulk and a squealing girl who should probably be doing her algebra homework instead... Nothing in his unlife felt more pathetic than chatting online while his centenarian roommate had crazy monkey sex with his not-quite-jail-bait girlfriend. He felt pathetic.

That was before he had found her. The girl on the screen changed everything for Doyle.

They hadn't started as a long distance love affair. It was an accidental meeting. Doyle had started going backwards a little bit from message boards to chatrooms. It was an easier way to find like-minded people. He wouldn't tell you what kind of chatroom it was where he met her, but he had made an impression by being Doyle. He had never thought that his attempts to be an overly-educated man would ever get anyone's attention, but he'd said something smart, a thing he couldn't for the life of him remember and she found him. She thought he was smart. That was how he attracted the attention of MurderDoll_Marcie.

She had enjoyed his personality. Humility wasn't something you often found coming from confirmed bachelors on the internet in her experience, so it was why she had sent him a private message in that chat room. Doyle had never spent so long talking to another person in his life that he wasn't in the room with. During the initial four hour conversation, they started exchanging e-mails. Many people would have thought this was unusual. After all, who these days sits down and writes long and endearing love letters to someone in the digital age. The answer to this question was Doyle Lanagan. At the risk of making him sound like a terrible stereotype from romantic vampire novels, his ideas of Victorian courting had served him well in this day and age. It didn't hurt much that MurderDoll_Marcie was someone who was looking for exactly that kind of romance. Doyle worried that he'd found himself a Bella, but he told himself to not stress about it. This wasn't a real relationship after all and they would never ever meet for real. You could toy with a Bella and not make her your girlfriend.

Part of Doyle felt absolutely terrible about this. He could justify it to himself. She wasn't "real" anyway and was more likely out to get something from him. Doyle just knew that she was some sort of trick being played by some troll who was going to reveal he had a penis the second things got compromising or try some scam for money. Truthfully, Doyle didn't care and that more than anything made the annoying, practical part of his mind sit down and shut up. He had started taking Carson's advice on this matter. It didn't matter what they were doing because it wasn't a long term event -- this was only for the here and now and Doyle was enjoying himself, so he could only ride this out for as long as he needed. That philosophy got them over the hump of two years. He spent that time with her and enjoyed himself, whether or not it was real.

It wasn't hard to keep the important things from her during that time. He'd learned how to talk about himself from his years of practice at being a vampire. If you learned how to charm prey well enough to stay undead (instead of just dead) as long as Doyle had, then you learned how to talk right. Besides, she spoke more about what she was doing in her life and that was fine. Doyle liked learning about her. He had learned quickly a few things about her over the conversations. She and Doyle had taken similar classes at McKean State, but not at the same time. She was working on a PhD. She had a thing for old world literature and thought there was something charming about letter writing. It was a lost art and she thought it was a shame. Sometimes, she wished she'd been born in another time, but she was realistic about it. She knew that there was nothing romantic about the life Doyle had lived -- not that she knew he'd lived in those times -- it had been hard and terrible. She could just enjoy it from the safety of her own life.

He talked about himself carefully to her. This was where he had gotten good at the word "something" and half-truths. Doyle or, as he was known online, aifeala_47, never revealed too much about himself, just enough to find out more about her. He told her that he was a widower and had children who had died very suddenly, which was why he'd left his homeland to come to America. He didn't tell her about his condition or his age and he was never going to. It was really for the best, Doyle resolved. Some things needed to be left out. What he didn't expect was to start to slowly fall in love with her as they exchanged their e-mails. He printed them out and kept them in a carefully hidden place away from the sight of anyone else. They sat in their own box under his bed, next to the things he'd kept from Molly. It was his secret place where he hid things he liked. He had never told anyone of those things except Her. She'd found them once and mocked him for so very long. Doyle tried hard to keep the shadow of Her life out of his affair with MurderDoll_Marcie. There was nothing he wanted more than to never have the whisper of Her influence ruin this courtship. Doyle didn't need Her help. He could do that all by himself.

The fateful day that Doyle tried to ruin his relationship with MurderDoll_Marcie started with learning how to look at profiles. Doyle hadn't quite gotten to social media, but he had started with instant messenger. It was how he and MurderDoll_Marcie started talking out of chatrooms and in real time. When Doyle had nothing better to do, he looked at the profile that was attached to her IM account. That was when he learned two things that would change everything.

First, Doyle discovered that the girl he'd been talking to was the night librarian at Goodchild Memorial Library. He had been starting to feel guilty that he was cheating on MurderDoll_Marcie with his crush on the librarian, but that was impossible now that they were the same person. This made Doyle feel much better about his life in general. At least he was only lusting sinfully after one girl.

The second thing he found out was the origin of MurderDoll_Marcie's charming name. MurderDoll_Marcie had a link on her profile that Doyle had to click. What it led him to was seeing her in a white lacy undergarment with a white cotton corset. Doyle knew those clothes. He'd seen the outfit once when he'd been walking around the pier and caught sight of a woman stripping in the penny Black Mariah. This wasn't something a good woman would want you to see. There was more to it than just the shameful lack of clothing. She wanted people to see her in those clothes. She looked over her shoulder as her hand gripped the laces of her corset. There was a slight smirk that forced her dark brown eyes to dance with seduction. In the span of thirty seconds, Doyle could tell you how many tattoos she had on her body and he instantly hated himself for it. Doyle subconsciously put on his Victorian gentleman hat. A proper woman would have been mortified by being photographed in her undergarments. There was something very naughty about this. Doyle was embarrassed and aroused all at the same time.

After he asked for divine forgiveness, Doyle debated not talking to her anymore. He couldn't live with the lustful urges that followed. He'd had an honorable relationship with her and now he was seeing her as something else. He saw her as a soft thing that he wanted to put under his nose and breathe in her feminine scent. He suspected that she smelled like cinnamon and he wanted to explore every part of her elegant frame. He couldn't do this with her. These lustful urges were wrong in his mind and he could not do this dance. He couldn't count how many nights he spent clutching his rosary, attempting to find any breath of clemency. She wanted him to see those pictures, he finally resolved. Perhaps she thought it was art. People did things like that. This made Doyle feel guiltier. Art was supposed to be inspiring and not leading people to sleepless nights of unclean thoughts.

Doyle was terrified. He'd never been so desirous towards a woman he'd never met. He didn't know what to do. Doyle stopped talking to her. For a moment, he even debated throwing his laptop away. It was a mere week before he returned to his digital companion. He didn't tell her why he had stopped communication, not at first. After a while, he couldn't take the deception any more than he could bear his lustful feelings before (immortality notwithstanding, it sometimes just flat out sucks to be Doyle). In a five page e-mail, he explained why he had stopped talking to her. He felt he had to confess to the quiet of lusting after her. He felt he had spied on her in her undergarments. He told her that he'd understand if she didn't want to ever speak to him again.

She didn't e-mail him back. She instant messaged him instead.

MurderDoll_Marcie: Yea, that was a part of a photo-shoot I did for the Murder Dolls. It does Victorian pin ups. Want to see the rest?

Doyle hesitated (but not very long) before agreeing to see the rest. Within seconds, his inbox was flooded with jpegs from her. Doyle had only opened a quarter of them before he felt the same wave of guilt and arousal as before. It only increased with each image that showed more of her tan-toned skin. Had Doyle been a living breathing human, beads of sweat would be rolling down his furrowed brow. He glanced back at her hardened nipples peeking through some gauzy lace thing. Doyle tried to blush. It wasn't working for him. She sent him another message.

MurderDoll_Marcie: Did you get them yet?

Aifiela_47: Yea

MurderDoll_Marcie: :D Cool! What do you think of them?

Doyle was dumbfounded with a sudden panic. A man who was normally eloquent found it impossible to find the right words to express his feelings on her inked naked flesh. The context of their interactions had changed. This was a level of intimacy that he wanted, but had always been afraid of asking from her. She was also very forward and that scared him. He stared at his screen, attempting to muster something to say. He had to come up with something. He resisted the urge to announce that he that he needed to go to pray. Slowly, he typed something, anything.

Aifiela_47: I didn't think they were terrible. A little surprising, but not bad.

Doyle brought the heel of his hand against his forehead in a disbelieving face palm. This had to be the most awkward conversation he'd ever had with a girl. At least she couldn't see him fidget nervously. Doyle buried his face in his hands.

MurderDoll_Marcie: Well that's pretty good coming from you ;) I'll take it as a compliment. LoL.

Doyle breathed out a sigh of relief (reflexively, of course. He didn't actually need to breathe). She had taken his words as a joke. Doyle leaned back as he watched the screen. Her next words to him changed the course of their relationship forever. They hadn't seen it coming. She had anticipated the conversation of course, but could not have foreseen it going like this.

MurderDoll_Marcie: You've seen my naughty pictures. When do I get to see yours? It's only fair to trade.

Doyle did what any sane, rational person would do in this situation. He slammed his laptop closed and stood up. She was getting too close for his comfort. He paced for a moment. He could apologize to her later, but that wouldn't help now. He'd still be uncomfortable with all this. He'd deal with her later. Tonight he was going to Pitch's.

XI.   Carson O'Brian Sing The Blues

Now...you hear me now!

A hard-ridden Crown Vic rolled over the cobbled stone and down a twisted one-way street. The car sputtered as it lurched forward and suddenly stopped as it found its way into park. Asher Stone stared out of the window as Karl Spangler turned the ancient vehicle off. He wasn't quite sure what he was expecting, but Asher was looking at a pinup red devil grinning at him from what felt like a decade away. She gave him a repetitive wink as she kept her large smile on her face. She assured him that the bar was open. Asher wondered if Karl was playing a cruel joke on his first day on the job with the Department of the Arcane. Asher had been in recovery for two years before joining the supernatural regulatory agency. As a rule, he avoided bars because it was far too much of a temptation for him. So when Asher saw the sign for Pitch's Bar and Grille, he became irritated. Karl knew that he was a recovering addict. Everyone knew that Asher was a recovering addict. It was the first thing that came out of Asher's mouth. Even if it hadn't been in this particular case, Karl knew just about everything due to a side effect of his demonic possession. Therefore, stopping at a bar was offensive to Asher who knew that Karl was well aware of his situation.

Even if this was a joke, it wasn't funny.

"Pitch's." Asher repeated. I say repeated for those people who have read the first book (Spring Blessings -- if you haven't, it's a damn fine read for one thing, and for another, you'd know who Asher is, so I suggest you read it). I know it took me a while to get back to you guys. I know it was worth it.

"Oh, good," said Karl dryly. "You can read. That saves me a step later. Yes, this is Pitch's. You aren't here to have a good time. Tonight, we are here on official business."

"In a bar...on karaoke night."

"Don't be snotty," said Karl. "There are plenty of good pieces of information to be learned from being in a bar. Ever see Casablanca?"

"Yea, you do know I am a recovering addict...right?"

"I do, so let me put it this way. You order a drink and I will break your neck and devour your still beating heart."

"You've thought about this a lot, haven't you?"

"Every day since you joined...however, we are here on Department business."

"But you asked me what I knew about varies. I guess this is a vampire bar."

"Pitch's? Nah. The only vampire bar in town is the Standish Club and the Southies won't go to a Northern Bar. Pitch's is sort of neutral ground in the supernatural community. We are coming to provide assistance to the Gaiman P.D. They are coming to integrate a pair of vampires. They can be difficult."

"So, we do this a lot?"

"We try to keep out of their business, but with law enforcement this lines blur. Come on."

Karl pulled his old frame out of the driver's seat. He started on a deliberate path before Asher could even start following him. He stopped at the man in a cheap suit leaning against a dated Volkswagen Jetta. The man eyed Asher carefully. For a moment, he looked very disappointed. Then he spat black tobacco juice into a plastic soda bottle.

"My Norvita," said the man, as he looked Asher over, taking in the lines of ink that peered out of the cuffs and collar of his dress shirt. "you've gotten more handsome and covered in tattoos since I saw you last. I am at a loss."

"Are you going to hit on all my partners?" Karl asked almost jovially. This threw Asher for a loop since in all his experiences

97

with Karl he'd been so serious. "I will not be responsible for what happens if he starts deploying Norvita's personal tactics towards you."

"I don't know... if he's who people say he is...I might let him."

Asher blinked quietly looking between the two.

"Asher, this is Weston Lewis," Karl explained. This explanation did not enlighten Asher at all -- he was more confused that there was someone Karl liked enough to joke with. "Weston here is the Department's point man at the Gaiman P.D. Anything weird comes to the PD, he gives it to us. Weston, the part of my lovely partner is going to be played by Asher Stone this evening. Norvita has other work with Aguirre and Dira up in Twillingast tonight."

Weston Lewis extended his hand to Asher. After a few seconds hesitation, Asher took the policeman's hand and shook it. Weston Lewis gave Asher another once over.

"Stone, you said," he remarked. "Are you Stephen Stone's kid?"

"Holy shit!" Asher exclaimed. For those of you who aren't aware, the above question is quite commonly asked of Asher. "Did everyone in this town know my dad and not tell me?"

"I don't know about the secrecy, but your dad was magi royalty." Weston Lewis spat into the bottle again. "I didn't meet him myself, but I've heard stories. Dad talks about him all the time... it's cool though. I won't bring it up. People like to confuse me with my family too."

"So," started Karl dryly. Things were moving off topic and they had business to attend to this evening. "do I want to know what the South Gaiman brood did this time?"

"Man, I wish it were the South Gaiman Brood. Hell, it would make shit easier if it was a rogue faction of vampires. But it's just these two."

"Two trouble-making Southie vampires. Turn them over to the brood chiefs."

"Yea, Karl, I know. I wanted the Department on hand when I talk to the brood chief because its him and you two seem to get along. Shall we?"

"Lead on, MacDuff."

Weston Lewis tossed his blackened spit bottle into a trash can as he walked into the bar. Karl followed behind with Asher bringing up the rear. Despite his apprehension, Asher had heard of Pitch's. Iago, Asher's former best friend and drug dealer, used to rave about the place. Of course, by the time Asher had wanted to go to the bar, Iago had been banned from Pitch's. Asher didn't know what Iago had done, but he could guess. After all, Iago had tried to kill him.

Asher glanced around the bar. He was taken aback by the bar in itself. Based on the scantily clad neon devils outside, Asher expected something else would have been the décor. Instead, he was greeted by a bar that could have been the bar set from any sitcom. The wood had an amber hue in the dim light. The windows were tinted with an elaborate Tiffany glass. Asher tried hard not to stare at the monstrous patrons who spoke to each other in a low hum of noise under the sound of someone singing "Girls Just Want to Have Fun" off key. He glanced over to the bar. The Bartender glanced at Asher and gave him a respectful nod. Asher felt his jaw clench as he stared at the bartender. Hurriedly, he tried to catch up with Karl and Weston Lewis.

"Karl, Karl," Asher hissed in a whispered tone, "the bartender has horns."

"Of course Pitch has horns," Karl reassured him. "He is a demon, after all."

"A demon?" repeated Asher blankly. "Why is he...."

"Because Pitch is more complex than Department regulations. John Rose and Pitch aren't typical. I have a book you should read on the subject. It's very informative."

Before Asher could respond, he was distracted. On the stage was a wispy androgynous elf belting out "I Will Survive" in an octave that Gloria Gaynor wouldn't have dare attempted. Asher cringed as the glass in the windows shook. Asher hated bars on karaoke night. Everyone thought they were Bette Midler after a few drinks. He stopped as he felt arms wrap lovingly around his shoulders. There was a body writhing gently against him. It didn't take long for Asher to figure out who was trying to leech power off of him.

"Oh, hey, Norvita," Asher said awkwardly. "I thought you were at the crazy house tonight."

"I was." She whispered in a husky, lust-filled voice. Her fingers brushed over the front of Asher's pants. "Then I was done, so I came here. Hey Asher, guess what."

"What, Norvita?"

"I'm not wearing any panties. Wanna feel?"

Asher looked down at Norvita's alcohol-paralyzed eyes. She licked her lips as he contemplated the options of verifying Norvita's claims. There were three problems with that idea. One, Norvita was drunk. If Asher had learned anything from his days as a junkie, it was that it's always a terrible idea to feel up a drunk girl, no matter how hard she throws herself at you. Make no mistake, Norvita Patel was very, very attractive and – in her inebriated state – was throwing herself at Asher like he was a life preserver on the Titanic. Asher knew better though. There was a special hell for people who took advantage of drunk girls.

Two, Norvita was rumored to be in a relationship with a vampire. It was the thing that had gone with Norvita Patel despite her family's status in Gaiman Heights. The wild party girl granddaughter of the solemn Swami Patel was hooking up with a vampire. It wasn't shameful. There was a running joke of psychics who hooked up with vampires for obvious literary reasons. It might not be true, but Asher wasn't going to risk it.

Three, Asher was engaged to Natalie. Natalie was better known as Doctor Campbell unless you were a changeling. Then she was Lady Natalia, ruler of the Outer Lands. Natalie had been crowned as such when she had gotten lost in the Hedge and accidentally married to Lord Oberon. She kept her position without consummating this union because she'd learned to play cards with the kids in the pediatric oncology department (long story). Since then, the marriage had been dissolved between her and the king of the fairies after she had exchanged a basket full of Pocky for her freedom. Asher loved Natalie. She was the reason that Asher got clean. When she met Asher he'd been sleeping in her dumpster and because of her own personal nature of helping strays she gotten him cleaned up and off the streets. Two years later they were still in what was probably the healthiest relationship Asher had had in his adult life. Asher weighed his options and chose that it was better not discovered whether or not Norvita was wearing panties. He stiffened as he looked around for an exit.

"Karl," he begged loudly. "A little help?"

Karl stopped and then turned. He watched Norvita and her drunken seductive dance. *Huh*, thought Karl, *must be after ten on a Friday*. He dug into his wallet and gave Asher a five dollar bill.

"Tell the DJ to take a break and play some Katy Perry." Karl instructed Asher.

"With a five?" Asher asked.

"Trust me."

Asher took the five from Karl and, with Norivta still clinging to his body, he tried to move towards the DJ booth. Karl let out a quiet sigh as he looked back at Weston Lewis. Weston Lewis quirked a brow.

"So," he said. "The rumors about him are true."

"We both know that Norvita needs little convincing to throw herself at someone when she's drunk," said Karl. "But, yea, he's one big piece of magic candy."

"How's he working out as a partner?"

"Not bad," said Karl. "It's nice to have a partner that listens. Part of me enjoys having someone who isn't a pain in my back side."

"And the other half?"

"I want to rip off his head and drink his blood like a wax bottle." Karl said flatly.

Weston Lewis nodded slowly. It was this kind of statement that occasionally worried Weston Lewis when working with the Department. Karl was walking a fine line between humanity and the bestial creatures. Karl had been possessed by a demon. As a result of the possession, Karl became a part of the Marked – a group of unveiled who retain a part of the demonic parasite left in them. A constant concern of the Marked was losing their humanity. He couldn't gauge if Karl was joking or not, but hoped he was.

They were interrupted. Weston Lewis glanced towards the dance floor as a saccharine-sweet pop song pulsed through the air. Norvita squealed as she danced with herself in a drunkenly provocative manner on the dance floor. She was good at making grown men feel guilty about their elaborate fantasies about her and the things that they'd like to do when she danced like that. It was okay to think about those things now though. When she was drunk, she forgot that she was a psychic and stopped Listening. Asher finally returned to the seasoned law man with wide eyes. This might have been the most traumatic event of his night. Asher kept his head down, avoiding eye contact.

"That…that was awful,"he muttered in bewilderment.

Weston Lewis and Karl didn't respond. They just quietly chuckled as they walked towards the back of the bar. Asher knew then that this was some sort of hazing. Norvita's attentions had to be some kind of punishment. The three men walked towards an isolated table where a lone man sat. Over his head hung a dark blue flag with a bright orange sunburst. The man looked up at the party deliberately, slowly, as if he were only just now sparing them his attention now that he'd finished a chapter of his first edition of James Joyce's Ulysses that he closed and placed next to his untouched Guinness. He leaned back, looking at them. For a moment, Asher felt himself lose a little bit of control. The hipster at the table looked like a bad stereotype from Darby O'Gill and the little people. If he had a wilty Irish accent to go with that outfit, Asher would lose it completely.

"Never took you for a Finnian, Doyle," said Karl, by way of an opener. "I thought your people exploded in sunlight." He gestured at the flag.

"Being under the Warrior's Flag gives me the comfort of th' Auld Country. I'm not a fan o' the politics of the livin', but I do miss me homeland and her sun." Asher bit the inside of his mouth as he failed to suppress a surprised snicker.

Doyle pursed his lips as he eyed the tattooed man. "They give you a new one already, Karl? He's not nearly as pretty as Norvita, but he smells a lot better."

Doyle leaned forward with a hungry growl.

"You and I, boyo, should sit down and discuss eighteenth century lyrical poetry sometime. If you're lucky, I'll even buy you dinner."

"Oh, um," Asher stammered. "I'm not ga…"

"No." Karl cut Asher off flatly. He knew where this conversation went. "He's not for eating."

"Eat?" Doyle's eyes went wide as he feigned innocence. "Did I say eat?"

"Doyle, you are fully aware of the Winnipeg Treaty of 1922. You know that it is expressly forbidden to feed on magi without permission -- assuming his blood doesn't make your head explode," Karl lectured. "More importantly, Mr. Stone has an incantation on his jugular that'll shatter your fangs if you even try to bite him so…no."

"So, the story is true," Doyle said. "Nice to know…"

"Besides," Weston interrupted. "You're not the "seduce and feed type." That's Carson. Speaking of which, where is that sociopath? Did you two finally break up?"

"Carson is having himself a heart to heart with a wayward soul who found herself in this bar and was being eyed by a Northie who has been politely told to never come below Pratchett Street ever again," Doyle explained. "I suspect that he's attempting to get her back to the convent or the girl's school or wherever she came from. Don't worry, he'll be back in. He's on the card next. I think he's doing Journey tonight. Can I go ahead and assume you are asking where he is because you aren't really here for the stimulating conversation or here for the performances?"

"Doyle, Detective Lewis here would like to talk to you about some odd brood activity. We are here as a courtesy on behalf of the Department of the Arcane."

"That's right nice of you, Karl," Doyle said calmly (not the good kind of calm; more like calm before the storm...).

It was then that Carson joined the party. He slid into a chair beside Doyle, wiping blood from the corners of his mouth with a sly smirk. From the instant that Asher laid eyes on him, he knew there was a difference between the two men. Carson seemed to be enjoying the fact that he was a vampire, as opposed to Doyle who seemed to be living in some sort of Hollywood-made stereotype. He wasn't sure what it was. Where Doyle was Bella Legosi, Carson seemed to have a more Keifier Sutherland in Lost Boys quality to him. He had learned to live a happier life with his condition. Then again, many loving relationships had been between opposites. He and Natalie were the same story. Maybe it was so with these two. They seemed like a very loving couple.

"Well, that was bullshit," announced Carson bluntly. He looked at the men gathered around the table with a disgusted furrowing of his brow. "What the fuck is up with Bulls at our table? Though you guys are smelling pretty fucking amazing right now."

Doyle gave Carson a cold look.

"Ni Asher Stone ithe." Doyle said matter of factly to Carson -- almost too loudly.

Asher was confused by the sudden use of a different language, though he did catch his own name in there. He chalked this up to the fact that this might have been his first day, so what he knew about vampires did come from watching movies and reading books. He also knew that the mundane world never got things right about what went on beyond the veil. His employment with the Department had taught him that much. This is why you should have read the first book. It's okay...I can hook you up.

"Stone, eh?" Carson said, looking Asher over almost as if he were impressed. "You some sort of relation to Stephen Stone?"

"Yea." This confirmation made Asher seethe. He knew that he was going to have to answer this question forever. He was also preparing for someone to tell him how great his dead father was. "He was my dad."

"I knew your old man," Carson began the predictable response to Asher's admission. "He was a mother fucker. I think he owes me and Doyle like ten dollars or some shit."

"Carson," Doyle said calmly (yep, still kind of scary calm). "Detective Lewis would like to have a word with us."

"I know what you two have been doing lately." Karl started. "You left me voicemails and quite frankly, Doyle, your Carson voice is silly at best."

"What the fuck, Doyle?" Carson muttered under his breath.

"We don't know what you're talking about," Doyle stated quietly.

"Yes you do. You two think because you are big and bad and take care of the broods that you can start busting heads in the mundane world like you're superheroes or something."

"Well," Carson said. "I did want a Carson supersuit once. I thought liked that Nolan shit. That'd be pretty fucking bad ass. Then we saw the last one and I ain't married to it. And I don't like giving up my leather jacket."

"Guys," Weston Lewis finally spoke. "I appreciate that you have a lot of free time on your hands. The undead immortality leaves you with that, but I can't have you hunting down people and turning them into the police. There are vigilante laws that we have to consider and seriously, guys? I don't want to tell the D.A. that I got a call from a vampire. That sounds insane."

"Hunting?" Doyle did his best to sound horrified at the implication. "We aren't hunting anyone."

"See, you have that shit all wrong," Carson interjected. "Me and Doyle was just hitting some balls from the top of our building when we seen those Nazi fucks chasing that skinny faggot."

"Carson." Doyle interrupted.

"Oh right, they don't like that...homo. We thought we just needed to do the right thing and save that kid's life. We enlightened them as to the errors of their ways and they felt so bad, they beat the fuck out of themselves."

"The skinheads are one thing," Weston replied. "I know the missing kid case from St. Nicks wasn't called in because of you guys. I know that you are probably already tracking the serial rapist that's moving through Old Gaiman right now. But do you understand that when you work like this it makes it harder for the police to do their job?"

"So if I'm to be understanding this," Doyle summarized for a moment, "you are upset with us for saving lives in a part of the city that you never get called to anyway and then turning over the mundane criminals to you. You'd rather us turn a blind eye to something that draws more attention to our neighborhood from the mundane, which causes there to be more problems for us and the Department."

"You don't come into my house and start some shit and think we ain't going do somethin'." Carson started.

"Guys," Weston Lewis was starting to sound tired. "I get one more phone call about this, I will have to tell Prudence. I don't think she'd be happy with her brood chiefs causing problems."

There was a moment of silence as Carson and Doyle looked at each other. They leaned into a huddle, turning a sinister eye to Weston Lewis as they spoke to each other in hushed Germanic tones. It wasn't a language that Asher knew. He furrowed his brow.

"I didn't know that vampires had their own language," Asher whispered to Karl.

"They don't," Karl said. "North American Vampires work in English since the majority of them speak it. They're speaking Gaelic. Irish Gaelic to be exact. I don't know if Doyle spoke it before he died or not, but I suspect he taught it to Carson just to be able to circumvent authority. They don't like cops and detest any authority that isn't their own. The difference between them and others like them is that they are somehow civilized enough to know they need to work with us. It's an 'us/them' sort of thing." Karl shook his head. "You can take the boys out of Offalay, but you can't take Offalay out of the boys."

The pop music stopped with a static crack. Attention was turned towards the stage.

"And now it's time for one of Pitch's All Stars," announced the DJ. "Carson, get your happy ass up here."

Carson gave the group a smug grin as he started towards the stage. Norvita pouted drunkenly as he put his arm around her waist and dragged her on to the stage with him as he reached for the microphone. Quickly, he swung into a Bobby Darin classic. Within seconds, Carson's voice filled the bar.

"To talk like a masher, he has got a lovely singing voice." Doyle shook his head. "I'm surprised he went with "Beyond the Sea". Usually when he does Bobby Darin, he typically goes with "Mack the Knife". Means a lot to him because we saw Threepenny Opera in Berlin. I've never seen a play so happy to be performed among the smell of death. This is him showing off. He must've had a fight with Norvita before they got here."

"Doyle, I mean it," Weston Lewis tried to bring the conversation back to his point. "Stay out of the justice business."

"I assure you, Detective Lewis," Doyle said smoothly. "We won't be arousin' your suspicions anymore. You have my word."

"Good," Weston Lewis said with all the sincerity he could put into his voice. It meant enough to him that Doyle had bothered to lie to him. "Gentlemen, if you'll excuse me, we're coming up on review week. You boys have a good night."

Without another word, Weston Lewis left, thankful that he was leaving. The last thing he wanted to do was be in that bar after midnight. That was when the real freaks came in to Pitch's. He glanced back at the table. Doyle's envy of Carson became evident as a scowl crossed his face while Carson crooned to a drunk and admiring Norvita. Weston Lewis, at that moment, let go entirely of his crush on Norvita. Lusting after someone or something that he'd never have was going to make him a bitter old man like Doyle. He just couldn't be like that.

Karl stared at Doyle. He suspected something odd in Doyle's words. He wasn't ready to trust him at his word at this point.

"You're really going to comply with a police request?" Karl questioned.

"Of course I am." Doyle replied. "I wouldn't dream of endangering our chances of having a quiet life."

Karl nodded as he glanced back at the stage apprehensively. Nothing had been settled right and Doyle knew it. He had been hoping to at least stay under the radar or for a slightly warmer reception of his and Carson's efforts. The results weren't what he'd hoped, and to beat it all to be threatened with Prudence. Doyle could not let that eventuality happen. He knew what he was going to have to do and that bothered him. He would justify it later, but this was his purpose in the afterlife. He and Carson had to keep hunting, otherwise he'd never feel whole. They just had to be careful and not get caught.

XII. The Love Song of J. Ellis DeWitt

Eighteen Years Ago....

There is something that unites us all. The theologians call it God. Scientists call it physics. One old woman in Bavaria called it fate. We are all united by fate, according to Dagmar the blind prophetess of Bavaria. She goes on to talk about something that is far more important. The world is moved not by the actions of wise men and their desire for power but what we will do for the ones we care about and what we will do to them. Love can hurt people to the extent of its depth for those people. And when those lines blur, fates are bound and ties are not only cut but changed.

Prita Patel had no intention of following the path that fate had set out for her. She had made it her mission in her life to be what would have been called a shrew by most. It wasn't easy to know her and she liked it that way. There was nothing but a push to make her a part of a society that she never wanted to be a part of. She wanted to be like the others she knew in town and at her school growing up, but that was simply never the case. She never felt like she belonged. Part of that was the feeling of being an outsider in a new land. She was too new to America to fit in with the culture. Prita was the first generation of her family to be born in the New World. She wanted nothing more than to be westernized and a part of America, just like many immigrant children wanted, yet this was impossible for Prita. She could believe that it was her skin tone or her ethnic background. She knew that she wasn't a part of this culture that was so easy to blend into -- a country where old traditions were quickly lost in a plastic veneer of red, white and blue. Prita could not assimilate because she was treated like a princess by her immigrant community.

Her father was a holy man who left India in the days after the Lace-Keller Act of 1946. Before India had been liberated from British rule, their lives had been very easy even if there was poverty. They were very comfortable to say the least. Prita's father was a holy man and a healer. It was something of a coup for him to marry but he'd been given a wife and she was quite noble born. They were a holy couple and that was their fate. Vivek and Utarra Patel were a very powerful couple in their community and respected by all. Not even the English could deny the presence of the holy man. He saw the future and they knew that was he was very real. He also knew what he had to do when the world started changing. So when it came time to leave, they immigrated to the United States (something the holy man's wife would be upset about for quite a few years). This was a fortunate turn of events for them, as they readily found a community of prestige. The year before they arrived in Gaiman Heights, Edgar Cayce – the sleeping prophet – closed his eyes for the last time. There was a vacuum. In it came people like Jane Roberts and, of course, Swami Patel. He, as his wife pointed out, traded his holiness for parlor tricks.

"I did no such thing," he often told her. "We were offered gifts and food for what I did in our homeland. How is this any different? We are just given money."

"At least we could have still been English and I could get a proper cup of tea." She would repeat.

Prita had been born with a measure of that same holiness of her father. She became the latest heir to a line of holiness that had stretched out for generations before her birth and long into the future. Prita could read the auras of people. She could hear thoughts of other people. She could sense pending doom when it hung in the breeze. For lack of a better term, Prita was a psychic.

It wasn't a hard burden for her to bear. Like all gifts, people accept their talents when there is a supportive home life. Her father wasn't the first psychic in the family and she wouldn't be the last. As long as they could remember, they had always been a family of soothsayers. Prita was the first daughter born in seven

111

generations. According to her mother, she had the honor of uniting two holy families. So it fell to her mother to marry Prita off to any number of boys back in India. The cliché of the shrew fit because Prita had herself become a cliché. There was not a single suitor that she cared for and she made that clear. The last thing that she wanted was to be a princess in the life of some obnoxious prince. More importantly, she knew what they were all thinking. They had found a chance to up their societal status with a match in the lineage of a holy man. She was not their prize to have and to show. She would not be any one man's woman. Prita scared off any and all potential suitors as often as she could. This irritated her mother who would spend hours yelling at her for not listening. Her father was calmer about the whole thing. He understood those problems all too well.

"One must find the soul that completes them," he would say. "I was fortunate enough to find a woman willful enough to now share her thoughts and she gave me a willful daughter. That willful daughter will find the soul who completes her."

Prita chose to remain alone and an incomplete project in her mother's eyes. She didn't like dating American men either. Men found her exotic and she found them boring. She had to work on something else that was more important than dating fools for the fun of it. She knew that she couldn't trust her bloodline with anyone. She felt that it was time for her to let her family powers die. She knew this through her second gift. Prita, like all the women in her bloodline, had dreams that seemed to come true. Prita watched things come to pass that she had seen unfold in her mind's eye. It was a nightmare and she wished it on no one else, her potential children least of all. She had even seen her fate. She would fall in love with a man and her fate would be tied to one man. She would bear him a child and he would end her life. She knew his name. Prita feared the day that she would meet J. Ellis DeWitt.

She knew that she would never really shake her fate; that is why it is called fate after all. What she believed was that she could change her fortune if she tried. If she couldn't, then there was nothing she could do and her very being recoiled from such helplessness. She knew that she had to try to keep herself away from being twisted into a path, but she couldn't deny the world the use of her talents. That was very reason her family had these gifts. There were stations and places where roles had to be played sometimes. Prita did her brief stint on the circuit with her parents, before she started working in a more humane way. She chose to work for an organization that could make a real difference. She was a part of the Department of the Arcane. If she was looking to walk away from her own fate, this however, was not the path to walk. Her life was going to lead her right into the path of the man who would end her life.

Through the forces that she did not fully comprehend, Prita was introduced to J. Ellis DeWitt.

The DeWitt clan had been hunters for the Flemish Bankers looking to make a life in New Amsterdam. They would have remained if it weren't for the curse of Heller DeWitt. As the story goes, Heller courted a young woman who cursed him. And when he returned to his family, the livestock died, children went missing. It was clearly black magic. Because of the shame, the DeWitts left for New England to make a different life. It was the same life that they had left only instead of Flemish bankers they found themselves aligned with the Clan of the Flaming Sword.

The long line of hunters resulted in J. Ellis DeWitt. He too was the son of legacy. He hunted like his father and grandfather. J. Ellis DeWitt also had started to think about his fate. Perhaps it was just the natural thoughts that came with young rebellion or perhaps it was something else. The Flaming Sword hunted like other clans, he had a life altering experience that would change the heart of any soldier. On his last hunt with his clan, they had walked into a rookery. For those of you who aren't aware, a rookery is where young dragons are hatched and spend the first few years of their lives. His clan smashed the eggs in the rookery of House Grendel. He watched as his family murdered hatchlings who had changed their faces to those of small children's faces and begged for an end. Even their mother couldn't stop it. After everything was done, J.

Ellis DeWitt could no longer take the unjustified death. When things were cleaned up, he stealthily took the last surviving egg and hid it somewhere for safe keeping. He then turned himself over to the Department of the Arcane.

It is the Department's policy to have a new contact screened by a psychic. As such, the first person to have contact with J. Ellis DeWitt was Prita. When she walked into the interrogation room, she felt her body freeze and her heart sank. After so many years of avoiding the truth of things and working hard to not be on this path, he was sitting there looking up at her like she knew he would be. He was everything she knew that would be. Forgettable handsome face, studded with three day old stubble. He watched Prita with passive brown eyes as she walked into the impersonal room. This was the moment that she knew that this was the life she was going to live. She wanted her fate now, any fate, if it meant being with him. She looked away with a flush haunting her cheeks.

"You're having a hard time looking at me." He pointed out passively. He had a smoky voice that crackled in her ears. He ran a finger over a jagged scar that ran from his hairline to his upper lip. "I was seven when I went on my first hunt. My dad thought I could handle it so we went off. We came across a griffin nest. Momma got ahold of me. If I hadn't shut my eye, I would have lost it. I killed the thing though. I guess my fate was sealed."

"Mr. DeWitt. I'm a Hindu," she said coldly. "I don't believe that fate is something that we are not able to control. You are not predestined to be a killer because of a nasty scar."

"I think you're lying."

"Based on what information?"

"Based on a couple of things. I know that you, like the rest of us, know that the fates conspired to put you where you are. You think I'm some sort of monster because of how you are acting."

"I'm sorry," Prita continued with a cold snap. "Are you a psychic, Mr. DeWitt?"

"No, but you are. I thought your type believed in visions and such."

"Precognition is not the same as being a fatalist, Mr. DeWitt." She shook her head. "There is a Sanskrit proverb my father is fond of. Yesterday is but a dream, tomorrow but a vision. But today well lived makes every yesterday a dream of happiness, and every tomorrow a vision of hope. Look well, therefore, to this day. I'm more concerned about the now, Mr. DeWitt."

He smiled as he leaned back in the plastic chair. The carelessness of his actions made her feel uncomfortable. She wanted to hate him for what she knew he had done and would do, but how could she? Loving him was a part of her fate. Unless she could resist him. She had more important worries. Prita sighed as her eyes closed carefully. She breathed deeply, pushing her thoughts away from her body as she entered a trance. She visualized a small box that she was trying to open which represented his mind. The box opened and there was nothing inside. This was a new thing for Prita. Whether she wanted to or not, Prita could read the thoughts of everyone. No one could be exempt from her probing except him, evidently. There was nothing. She opened her eyes scowled at him. J. Ellis DeWitt chuckled as he rolled up his sleeve to show her the tattoo of a flaming sword.

"Part of clan ritual. We walk into the light and become filled by the Spirit. After that, we develop different skills. I can't be read by psychics. Useless and weird…right?"

She knew that warm sensation that burned up her back. Her heart pumped harder and faster. The fates were pushing them together.

"Is that why you were leaving?" She stammered while trying to keep her composure. "Because of useless powers?"

"I'm done with the fight," he said finally. "I'm not a part of a war that murders children and a mother who couldn't fight back. It's not fair to anyone. I don't know if they were evil but I'm done."

"You could reconsider, the Department always needs men like you."

"And do what? Another fight? Another war? I spent my whole life being told what to do and who to do it to. This is just the other side of the same damn battle. I'm done with the fight. Get your scribes here and I'll tell them anything they want to know, but after that I'm out."

In the span of forty-eight hours, J. Ellis DeWitt told the Department everything that he'd learned in his years as a hunter. It was a long period of time and often repeated. He knew that he wasn't offering them anything that they didn't already know, but he really didn't care. He offered what he had and that meant he could move on with his life and be something else.

Over the next few months, J. Ellis DeWitt became a mundane citizen. He got a job that no one would have ever known about. With the the proceeds he got a house with a puppy. Then he got himself a girlfriend.

He had liked Prita from the moment he saw her. She walked in with a cold and careful look that meant he was going to have to work on her to become his friend. It wasn't easy, but with his determination he was able to convince her to like him. And then like worked very hard to be love. She knew that it wasn't going to be that hard to convince him to be in love with her. A long time ago Prita had finally resolved to be with him. No matter what choice you make, the big parts of your fate always happened. He was her fate.

It was him. It had always been him.

They got married two days before she went into labor with her heir. Her mother was disappointed by this and told her so throughout the ceremony and labor. Prita didn't marry a Hindu boy and that was shameful. Of course that shame really only lasted long enough to suddenly realize that she was a grandmother to a bright-eyed child. The stage would be set around this girl. Her grandparents knew the moment they saw her that she had eyes to see the future. She was going to be a light bringer.

The only person who was more excited about the daughter being born was her father. J. Ellis DeWitt had fallen in love with his daughter. He had never created something that was so good and there she was. He knew that there was only one person who he would be devoted to for the rest of his life. He quit his job to be a stay at home father. She was more important than anything else that he could do.

Prita was not happy with this development. She knew that he was a devoted father and a loving husband but she knew that there was something that bothered her. He was more attentive to them and he knew that she was going down a path that she couldn't control. That's what really bothered her more than anything. She couldn't figure out what her path was. Since the birth of their daughter, she was not able to read the future. She was concerned with this turn of events and she discussed it with the only person who knew how to help.

"It is not a good or bad thing, my child," her father told her, trying to reassure her. He poured her more tea. "Your time with the gift is over. It is her time now."

"What does that mean for me, baba?"

"No one truly knows, no one."

But someone knew.

Every clan of hunters has a ceanne or leader of the clan. Not only is the ceanne the general of the clan but he is also the spiritual leader. The ceanne of the clan that J. Ellis DeWitt belonged to was the black cloud in Ellis's mind. The ceanne didn't have a name or at least not one anyone knew. There was something wrong with him and his self-assured smiled. It was cold and never left his face. He had never shown any respect for the work but seemed to know everything about the blackness. When he thought about it, J. Ellis DeWitt had figured that this was what bothered him about the Clan of the Flaming Sword. He commanded their conquests. They had been successful, but to what end? He had asked but all he could remember was staring into those cold blue eyes and learning nothing but that his soul could be ripped apart. He had kept himself under the radar since leaving, but he knew it would only be a matter of time before he was found out by their Ceanne. He could be found by the man.

He found J. Ellis DeWitt on a sunny day towards the end of his life. Ellis had taken his daughter to the park to enjoy the mild summer day. A cold wind wrapped around the two of them as a cloud of black smoke covered the sky. Then, he was sitting beside J. Ellis DeWitt. Ellis gripped the stroller, turning his child away from him as he stared forward. He couldn't look at this man for a long period of time.

"Joren," said the ceanne, with perfect enunciation of each syllable. "It has been a long time."

"Not long enough." Ellis replied coldly. He was thankful that his daughter was asleep. There was something unsettling that he was afraid of her catching from the ceanne. "If this is about me coming back to the clan, we both know how that ends."

"With us beheading you as a traitor?" The ceanne laughed. "That would be silly. You still have a job to do."

"I left...remember."

"Yes and you laid with a filthy sand niggress which I could forgive if it weren't for the unholy blood that pumped through her veins, and then you sired a mongrel. This is not acceptable...that is why before you cleanse yourself with fire you will correct this error."

"If I don't?"

"There is no negotiation... you will do what I say."

Ellis got up as fast as he could, but it wasn't fast enough. The ceanne pulled him back on to the bench with a hard push. Elis struggled under the fierce grip as the ceanne leaned against his ear and whispered lowly in a language that he didn't recognize. Something wormed its way into his ears. J. Ellis DeWitt's eyes glazed over as he stared forward. The error of his ways had been shown to him. He was sure that the path was laid out before him. He had created a monster with a pagan whore. This was a sin that he had to rectify with blood. The Ceanne let go of him and departed. J. Ellis DeWitt looked at his daughter with disgust. He could have smothered her there while she slept, but this doesn't belong here. He would prepare for everything. Besides, she should die with her mother.

He started the ritual of purification simply enough. He'd laced his wife's food with holly and wormwood. He prepared his gun with the shiniest and most painful silver bullets. He set the table for the last meal that waited for Prita when she came home. She knew that this was her last night when she walked through the door. It was the dream that she knew all too well. This was her last night and she was afraid. She knew she would go down, but she'd always hoped that her child wouldn't be there. She only hoped someone would find her before he killed their little light-bearer.

"You're going to murder me tonight," she said, sitting at the table.

"Murder implies that you have a soul," he told her. "You are not even human, so I doubt you have a soul. You and the Halfbreed won't be murdered."

"Eli, our fates are tied. I knew that the day I met you,"she said as she stood. "But you don't get to choose Noorie's fate for her. She goes with us over my dead body."

In the history of last words she didn't chose bad ones. She felt her body lurch forward in an effort to get out of the house and draw him away from where their daughter slept. Her plan had worked, drawing him out into the street as she ran, only stopping when a bullet pierced the back of her neck and traveled into her brain to bring her body down. She dropped on the cold street with a soft thud.

"Joren, stop. You're hurting me." He swore he heard her say that.

J. Ellis DeWitt only realized what he had done when he heard the sound of sirens behind him as he stood over Prita's body trying to process what seemed to have happened and decide what to do about it. The inside of his mouth was dry and on some level he could hear his daughter screaming in her crib. He didn't hear the policeman demand he put his weapon down as he looked up to his apartment.

"I'm sorry Noorie," he whispered as he took a step forward.
"Please forgive me one day."

J. Ellis DeWitt raised his weapon as he took a step forward and into a hail of bullets, each one avenging the blood that he had spilled over the years. He flew back to land next to his beloved Prita.

This is not the end of the story.

The end of the story is the patrolman who took a look at the apartment that had been shared by both Prita and her ill-fated J. Ellis DeWitt. He'd been the one who walked upstairs to hear a child. In the midst of chaos and bloody death outside, she had opened her eyes and become terrified. She had started screaming, which was good for the patrolman. He bowed down and picked her up. The small child looked back at him and gave the policeman her very first smile. Her small fingers reached up and played with his name badge.

"You like that? I'm not fond of Spangler," he said to her. "But you can call me Karl. I'm going to make sure you're safe now."

It would be later that Karl would reflect on the things that Prita had always known and in her last moments had come to accept. He would watch the daughter of the hunter and the holy woman grow up and shake his head at her sometimes. He would have to admit one thing to himself though. Fate was a funny thing.

XIII. Punk Rock Girl

There were two libraries in Gaiman Heights. There was the Murphy County Public Library which had been set up as a part of the library system. Within Gaiman Heights there were at least three branches that served downtown, north end, and the suburban regions. Then there was South Gaiman and Old Gaiman which bordered on the campus of McKean State University. Looming on the edges of the older part of the city, was an old house. This building had the pleasure of being the second oldest building in Gaiman Heights next to what many mundane people called the customs building that sat at the center of Harmony or Old Gaiman and had the fond nickname of the Spire, for the architectural feature it had which looked over all of the city including the library. Often there was an old man who would pace at the top of the Spire, randomly yelling at the city.

The library hadn't always been a library, but had at one time served as a private residence for the oldest resident of Gaiman Heights. Prudence left her home when she became queen to live in what is called Trublood Manor but as a Puritan, letting something so well built go to waste was not in her nature. So she donated the home to the city under the condition that it would be used as an educational center and that she could control the content. She dubbed her former home the Robert and Agnes Goodchild Memorial Library in honor of the two ghosts who had taken up residence in the basement. Goodchild was a unique institution, as it had two very interesting features. One was the selection of books. Prudence in her long life had become a collector of sorts.

Her personal doll collection stayed in the throne room of her palace and her book collection had gone to the library which had led to some unusual tomes in its stacks. The other unique feature was the fact that it was a twenty-four hour library. It had never been closed. Because of this, the chief problem with Goodchild Library had been staffing until they had found Marcia Marquez.

Marcia had moved to Gaiman Heights almost a decade ago. She was barely seventeen when she moved into a dorm at McKean State with the help of her father, mother and uncles. They were close family and it was hard for her to leave. She'd promised herself that she'd make something of herself and with her use of modelling skills and clever marketing tactics she had been able to finance her way through undergraduate and into graduate life. That was when she became employed by Goodchild Library, which suited her very well. She'd never admitted to her parents what she did for money even if she never found anything shameful in being with the Murder Dolls. The Murder Dolls had celebrated the beauty of women in a long forgotten popular culture scene and in alternative styles; it was art, but something always felt wrong sharing that with her parents. They weren't conservative in any way, but something about her posing provocatively and engaging in that kind of behavior would have broken her mother's heart. Some days she wondered if that was the last thing that pushed her mother to the edge when she was dying. That's when she settled on being a sexy librarian instead of a sexy pin up goth nerd.

She sighed, propping her head up for a glance around the empty library. Night in a library was boring, even with the ghosts, and Saturdays were the worst. She was extremely bored since her pen pal had flaked out on her yet again. For the past two years, Marcia had been writing back and forth with someone she only knew as Afielia_47 who had been something of a timid soul. She knew that it sounded completely pathetic to say it out loud, but there was something that she'd liked very much about him. Perhaps it was true that you could learn more about a person when you didn't see him face to face and he seemed to have an old soul that she was very smitten with. She would sometimes call him her online boyfriend. That seemed extremely pathetic to her, but it was true all the same. She'd fallen in love with him and that's why she felt comfortable with showing him her pictures. He hadn't been comfortable with it so he stopped talking to her. She shrugged it off for the time being. She was going to have to find a new way to spend her time. He filled so much of it. She was going to miss him.

Marcia had begun to fill her quiet time with an expedition into the back shelves of the library that were often untouched by many people even though they were quite rare. She had found herself a stack of books to start reading. The one she had picked up first was by a local author by the name of Carter Lewis. It was beyond interesting to her. He wove stories about tracking beasts and violence in the cobbled streets of Gaiman Heights. The death of his brothers at the hands of the She Wolf. The love of his life fighting by his side. How could she not fall in love with these stories?

The electronic bell chimed suddenly, trying to coax Marcia out of her skin. She glanced up to watch a quiet man in a tweed suit walk into her library. It was Saturday night in the summer. The only people who came in at that time were either drunks looking for a bathroom or Karl. It was cool to have Karl there. Weird things and people stayed away from the library then. It would be fair to say to say that Marcia had a bit of crush on Karl. He was a better educated, older man than she'd seen. Part of her had hoped that her digital boyfriend was Karl. She'd figured out that he wasn't that. Karl was roughly twenty years behind the times. Her boyfriend was just five years behind. She was going to have to deal. Still, Karl was a good friend. It was like having a professor. Karl ambled towards the counter and leaned forward with a smile. Marcia put her book down.

"Doctor Marquez," Karl said in a cheery tone as he set a bag full of books down. "How is the queen of books?"

Marica rolled her eyes as she reached into the bag. With deliberate professionalism, she started to scan books back into the library. She was trying to delay Karl's departure. He wasn't bad to have around. He could be here all night if she let him.

"You say that like my father," she said, rolling her heavily made up eyes. Karl had the amazing luck of being surrounded by strangely attractive women he never had an interest in or at least that he wouldn't admit to having an interest in. "You just need to say it in Spanish."

"I didn't know your father spoke Spanish. You told me he was a realtor from Gaithersburg."

"He's been taking classes. He's starting to threaten to take my little brothers to the village where my grandfather was born. He won't do it. It takes way too much work for him." She looked at the cover of a book and then smiled. It had been a favorite of hers as a child. She looked at Karl. "Did your girls like this one? It seemed like it might be up Annie's alley."

"She said that it wasn't scary enough. She wanted more ghosts." Karl chuckled. "I hesitate to share Grimm's Fairy Tales, but man cannot live on R.L Stine alone."

Marcia chuckled politely. It was the kind of chuckle that you cultivate while working in a library. She didn't mean that it would be polite.

"Ever worry about how weird your kids are?" She stopped before she picked up a book that she was reading. "You could try this. I picked up it thinking it was some other weird fantasy book, but its like some kind of horror fantasy set in Gaiman Heights. It's a little bloody, but a really gripping read. Whoever Carter Lewis was, he was pretty brilliant."

Karl took the book with a sour grimace. He knew Carter Lewis. He was a haggard old man now and there was something harsh about him. The things he'd seen and lived through only to be denied a peaceful life made him angry. He never told you that. He always tried to be personable. That was reflected in the small battered book in Marcia's hands. He took the book with a nervous twitch. This book wasn't supposed to exist and he knew that, but what you think you know isn't always the case. He looked back at

Marcia with a scowl. She thought it was fiction and that was just fine. He forced a smile at her while flipping through the pages.

"Where did you find this?" He finally asked.

"It was in the back where no one ever goes. I've never met Lady Goodchild, but she has a love for books. Many of them are very rare. I mean the nerds from Beinch Library come down here for vacation. I always feel bad for the cleaning staff that week. Have you read that one?"

"No, but his son Weston Lewis was my partner before I left the force. He's Carter Lewis' youngest son. You should listen to him talk -- he's got some great stories. Never be alone with him when he's had too much to drink though."

"He sounds fascinating," Marica sighed wistfully. "Vampires and witches. Wouldn't the world be more interesting? Maybe not as safe, but I don't know. He makes it feel so real. It would be kind of cool if it were real."

"I don't know about that. The world is pretty strange."

"I guess. Just nothing cool ever happens here."

Before Karl could speak, the bell rang. Marcia looked up at the door. Doyle had been an infrequent visitor. He never said anything to her. Doyle had never quite fully understood libraries or how to talk to cute girls in libraries. She wasn't threatened by him. He just seemed out of place. Doyle stopped looking at her feet and they locked eyes. He felt himself twitch before he started off towards the back. Marcia became flushed as she felt her feet fumble. She knew it was him. The man she could call her friend. The man she had fallen in love with through scrolling text on a computer. She covered her mouth as her heart rapidly pumped nervous blood. Karl had said nothing between these moments as he leaned back against the counter with a cocked brow. Karl carefully gave Marcia a sideways glance.

"Him," she whispered. She found herself suddenly conflicted. She liked Doyle but now the tide had turned and things changed.

"Hmm?" Karl said, pretending to not have heard her.

"Oh, nothing," she said quickly, covering her shock. "My loner weirdo is here tonight. He's not a problem. He's just a little…"

"Creepy?" Karl finished for her. "Doyle isn't creepy. He is just old fashioned."

"Old fashioned?"

"Victorian to be exact," Karl said quietly. "By that I mean he's, well, foreign. He's just from a very old world."

"I think I knew that," she said quietly.

"That means that Doyle has some repressed emotions about courting and the opposite sex. You want him to leave you alone, you just need to tell him that. Or he won't do it."

Karl squinted.

"You do want him to leave you alone, right?"

Marcia looked away, clearing her throat of her own embarrassment and then she shrugged.

"I don't know..he's…"

"Go talk to him. If he's too much for you, then you can tell him to shove off."

"What if he gets violent?"

"He won't, but if it makes you feel better." Karl started to write a number down on a piece of paper. "You feel threatened, call this number and tell them. They'll take care of him."

"You ever going to stop sounding like my dad?"

"I'm someone's father. That's what we all look and sound like. Go talk to him because you want to. Now if you'll excuse me, I have to go pry a nineteen-year-old off of a scared new recruit."

She watched as Karl walked out of the building. She breathed in as she brushed her hair out of her face and straightened a skirt that didn't need it. She walked towards the back table in the reading room that Doyle had rushed into. There was a moment's hesitation as she watched him with his book. She could go back to her desk and he wouldn't have to know she was staring at him.

That was before he turned his head towards the door listening to her nervous twitching. He knew she was there and there was nothing else he could do.

"I know who you are," she said finally.

"Oh?" Doyle said coolly. He leaned back in his chair, staring at her. It was an odd posture for him, but this sort of thing seemed to work for Carson. "Who am I?"

"Aifiela_47."

Doyle leaned forward and glanced up at her carefully.

"Since that was figured out and you're acting like I'm right, I'm going to guess you know who I am. Are you stalking me?"

"No, just come here for the peace and quiet. Not you specifically, but you are an added point." Doyle stopped. "I'm going to stop talking to you."

"No," she said quickly. "I was trying to be funny. I'm kind of relieved that you are who you are."

"Oh."

"Look, I'm sorry about weirding you out about the pictures. I just wanted...I like you and I didn't know where to go with this so..."

"Courting. We could go courting."

"That's dating right?"

"Yea...sure."

"Cool...we can go out on a date."

"Good. Good. What do we do on a date then?"

"I don't know…you could ask me to see a movie…that's what we do in this country.'

"Right okay. We can do the moving pictures."

"The Cerberus Cinema, 8:30, Sunday. You gonna to tell me your real name?"

"Doyle Lanagan. I'm Doyle Lanagan." He stopped for a moment, his head craning out as he heard something unusual. "I need to go. I'll see you on Sunday."

"Right…see you then, Doyle Lanagan."

Doyle smiled before he ran out and into the night. There was something that needed his attention. He then hoped that he could talk with Father McCreely after that. Marcia furrowed her brow in fear that she had made a mistake by linking up with an odd man. Then something crossed her mind. She somehow knew that name. She shook her head as she walked towards her desk. Slowly her fingers fumbled through the book. She blinked weakly and terrified. Next to the words "Doyle Lanagan" was the word vampire. She shook her head. That was just another strange and unusual coincidence of her day. She would never be that lucky. .

XIV. From the Department of the Arcane Training Manual

Chapter 82-9b: The Winnipeg Treaty of 1922

By this time in your training you have experienced what you need to know about vampires and vampire society. What you need to be fully aware of is a key reason that the Department of the Arcane involves itself on occasion when it comes to vampiric society. This reason is the Winnipeg Treaty of 1922.

The Winnipeg Treaty of 1922 is a document that ended hostilities between hunters, vampires and werewolves. While there is not an outright love between these three groups, open warfare has been ceased and agreements between the three have been reached. If there is a major conflict that cannot be resolved by the parties involved, then the offer to mediate will be thrown over to the Department of the Arcane.

In this section, you will learn the basic history behind the treaty and why it is very important today for you to be fully aware of it and its implications.

The Treaty of Winnipeg was drafted after the shift in defense following World War I. This signified a break between the European Congress and the North American House of Burgesses in the vampiric community. When it was decided that they could no longer work together as an international group, this discord was considered a rogue act by the Communion of Hunters who attempted to wage war on the newly founded vampire states. Oddly enough, the vampire's longtime rival for territory, the werewolves, came to the aid of the vampires which then led to a violent and bloody war. This war ended after the negotiations conducted by Seth'rel of House Grendel. It has been signed by Ward Lewis, Bruno Sunbear and Claudius Faustino.

This agreement states that the vampires promise to stop hunting to kill on tribal lands and stick to their traditional outside grounds of hunting for vampiric peoples. Hunters in turn promised to not hunt either vampires or werewolves unless it becomes necessary to curb these people's wrongdoings. Indirectly, this also limited the types of people vampires would feed on, though they will indeed tell you that their exclusions were not giving anything up since these dietary selections were falling out of vogue anyway.

What this did on a larger scale was give werewolves a new level of power in North America. The Skinwalkers are the first creatures to have settled this new continent and much like their mundane counterparts they were often overlooked in the affairs of the new world. This was not assisted any when they interbred with early Conry people who settled in the interior. The Conry are what simply need to be known as werewolves from Ireland and Scotland (and they will tell you the fine differences) who settled in the Appalachian Mountains during the 1800s. Since these clans were often overlooked by European society, the natural intermarrying of skinwalkers occurred. As such, isolation had made them less desirable to deal with until, of course, war came to the vampires and hunters which afforded them a way of gaining a political foothold. With the signing of this treaty, the werewolves were now respected members of supernatural society. Not only this, but a form of protection was extended to the Maccon as well, who are the non-changing families of the werewolf tribes.

Significantly, this aspect of the treaty limited the power of hunters in North America. With the involvement of the Department of the Arcane, many hunters were no longer so hot on the path to hunt and find and slaughter. Instead, many of them joined an allegiance with the Department to work directly with them. There were, of course, some holdouts who felt they could not trust the department. While these are few and far between, they were unfortunately some of the most dangerous. We will discuss that later in this manual.

The long term ramifications of this treaty have created some unusual outcomes. If it had not been for this treaty, then the war of Vampiric succession might not have ever occurred. However, because of this treaty, the involvement of two or more factions had in fact caused a change in how things could be done. While we will not directly be involved in outright wars, if there is a buffer needed only in the strongest of situations will the Department interfere in the lives of these three ruling bodies who have set out to regulate themselves.

XV. Heart Shaped Box

Now

Jacob grumbled as he slipped back into the small hotel room that he was sharing with his dear Rachel. She'd been asleep for hours because that was better for all of them. The nightly excursions out hunting were something he couldn't explain to her. He'd been acting weird since they'd left East Tennessee or that's what she told him. He'd gone from his typically jovial self to something far more upsetting and she was starting to worry about him. It wasn't necessarily worse, but he was different. He would shrug it off. There was no point in telling her. She wouldn't be a part of it when it came. Things were changing because he felt a new world coming.

They stopped in Gaiman Heights which wasn't the original plan. He told her that the Renard Brothers were paying for them to settle there until the job was complete. Once it was done they'd pay them the rest of the money they were owed. Rachel hadn't questioned it. He'd grown in his abilities and had convinced the hotel manager to let them stay for free. That was until he'd been found out in a way. Then he had to start stealing. That wasn't hard to do. He had been able to establish a connection with Her and since then She had been teaching him skills he would need to serve Her. He had become excellently adept at stealing and moving stealthily in the dark. It was why he needed to escalate his hunting. He had proved to her that he could take a life. She had listened to him as he told her everything he was going to do and what he did. Things had worked out for Jacob and the love of his life. He'd free himself from Rachel and they would be together.

Jacob had chosen his hunts to be in Gaiman Heights because that was where Her throne had settled. His intentions were simple. He had to find a mate and some manner of clue to how to liberate his Mistress from the bonds that had held her in captivity. Both of these things were in the city that he'd chosen to hide in for the time being. Jacob gladly followed his orders. As he saw it, what could he look forward to when they returned to Halifax? Nothing good, he'd convinced himself. Rachel would still listen to her father who thought Jacob was a waste of a human being even if what the Renard brothers promised to pay would set them for life. He knew that Rachel never really loved him or, at least, not like She loved him. She saw that he was to Her something to be treasured and held on to. They needed each other and she could treat him like he deserved to be treated and he knew that.

He'd fallen in love with Her.

He knew that he was in love with her the day that they met at the Farm. Her ghostly spectre was all she could muster to tell him what she needed and he gladly accepted. He'd been living her life for her since that day. It was love and sympathy. Jacob was a motherless child and she was a mother whose children betrayed her. She was a glorious queen who had been deposed by an imposter sister who had tricked a world into believing she was a true heir. Jacob felt the pangs of sorrow from her tale and her song and knew that what he'd found was his fate. He would sit at her side and restore her to her Glory. Only then would neither of them ever be lonely again.

He couldn't wait to see her to tell her of his adventures. It was the only reason he'd settle down beside Rachel at night. He saw her in his dreams. It started the same way every time. Jacob would hear a noise from just outside a door in their basement apartment. He'd get up to see what it was, careful to not wake Rachel which wasn't hard. Rachel was always in a deep sleep. Jacob's eyes would search the black until he heard another noise and there was a bright light seeping out from under a door. Then he would hear her humming her sweet thick song and he knew it was okay to walk towards the door and open it

Jacob always found himself in a moon-kissed glen far away from where he had fallen asleep. If felt like somewhere just outside of reality and in a place where romance novels became real. Jacob would be lost in confusion until the heavy scent of freshly blooming oleanders flew towards him on the waves of a sweetly perfumed song. Her voice would lead him over a small hill into a valley through which flowed a blood black lake. His eyes would search until she lit up his vision like she was the holy Virgin.

She was the most beautiful thing he'd ever see every time. Her smooth white skin showed a soft illumination in the white glowing light that radiated off the surface of everything. He'd watched her blood red lips curl gently into a smile as she walked towards him. That's when his knees would buckle and he'd fall to a kneeling position. This was their standard every night. Her pleasure in his willingness to submit had made him sit high in the pantheon of pets. He knew that and that made him feel terrible about his failures as a hunter. She settled in her grand throne.

"*Mon chere*," she said in her husky French accent that seemed heavy with intent like a rich cream. "You don't have to be all the way over there. Come, pet, sit at my feet."

Jacob had learned to not wait at her command or when she showed her grace to him. He crawled forward towards her as she sat, finding his place against her bare feet. Her hands would guide his head to her lap, pushing the skirt up to expose her bare thigh just inches away, teasing him with her musky perfume. She'd stroke his dish-water colored hair gently. Part of Jacob knew this was wrong. Something "off" felt like it was taking hold, but he no longer cared. He was completely devoted to Her.

"How did the hunting go?"

"I haven't found the one yet, Mistress. None of them taste like you ask. I have been looking carefully. Each of them seem less than perfect. I did see one though. When we went to the library the other night. The one at the Goodchild library. Rachel said she looked like she had mental problems."

"I know who you speak of. She won't be easy to get to, you know."

"I know, but I have a feeling about her. She has the book we need. I think she might be the one."

"Not Rachel?"

"No, Rachel is so plain. This one is extraordinary. I showed you her pictures."

"Of course, her." His mistress smiled a knowing smile. "You'll have her. After all, a woman who poses like that for pictures is just waiting to be taken. You've proven your loyalty and for someone with your condition that is so much to say."

"Mistress, I am not normal as you know, even for my kind. You and I are kindred and alone. I could never be so cruel to you."

"I know, my blue-eyed boy," she said sweetly. "I know you weren't able to get to her, but did you get the thing I was looking for?"

"No, not yet. They said that someone had taken the book with them. It is her, Mistress. That's how I know she's the one. She is begging to join us."

"Then you will retrieve the work for me and if she resists…you know what to do."

"Yes, Mistress. I am ready to offer you a life. I cannot wait to fulfill my promise."

When he woke up from this intoxicating dream, he knew what he had to do. Ascension meant that he had to become more interesting. It meant sacrificing his old life for a new one. Rachel was the first offering he made to his Mistress -- the woman who would be the goddess. He'd been right about her not being perfect enough. Her blood tasted exactly like everyone else and that meant there was nothing special about her. He'd hope that it was deep enough in the woods that she wouldn't be found until he'd be transcended but soon enough for her father to have peace. The only thing left was to find the librarian who had his key to resurrection.

XVI. Graceland

Now

There was one attractive woman that Karl wanted something to do with in his life. She had a standing appointment with him on Fridays at noon. Every Friday at 11:30, he would climb the spiral staircase in a Victorian house to her office on the second floor. He'd sit in an overstuffed chair that felt like a prop from a stage performance of Alice in Wonderland overlooking a back street through a large window. Every movement she made was delicate, like a John Waterhouse painting. She would write notes in her books with soft white fingers making elaborate movements as he'd settle into a chair. The individual hairs of her fine white fur would be outlined with the glow of intruding sunlight into her office. His favorite part was attempting to watch her walk along the wooden floor with silver pressed hooves which made loud clops on the floor like a pair of thick heels before she attempted to sit in an adjacent chair with an ounce of modesty that came with her clothing choices. It wasn't hard sitting in a neat sweater and a pencil skirt. By that point, Karl would be thoroughly distracted by her elegant, long face, crowned by curling silver horns that glittered like an elaborate elfin tiara. He couldn't help but smile at her before he said anything. She would smile back at him.

Life was hard for people like Karl. Being unveiled is very traumatizing for the mundane and rarely do they know how to cope. While the rest of us have the luxury of ignoring whatever supernatural trauma has happened and shrugging it off as solar flares or unusual coincedence, it is not that simple for Karl and people like him. Karl had been possessed by a demon. As such, he had been left with the ruminates of that possession. People like

Karl are called the Marked; named after the ward that is tattooed on their wrist to protect them from future possessions. It's hard for the Marked to return to mundane society after a possession because of the actions committed during the Possession. Without the support of a community, the Marked run a high risk of attempting to become possessed again or far worse.

Karl feared the day that he would finally fall. The day that the progressive leftovers of the demon who had ridden his body for eight months would finally consume him and his soul and he'd become a demon himself. He did what he could do to fight that off. That was why he had a standing appointment with her. If there someone who understood his plight, it was his therapist. She might have had it worse than him.

Fairies are quite fond of sex and they spend a lot of their free time having it. A fairy will not deny this and will happily tell you all the weird things that he/she/it has done during the act of intercourse. Of course the world is not overrun with fairies like one would imagine based on the amount of time fairies engage in coitus. This is almost evolutionary defense in the regard that a live birth of a fairy is very, very rare. It is known that there is only one court where fairy children are born and only one person knows that ritual to perform for a fairy born child. She also guards that secret and only does it as a great honor. What this means is that often fairies wish to have children for whatever reason they choose, yet are unable to produce their own. For this desire to be fulfilled, they will capture mundane children. These children grow up in Arcadia which is extremely difficult for a child, but children are amazingly adaptable so they learn to change who they are and what they are to live in the land of fairies. Many may think this is giving up a piece of humanity, but there is nothing more human than learning to survive in an unusual environment. That doesn't mean that they don't remember what it is like to be human. If they do, they eventually return to this side of the Hedge. She had and Karl knew that must have taken so much strength he couldn't bear the thought of it. He had fallen in love with her, but he couldn't dare breathe that word. She was currently serving as his therapist.

He could never say anything about these feelings to anyone. He knew what would happen if he did, she would drop him from her service. Karl could not afford to lose her from his life. This type of interaction could not be gotten from anyone else in his life.

He was constantly surrounded by people who thought he was getting ready to go insane. Weston Lewis seemed to talk to Karl like he was ready to snap. Karl's ex-wife, Monica, never checked in with him unless she wanted something. Norvita was like talking to a sociopathic eight-year-old and as for Asher? Karl didn't want to think about Asher. He was the most powerful being that he'd encountered and that made Karl very uneasy. This place was a safety zone for him and a safe place to be in, and she did that for him. If he lost Doctor Chevre he would lose his safe place.

Karl pulled his head out from his hands as she sat back across from him in the chair. She cringed as she looked at him. He looked sick, like he'd been fighting off too much tired. Karl hadn't been sleeping, that was obvious to her. Maybe he couldn't shake the tired from his bones. She looked over the edge of her glasses gently with a warm smile, as always suppressing her fear for him. A lack of sleep was a sign that things were about to start going down a path that he couldn't come back from. It made her sad to know that one day Karl would fall and become demonic. There had been great potential for Karl and he'd been able to fight off the changes better than most of her patients. She then had to remind herself. He was tired and still talking to her. If nothing else, it meant he was feeling the effects of his condition on his human body and taking the proper actions to deal with it. She was happy for that.

The real problem would be when Karl stopped feeling the side effects of being alive.

"What's bothering you Karl?" she asked finally.

"Who said something was bothering me?"

She pushed the black line glasses up while peering over the rim with a gentle scowl. She was never going to say anything direct to Karl but there was a look she gave him. It was a perfectly good look of disappointment she kept on tap for when someone lied to her. He couldn't tell if it was supernatural or just a level of skill she'd achieved, but she never questioned him when he lied. All she did was look at him and he'd crack. He sighed, facing the Look.

"I'm not sleeping anymore."

"Are you having nightmares again?"

"I wish. I'm not seeing anything. What it is, there's a feeling that settles on me. I can almost feel someone sitting on the edge of my bed staring at me. There's nothing there I know that but I feel them. I'm afraid it's the other me. I don't want to say anything because you'll…"

"I'll what?"

"Take my badge," Karl lied. "I can't lose that again."

"Karl, in this situation I would be very concerned, not because I think you're crazy. Far from it, I think if you weren't so sane, you'd be dead by now. What are you seeing?"

"Nothing, just shadows. No voices. I think I'm just so tired."

"Has your body temperature gone up?"

"No. I am little scared of what it might mean. There's this kid who's not even sure what he is, but he makes me nervous."

"Can you avoid him?"

"No, he's been paired with us for reasons that I don't know."

He looked back, waiting for her to speak. She was staring back at him, waiting for him to continue.

"I'm worried," he said finally.

"For you?"

"No, I'm to fall, but not because of him," Karl explained. With this kind of power... it attracts attention. I'm afraid of what might come after him and what they might to do to get him."

"When you see the shadows does it feel like someone trying to get in on you?" Karl nodded at her question. "Show me your mark."

Karl rolled up his sleeve to show her the simple tattoo on his wrist. She inspected the carefully worded Latin. The words were perfectly spaced and untouched.

"It's not demonic," she said quietly. "Maybe it's the new agent. Who is he anyway?"

"Asher Stone. He's one of them."

"Oh," replied the Doctor rolling aside her mismatched idea. "Maybe it's something else then."

"What?"

"Anxiety. It's not common among the Marked, but it's not uncommon. Anyone going with you on this trip to Tennessee?"

"No, I go alone. Kids can't take off and Norvita hates the South."

"Maybe you can relax on this trip. It wouldn't kill you to learn how to relax. You're always happier when you come back. Maybe you just need to get away. Sometimes I think you'd be better off if you weren't here."

"Wouldn't you miss me, Dr. C.?"

"As a patient? Yes. But making you stay for my wants isn't good for either of us."

She sighed as a soft bell chimed on her desk. She glanced back at her clock in disappointment. These hours were far too short.

"That's it for today, Karl," she said sadly. "Be safe on your trip. I'll see you when you get back."

"Want me to send. Want me to send you a postcard?"

"Sure."

XVII.   The Hunter Gets Captured by the Game

Now

"Did you really tell them that we'd stop hunting?"

Doyle gave Carson a glance quickly as he returned to tracking their target. His hearing might be perfect, but he couldn't afford to lose the quarry because of a stupid question distracting him. He hadn't been hard to find really. Their prey walked with a noticeable pressure on his left foot causing an uncomfortable shoe to squeak and was two sizes too big for him to boot. Either their target was poor or someone who didn't know him all that well bought him those shoes. Doyle had felt guilty about his thoughts when it came to their target. He had crafted a narrative about him. He was being sent out on a mission. From what they had gathered, there was someone hunting women in South Gaiman. They'd each been sexually assaulted after being stabbed. Not fatally, but enough to draw blood. Carson and Doyle knew what that meant. It was only a matter of days before the papers called him the vampire of South Gaiman. That was bad for the brood and they had to take care of it.

The more Doyle thought about it, the more it felt awful. He was wearing oversized shoes that someone had bought for him. So he loved that person. Was he or she sending him out on these hunts? Something about that bothered Doyle and Carson more than they wanted to admit. If it hadn't been for the feeling of apprehension that came with it, Doyle would have wanted to do this on principal alone. Carson and Doyle each had their own triggers. Carson's home was St. Nicholas and he took anyone who messed with the kids there as someone attacking his little brothers and sisters. He also had grown up in a time when pedophiles could prey on the innocent lost children and no one could stop them. He would see people burn for that. Doyle didn't like pedophiles any more than the next self-respecting vampire, but his trigger was a little more personal. Doyle's angry spot was for another kind of criminal.

When Doyle had been a younger man, he'd had a favorite aunt, which happens frequently in large families. She was a couple of years older than Doyle and was really more like a sister than an aunt. He kept himself close to her as the oldest boy of his clan. Doyle had been the one who found her on an autumn day. Her hazel eyes dancing with terror as her face was forced down in the dirty hay of the barn with the O'Leary boy rutting shamefully on top of her. He could remember the taste of blood as he swung his farm-worn hands into the face trying to pull him off of his aunt. He never knew if the O'Leary boy saw any sort of justice, apart from his uncles tracking him down when they were told of the event. Doyle just knew that she was never quite the same after that. The baby she'd given birth to was given to a nun and then she lost her mind. Doyle had also been the one who'd found her body that winter.

He knew this man wasn't the O'Leary boy. He knew that stopping him didn't make up for an injustice that happened a century ago that he could not stop. What Doyle also knew is that this was going to make him feel better. It would be one less sin that weighed on his soul. This was redemption that he craved and desired. Justice would not be his, but a feeling of vindication would be and that meant he would be violent. It would be bloody. He would destroy this man and it would have nothing to do with justice. This was about vengeance. He hoped he could keep that from Carson. Carson had been Doyle's responsibility since they betrayed their mistress. He'd saved him from the fate that he almost collected due to his loyalty to the She Wolf. One of those things was leading by example. This was the example of something he didn't want Carson to do. Doyle wasn't that concerned about the finer distinctions in motivation, as Carson wouldn't know the difference.

They came close enough to find where the trail stopped. Their prey had found his prey and for Doyle that was exciting. It was like a big game hunter that was tracking a predatory beast on the Serengeti. They were hunting a hunter. He wasn't going to hear or see Doyle until it was far too late for him to do anything. This one was getting ready to pounce. They could stop another attack and that made Doyle feel powerful. They had to move fast. He'd found what he was looking for. They had to strike. He would regret crossing paths with Doyle and Carson.

"I said we wouldn't arouse suspicion," Doyle finally answered. "That just means we cannot get caught."

"So, what, we're going to start calling the fuzz when we are suspicious of a crime. That's boring and you know it."

"No, I'm just going to do that thing we never talk about that I'm really good at."

Carson found a smirk cross his lips eagerly. He knew what Doyle was going to do and he thought it was pretty amazing. Vampires have different skillsets, much like human beings. These skills can be based on one of two factors. The first factor is what skills the progenitor had. Vampires have some universal skills, but others are stronger than others. For example, some are able to fly or turn into a bat better than others. These can be passed from one vampire to another. There is the story of a vampire who switched from being left handed to being right handed from his progenitor.

The other factor is the natural skills of the person prior to their conversion to vampirism. Doyle was always a well-spoken, thoughtful man who had been empathetic in life. As such, his enhanced vampiric ability was to speak to people to convince them to forget what had happened to them. This is a surprisingly common skill. Before you die, you will cross paths with a vampire. In fact, you are more likely to be fed on by a vampire than you are to interact with a ghost. Of course, you won't remember this attack because a vampire will tell you to forget this attack and you more than likely will do so. Human beings are very willing to forget meeting a vampire because we are wired to just disbelieve anything that is said to us, like you just disbelieved me telling you that you have been or will be fed on by a vampire. But while you laughed, did you check your neck for scars? Doyle was much better than that when it came to this skill. Doyle had the ability to slide into a person's brain and completely rework their memories. This was something Doyle hated doing. He could feel the people working around in his brain too, which meant that he could feel that person under his skin and that he knew things about them that he couldn't forget. Their secrets, their wants. It was all very, very upsetting.

"You serious?" Carson said excitedly.

"Do we have any other choice?"

"None of which are any fun for us. It's pretty cool when you do it though. It's one of the Dracula tricks. It's like you are a real vampire."

"You turn into a dog. That's something we're supposed to do. I've never been able to transmorph."

"That's a bat but I ain't never known anyone into a bat. Wolves? Sure. Cats? Only if you're a fag. There was that one guy, Jesus, what was his name? You know who I'm talking about, that crazy Spanish guy?"

"Juan Carlos Hoffman."

"Yea, that guy. That fucking guy. He was such a weirdo. Remember he used to turn into a llama or some shit. Man, I get fucking sick of those racist stereotypes. You tell people that you're a vampire then you're supposed to be a fucking able to do mind control and turn into a fucking bat or whatever. Shit, I'm going to punch someone in the vagina if a Bella asks me if I sparkle."

"We're not really a race, Carson. More like a species diversion."

"You know I mean. We ain't all the same and that pisses me off. Ain't that hard to talk to one of us, is it? Like the pictures. That shit is the most annoying. I ain't never seen one that even got close. Except that one....you know with Frank Longora. That's a Dracula who fucking loved being a vampire. Like us...well like me."

"What about <u>Let the Right One In</u>? That was a fairly accurate one."

"Yea and I ain't gonna watch some creepy ass little girl in a vampire movie. If I want that, I'll have tea with Prudence. I'm just saying it wouldn't kill them to talk to us."

"We aren't a sharing people with outsiders. We probably would eat them. Besides rumors are rumors for a reason. We can't control the mass media."

"We should be able to. With the age and wealth we have, we should be able to control. At least we should have a decent vampire flick out there. Something that doesn't offend my refined taste."

"Bring it up at the next conclave. Prudence might have some money for it."

Carson snarled as he listened to Doyle's words. In an effort to survive, vampires have a very complex government society. They are ruled by a congress of elder leaders who are called Burgesses (as you know) who make rules for vampiric communities. Below them are the princes and kings and below that are hounds and sheriffs. Each group holds meetings. The neighborhoods which call themselves broods meet weekly. The queen can call a congress on the new moon. This is when major things were discussed. They would be able to discuss things like Carson's complaints. He also knew that he would get shot down.

Doyle stopped and stared up. The trail ended at a converted five story building. There was a familiar scent that radiated from the building. That bothered Doyle because he knew that something was coming. Doyle watched a dark figure climb the side of the building and slither into a semi-open window. When the figure pried the window open more, the smell grew heavier. Doyle felt himself lean forward with a small snarl. There was someone he knew in that building and something about that made Doyle want to hurt their prey more. He looked at Carson cautiously. He hoped that he didn't smell it. If he did, Carson didn't care. He was far too busy being amused by the clumsy antics of their target. Doyle hoped that he didn't notice the scent to pick up on it. Or at least that he wasn't familiar with it.

"Will you look at that, Doyle? Stereotypes abound." Carson laughed. This confirmed Doyle's suspicions that Carson was distracted. "Some fucker trying to be stealthy in our city as he sneaks into a dame's apartment. You'd think they'd learn to not being so fucking obvious. Ain't nothing I've seen sadder. You, Doyle?"

"Lots sadder than this. Orphaned kittens lost in the rain. Old women who aren't visited by their grandchildren." Doyle looked up. "Shall I, or do you want this dance?"

"I had the last one. You can have this one."

Doyle nodded before he backed up to take a running leap up the side of the building. Doyle had been embarrassed by his anamorphic abilities, but he had quite the vertical leap, as do most vampires. With very little effort he'd gotten to the side of the building as he climbed up quickly towards the open window. Within seconds, Doyle had gained entry into the apartment. A scent he had dreamed about for two years filled his nose, forcing a territorial snarl to rumble under his tongue. Doyle felt his stomach sink. He knew she was here. His prey had chosen to attack someone Doyle was starting to care about. He had stopped this all from happening. He walked with his head down, looking over the framed movie and concert posters. He walked along towards an open bedroom down the hall.

Street lights and the moon cast a yellow light and shadows over the form of a sleeping woman nestled safely under a sea of blankets. Above her was a shadow staring down with his head maliciously cocked to one side. His fingers ran over her light-bleached face. Doyle could not wait. He knew what this thing had done to the shadow. Doyle stepped forward on light feet and snatched the shadow out of the room with a fluid motion, taking him out of the bedroom back into what Doyle assumed was a living room towards the open window. They had to leave as quickly as possible. Doyle could not risk violence in her apartment. Not at this point.

What happened next was very confusing to Doyle, but I will try my best to keep it as accurate as possible. Just as they passed the couch, the shadow ripped himself away from Doyle's grip and shoved a shoulder into Doyle's back pushing him forward. This was very surprising to Doyle. Not many could be stronger than him in a fair fight without being something extra. As such he lunged at the shadow. The pair of tumbled towards a wall with a heavy clap of noise. Doyle pinned the shadow against the wall with a growl.

"Hey, man, get out of my way," whispered the shadow carefully.

"No. You don't belong here."

"I do more than you, Doyle," said the shadow. "Let go of me."

Doyle's fingers let go of the shadow as he backed away. He didn't know this shadow but somehow shadow knew him. Something hit Doyle in places that made him drastically uncomfortable. He didn't smell like it himself, but someone attached to the shadow smelled like death and joyous suffering. Doyle found his fangs dropping out of his mouth with a snarl. He had to destroy who or whatever this thing was.

"How do you know who I am?" Doyle growled.

Somewhere on a high hill there was a car that drove past, lighting the inside of the apartment. In that flash of light, Doyle saw the face of a sickly man who had not seen sleep in three days or more before disappearing into the darkness. Doyle was filled with apprehension as he watched for a moment, his fingers gripping the shadow's shirt tightly. The shadow gave him a grin with a hollow laugh that was followed by a wheezing cough.

"She knows you. I know Her and She knows me and We are all together," said the shadow.

The ring of familiarity punched Doyle in the face at his words. He should have not been surprised that She'd learned how to drain a victim psychically. That was most devastating. That meant she was still alive which had always been Doyle's greatest fear in life. He looked back at the shadow. For a second, he saw a glint of jade green flash in the shadow's eyes. If Doyle were half the man he wanted to be, he would have killed him there. This would be something he'd regret for the rest of his days and he knew it, even as he let go of the shadow quietly.

"We will speak again," said the shadow before he disappeared out of the apartment.

He told himself that it wasn't true. There was no way that could be the case. And yet the shadow slipped off without incident or word from the apartment. He couldn't have frightened him away, but Doyle couldn't chase after the shadow -- not until he had figured out what was going on. If She could possess someone then she was more dangerous than he'd thought. Doyle shook his head as he looked over the edge of the window. Carson stared up with his arms crossed staring at him angrily.

"What the hell?" Carson called.

"He ran on me. Try down the alley." Said Doyle.

"Seriously? You are usually faster than that."

"Carson…just do it."

Carson nodded before he ran off. Doyle took a breath before he started to shut the window as he started to leave.

He smelled her before he heard her creep up behind him. That action was not nearly as subtle as she thought. She rolled her feet, keeping her steps soft, but she smelled like warm cinnamon that dotted the top of warm, fluffy pastry. Doyle savored the moment of her walking behind him. He turned towards her in enough time to see the silhouette of a heavy wooden object raised threateningly over her head. Doyle had a split second to decide whether or not to take the hit. While he was deciding his instincts kicked in and he dodged, only to tumble into the couch. Her swing smashed into a lamp. She swung at him again angrily which connected this time and Doyle let out an anguished cry, as he covered himself.

"Oi!" He yelled.

"You fucking pervert!" She screamed. "Get out of my apartment before I call the police!"

"It's bloody hard to do that when you are trying to beat my head in with a…Is that a cricket bat?"

"Jai alai. I play Jai alai. Wait, Doyle? What are you doing in my apartment?"

"Oh, I came to borrow a cup of sugar."

"Yea, I am going to go ahead and call the cops," she said, turning towards her phone.

"No, wait."

She stopped as his fingers gripped up her wrist. He stood up quietly looking at her with his powerful expression. Invading moonlight played over features that had twisted into a severe understanding as she looked up at him. He'd gotten her into a position that he was eagerly looking to exploit for his safety and hers. He attempted to keep his head straight as he felt the pleasure of warm skin against his. Her lips parted as she waited for him to explain himself and he knew at the very least that she would believe every word that he would say to her because, simply, he would tell her to. Part of him felt guilty about this, but their survival was more important than complete honesty and he knew that. He brushed his fingers over her cheek, watching her eyes shut relishing in the touch. If they'd met even a decade ago... the things he would have done to her while in this state. Oh, yes, he could be a bad and wicked man.

"I will only tell you once because I can't say it again," he said. "I'm not here to hurt you, but to save you. There was a man in this room who was looking to harm you and he got scared off. He won't be coming back. I'm so sorry."

"For what?" She said in a dreamy state. "You saved me."

"From him, yes. Not from me."

Doyle pulled her head back, bringing it to his lips in the way that only a man who understood modern romance by reading the poorly-crafted harlequin novels that were left in his toilet by a teenager who barely understood it himself and his excitable psychic girlfriend. He let out a breath that passed against his lips in pure instinct of what would come next and that he yet knew was not going to be the case. He sighed as he constructed a peaceful night's sleep of quiet and meaningless dreams which this awkward moment would become a part of. He'd already formed his plan of tucking her in and leaving quietly to never mention this to anyone ever again.

That was, of course, before things went in an unexpected direction.

Maybe he was trying too hard, but somehow he screwed up. He let too much of himself slip into her mind and this left him in a position where he couldn't continue. He'd seen things that he shouldn't have seen in her person that should never be shared. This is where he screwed up and let too much of himself go. He let her know about the awful things that he'd done. When someone shows you mentally what deeds they've done which they consider black, it leads to an interestingly distorted view of it. Not only are the facts there, but also the guilt that is associated with the act, which proved to be extremely overwhelming for Marcia. She let out a wail as she found herself on her knees. Doyle looked down awkwardly, trying to help her back up which he sort of managed by draping her in the vicinity of the couch.

"What are you?" She asked as he stretched her out on the sofa.

"Very sorry."

"Get out."

Without another word, Doyle left her apartment with a quiet dignity, attempting to get himself to a place of understanding. He felt less bad about how it had gone than he thought he would, but knew this was not something that he needed to ever do again. Marcia lay on her couch holding her body with a soft shaking motion. When she had a moment to cope and sort through things, she was going to make a phone call. Things here were starting to get very, very confusing for her.

XVIII. **The Mage, The Nexus and the Garden**

Now

Asher Stone sat with his legs crossed, looking around his mother's back yard as the day started relax into late afternoon and head towards evening. Swings that had been bought for a younger set of people swung in the breeze almost to the rhythm of an academic baritone yelling at someone who wasn't doing something right. There were many things Asher liked about Brady, but his superiority complex wasn't one of them. Brady was a professor at McKean State and it showed. Lately it had been cropping up around the rebuilding efforts on the house after the incidents of the spring in which a manticore tore apart the house. Then he heard the semi-timid voice of another. Jordan had started to show himself to be a little bit more of a man since they got back from the last dig. Everything was changing and his baby half-brother was growing up. Asher thought that was pretty cool. He didn't know what they were fighting about it now, but he didn't care. Whatever it was, Asher was at least happy that it wasn't drawing any attention to him.

Don't get Asher wrong. Brady wasn't a bad guy. He and Asher just didn't see eye to eye these days. He'd been Asher's father since his own had died years ago and Asher had been grateful for the influence of a strong male role model, but Brady just didn't quite understand Asher and his mother and some of their choices in faith. He didn't approve of what he considered a waste of time in alternative spirituality. Asher blamed part of his problems with addiction on this awkwardness. Brady had no patience for his mother's Pagan faith. He thought that this influence was the reason that Asher had no choice but to become a tattooed junkie by the time he was in his twenties. His mother had been odd when it came to faith, sure, but Asher had let go of that

155

anger now that he sat on this side of things. It had only been lately that he appreciated why Brady thought these things. Asher had only recently been made fully aware of what his mother believed and why. Asher was the son of a powerful witch and what people referred to as the Prince of Gaiman. He hadn't known this until the aftermath of the manticore breaking into his parents' house last spring and destroying the split level. Brady hadn't been aware of his wife's and stepson's or even his daughter's talents. Asher wasn't sure if that was a good thing. He couldn't imagine not telling his fiancé about the life he was living now. Brady was normal and never knew. Asher wasn't sure if he could ever live with his own personal Darren to his Samantha. The more he thought about this, the more it made Asher sick.

He hated his mother's relationship with Brady. It wasn't only the fact that he had married his mother. Asher's father, the Great Stephen Stone, had fallen into the void when Asher was very small. He could remember his father if he tried, but he generally chose not to worry about that. Whether Asher liked it or not, Brady had been more of a parent to Asher than his own father, even if things were always a little odd. What Asher hated was the lack of communication between Brady and his mother. He understood that there was a rule to keep the mundane safe from the world that no one could control and that was fine. He wondered if someone like Karl's marriage would have survived if there had been some kind of honesty in his life. He suspected that Karl was bound in secret to never share the experiences of being a demon or his downward spiral with anyone. He couldn't imagine not telling Natalie, the woman who'd got him clean and sober, anything that happened to him ever. Of course she'd spent some time herself on the other side of the Hedge in the land of fairies that did strange things to a person.

He contemplated this as he watched his mother walk to the makeshift meditation pit. He had fond memories from summers past of this pit when it had been his sand box. Then again, there were no young children in the house anymore so what did he expect? She knelt down, setting a tray between the two of them. He kept his eyes trained on her as she carefully poured hot liquid into two different cups. He wouldn't lie to anyone who asked. This kind of ritual scared him. Asher's life had been a series of events that were either terrifying, confusing, or -- most often -- both. That had led to lies about what happened to him and sometimes the removal of memories. Even though he had agreed to live in this world now, part of him was afraid that they would take everything away from him. The other part of him was afraid that he would go back to his own path of self-medication that had been riddled with drugs and paranoia.

Deep down, Asher was really afraid of what he'd find out about himself.

She lit a stick of incense. Asher watched the white smoke waft between of the two of them thinking this was a little silly. Why would anyone do this outside?

"I know that look," his mother said softly. "I've known that look for longer that you've been making it. Sandalwood cleanses the area of impurities. Any negativity that surrounds this place will be purged."

He looked at her as she finished getting the ceremonial work done. A crease folded in her brow as she worked with some intensity before looking back at him. He felt his body seize. There was never going to be a time when that sad smile didn't scare him. Something he wasn't sure he could cope with was about to happen.

"I'm sorry sweetie. It's not what you think," she explained. "The last time I did this was when you father invented the ritual."

Asher felt his heart beat faster with excitement. Due to whatever reason, his mother rarely spoke of Stephen Stone. What little he knew was that his father had been a powerful mage born to the highest of witches, the Crone, and had taken a noble dive which meant that every time Asher was introduced to a new person they'd ask the same question, much to his perpetual irritation. He hadn't known his father, but lately he'd been learning a lot through his interactions at the Department of the Arcane and now through his mother. He held his jaw tight as he listened.

"It seems like a Pagan thing, but your father's mentor was Kenta Nakamura. Kenta was a big fan of using meditation to focus your talents. They both thought that all magic users could benefit from meditation to unite with their magical avatars. I honestly don't think that your father ever wanted to be a mage. I think he was only a mage because he didn't know what else to call himself. At the end of the day he thought the distinction between witch and mage was foolish."

Asher felt pity for his mother when she talked about Stephen Stone. There was always something very sad about it. She loved Brady, of course, but it was as if there was something more powerful in the relationship with her first husband -- a love that went beyond and that she would never quite get over. He knew this, when she talked about his father, there was a peaceful grin on her face. No matter how hard he tried, Brady would always be second place. It was in times like that that Asher would pray that they would get divorced already. Not because he hated Brady, but because she needed to stop lying to Brady.

"People treat his memory like he was some kind of king. I guess he was sort of revolutionary. Is that why you fell in love with him?"

"Partly," she said. "Your father was sometimes too good for this world."

"I don't know if I understand."

"Your father saw the best in everyone and thought that it could be brought out. When I met your father I wasn't a good witch and without him telling me that I had a place, I probably would have still been wicked. Now drink up, your tea is going to get cold."

Asher took a breath before bringing the hot liquid to his lips. He carefully drank the tea with a contemplative thought. He'd never been terribly trusting, but this was his mother and she was trying to help him connect with his inner power. That was the Nexus. The Nexus was the center of all magic and was quite powerful. He'd spoken to her once that he was aware of and replicating that was the exercise of the day. He shut his eyes, trying to focus on something. He thought of gardens like a mind palace and saw the blackness of the inside of his eyelids. He let out a grunt as he tried to will himself to create a place to meet with this avatar. His mom sighed.

"Asher stop. You are trying too hard," she said, trying to keep her voice soft. "Let your mind wander and it'll come to you."

That made no sense to Asher at all. If you tried too hard, then you could do anything. Asher became frustrated as he could find nothing to think about except how frustrated he was becoming about not having something to think about. He was very angry about it. Asher let out a frustrated grunt. His mother sighed again.

"Stop, just stop," she quietly repeated. "Just relax and it will come to you."

"I don't what that means," he said, mostly to himself.

"Asher Pennywise Stone," she said in her stern mother voice. "Relax."

Asher sighed as he thought again to himself. He couldn't just relax. His mind raced from one subject another so quickly that it was hard for him to hold on to anything in general. This was not how one meditated.

She's right you know. Part of the reason you had a habit was you couldn't figure out how to relax.

Asher opened his eyes to his head spinning. He found himself standing in a garden that he knew to be the atrium in the back of the Department of the Arcane. This was where his adventures had started with the Nexus. Slowly, he stood up and walked towards the open clearing as the leaves shook around him.

"Sorry," said a voice that danced like ice through the trees. "I got impatient waiting on you to figure things out, so I did it myself. This garden is pretty peaceful. I thought it might help."

"You hijacking my body doesn't help. I thought I was crazy when you used to do it when I was younger and not tell me."

"You never spoke to me. We could have figured it out together. You wouldn't be the first vessel to lose his mind and won't be the last."

"What are you? I mean really."

"I don't know. I have long since forgotten what I am or where I came from first. It seems unimportant really. Most call me a nexus but it's not what I want to be called."

"What do you call yourself?"

"Doug."

"Why?"

"Why not?"

"Do you always whisper through the trees?"

"I haven't tried a body in a long time. I suspect I could now."

The tree trunks shook as lighting crashed behind them violently. Doug slowly walked out of the trees with her long mirrored frame coalescing into solidity. She had Asher's hair and jawline. Her body was dotted with his own familiar tattoos. Asher furrowed his brow, looking into her bright inhuman blue eyes.

"You're a girl."

"I am of no gender, really," the Nexus replied. "I prefer to think of myself as She."

"Named Doug."

"I ask you not to judge me."

"I can't. You are a part of me and that would be judging myself. That's not ended well for me so far."

"Fair enough."

"Doug, why did you choose me?"

"I saw your father and your mother and knew you would great with or without me. I wanted to be with you when you were great."

"That's not fair. I didn't get to choose."

"And it is why I've been careful to not interfere. Now I cannot wait anymore. When we must be protected, I will teach you how to work with me."

"I…"

"No, it's not time yet."

She pushed her lips to his and blew gently. Asher found himself falling backwards with a feeling like sliding through a painful sieve until he landed on his back. He looked up at the sky and watched the trees. He looked back at his mother who sighed yet again. They didn't need to say anything. He just knew that things had to be ready for him.

XIX.   Post Mortem Engagement

Now

No one ever really quit hunting. You were born a hunter, you would die a hunter. Carter Lewis knew that better than most. The only thing you could do is hope that the next generation was going to be ready to pick up the fight. You taught the younger ones as much as you could. He had given his sons and daughter all the knowledge that he'd acquired before he was even born. The fight would never be done and now he knew it. The more he thought about Prudence's concerns and words the more he knew she was right. War was coming. It had to. The She Wolf had been quiet for too long. The demonic hordes of the eighties had been fought back and the College of the Black Thrush was all but gone. He knew that something had to be coming. If the Nexus had been awakened (the biggest news in the supernatural world in a long time) then this war would be coming. Carter Lewis hadn't been sure if he was going to live to see that war. The more he thought about Prudence's concerns though, the more likely it seemed that he certainly would. War was coming and he was getting too old to fight. Truthfully, he didn't care if he lived through this one. If Margaret had been alive, then he might have fought with everything he had, but ~~not~~ there was nothing to live for now. He had to get the rest of them to survive. It was time to build an army and an alliance for a time he wasn't sure he would see. Now didn't matter so much anymore -- they had to prepare for the time to come.

The Lewis Clan had always been on the front lines of the wars that came. It's what his people did, starting with Giuseppe De Ludovico. He had been the first of the Clan to hunt and he hunted on the streets of Florence for the wealthiest of families. He was remorseless when he had to be and this earned him very little respect by those who hunted him in return. Giuseppe lost his first family in a violent bloodbath as the Harpies of the Under City claimed vengeance for the murder of their queen at the wedding of her daughter to the Beast of the Black Woods. In a normal story this is where a man changes. Sometimes they go on a trail of bloody vengeance until everyone is dead. That only worked in the movies and Giuseppe De Ludovico knew he would be dead in a matter of weeks, should he take that course. He could have given up and gone to a monastery, but that wasn't right for him either. He was a hunter by trade and chose to keep going so his family wouldn't have died in vain. He instantly decided that this tragedy was an experience he should never have to go through again. Within weeks he pledged his allegiance to his Holiness Pope Leo X. Armed with blessing of the Vatican, Giuseppe and his heirs hunted throughout Europe, establishing the De Ludovico name almost as a franchise for hunting. Each heir learned a threefold lesson from the patriarch. Always keep your family close, because they'll be your only ally, always have a patron willing to protect you from what evil may come, and always evolve yourself when you need to in order to survive. It's how Andrea De Ludovico became Anderson Lewis and gave rise to Milan Lewis. And it was why Carter Lewis was standing in the middle of DeWitt Hardware. It was time to evolve again.

The hunting families had been hurt by the Vampire's War and the paladins had been driven out of the city. The Department took over where the paladins gave up. The families hung on because they had to. The only two who remained were the DeWitts and Lewis Clans. The DeWitts were the last of the Clan of the Flaming Sword in town and had shied away from that life. They'd come to the idea of being respectable when Ellis had married Prita Patel. That was why things became much worse when Ellis did what he did to Prita. The Patels were one of the respected names in the city of Gaiman. When the heir-apparent to the Great Swami Patel was slaughtered, the world turned on them. It wasn't fair to them. To hear the Swami tell it, Prita knew what was coming with Ellis. She could have avoided it, but went along dreamily with her fate. Carter Lewis feared that it confirmed their beliefs that they would never be a part of the city and they were simply waiting for the final battle. No one spoke to them and they stayed away from the supernatural world, firmly planted in the confines of the mundane world. The big box stores had all but driven everyone else out of Gaiman and yet here the DeWitts stayed. It was time for families to be at peace. Carter was terrified of what might happen.

The patriarchs of the two families had been rivals since they were young. They were rivals when it came to grades and sports, each attempting to best the other. The ultimate showdown had been for the love of Margaret Hauge. Margaret was had been arranged to marry Alistair DeWitt until she met Carter Lewis. He was sure he did a few things to make Alistair look bad in her eyes, and some of his motives were underhanded. He just assumed that it couldn't have been *all* him. If she loved Alistair then she wouldn't have been swooned by anyone else. Maybe he regretted the competition but he'd had nearly forty years with the woman he loved and five kids. He wouldn't take any of it back.

Carter stopped halfway down one aisle and watched a young woman stock a shelf. If he didn't know better he would have sworn that she looked like her mother. Margaret's best friend in life had been Cait DeWitt. They'd known each other since they were children and had grown up to be fine women together. Ultimately Cait had become Alistair's wife, which had always bothered Carter Lewis but he never said anything. Margaret remained close, Carter didn't have to. This girl had to be their daughter because they might as well have been clones. He cleared his throat to get her attention. It worked without an ounce of startle. She was a hunter all right. She gave him a smile as she eased off the step ladder. She looked like her mother and somehow that made him miss his Margaret more.

"Can I help you, sir?" She asked.

"Hey, Kelsey," he began. "You don't remember me. I'm Carter Lewis. Your dad and I used to be friends. Is he around?"

Alistair DeWitt never gave up being a hunter. He was just waiting for the day when the hunt would come back for him. He was training and keeping himself up to date on what he would need to do. He kept his beard trimmed and short as his hair, ready to go into battle when need be. Even his back office was ready for an ambush with the weapons and tools of the trade ready for a fight. It was why Carter Lewis was surprised that he was greeted with a handshake and a smile as opposed to the pointy end of a crossbow when he walked into the office.

"I wasn't quite sure what to expect." Carter Lewis confessed to the old hunter. "I half expected you to take a swing."

"For what?" Alistair DeWitt replied, as he poured himself and Carter Lewis a glass of scotch. "Something that happened four decades and ten kids ago? I can't be mad at you for that. It worked out better for both of us anyway. Cait and Marge never held it against us and really the alliances fell apart during the War anyway. I'm too old to be angry."

"That's part of why I'm here. Al, I think it's time we do an alliance. My numbers are small and so are yours. I don't have a lot of time and I don't want there to be any questions on it."

"Carter, you sick or something?"

"Something." He couldn't mention the fears of Prudence. Alistair had never trusted a vampire to tell the truth. "War is coming Al, we both can feel it and it's going to be bad -- just as bad as the last ones. I think we are the ones to have to give a front. We should be one family."

"I'd say we need to run this by the Communion, but I don't think they give a shit about it. An arranged marriage hasn't happened in over a hundred years. You sure of this war?"

"Vamps are spooked and the Nexus is awake. I'm very sure of my war."

"I can't promise my kids will go for it, but I'll see what I can do. 'Course the only one that's still single is Kelsey."

"If she's anything like Cait, she'll be a great daughter. I would be honored. You know I think she could be great with Weston."

"Weston and Kelsey DeWitt-Lewis. Your blood is my blood Carter. My home is your home. When war comes we will stand together as one. So mote it."

XX.   I Should Tell You

Now

Carson's words were unmistakably louder as they always were when he was either very amused or very upset. Doyle wasn't sure which one it was when Carson started to recount their misadventures of Thursday night to Norvita. It had started as shame before Norvita's eyes started dancing, which had turned to amusement on behalf of Carson. The sound in the bar started to drop, which made Doyle more embarrassed as the seconds passed and the feeling of eyes judging him settled on his shoulders. He had tried to figure out what had created his failure to perform and the answer was still eluding him. He hadn't been able to put his finger on why he failed. Maybe it was because it was Marcia. There could have been an issue with that. Doyle hated doing his "hat trick" as Carson had called it and it was harder to do when he liked someone. He would not admit it was the shadow who had thrown him off. The glint of green eyes and the possessed soul that called Doyle's Mistress his own scared Doyle like no one could understand. He should have told Carson about it, but those words failed him. He couldn't exactly share a fear that he wasn't entirely sure was true. Instead he'd spent his time trying to convince himself it was the former of the two. It was the girl that he'd been in love with for two years that had thrown him off his game. He shook that from his mind as he settled down, trying to make his lanky frame as small as possible. Doyle's hands attempted to casually hide his face when Norvita leaned forward, batting her long lashes at Doyle.

"Then, he comes running down the street like his pants are on fire, heading towards St. George. Apparently, he froze up doing his hat trick." Carson concluded as he let out a laugh. "What the hell happened up there, Doyle? She naked or something?"

"What?" Doyle said, pretending to be slightly distracted.
"Nothing, it was a bad night."

"Whatever, you don't hunt often, but you don't let someone go and you don't freeze up. Ever."

"Something threw me off. I just don't know what."

Norvita blinked as she scooted closer over next to Doyle. He fidgeted to move away from her gaze. She grinned at him, watching him get more uncomfortable, which made her only slightly more amused. She noted the motion of worry that crossed Doyle's face, but deep down she suspected he had been in the house of a lady who he intended to court. As a rule, vampires are very hard to read for psychics. Doyle was especially hard to read, but she didn't need to read Doyle. She had a line of questioning that would help her figure it all out completely.

"Who is she?" Norvita finally said with a soft blink.

"Who?" Carson stopped.

"No one.," Doyle said too quickly.

"The girl that Doyle likes," continued Norvita. "She lives in the apartment you guys were at."

"I said no one." Doyle said definitely.

"We went into apartment of the girl you liked?" Carson's tone had gone back to angry. "That wasn't the reason things went to shit -- because you were up there to fuck some chick?"

"No," Doyle said defensively. "It was a random happenstance. I didn't know it was hers. Not until it was too late."

"So…there is a girl you do like," Norvita concluded with a satisfied squeal. "I totally was bluffing, but that is awesome."

"Yes, there is a girl, I do fancy a girl."

Norvita let out a hard and loud giggle that echoed triumphantly throughout the bar. Carson and Doyle growled as her laugh pounded at their sensitive ears. For a second, as their ears rang violently, Pitch's bar seemed to be lacking noise entirely as all eyes stared at the party. Norvita sat back down with a smile, finishing her Rum Runner.

"The question remains, who is she?" Norvita asked again, batting her lashes at him.

"No one you know," Doyle growled at her.

"Wait, I bet I know who it is," said Carson. "It's that naked chick on your computer….the one from the library."

"It wasn't her. That's no one at all. Just stop."

"Well, if you don't fancy her, that would explain why you are sitting here instead of going on your date with her."

"Wait, Doyle had a date with a librarian who sent him naked pictures?" Norvita asked in disbelief. "Seriously, are you gay?"

"No, Catholic."

"You have to be. I'd invite her up to see my etchings, even without the dirty pictures," Carson commented snidely. "Prudence hired a fine looking lady to run her library."

"Wait wait wait," said Norvita. "You stood up MurderDoll Marcie? Doyle, as a straight woman who would totes be gay for a Murderdoll, that's fucked up."

"How is that fucked up?" Doyle yelled. "You stand Carson up all the bloody time!"

"That's different." Norvita replied sharply. "Carson and I are in a relationship. I'm allowed to stand up Carson. If Carson were a hottie like MurderDoll Marice, then that would be a different kind of different. You don't stand a hottie up on their first date with you."

"Doyle, you totally fucked up." Carson said, returning from his momentary distraction of a moment while enjoying the notion of some girl on girl action with Norvita. He stared towards the doors of the bar. He blinked. "Refresh my memory. MurderDoll Marcie; a little gothic with a strong resemblance to Delores Del Rio?"

"Wait, are you looking through my computer when I'm not around? Those aren't for you at all!" Doyle yelled at Carson. "How could you?"

Carson didn't say anything. Instead, he nodded towards the entrance. Doyle narrowed his eyes before he turned in his chair. Slowly, his eyes widened.

"Christ Almighty." Doyle whispered.

There are very few things that are scarier than a woman storming towards you. Doyle didn't know them. Marcia marched towards the table, towards Doyle, radiating justified fury. Doyle, being the clever man he was, attempted to use both Carson and Norvita as shields which lasted just until Carson and Norvita carefully moved to the table beside him. Norvita watched eagerly with bright big eyes and complete fascination. This was an amazing story. Doyle smiled softly at Marcia. It was not going to work. Hell hath no fury like a librarian scorned.

"You potato-sucking son of a bitch," Marcia began, yelling over the crowd in a sharp register, which was jarring even to Norvita, who had known it was coming.

"I know!" Norvita interrupted. "It's so not like him. We're both very disappointed in Doyle."

Carson wasn't sure what kept Norvita from dying in that moment. He suspected that it had something to do with the fact that Marcia was very much more interested in Doyle. At this time, it was wise to make a peaceable exit.

"Oh? Did we have a date for us?" Doyle tried to cover for himself. "Must have slipped my mind."

"You strike me as someone who doesn't forget a lot," said Marcia coldly. "You also strike me as someone who needs to explain yourself to me."

"Well, it was nice to meet you, Marcie was it?" Carson said, loudly interrupting the scene. "And we would love to stay and chat, but me and Norvie are off to get a cheeseburger. You ready, Norvie?"

"Oh, I'm so not ready to go," was Norvita's dismissive reply to Carson.

Carson stood up quietly. As a kid who had seen his dad and mother fight one too many times, he knew better than to watch a couple fight. He wasn't ready for this drama. Instead, Carson picked up Norvita and threw her over his shoulder. Norvita squealed her protests half-heartedly, feet kicking as they disappeared from the bar. Doyle sighed as her demands to be put down faded from hearing. Doyle watched his ladylove as she sat down across with him and met his eyes squarely.

"Why are you avoiding me?"

"I'm not. I just forgot."

"You are terrible at lying to me. Are you scared of me because of what happened in my apartment?"

Doyle snarled to himself quietly. He had hoped that something had stopped from her remembering. He didn't even do that. Now, he had to worry about what had happened and how much she did remember.

"It wasn't me," he tried again.

"Right." Marcia said bitterly. "It was some other Irishman named Doyle who I hit with my bat and he left all the horrible things in my brain. I STILL have nightmares. You owe me dinner for at least that."

"It wasn't my intention to do that. I'm very, very sorry about that."

"Then Doyle, what was your intention? Were you trying to erase my mind?"

Doyle gave her a sober look, but said nothing. Marcia found herself shaking her head, horrified.

"Oh My God! You were!" She yelled at him aghast. "I don't believe it. What the hell is wrong with you?"

"You don't understand. There are things about me that I can't even begin to explain to you. I wish I could."

"Don't do this dramatic bullshit, Doyle. I KNOW what you are."

Doyle found himself becoming more terrified than her. He dug his nails into the table, leaving dents from his grip. His instinct of self-preservation was kicking in. He couldn't hurt her. He knew that he shouldn't let himself do that. They were dancing very close to death.

"Do you now?" He said carefully.

Marcia rolled her eyes at him as she looked at him flatly and shook her head.

"I work in a library that has a large collection of rare books. Carter Lewis wrote in great length about his exploits as a hunter. I thought it was fiction until you were in my living room. I'm not going to say it out loud because that just seems weird. I just know what you are."

"It does seem weird, but books do that, don't they."

"Only the bad ones," Marcia said quietly. "Where does that leave us?"

"Well, I owe you dinner for what I did."

"Well okay. That's a start."

XXI. Another Excerpt from the Journal of Virgil Blackmore

I am unable to sleep at night anymore because of the voices inside my head. I thought that my delirium was coming from the unseasonable hot weather we are having, but it is not. I am plagued with a nightmare that I am not able to explain. This vision starts the same every single time. I am out on a hunt on the back road. I do not know if this is the Crowe Trail but it very well might be. Then I spot an elegant deer with soft eyes. The doe and I lock eyes like we are familiar with each other before she sprints off. I follow her through the forest until we reach a blood black lake. The deer is there with a few of her fawns and a buck. Before I can level my rifle, a pristine white wolf bounds over and expertly executes the family by the lake. The wolf raises her head to look at me and trots off. For a moment I am horrified, but I follow her.

After walking for what seems like forever we end up in Jessum's Hollow. It doesn't have the nightmarish visages that I recall from the night that we went down into that valley, but a throne room of skulls and bones lays before me. I try to turn to leave but I am stopped.

She is behind me with strong hands on my shoulders and her chin resting next to my ear. Her skin is cold and I can feel her on me. Her body aches for my touch and calls out to me in a way that I have never known from a woman. I find myself stumbling and falling. The next thing I know I am lying on my back. Then she is on top of me, straddling me like I am some sort of quarter horse.

Her hips grind into mine and she is desperate for me. I find myself wanting her to be with me. I am desperate for her too. She smiles down on me with powerful eyes.

"I do not know what I must do to get your attention." She says in an accent so thick it hurts. I've only heard it once from our time in New Orleans. I was in the hands of one of those quadroons who showed me things about pleasure that my good wife would never do. My mind races through fantasies that I thought I would never see again. And there is this pale-skinned woman who brings it all back. I am confronted with another Cajun woman. "I showed you we are similar by punishing your pets who ran and you still won't talk to me so now I must do this."

"Why are you doing this?"

"You are something I want...*mon chere*."

"Am I going to die?"

"Soon."

She leans down and bites my neck violently. It is this time every night that wakes me up. When I check my neck for marks there is nothing, but I am too disturbed to go back to sleep. I retire to my study to find myself drinking whatever I find until I am reclaimed by dreamless sleep.

Yesterday, Mr. Carter found me in the study before my wife and children awoke. He had Henry clean me up, as well as the pile of sick that was at my feet. We sat in the kitchen as he fed me a steady stream of black coffee and sourdough bread.

"I take it that you've seen the vile Cajun woman, as your father would call her," he said. "I was afraid that the stories about the curse might be true."

"Curse?"

"When your father bought this land from the Rahn's, he was told that there was a place where an old witch lived. She'd become lost on her way from the march down to New Orleans from Acadia. She tormented his family until they bound her in a cave. The one that was out by the cemetery. Your father didn't believe the story, so naturally we did away with the blocks. That's when he started seeing a woman in white. Said she could be a wolf sometimes. People talk about wolf men all the time so I thought he was just messing with me until he told me about the Cajun woman. She tormented him for years until he killed himself. I found your father and figured it was her. I've prayed that she wasn't coming for you too, and well...I was wrong."

My heart breaks when he tells me this. Mother never spoke about what happened to Father, but I know that when I was sixteen that I took over the farm after he died. I don't remember much of the funeral or even what killed him, but this revelation is terrifying to me.

"Are you saying that my father was insane?" I ask with the words sticking in my throat.

"That's one way of looking at it. I think that there was a spirit that was too strong for him to fight and I think she was going to do something terrible to you and your family if he didn't stop her."

I think about Mr. Carter's words and I know what I must do. I did not believe in ghosts before this moment, but if this tale is true then I know what will happen. The family of deer are my wife and children and the wolf will kill them just to get to me. She will do whatever she must to end my life.

God forgive me for what I must do.

XXII. **Mud on the Tires**

Karl looked up as the "Fasten Seat Belt" sign lit up above him as a bell dinged gently as the plane prepared to do its final descent over the ancient mountain range that was the spine of the East Coast. Karl let out an irritated groan as he put his tray table up. This was the one thing that he couldn't stand when it came to flying. Because of his oddly bulky frame, it took Karl forever to get comfortable but once he did and started to distract himself, it was always time for his plane to land. He would always figure out the exact right position on the last leg of any of his flights. He never had time to get comfortable on the first leg from Herbert Field outside of Gaiman Heights to Hartsfield-Jackson International Airport in Atlanta. That often took less than an hour but would end in the black hole that was the Atlanta Airport. Atlanta was a black hole for his valuable time -- life moved slowly there to be sure, but he would lose hours in the various concourses as he made his way to each small airport, always checking the boards to see that his flight had been moved to yet another distant plane of existence (yes, I made the pun on purpose -- I think it's hilarious). It was like his own personal hell, but you didn't go south of the Mason Dixon line without passing through Atlanta. It was the only thing that he'd ever seen of that city, so Karl assumed that Atlanta was nothing but an enormous convoluted airport.

Despite this irritation, Karl was still very excited to be going south. For the last three years, he did branch inspections for the East Coast. What that meant was that it was Karl's job to check the lonely stretches of road like the one from Roanoke, VA to Knoxville, TN. And he loved it. It was rare that Karl got to take a break from the life that he had been thrown into and this was his break. He always came by himself. The girls couldn't miss school and Novita never liked going south. Whether she was going to ever admit it or not, Norvita was a little bit racist and she disliked white people from the mountains in particular. Besides, this exact location was always a little more complex. Things were different in the Watauga Valley office. It was a little more laid back and quiet and Karl was fine with that. He thought about that on his flight when his mark started to ache. He was going to have to give this job to someone else when he finally fell and he regretted that. The day that Karl and everyone connected to him feared was on the horizon. The tattoo that kept him safe from demonic possession would eventually break. Then he would fall from humanity and violently become a demonic. His only hope would be that he could get Asher trained and down here. If he could do that, then Asher could take over. When that happened to his satisfaction, Karl would sit down and drink a bottle of scotch and salt the rim of his gun and end it all. When he felt that Asher was ready, it would be time.

Karl tried to push that morbid thought out of his head as he walked down the old concourse away from the twelve seater plane that he'd just spent the last hour and half on. The concourse was a relic from a time when they thought the town that they were building was going to be bigger than Charlotte and clearly they fell short in the estimation. Everything in this airport had been upgraded slowly so they could keep up with the city's growth and yet it had fallen shorter with every moment. They had given up on the upgrades around the early eighties. Karl walked along the bare terminal until he arrived in the waiting area. He laughed to himself as he looked over the woman who was waiting for him. She was always going to be the one waiting for him. He knew this because she was always waiting for him in the exact same outfit. She was wearing a pair of well-worn jeans that matched a black t-shirt that was at least fifteen years old and was marked with a number three. She thought that the first time she wore it, it would scare off Karl. It hadn't. Karl didn't scare easily and now it had become tradition. He enjoyed the familiarity. When he walked up to her, she was pulling her blonde hair back into a ponytail revealing a layer of black under that sunny blonde hair which was the current fashion in the area. That was something she was okay with. It was also nice to see she'd ditched the colored contacts and was now showing her blue eye mismatched with her brown eye. She wasn't comfortable with it, but she was only half wolf. Her father had been one of Those Crowe Boys and her mother was a woman who had never taken no for an answer. She'd been tough and had to be to not be made fun of by her new family. Karl grinned at her as he slung his carry on over his shoulder.

"Karl Spangler," she said with an accent that was pure East Tennessee. He grinned brightly as the familiar voice rang in his ears. "You're all by yourself again? I'm starting to think you're coming to see me."

"Jodell Crowe as I live and breathe." Karl said with a casual smug slur. "How's your momma?"

"Still married to Brycen," she answered with a bitter spit behind her words. Jodell's father had met his end at the battle of Sugar Hollow during the eighties, fighting a group of Necromancers back to their caves in North Carolina. Those Crowe Boys had kept their hollow safe. Jodell was never happy with this, largely because she didn't like Brycen. He was also one of Those Crowe Boys, but he wasn't a good member.

"When is she ever going to get it right?" Karl said sympathetically. He figured that there was never going be an answer to that question. He wondered if Jodell's fierceness would ever let someone right get a chance. Brycen was husband number four for her mother since her father had died.

"When you give up being a big shot up in Gaiman?" Jodell retorted sweetly. She'd been working for a long time on getting Karl to move down here and become husband number five. "Then you and her can finally get married. Ain't like you'd ever have to work. We'd take care of you and she'd feed you cornbread and beans all day long."

Karl laughed nervously at they walked to the baggage claim. This had been a dance that they did for as long as Karl had been coming down there. It was all in good fun, but Karl was always nervous that she was going to be getting serious about it someday and he didn't exactly have a plan for that situation.

"I don't know. Your momma raised you. I don't know if I can handle her," said Karl as he picked up his suitcase. "She might be too much woman for me."

The two of them walked out of the airport as the sun disappeared behind the mountains. She gave him a sly grin as they walked into the parking lot.

"I'd say we could head to Momma's tonight but I got my orders. The Blackmores are urgently demanding your presence at the estate. The house of Burgess got some sort of call from Prudence and I think they're ready to finally try to carry out their sentence. I don't blame them. The magi aren't exactly trustworthy."

"That cage wasn't made by magi," Karl said, "but I understand. Let's just get out there fairly soon."

Karl stopped as he looked at her. She was taking the time to listen. Karl and Jodell stopped at a black and red trimmed Chevy Beretta. Karl tossed his backpack into the trunk of the ancient vehicle. As she shut the trunk, Jodell gave a half apologetic grin.

"It's been rainin' for a couple of weeks before you got here," she said sadly. "The back road to the Blackmore's estate is all muddy, but the other main road to Hamptons is out so...."

"I'll just have to get over it."

Karl held tightly on to the passenger side handle bar as the Beretta careened down a muddy road, dirt flying out behind them. "Black Betty" by Ram Jam blasted loudly as the spinning tires flung mud onto the vehicle and on the trees around them. Karl let out a loud whoop as he gave himself over to euphoria. Karl had been officially voted all right by Those Crowe Boys because Karl was a huge fan of something called muddin'. The idea of driving through mud puddles was oddly liberating for Karl. He had no doubt that he would be tearing through the countryside on an ATV before he went back to his life in Gaiman.

Sadly, the fun was short-lived as the back of the Blackmore Estate came into view. Jodell parked the Beretta in the circular driveway that would have served as a carriage arrival, then involuntarily snarled, feeling apprehension creeping up her spine.

"You don't have to follow me to the porch," Karl said. "I know you have no love for the Blackmores."

"My orders are to make sure that you are with the Blackmores safely," she answered. "If I dump you on the porch, Thursday and Trumper will have my ass. I'll be here until someone answers the door."

Karl knew better than to argue with that. Arils Thursday and Edmund Trumper were senior field agents. If anyone didn't follow their orders, they would be punished. Karl knew that he wasn't going to do anything to get Jodell in trouble. Instead, he pulled the gold stitched rope, letting a slow chime ring out. After that, a door opened quietly. Karl tried to smile politely at the serious dark-skinned man. He was handsome and well-dressed in a suit that was almost a century out of date. He looked over the pair on the porch with hollow eyes that were set in a gaunt face. Karl recognized that expression as belonging to someone who remained ageless and on the corners of death. That only came from feeding on a vampire for so many years. Henry was the mortal servant, of if you wanted to be crass, a Renfield to the Blackmores.

"Mr. Spangler," said the man with a refined voice and well-planned manner. "Miss Crowe, good evening."

"Henry," Karl's tone changed drastically. He was ready for a formal situation. "Good evening to you. Are the Lord and Lady Blackmore in for the evening?"

"Of course, Mr. Spangler. The Master has been expecting you for dinner. Shall I tell him that you and Miss Crowe are calling on him this evening?"

"Just Karl. I'm going to be heading out, Henry," Jodell said quickly. "The smell in your house is hurting my nose and I'm not about to say something to insult your Master. Give me a call when you are done, Karl."

Jodell gave Henry a sneer as she turned to leave. Karl furrowed his brow as he watched her drive away.

"Henry, one of these days you'll have to explain to me the tension between Those Crowe Boys and the Blackmores. It seems odd."

"Honestly, Mr. Spangler, I think it has less to do with any actions of individual members of any party. I believe that it was something to do with cultural stages that proceed from their own misconceptions. Shall I show you to the study?"

"Please."

Henry stepped out of the doorway, permitting Karl to enter the home. He led Karl down the hallway to the study where Lord Blackmore was waiting. Virgil Blackmore had grown into his role as the Lord of the Watauga. He had FDR to thank for the steady increase in his subjects and NASCAR for keeping the population steady and his subjects loyal. They were few, but they were loyal to their master who had invested in the ideas that had kept their food supply at home. He'd been concerned that things would die down until the heritage movement had happened. People became interested in historical sites and farmer's markets. That meant people were interested in the history of his home and the home that his father had built. He graciously let people come to visit the estate, getting a piece of the profits. The new century was kind to Lord Blackmore. Karl stood in the doorway as Henry walked over to a man dressed in a smoking jacket, leaning back in a chaise lounge.

"Mr. Karl Spangler to see you, my Lord," he announced.

"Show Mr. Spangler in and take his luggage to his guest room. We will join you for dinner soon."

Henry picked up Karl's luggage as he motioned for Karl to enter the study. Karl walked quietly into the study as the vampiric noble stood. Lord Blackmore grinned before embracing Karl happily. Karl had become a friend to most in East Tennessee and he knew that this was home. Lord Blackmore gestured to sit with him and Karl did.

"Karl, it is nice to see that the dog woman did not get you lost."

"She never gets me lost. She has a keen of smell."

Lord Blackmore chuckled.

"It's fortunate that she's useful for something. Most of them are not. How was your flight in?"

"Uneventful as always," said Karl. "How has everything been here? Nothing unusual, I take it?"

"So sad that we've gone directly into business. That's what I like about you. Get the important things out of the way, leaving time for the visiting? No, Karl things are quiet. Prudence told me that she's become concerned about her future. I suspect that she's pressed the Burgesses to make a choice. They tell you that all the kings and we are equal, but Gaiman Heights is our new world capitol and the queen of that city has more clout. Maybe that's why I agreed to keep that vile Cajun woman here. She hasn't moved though. Susanne tells me that she had a weird client group on a tour but she says that quite frequently. I assume you will be looking at our work on her cage."

"At twilight as always, but I'm pleased to hear that things haven't changed. I think I'm done with business."

"Good. Now it is nine o'clock and the Lady Blackmore has been working since yesterday for your arrival and if we don't join her soon, she will skin me alive."

If there was one person who had adjusted and modified her life better than the others, it was the Lady Blackmore. Throughout the years, she'd found that her brand of party hosting had not changed and she had been a brilliant mind behind a series of etiquette books on the subject. She still wore the finest fashions and made sure that the house was kept in shape. She was also a perfect hostess, as indicated by her courteously standing waiting for the men to enter the room.

"Mr. Spangler," she said politely. "I am so happy you have made it in time for dinner. I was afraid that dog woman wouldn't take our request seriously."

"She does her job well and I'm very pleased she did. Your house is of course, perfect as always."

"Aw, you're still very flattering, Karl. It's like you want me to forget that you brought trash into my home or like you even know that I'll rip your throat out if you find yourself discussing work at my dinner table. Do enjoy it please -- Henry has been working very hard on this meal."

Karl knew better than to defy the Lady Blackmore when it came to the things that were to occur at her table. Besides, he was more excited about the meal that was going to be set out before him than his routine inspections. Henry never got to cook for the living, so when Karl came around the food was going to be perfect. He knew that it would only be a matter of time for work. Tonight, he was going to be a good guest.

XXIII. **Because the Night**

Norvita thought he was terribly boring as she lingered in a doorway. There had never been a moment where she had felt more like an adult than as she watched Doyle throw almost identical pieces of clothing out into a messy pile on the hardwood floor of the bedroom. She'd started watching this insanity on a whim, but by now it had become somewhat amusing to her. Normally, Doyle would pull on whatever outfit looked like it worked for him and then go on with his day. Today was the exception to the rule. Norvita hadn't been quite sure if Doyle had ever gone on a date before or after he was turned into whatever you would call what he is. Then again, her understanding of nineteenth century dating habits were virtually nonexistent since that was just not something she thought about on a regular basis.

Doyle was actually on his first date ever and he wanted all the help he could get. The only person he could think of who knew how to date was Norvita. When she had arrived, she was dragged upstairs and asked to help him. She had been entertained by Doyle's awkwardness before she became bored. He wasn't speaking to her and quite frankly this was extremely frustrating. If she was going to help, then how was she supposed to do that without his interaction? Then, without warning, he pushed Norvita out of his room to get dressed. Norvita didn't leave though. She knew that if he didn't stop this process and get dressed soon, then he was going to cancel and she wasn't going to let him cancel. Not on a hottie that he had a chance to get with. She suspected that Doyle had settled on some sort of stupid looking brown suit with a dress shirt and some sort of colored vest.

After Doyle finally got dressed he opened the bedroom door, waiting for Norvita's approval. She looked up from the screen of her trendy phone with a brow quirked at him. She tried to pretend that this was a drain on her time, but that wasn't the case. She would never admit it to Doyle, but she was rather flattered that he'd asked her. She knew that her advice was always perfectly good and he finally asked her. She wasn't going to tell him that he had made her night. Instead she was going to plow through the path of him looking at her expectantly in the same suit with different tweaks here and there. The fact was that it was the fifth suit he'd picked out and night was pushing towards their date. If she couldn't help him now, then there simply was not hope for the rest of the night. Norvita was starting to really hate Doyle.

Doyle looked at Norvita expectantly, waiting for an answer. He gave a small spin before he looked at her again. She wasn't quite sure what to say to him because she wasn't quite sure if he was looking for a real answer. Norvita looked at him quietly while trying to choose her words.

"Well?" Doyle said finally, ending the silence.

"Are you off to help Mr. Herriot and Mr. Farnom birth the Copperton's new calf this fine marrow over in Dilby?" Norvita asked sarcastically.

"No one is going to get your Downton Abby reference in this house."

"That's why it was an All Creatures Great and Small reference. I know to go old school PBS British Drama with you two."

"How do I look?"

"You're wearing a suit?" Norvita said, still a little dumbfounded.

"So, it's a handsome suit." Doyle said defensively.

"One, no one ever calls a suit handsome anymore. You are handsome in a suit, which you are. Two, no one ever wears a suit on their first date. You're going to scare that poor girl out her mind. More so than she is already."

"I will not," said Doyle. "I'm planning on courting a girl and I would like to make a good impression and for that you dress smartly."

"Okay, fine you can wear the suit. I just wouldn't use the word "courting". I just think you're overthinking everything."

"Lots of people wear suits on dates."

"Carson's never worn a suit on one of our dates."

"Carson hasn't worn a dress shirt since VJ Day," Doyle replied with some irritation.

"Wait, you're telling me that Carson has VJ? Why wouldn't he tell me that? That would be important to share with a sex partner."

"Because you are thinking of VD. Carson doesn't have VD. He hasn't worn a dress shirt since the end of World War II."

"Then why just not say that instead of worrying me about the clap?"

"Because I didn't think it was going to be an issue," Doyle said through gritted teeth. "You aren't helping."

"Of course I am. I just don't hold hands. If you don't like my help, go talk to your boyfriend."

Doyle let out a disbelieving groan as he looked at his shoes like a shamed schoolboy. Norvita just waited. When it came to social settings, talking to Carson and Doyle was like talking to pre-teens. Doyle finally looked up with a weak smile.

"I can't talk to Carson about this," he said quietly.

"Why? Are you afraid he'll make fun of you?"

"Well…yea."

Norvita's first instinct was to laugh at Doyle's embarrassment. Even Doyle was waiting for the shrill sound of Norvita's mocking laughter to ring through his ears. It was her custom of coping, since she had a tendency to think Doyle was too much. And yet, she didn't go with her first instinct. She smiled at him quietly like an old woman. Through her eyes there were generations of mothers looking at him with pride and pity. Doyle suddenly felt apprehensive.

"And he'll make you more nervous by barking orders at you," Norvita said. "You've never been on a date have you?"

"No. The last time I was romantic with a woman was Molly and we never dated. Carson'll tell me about the number of girls he's bagged and then what he does with you and…that doesn't help me."

"Yea, I'm not the pinnacle of romance, but okay. I'll see what I can do. What have you done so far?"

"I told her I had to make up for the breaking and entering and standing her up so I have a nine o'clock reservation at Ivo's. She's figured out I'm not human and I thought it wouldn't be too weird to go there and not eat."

"Well, I'm now super jealous of her. Carson never takes me to Ivo's. It's a good choice for a first date. Now, hold still."

Norvita walked slowly around him as she inspected each thread of fabric. He furrowed his brow in anticipation of her remonstration as she looked at his suit. She stopped and gave him a final once over with a smirk.

"It isn't my taste, but it does suit you," she finally declared. "One thing though, don't wear a hat. I know that is something you feel naked without, but your hair is perfect right now and a hat would totally ruin that. Also your hat that you always wear really makes your ears look too big and you are out make a good first impression. Other than that, I would stop by the Stop and Save and buy her some flowers. You need to go with pink and purple. It's a nonthreatening combination."

"I don't think she's a girl who likes flowers."

"Doyle, please," Norvita rolled her eyes. "All girls like getting flowers even when they say they don't. If she doesn't like them, then she doesn't like you and you need to know that now before it gets serious."

"Why are you being so helpful?"

"Oh don't worry -- it won't last. If Carson doesn't take me out tonight, I'm going to the library and cyberbullying some people."

Doyle hurried down the street trying to understand what cyberbullying was and why Norvita would do something like that. He wasn't quite sure it was a worthy endeavor but Norvita would not be able to cope with being too very good all in one day. He turned down the familiar path towards Marcia's apartment. Doyle was nearly 200 years old. He'd fought in two major wars, he spoke to the high queen on a regular basis and acted as an intermediary between his people and the Department of the Arcane. Any missteps in those situations could lead him to being nothing more than a spiked head waiting for the sun to rise and yet this was the most nervous he'd ever been. He tried hard to not crush the bouquet that Norvita had helped him pick out as he stopped. Marcia had been waiting for him on the steps of the apartment with her arms crossed. He felt himself twitch as a smile crossed his face. He had been expecting something special, but not a bright red dress that made the vision of her scream out at his senses in the darkened street. Her glance caught his and then she smiled, relieved at his continued existence.

"Oh, thank God," Marcia began, "I thought for a moment I was going to be over-dressed, but then you show up like you are ready to go walking on the moors."

"I..didn't…"

"It was a stupid joke. You look handsome. Ready?"

Doyle nodded quickly as he handed her the flowers. She smiled as she took a short inhale of the bouquet with a pleasant smile. Doyle felt the intensity of the moment pass as she started to settle into liking him. This had been confirmed by the fact that she leaned up and planted a kiss on his cheek before taking his arm. Doyle found himself escorting her down the street on their way to Ivo's. So far, this was a great date.

****

Light jazz played over the bar as Doyle felt himself becoming more excited. His eyes stared into hers across the table. His ears twitched at the light, meaningless conversation drifting around them and felt nothing but jealousy at everyone else's ease and wit. Doyle hated that he couldn't think of a single intelligent, interesting, or even boring thing to say to her. Instead, he found himself tapping out a rhythm on the table in a nervous pattern. He wasn't sure about what was happen on a date, but this was awkward to him. He had licked his lips preparatory to attempting to open his mouth attempting to figure things out, but for the first time, in a long time, Doyle was at a loss for words.

Marcia wasn't doing much better. This wasn't her typical date. Ivo's was a five-star restaurant and one of the most difficult places for people to get in. Ivo Warmace was an extremely skilled chef who created delicate and rare meals as well as the only troll to have a Michelin star (a fact not many people knew). Then, Marcia had to figure out the last time she had gone out on a date. She'd dated her friend from roller derby for a few months, but as far as a male date it had been a long time. The men who looked at Marcia's body of work had different types of expectations for what would happen on a date with her. Dinner wouldn't usually have happened and life would become awkward as the date devolved into explanations about boundaries and how one's work in a fetish film didn't necessarily reflect one's real life. Doyle wasn't like that at all though. The fact that he could tie her to a bed and do things to her seemed like a complete afterthought for him.

She put down the bits of roll that she was shredding on her plate while looking back at Doyle. He stopped tapping and smiled at her awkwardly. She returned the smile. First dates should never be this awkward. Marcia had to do something fast.

"I feel awkward eating in front of you," she said quietly. "It seems kind of rude."

"You shouldn't. I haven't eaten in a long time. I don't really miss it."

"I know. I read the book. Your kind don't eat conventionally."

"Oh, you see, that's where you're wrong. We can eat mortal food. It's something you try after you first turn and it's just not pleasant. I mean, first of all, food no longer has any taste -- it's just like sticking paper in your mouth and then there's just the vomiting. It's part of why I don't take communion when I go to church."

"You go to church?"

"Saturday night mass."

"I thought the whole church thing would cause you to blow up or something."

"You'd think that, but no, I don't. But we can actually eat, but when it ends in bloody vomiting and you just…"

Doyle stopped, looking at Marcia who was blinking at him rather blankly.

"I shouldn't ruin your appetite. Not exactly proper dinner conversation."

"No, probably not, but you know you haven't spoken to me all evening."

"I'm not very good at this."

"No, you aren't. Did you even date in the last century?"

"No. I haven't been on a date like you know it. When I courted my Molly, I would walk over to her home and spend the day and evening. She had brothers who would walk behind us to make sure we weren't doing anything wrong. Except the one time, she and I snuck away in June. There was this creek."

She was watching him with bright eyes and a slow smile. Doyle stopped.

"Should I be talking about my past and my wife? I'm not sure that's an appropriate conversation on a date with another woman."

"Normally? Yes, it's a bad idea to talk about your dead wife, but I think if she's been dead for over a century, you've hit the moratorium on it being a dick move. Just don't bring up the other ladies."

"The other ladies?"

"Doyle, according to Carter Lewis, you've been dead since before the Civil War. I would be foolish to think I was the first girl you tried to court in all that time."

Doyle looked down into his glass of wine.

"This is the first time. I haven't tried to date or court anyone since Molly died."

"Wow, really. Are you gay?"

"Why does everyone keep asking that?"

"Are you?"

"No, I'm Catholic."

"Doyle, you can be both gay and Catholic. It's not like one excludes the other. I figure if you are, then you should figure it out before we move forward. I've already put two years into this relationship, so I'd like to think we can move forward."

"I'm Catholic...not gay."

"Okay...you are super conservative. Gotcha. Was Molly your..."

"Wife," Doyle said, cutting her off. He knew where she was going with that question and he was not about to discuss it. Molly was not Her and the two should never be confused. "She was my wife."

"I get being guarded and careful about dating," Marica said with a shrug. "You'd think because of the MurderDolls I would be some kind of slut, but I'm not. I'm comfortable with my body and my sexuality and that's why I do the shoots. Guys just think I'm looking to be a slut and women look at me like I'm holding back the cause. It's why I liked you from the first. We didn't know each other and you didn't know I was a MurderDoll and that just didn't matter to you. I didn't know you were a vampire, so the baggage wasn't important. We can move forward without worrying about the past."

"You said it was okay to talk about the past."

"Yea, we can talk about our past. We should in fact, but I can guess it might be too much for either one of us to share too much too soon, so there is no pressure. I'm not going to sit here and ask you fifty questions about your life before you became a vampire or even about being a vampire. It seems a little silly. I mean every novel I ever read has that scene where the vampire gets interrogated by the protagonist. I figure you and I will get to know each other organically unless you want to play twenty questions."

"This is not what I was expecting. Things seem very complex."

"Yea, most modern dating is." Marcia smiled. "Where are we going after?"

"I honestly haven't thought that far ahead. We could do the motion pictures. I think that's what we were going to do last time."

"A dinner and a movie, how very 21st century of you, Doyle Lanagan. If I didn't know better, I would think that this isn't your first date. Can I assume you came up with this on your own or did Norvita Patel help you?"

"I came up with it on my own. Though she did help me with the suit. How do you know Norvita?"

"She uses the library computers for cyberbullying. I've seen the pages she goes to. I think she's bullying herself for whatever reason. That girl has problems. Why do you know Norvita?"

"She dates Carson. I'm waiting for her to just move in."

Marcia nodded slowly as she thought about it. This was the organic conversation she had hoped for, although sadly, it was about other people's lives.

"See, this is why people might think you're gay. You live with a guy."

"But I'm not in a relationship with Carson," said Doyle in some genuine confusion. "His creator is my creator, so in a way we're brothers. We're the only family we have now."

"Oh. Can I ask?"

"Is it common?"

"Yea."

"Not really. Most vampires have only one heir. We can become very competitive between each other. She just liked Carson more than me. He was stronger and more aggressive. I'm just more stubborn."

"She?"

"The woman who damned me to this state," Doyle said coldly. "If you'll forgive me, I'd rather not talk about her."

"Is She still around? Will I ever meet Her?"

"If I have my way in all of this? Never."

Marcia felt her body shake at Doyle's suddenly cold and violent glance. His hard expression stopped her line of comments, because she could tell this was not going to end well. She glanced up as the waiter brought the entrees. Doyle fought the scowl away from his face as his fangs dropped into the soft flesh of his mouth.

This was the last thing he had wanted to bring up during dinner. True to her word, Marcia dropped an uncomfortable subject. She had to do that. She was determined to make the next date go better.

XXIV. Tilly The Witch

Now

Karl watched the summer wind bend the green leaves and let the sunlight spill into the floor of the old forest. He sighed contently to the gentle sound of creek water splashing a gentle beat against wet rocks, as he walked along the carved dirt path. A sparrow took its time to let out a soft song that pushed through the trees and the late morning air. Karl took the time to sit on the bank of the creek and take a break from his travels to look up at the rusted train trellis that spanned the deepest part of the water. This was the part of the trail that no one walked down but the Crowes. They were the ones who carved it out years ago. This was the spot where Jodell's great-grandfather and great-grandmother had hidden their hand cart. The first Crowes settled the Cove just after the Revolutionary War. The first of the Crowes had been given this land for their service to General Washington's army or so the story went. They had come from Ireland for the same reason that most people had who'd settled around here. The Crowes were Conry. It wasn't something they were proud of. The very first Crowe was in Jamestown. He'd been hired by the colony to take care of the Powhatan Skin Walkers. That didn't work out well and by the winter he'd joined the pack and wandered off. There were no more records of Crowes until the Revolution came to the mountains. They'd figured out where this land came from and now it was a modern sacred place for Those Crowe Boys. This was the family spot where they became Those Crowe Boys.

One day, as the story went, the first of the Crowe Boys and his wife were on their way to work when a train came barreling down the tracks they were crossing. If they hadn't moved the cart when they did, they would have both been killed. Her great-grandmother cut her leg on the trestle, leaving a long scar on her thigh. It was the smell of her blood that had activated Jodell's great-grandfather's first transformation on that very spot and the subsequent attack had triggered her great-grandmother's first transformation. It had become the spot for following generations of the Crowe tribe to sit there and hope to see the Prince of Famori and receive the blessing of Cu Chulaind. All of her cousins and siblings had received that blessing except for Jodell. She cursed being the one who took the frailty of being a half-breed, without any of the strengths. Karl never quite understood it. If he could shed being a monster, he would gladly throw it off. There was nothing that Karl wanted more than to return to the life he had once lived.

He let out a dusty sigh as he sat on the creek bank resting. He was already tired. It was a mile further down that trail to town and three miles back to the Blackmore Estate. This was a choice that he'd made and now he was stuck with it. He could have called Jodell or asked for a ride from Henry. But of course, none of this was official Department business. This was a personal matter for Karl that Karl alone could attend to. He couldn't tell his hosts of his need to go see something on his own. No one would care to believe him. After a moment of rest, Karl finally stood up and started on his path.

It was around noon when Karl's feet finally met the asphalt of Hampton, which hung as a wide spot over the mountain from the Cove. Relief sighed from his lips as he started along the deserted road that went through the center of town. Hampton had chosen to remain small through the years and was taking today as slowly as anyone could in the East Tennessee summer. There wasn't anything loudly going on except for the call of young boys as they raced each other down sidewalk-less streets and somewhere a girl screaming at them to pay attention to her as she used a trampoline in a back yard. A town like this, Karl wondered if they even bothered with holding to the laws set down by the Department of the Arcane. With Arlo and Boyd brewing both moonshine and alchemy up in the hollows and those Crowe boys running around in the woods though, they had to. Unless they bowed to the authority of the medicine woman and that kept them in line. That had to be the case. Gaiman Heights wasn't the only place looking to preserve a traditional way of life.

That was, by the way, who Karl was on his way to see. On his first trip down, he'd met with her and had been rather impressed. The religious folk called her the witch of Ripshin Mountain. They may have looked at her with disdain, but they never quite tried to remove her from their lives. Even they knew that she was important. So they would spit bile and slander her name and she'd take their money just the same. Religious people were the best business a witch could ever ask for. They were the ones who would look for the extra protection from the evil powers of the woods. Tilly Lee Bowers never considered herself a witch. She'd never worn a pointed hat or ridden a broom. She had a series of cats on her property, but that was to catch the mice and rats on the farm and never once were any of them a familiar. What she did know was how read omens and what herbs that would work to cure and heal a body. She still would tend to her garden out back of her home and, like other shamans, had learned how to communicate with the spirits. Tribal life was still alive and well in the mountains and Tilly was their shaman.

Karl walked towards the store where Tilly did her work. It was the newest looking building in the town and it was made out of red brick between the last surviving Chevron station and a storefront church with the longest name he'd ever seen. Tilly's Beauty and Day Spa was designated from the other store front by a bright neon purple paint around the frame of the door and signs adorning the window listing the services offered, which always made Karl cringe just a little. Tilly did hair, nails, tanning, and general omen reading and sooth saying. That was the kind of thing that bothered Karl as an agent. Advertising your skills would have ended your practice in Gaiman Heights. Here it was just something else. No one in their right mind never told Tilly what she could and couldn't do. It was safer to let her share what she knew with the people in her tribe. If you couldn't trust your hair-dresser, then who could your trust with your future?

There were two men sitting on a bench that proclaimed "Enuf is Enough" who broke off their conversation to stare at Karl. Calvin "Cab" Byers had been married to Tilly since they were sixteen (when Tilly had their first son Darrell). They'd lived a life in Hampton that had always been. Cab had his best friend Herbert. Herbert wouldn't tell you, but he secretly hated his name because he'd been named for Herbert Hoover. The two men paused their conversation about how the coal industry in this country was being hurt by the Russians undercutting sales overseas in China.

"She's been waitin' on you since this morning," Cab said. "Damn nearly kicked me out of bed with her damn premonition. It's a rough one."

Karl made a face. A violent premonition was never good and one about someone specifically was worse. Karl instantly became worried about what it meant.

"Did she tell you what it was about?"

"Apart from the fact that you'll need a ride back to the vampires? Nope. You best get in there before she gets mad at you. You know how she feels about being late."

Karl didn't really need to hear anything twice. He squared his shoulders as he stepped into the shop. He was greeted by the familiar sights of the salon. The wood paneling walls were lined with brightly-painted candy pink and blue statues of Jesus pointing to his exposed heart and the holy Virgin Mary praying quietly next to yellow silk roses. The smell of hair care products permeated the air, along with twangy music that was either Old Time Christian or Country. Karl considered the couch with its five year old hair magazines before he realized she was waiting.

She was sitting in her barbershop chair at her station. The rest of the girls were out. She pulled her bright red lips into a judgmental grin as she read a story about some couple who had done something to someone in a three-month-old gossip rag. She arched a delicately penciled brow at something in that magazine, pretending to ignore Karl. He was being punished for being late.

"Am I late?" Karl asked innocently.

"Sure are, honey. The rocks too slippery over the hill?" she answered, finally looking up at Karl. "Have a seat."

With the wave of a pair of scissors, Karl was sitting in the chair, spinning towards the picture-lined mirror. Her vibrantly lacquered nails massaged Karl's scalp as she looked him over and contemplated what she would do with his full head of hair She leaned over his shoulder and began pulling various tools out and setting them on the counter. She shook her head as Karl fidgeted like a four-year-old as she covered him in the soft nylon bib.

"An eight hour flight and then a three mile hike just for a haircut," she said jokingly. "Can't find someone to do your hair up there?"

"Not the way I like," he replied. "Besides, I was in the neighborhood."

"Hell of a neighborhood, I'll get you all neatened up. How's life treating you, Karl?"

"Not bad," he lied as she wetted his hair down with a spray bottle. "Nora's starting kindergarten this year. I barely handled Annie going in. I hate it when they grow up."

"No one likes watching their babies get big," she said as she trimmed off dead ends. "I bet that's really hard when you can't remember her being real little."

"I don't remember anything about her being a baby. I would love to, but I don't know what else I lost in the blackness."

"You'll find out one day."

"Is that the premonition you had?" Karl asked, glancing at her in the mirror.

Tilly stopped mid-cut. She peered at Karl with a cold look. She knew what he was doing here. She was hoping that she wouldn't have to share it, but there they were. She sighed before going back to the cut.

"I don't know if you want to do this one," she said before she went back to cutting. "And I know you when it comes to premonitions.

You are looking for a reason to give up when you aren't supposed to."

"What do you mean?"

"You are supposed to be fightin', Karl," Tilly exclaimed. "I don't want to tell you what I saw because I know what you are going to do with it."

"Just tell me how long I have…before it all ends for me?"

Tilly gave him a sad look. His brow furrowed at her with a pleading stare. She typically lied to her people who would ask about the future, but this was important. She wanted to know what Karl wanted to know and he had to work through his time enough to get things ready.

"It don't end for *you*, but you'll have more than enough time," she finally said. "Want me to put in highlights?"

"No, not today."

XXV. **E-Bow The Letter**

Now

Jacob sputtered at the last drink of blood he was able to pull from his most recent conquest. The coppery tang had yet to convince him that this was a good idea, but he knew that at the very least he had to show Her that he was ready to accept whatever She was going to give him as a blessing. She had to know that he wasn't weak. He'd shown her since he left Rachel and had his run-in with Doyle that he was getting stronger. She would love him for that. He sat on the edge of a bed covered in blood as he started reading again. He had to find the one who could unlock the box that held his mistress. It meant not leaving Gaiman Heights any time soon.

There was the mention of a fairy. He'd had some sort of relationship with an emperor and the prison. He had to find this fairy. Jacob went out hunting for this fairy knowing that he was the next step in a glorious plan. As it turned out, the one they called Iago was not hard to find. Everyone knew Iago. He'd had a reputation among many in the city either by his true name or as a ne'er-do-well named Iggy Smith. He was a drug dealer and a part time street magician who hung out in the park that sat next to a river. The only problem with finding more than news of him was that no one had seen the fairy since the spring. Jacob had quickly gone from joyful to saddened as he couldn't find this man who had to help him.

"I am so sorry, Mistress," he muttered.

"You haven't failed me yet. Do not give up."

Jacob had to figure out where he had to go from there. He spent an hour asking people in the park about the fairy. He learned that no one there called him Iago. They didn't know where he'd gone, but they knew that there was a hole in the lives of many people without him. The street magician had supplied for quite a few, including the homeless who had symbiotically used the crowds his act collected as their own hunting grounds -- those who watched the magician for any length of time would somehow lose bits of their wallets. Now, however, drug use and other crimes had been down this summer. Apparently, Iggy was missed. Yet no one could or would ever admit to knowing what happened to him. Jacob was getting very frustrated with this turn of events. He sat down on a bench with a soft grunt and dropped his head into his hands. If he couldn't find the fairy, he couldn't unlock the box. The protective role of graveyard magic could be overcome with blood, but the box was fairy magic…that was harder. Without any other question there was a figure sitting beside him. He caught the vision of a man in a bright red sweater and matching red shoes. Jacob scooted away for a moment. There was a fever that swam in his brain and that worried him. It was aggressive and violent.

"I hear you are looking for Iggy Smith," said the man beside him.

"Yea…are you him?"

"No, I am not. However, I do know that he has been known to go to Goodfellow Comics. Have you tried there yet?"

"No."

"You should."

And in a moment the man was gone. Jacob looked around carefully and then blinked. A sane human being would be concerned about the sudden hallucinations. Of course as of long before this point, Jacob was no longer really a sane human being and took this latest vision as he knew it to be. This was a very, very good sign. He took his time to go on to find Goodfellow Comics.

After two busses he found himself at the right store. He walked in and was hit with the smell of print and sweat. His eyes suddenly traveled to the two people playing what looked like an elaborate card game. He sneered at them as he walked towards the counter. The clerk looked up from his book with big moss-colored eyes. He stretched as he watchd the nerve-wracked kid walk towards him. Jacob swallowed as he stood holding on to the counter.

"Can I help you?" the clerk asked.

"I'm looking for Iggy Smith," Jacob said quietly.

The clerk immediately let out an irritated sigh. "You are like, the ninth kid to come in here looking for Iago," he said. "He's in Twillingast. I can't say it enough it seems, but tell your friends. He's in the nut house and I'm not taking over his business. I'm not holding. I'm not selling pie. I'm not pumping. Holden Caulfield and Mary Jane do not work here. If you want to buy manga, comics, graphic novels, or look at the girls in the nudie booth, fine. I don't want your kind in here otherwise."

"Nudie Booth?" Jacob said, more confused about that than any other part of the sudden tirade.

The clerk motioned towards a large glass cage. In it, there was a petite white and purple Pomeranian and a small ginger tabby who were sleeping on top of each other rather peacefully.

"A dog and a cat?" Jacob inquired, his confusion not at all lessened.

"A NAKED dog and a cat," the clerk corrected. "That get you hot?"

"No."

"Yea, didn't think so. It's not getting anyone hot. We're going to have to change our tactics. The girls are going to be upset. It was their idea."

Jacob didn't ask anything further. Instead he found himself running out towards the bus. He has found out what he had and anything else he learned from this clearly unbalanced fellow was just going to bother him. The Clerk debated telling someone about the latest nutter asking after Iggy, but it didn't seem that important. It wasn't like the fate of the world was riding on it, and besides he was going to have to wake up Amaya and Penny.

Jacob was pleased with himself as he walked up towards the mental health facility. Somewhere back in his head was a soft giggle. She was pleased with Her good boy. He was working so hard for Her. His reward would be great.

Getting into Twillingast wasn't that hard for him. He was able to lie to the girl at the front desk in the visiting area. She gave him the words to speak and his natural talents helped him work it perfectly. He was so charming when he told her that he was Iggy's cousin that came from out of town and just thought he'd come by to visit. She smiled and called for the orderlies to escort him to the visitor's room. In a moment, he was alone.

"My clever, clever boy," She purred in his mind, "You are doing excellently."

"Thank you, Mistress," he whispered. "I love you."

Suddenly, the door opened quietly. Flanked by two orderlies, Iago sauntered in. He didn't look like a fairy. In fact, he'd lost what made him special back in the spring *(seriously, there's a book about that. You can go buy it)*. His hair was close-cropped to his head in a dull flat brown color that had fallen from its perfect quaff of days gone by. He'd been the Prince of Lies and his stay at the asylum had made that beyond clear. Iggy was the most difficult patient to deal with at Twillingast. He had been the one who nearly unmade reality and he was pleased with how far he'd managed to get in his scheme.

Of course, he shouldn't have fared as well as he did in his imprisonment in the asylum. He held on to his anger from the fall, but somehow the chaos had been homey for him and now he could cope. Eventually the anger would fade.

He was surprised to see the young man in the visitor's lounge. Iago had very few visitors -- mostly it was the people who went to Goodfellow Comics or some poor junkie looking for a fix. This wasn't one of them. Iago pulled up a chair and stared at the boy sitting with his head cocked to one side. When people mentioned fairies, he wasn't expecting him to look so common. Jacob sat leaning forward, looking at the sad blue eyes.

They sat in silence, staring at each other for a long period of time; each man trying to figure out each other. Iago grinned before finally leaning back, smug in the knowledge that he'd gotten what he wanted.

"They tell me that you and I are cousins," Iago began. Jacob nodded. "I know that to be a lie. I might have lost my flair at the hands of the most beautiful man I will ever know, but I can smell special. You don't smell like my kind of special."

"I have questions. I'm told you will share them with me."

"By who? The Department?" He leaned forward with a grin. "Did they tell you I broke the Patel girl? She's better than you. I'll eat you like a Gingerbread man."

"I'm superior to her because I have the protection of my glorious Mistress," Jacob said quickly. "I do not have the weakness of being a bastard."

"Who's your Mistress?" Iago almost laughed.

"The great wolf you put into Her cage."

"Oh holy shit, She's more fun than I thought," Iago laughed loudly. "I didn't realize she had zealots. Well fuck, She's recruiting from beyond the grave. That's awesome. So you want Her to get out of her collector's box."

"I read the book. I know I need your help."

Iago let out another loud laugh that echoed off the walls.

"Fuck, I know you need me for it. What's in it for me?"

"What do you want, fairy? Once She has been restored to Her Throne, She will have many things to offer."

"And She'll see me dead for the help I gave an emperor almost a millennium ago, before She was even a wolf pup. But I'll help you anyway, because I would be glad to see this world burn and I know that's what her pack will do."

"We can do that."

"Oh, I know you will." Iago leaned back and sighed happily in the moment. He had his power back. "I will tell you what you want to know."

Jacob smiled as he scooted closer to Iago.

"What magic do I need to do to open the box?"

"Oh, there's no magic. We don't do the magic -- we make contracts and this box has a very easy contract. Of course, it's the person who opens the box that will end the contract."

"The one who opens the box?"

"Yup."

"How do I find that person?"

"Ask the box."

"I have to ask the box who opens it?"

"It's really simple. Most things in life are. Good luck, I hope you succeed. This world is starting to fester."

Jacob wasn't exactly sure how to proceed with this piece of information, but like most madmen, he was going to move forward as if he knew for certain what he must do. He sent an e-mail to the Renard brothers telling them that he knew where the She Wolf was. If they wanted to get what they wanted then they would have to meet him at the Blackmore Estate in two days time. He would offer one of them to his Mistress and the other would be able to break any bindings that the graveyard would have. He sighed gently with his hand on a window in the back of the bus. He couldn't wait to finally meet Her.

XXVI. **Little Talks**

Now

Carson slowly let his glance ride over to Doyle who was picking at something. He found his eyes narrowing at his companion's continual fidgeting and shredding of a napkin as they sat at their usual table in Pitch's. This was irritating for Carson. Doyle had started to relax and ease into a calm and exciting life of dating a person which had made him easier to deal with. That was until Norvita, who was carefully gone this evening from the bar, had gotten into his ear. Carson didn't know what was said but he suspected that it wasn't something that Doyle could deal with. He'd punish Norvita for that later somehow, but right now he had to stop Doyle from kicking him in the shin as he nervously pulled around in his seat, shifting his position way more than you'd think a vampire would need to just to be comfortable. Finally, Carson put his foot down on Doyle's plain shoe which got his attention.

"Knock it the fuck off, will ya?" Carson yelled at him.

"Sorry." Doyle said quietly. "I'm just a bit…"

"Nervous? No shit. I don't know if you can kick me hard enough to bruise, but I'm about to figure out how to tie you down. What's got you prancing around like a caffeinated monkey?"

"Well, Marcia and I have been courting for a while now….."

"Yea, big fucking deal. You haven't scared her away yet. For that you should be proud."

"Norvita tells me that there is a three month rule which we've exceeded."

"That I'm sure she didn't follow herself; three months for what?"

"That's when a woman expects to be intimate...physically with another person."

"You mean fucking."

"Well, yea if you're going to be crass about it, then fucking."

"Doyle, I don't know what you are worried about. Fucking the living is great. They smell amazing when you are on top of them and are so warm. You're missing out."

"I....."

"Okay I know you ain't a virgin, but I'm like the only person in this bar who's seen you naked."

"Carson!"

"What's your problem?"

"I like Marcia quite a bit and I know she likes me. I just...I don't think it's right, you know morally."

"Holy shit, Doyle. According to most people we have been forsaken by God. Us living is a sin against the Almighty."

"What if we aren't?"

"Are you really worried he's going to frown on you getting it on with someone who tolerates your shit who isn't me? And I ain't planning on fucking you any time soon."

Doyle sighed, knowing that his point was lost. Carson just happened to be more blunt and to the point. The notion of an immortal soul was not something Carson worried about. Doyle found himself burying his head in his hands. He needed to consult with someone else and was concerned that he might not be able to find the priest whom he'd been avoiding since he'd started dating Marcia. That was quite all right. As if an answer to his prayers, Arthur McCreely limped through the door of Pitch's. Doyle felt relief as he saw the priest head right towards his table. Even the priest was happy to see Doyle was all right. Odd things had started happening around town and he had been concerned that Doyle might have been missing.

The priest slowed his pace when he felt the bar grow quiet. He felt himself become uneasy as he watched eyes stare at him and heard the sudden intake of suspicious breaths filling the air around him. This tension in the atmosphere was terrifying for him, like he was back in the Sand Box. These people felt threatened by his presence and weren't sure if they could trust or kill him. He felt the same way as blood pumped through his veins in double time, preparing a fight or flight response. Pitch glanced up from the glass that he was cleaning and looked at the priest carefully. He nodded politely at Father McCreely, who nodded back. As if nothing had happened, the bar went back to its business and ignored the mundane priest. Father McCreely resumed his path to the back table.

"You'll forgive me if I don't ask your permission to sit," said the priest, as he pulled up a chair beside Doyle. "Limping isn't my strong suit."

"Unless you're a pirate," Carson muttered, not quite under his breath.

"You must be Carson. Doyle's told me a lot about you."

"Yea, and who the fuck are you, peg leg."

"Carson! Be polite to the Father."

"It's all right Doyle. It's a fair question. Arthur McCreely."

"You're the priest at St. George's. Ain't that a bit of a walk?"

"Well, yea. I haven't walked that much since PT training. It's a good mile or two from here."

"Why would you do that?" Doyle inquired.

"Because I keep hearing stories about children being saved from pedophiles and gangs being driven from the streets and I hadn't seen Doyle in almost three months. I started to get worried. Sister

Jack told me that you boys hung out down here. She speaks highly of you two, so I figured I'd go out and do some mission work."

"That's sort of stupid," Doyle said.

"No shit," Carson interrupted. "We might be cordial enough, but no one else is in this part of the city. You're lucky they didn't eat you at the door."

"Don't treat me like I'm a babe in the woods. St. George and the Dragon has such a colorful history that the Archdiocese would like to pretend it doesn't exist. I knew it would come with tests and I can only pray that I pass."

"You know about the pedophiles and the gangs?" Doyle said quietly.

"I know that there are a couple of people who are combing the wolves from the lambs. I know that Sister Jack's lost sheep came home safely. I don't need to know how that happens; I'm just happy there are hounds cleaning up the crowd."

Carson grinned stupidly for a moment. He might not have been a practicing Catholic, but a compliment from a priest and nun was always very important.

"You are my hero right now, Father," Carson stated, sparing a moment for a quick I-told-you-so look at Doyle. "And you couldn't have shown up at a better time. Doyle is need of counsel for his fucking problem."

"I'm pretty sure, Carson, that the Father doesn't want to hear about that," Doyle cut in quickly. "I'm sure that's actually highly inappropriate."

"Well, erectile dysfunction is a serious problem that affects many mortal men. I don't know about you guys. I'm not a doctor, just a priest."

"It ain't like that," explained Carson. "Doyle has this chick he's been seeing for a while and he's worried that she's going to want to fuck."

"What's the problem?"

"Doyle was born on the other side of Vatican Two."

"Oh…jeeeze. Okay," said the priest. "Well, that's great he's got someone. Is she cute?"

"She's a MurderDoll," Carson said with a wink.

"MurderDoll? Nice. Which one?"

"How do you know the MurderDolls?" Doyle asked angrily.

"I did two tours in Iraq. Do you think I didn't see some of those pin-ups? Which one?"

"Marcie," Carson answered.

"Well she's a really cute one. Doyle, what are you worried about?"

"I don't think it would be right for me to betray my personal morals for this modern society's conventions. What if she wants to be intimate?"

"Intimacy doesn't involve sex all the time," the priest began. "It means sharing yourself with someone and sex is simply the highest form of that. A woman wants to share that with you, it's a wonderful thing and I think if you are ready, then you should go forward. Hell, Doyle, not everyone lands a MurderDoll. There are guys I know who are happily married who would still be jealous of you finding an attractive woman who understands and desires you like that."

"It's just a sin to have sex out of wedlock," Doyle reminded the priest.

"Doyle, being promiscuous is a sin. Using contraceptives is a sin. Are you planning on sleeping with another woman while you're with this girl?"

"No."

"And in the unlikely event that you get her pregnant, what are you going to do?"

"I'm going to marry her."

"Then where's the sin, Doyle? If you do what you are planning on, then there's no hell-worthy trespass."

Doyle nodded before he got up and left unannounced from the table and walked off into the street. Carson and Father McCreely blinked and watched each other for a moment.

"Is he always that weirdly obsessive about rules?"

"I blame the Curse. None of us are right in the head when we go into it and I think it makes us worse the older we get. Weird things we did when we were alive just get worse. I guess he was OCD beforehand. You lie to him?"

"Probably, it's really all up for debate. Jesus always came down on the side of Love and Respect, so that's what I'm going with here. Doyle hasn't been to confession in weeks, so I assumed things are great for him and I don't want to fuck that up. Sox's playing tonight."

"Yea, can I buy you a beer?"

XXVII. **On Vampires**

Oh, hello there. I'm very sorry to interrupt this very interesting story. I hope you are enjoying it and I do know that there is a bit of naughtiness coming up that you are no doubt anticipating. I feel bad distracting you from this salacious storyline, but I really feel like we haven't talked much in this one and I just want to touch base with you as the reader. How are you doing? I hope you're enjoying this book. I worked very hard on it, as you might be able to tell. If you haven't read the first book about these characters, I know I've said it quite a bit, but you can go ahead and pick that one up. I would be very grateful and I bet you'd like it.

Now you may be learning quite a bit about vampires as this book goes on and I really do hope you are because it is actually quite important that you do. Here are a few things that you need to know before going on because they are good, important things they will save you some sanity down the line. You see, you will, before you die, meet a vampire.

Vampires are the worst kept secret of the supernatural world. This is because other creatures earned how to hide themselves from the mundane world, but it is harder for vampires to do this. Part of this is due to their still human nature. All vampires start out as mundane and it's hard for many to let it go. It also has something to do with the conversion into being a vampire. The ability to hide your true face has been shared through other supernatural communities for generations and yet no one cares to share it with the vampires, because vampires make people very uncomfortable. This makes it difficult for them to gain the trust of anyone.

Another thing you should know and that you may have already figured out is that vampires are lonely people. When you are a walking corpse, you miss the people who you left behind. Many of them, more often than not, will attempt to try to blend in with human society for both food and companionship. Of course vampires stick out in human society like a sore thumb. Sometimes people catch the pale skin or notice the person at the party who's not drinking, but generally it's mostly because they are the ones who are trying very hard to look like they belong there. They never will.

Vampires are walking corpses who feed on the blood of the living. Unlike other re-animated corpses, vampires retain their memories and personalities and are intelligent. While theories about why vampires exist vary based on many factors, most people do agree that vampires are superior dead things.

They are quite sturdy creatures. Whatever magic brought them into existence left them less susceptible to the normal death that they would have experienced as a mundane creature under similar circumstances. You can shoot, stab, strangle, and so on and the vampire will merely find you dull. The capacity for regeneration after the turn is difficult to understand and is still being studied by vampire scientists -- who, by the way, you should always avoid because, well, it's best not to think too hard about that one. Just do it.

Most vampires are very strong. This is based on something that one cannot explain fully, but somehow they do find additional strength that comes from being a vampire. Some theorize that with their diminished ability to feel pain and disregard for death, they are simply pushing the human body to perform feats it already can do, but that the majority of us hesitate to attempt. They are also very fast. Vampires will tell you that both of these things are products of learning to be a hunter but this is a lie. The truth of the matter is that vampires do not know why they are faster or stronger than humans because it is simply magic that they have never truly explored. All of this is attributed to the belief that vampires are not comfortable with the level of magic that is in their body (hence their tendency to mope and brood and otherwise fail to self-actualize). Witches and the Magi will tell you that human beings have a level of magic in them whether they are aware of it or not. They will postulate that this is why vampires have different skills based on their predator nature and become hunters. Many believe this "flavor" of magic is brought to the forefront of a vampire's being through something called the Ritual.

The Ritual is the only act of magic that a vampire will admit to existing. This comes from the Codex Vampirica which contains the ancient magic of vampires. No one has ever seen this book, but the Ritual has been passed down from the elders throughout many vampire lives. It is not surprising that New World and younger European vampires have ignored and dismissed the Ritual as Old World nonsense. That does not mean that many vampires don't still perform the Ritual though.

If you are to see one magical act from a vampire, it would be the Ritual. The Ritual is the last rite one performs before being converted into a vampire. While the origins are unknown, it is widely believed to have been written by the Father of all vampires, Strigori. Strigori is the writer of the Codex Vampirica. What exactly happens in the Ritual is very special and rare and is not even known to the Department of the Arcane.

For those who are uneducated, the Ritual would seem be what most of Hollywood would play off the Kiss or the mere conversion of human to vampire. Do not, under any circumstances, call it that. You should never refer to this act in such simplified human terms. Vampires will tell you that they are very offended by Hollywood's portrayals of these scenes because it downplays the Ritual.

Vampires do have a form of government. They have a group that enforces and oversees the rules that they all live by, which is the House of Burgesses. This controls all of North America. The South American vampires and other continents have something else they call different titles, but the function amounts to the same thing. These people rule on the highest and most important things. Once a person is elected as a Burgess, they never leave.

Next level down are the Imperial Masters of each region. Old leaders are the ones who find themselves being put in charge of the large scale business of vampires. While they are under the direction of the House of Burgesses, imperial rulers often will do what they please. They enforce the basic rules which keep them safe. They also hear problems between groups of vampires or broods. Each Brood is basically a neighborhood in vampire world. Broods are led by the captains or sheriffs of each neighborhood.

While you will meet a vampire in a bar by himself, do not assume that they live by themselves. Vampires are like humans and often need a community to survive. That is not say that they always live in this way, it is just more common to find vampires living in broods. There are families of vampires, but this is more rare and very difficult to maintain without serious hierarchical rules.

Elements of the stories about vampires are quite true, if they are based on the old stories. Vampires feed on blood of the living. It had been long believed that they could survive only on human blood, but they are actually able to feed on the blood of anything to survive without any adverse effects. Animals do not taste as good as humans, but it is good in a pinch. Part of this whole preferring human blood is also a wonderful way for vampires to find people that they can connect with -- as much as one can connect with one's food source.

There are also stories of vampires drinking from other vampires, but no one speaks of it loudly. It would be like talking about your kinky sex fetish at Sunday Dinner.

While we are on the subject of the old stories, do not rely on them to help you get rid of a vampire. While garlic is, indeed, repugnant to vampires, it won't repel them. If the vampire is looking for you, and you are wearing garlic, because of their keen sense of smell they will only find you quicker. In fact, they might attack you out of spite for doing something so foolish. Religious items don't work either unless the vampire itself is convinced it will. It's more psychosomatic than it is about the soulless nature of the creature, but certainly don't expect a cross to work on a Muslim or Jewish vampire. In fact, some vampires will also attack you faster because of it.

There is something from the old stories that does make vampires very upset and can kill them, and that is a fire. Vampires are quite allergic to fire and have been known to burn faster than most creatures quicker due to their highly flammable nature. If you plan on going hunting for vampires, then by all means learn how to make fire bombs.

The other thing is sunlight. They burn very fast in the sunlight, again due to their highly flammable nature. You could also stop a vampire by staking them through the heart I suppose, but good luck getting close enough to do so. Vampires are very strong and fast as I said, and will see the stake before you even have a chance to get it into them. Your best bet is shooting a vampire with a hemlock arrow or bolt from the maximum range you can do so (best to be downwind too). Hemlock is very poisonous to many magical creatures and has been seen to be the only supernatural element that can stop a vampire in its tracks (so forget silver and holy water too, ok?).

A surefire way to kill a vampire is by pulling out all four fangs. Not being able to regenerate from drinking blood -- which I shouldn't need to tell you they do use blood to regenerate, I think we know that -- a vampire will starve to death. This is a hell that few people want to deal with (convincing a vampire to sit still for the tooth-pulling would be unpleasant, as well as then having to deal with a very angry, hungry, dying vampire. If you're going down that road, you'd best have a very good plan or be very, very desperate).

Well, I hope this has been informative; I'm sure some of it will be relevant to the story before too long... Who's ready for the naughty bits?

XXVIII. **The Cave**

Now

Karl watched as the sun crept behind the mountains, casting shades of pink and red on to the clouds that were ushering in a blue-purple dusk over the valley. The timing was finally perfect. The soft white light of graveyard pixies started to dance around the grave markers like Christmas lights. They were out protecting the dead from evil and from the living. It was beautiful and Karl couldn't care less. He paused in his pacing as he scowled. The waiting always made Karl impatient. He knew that he had to work with other creatures in the community and he had accepted that. What he didn't like doing was working with the fairies. It was extremely difficult. For one, you had to have them swear three times to do or say anything truthfully or they could jack you around all day. Second of all, they were extremely unpredictable as was illustrated by the situation right now. The childlike nature of this fairy had forced her to climb a tree and refuse to continue what she had been contracted to do, much to Karl's irritation. The cop side of Karl knew that they had move quickly. Any evidence of wrongdoing was rapidly disappearing. Of course, the cop in Karl would know that he had to do something different from his first instinct. He had to stop thinking like a cop. The hardline policeman in him was going to make the fairy he needed much more unlikely to come out of the tree. Instead, he had to think like a father. If this were one of his daughters, what would he do? Karl softened his expression as he stared up at the shaking leaves of the oak shade tree. He placed his hands on his hips and stared back at the bright blue eyes watching him from the leaves.

"Amaya," Karl began with his most fatherly voice, "Come down from that tree right now."

"Nuh-uh," replied a tiny water-bound voice that fell off the leaves like a summer mist.

"You promised me and swore it thrice. You know you can't back out of this agreement. You made a contract and you know what happens to fairies who break contracts."

"They are eaten by the Maw," Amaya answered quickly. "But you didn't say it was scary down there. I don't want to go down there."

"I know it's scary, Amaya. Lots of things are really scary, but maybe if you didn't think about how scared you are it might be easier. Quicker this gets done, the quicker you get to go home."

"It's still a scary-looking cave."

"Well, then don't think of the crypt as a scary cave."

"Crypt?" Amaya said slowly as black clouds swirled around the tree. Her voice pitched up a nervous octave. "Like where they keep dead people?"

"Well, yes, Amaya, that's the exact definition of a crypt. Did that help?"

"No!" Amaya squealed as the quickly-forming clouds coalesced into heavy rain clouds that dropped big wet drops on his head. "That makes it worse!"

"Fine, you can go back to pretending it's a cave."

"I can't! You said it was a crypt. You can't take it back once you say it!"

"Amaya, sweetie," Karl said mildly. "What do I need to do to calm you down?"

"I...I don't know."

"Do you want me to get Penny to come and talk to you?"

"Penny's with me in the tree."

A curly-haired girl lowered herself from a branch much like a three toed sloth. Her head hung upside down, letting her drape down like Spanish moss as her big eyes looked at Karl solemnly. She let go and waved at Karl as she rocked back and forward on the branch.

"Penny," asked Karl. "What are you doing in the tree?"

"I'm really good at climbing," Penny said quietly.

"Penny, will you help me get Amaya down from the tree?"

Penny saluted and raised herself back into the tree towards the limb that Amaya was hiding on. The leaves shook as they talked to each other. Whispers cascaded through the rain breaking from the sky. Karl checked his watch and the sky as the negotiations continued. They had only a short window before the sun went down and they would not be able to do what needed to be done if this didn't get moving soon. There were only a handful dates that they could do this at all and he had to know if things were being held together on the She Wolf. He'd asked Amaya to do this out of all the fairies he could have asked because she was quite cheap. He reflected on how quickly that advantage could turn to a disadvantage until finally a chalk-white face peeked down from the leaves.

"Will you do it for an Amaya snack?" Karl asked quietly.

"Two Amaya snacks," she demanded. "A diet Mountain Dew and me and Penny get to hold hands."

"Agreed," Karl said.

Penny slid out of the tree first with her huge eyes looking around at the dancing white magic flowing through the cemetery. She stuck her tongue out, trying to catch sparks on it. Karl had always wanted to ask how hard Penny had been dragged through the Hedge to make her that crazy. Probably best not to know. Amaya followed gracefully behind Penny. Instantly she took her changeling's hand and started into the cemetery. The pair stopped at a cave that rose out of the middle of the grave markers. The leaves of ivy that tried to choke the life out of the grass swayed in the wake of dancing pixies. They stood in front of the wrought iron gate that separated a large stone casket from the rest of the world. Amaya leaned forward, watching the words written in a language she used know better dance in bright pinks and purples. She felt Penny squeeze her hand once.

"Come on, sweetheart," something whispered to Amaya. "I won't hurt you."

"No, mean lady," Amaya announced loudly. "I won't let you out. Come on, Penny."

Penny and Amaya skipped away from the crypt quietly. Karl looked at the two expectantly.

"She's awake," Karl said, slightly miffed at Amaya.

"Yea," Amaya said. "But the pretty witch magic needs something really evil to let the gate open to get to the ward. That's what the pixies say. And the wards won't come off unless that happens."

"So Puck's done a really good job locking it tight then. Someone should have mentioned that before now."

"Puck didn't set up this prison."

"Who did?"

"I don't know. It's a mystery to everyone." Amaya glanced back. Her grip on Penny's hand got tighter. "Mr. Karl, can we go?"

"Sure, I'll have the Snickers bars and Mountain Dew sent to you at Puck's."

They didn't wait to hear the promise of sugar and caffeine thrice. Instead, Amaya opened her portal and ran through, tugging Penny behind her. It was gone as soon as the doors were shut. Karl shot an uneasy glance to the rising cave. Another wave of tired hit him like a cartoon brick wall. Getting old, he decided, sucked. He finally turned to leave as he walked up the hill. He stopped as he felt eyes watching him march away. Karl reached for his sidearm that was always professionally planted on his belt as he looked around for a moment. Someone else was here and this was never a good thing.

"I don't know who's out there, but my name is Karl Spangler," he called loudly. "I'm with the Department of the Arcane and since you are this far out, I assume you know what's here and I will tell you that you are in violation. I'm only saying it once that you need to leave before I am forced to apprehend you."

Karl waited for something to break, but there was nothing so much as twitching among the twisting shadows of the graveyard. Perhaps it was his own paranoia, which would really seem more accurate than his assumptions. He turned back to the hill to see Henry standing at the top of it.

"I am sorry for intruding, Mr. Spangler. I find the fair folk unusual and wanted to see what their actions might be. I do hope that they found what they were looking for."

"Unless she's going to tell me something else, there's no more action to take. Amaya is many things, but she's surprisingly honest. She's locked up tight. Something happen, Henry?"

"I believe so. The Lord and Lady have been called to Johnson City for the evening. I suspect that the justice committee from the House of Burgess have arrived."

"That never sounds good. Something happen?"

"I believe they are hammering out details within their own ranks to agree to execute Her. I believe they informed the Lady Goodchild first."

"Oh," Karl felt invisible eyes on him again, making his back arch. "How is your master taking it?"

"Surprisingly, quite well. He might have been devoted to Her while She walked the earth, but she did murder his children and everything he loved. Lady Blackmore took a couple of their herd to go with them. I don't expect them back until the wee hours. I apologize that you'll be dining alone."

"Or I'll just dine in the kitchen. I know you're forbidden from eating on the good china."

"I would be honored, Mr. Spangler."

Karl glanced behind him again as he walked up the hill. If he had let his glance linger for just one more second he would have seen a figure walking among the pixies towards the great cave crypt. Jacob watched as the men moved to the house and the lights flickered around him. He settled against the stone and iron cage and sighed, leaning close.

"Yes, I heard Mistress," he said. "We have to move now."

"Tonight," something whispered back, almost audibly. "We end this tonight."

"Yes, Mistress. As you command."

XXIX. **Dangling Conversation**

Now

As the time crept towards midnight, the air grew cold. The breeze wafting down from the mountains started to take on that crisp, chill edge that ushers in late summer as they started through the Catholic Cemetery. She leaned against him while he searched the moonlit rows of graves of those who were but sleeping, waiting for the second coming of Christ. She reached for his hand as they walked, which he gladly gave to her. He found that he was very greedy for her touch and her body heat. She leaned closer to him which made him feel hungrier for her. This was a big night for Doyle. Tonight he was going to introduce her to his family. If things kept going the way he'd hoped, this was where they needed to be. Marcia looked up at him, her eyes dancing with excitement. If he never touched her more than this, it was fine. This was a level of intimacy that she had never thought of experiencing. Doyle hurt, but this was something he'd never shown her before. Carson had never gone here with him. Doyle stopped at a large white statue. The saint smiled back at them quietly with passive knowledge. The lamb in her arms looked like it had long given up the struggle as they stood above the name of Lanagan. Marcia leaned against Doyle with a soft sigh.

"I was wondering when you'd bring me here," she said quietly.
"Your daughters?"

"The two who died in America. Molly and the others are back home. I can't remember where they were buried. Part of that memory is gone from my mind. They were in one of the mass graves. If my memory of that time wasn't so spotty I'm still not sure I could tell you where they were."

"I'm so sorry Doyle. I can't imagine what it must be like standing at the grave of your child, let alone being in a constant state of alive. That's not the Virgin Mary though, is it?"

"It's St. Agnes. She's the patron of young girls. It's not uncommon to see the Holy Mother all over the place though. I want to at least not get them confused."

"Of course; they're special. Do your kind ever forget your lives as humans?"

"I don't know. It's a fear of mine. I don't forget my children and my family. But the Strigori and the elders have long fled from contact so I don't know. Claudius has never forgotten and he's the oldest vampire I've ever met."

"Maybe I'll be around to find out with you." Doyle looked down at her with a furrowed brow. "What? We've gotten this far, do you think I'm leaving? Nope, Boyo, you've got me for as long as you can."

"Despite the condition?"

"One day Doyle, I hope you learn you are so much more than your disease. You have more to offer than you let yourself."

Doyle chuckled.

"What?"

"Nothin'. You just said it like Molly. Have we gotten to the part of our relationship where I should stop talking about my dead wife?"

"Well, according to Norvita, yea we shouldn't talk about her. Of course, Norvita is the same girl who gets jealous when she thinks the waitress at El Taco Libre is flirting with Carson, so she might not be the best measure of a relationship. Me? I'm not jealous and you like remembering her."

"Are you sure?"

"If you want to talk about Molly, I want to hear about Molly."

"Did you ever see the one where John Wayne plays the boxer who goes to Ireland?"

"The Quiet Man?"

"Yea, she looked and acted like Maureen O'Hara in that film." Doyle stopped. "I can't remember what she really looked like though. I have this idea of what she looks like, but I can't be sure it's real. I had a photograph made once, but it's in black and white. It doesn't seem real anymore."

"Do you miss it -- being with a family like you were?"

"Of course I do. My family, everyone I loved at one time is dead."

Her arms held on to him with a warm hug. His arms reached up to grip her as his brow furrowed between confusion and a contented purr that left his lips. He almost shook with surprise at this comfort. His lips twitched with an unfamiliar impulse. He wasn't hungry, but he did want to put his mouth on her.

"I think you forget in your grief that you do have a family," Marcia said quietly as she hugged him tight and snuggled her head into his chest. "Maybe it isn't conventional. You have Norvita and Carson and maybe one day, me."

Doyle's reaction to her words was to grab her and give in to that impulse that twisted through his face. He tilted her head back eagerly as his hands pulled her warm body closer to his. Hungrily their lips met as he gripped her moonlit hair. Doyle found that his logical mind was running wild and screaming at him to stop. That was quickly drowned out by his senses as they worked overtime. She felt so warm and tasted so good. Doyle was getting lost in those senses.

If anyone was hesitant to fall into this relationship it was Marcia. She hadn't expected to be standing in a graveyard kissing on Doyle with eager anticipation. She was the one who'd made contact and this sort of relationship was as unusual as it was oddly arousing. This was another level to their life.

Doyle broke away from her kiss, only holding on to her closely. She gasped excitedly and looked at him. She blinked as she held on to him like she'd never let go. Doyle smiled again, holding her close.

"What?" she whispered. "What did I do wrong?"

"Nothing. I just --"

"What?"

"It's okay. I'm not gay."

* * *

Marcia settled gently on the pristine white sheets with a seductive smile as she watched him shed the last piece of clothing. He slid on top of her carefully. Her fingers played over his bare chest and he furrowed a brow as she stopped at the raised stitching crossing it. He flinched slightly as she slowly figured out that the word read "mine". She did not let it linger because that was not what she needed to choose tonight. She wrapped her arms around his shoulders as he brought his nose down onto the soft skin of her neck, breathing in her scent that he'd been falling in love with. She parted her legs and pulled his body against her hips. She pushed herself against his exposed groin, desperately trying to coax Doyle into a state of arousal. He brought his head back to her lips, pushing down against her and trying to restrain his eagerness to keep it from becoming a state of aggression against her. She pushed him away as her body writhed when she felt a mounting pressure building from her hips up to her torso. She watched as his lips twitched apart showing his fangs glinting at her. She shifted under him.

"I have to…er"

"Go ahead…please," she gasped, thinking in the back of her mind that in this state, she'd probably agree to, or beg for, just about anything. Filing that cautionary thought away in the back of her mind, Marcia flung all of herself into this moment of passion with her predator-boyfriend.

Doyle sank down along her body, planting a line of kisses on her skin. He pressed his nose against her skin smelling for a thick vein. He found a good vein running down the side of her left breast next to her nipple. Doyle rested his head against the skin and settled on the right quietly, wondering if he was really about to do this. She twisted then, pushing her breast against his sand-papery tongue, licking to bring the vein up and puckering the purple skin up to his eye level. She let a moan escape her lips as she brushed her fingers through his hair. He opened his mouth, letting his fangs descend into the soft skin of the breast. Marcia jerked up reactively, letting more blood spill out the open wound and into his mouth as she let out a loud moan of pure pleasure as she bounced in the rhythm of his swallowing. Her pupils dilated as unspoken pleasure tingled off every single nerve ending. The pheromones that she released in that moment invaded Doyle's nose and spilled on to his lips, intoxicating him with her passion. He couldn't take it anymore. He brushed his tongue over the wound, sealing the skin. She let out a soft grunt as she begged him to push into her. Doyle had never quite been able to turn down the demands of women. He contorted his body until he met with the familiar push and pressure that came from a joining act. Her body eased into a steady pace that only came from good old-fashioned Catholic love-making. She somehow sensed he could do better than that and they would of course work on that at a later date, if she could hold on to that thought long enough to file it away... It slipped through her mind like a dream that rolled on the tip of her toes and was kicked off to the ground like discarded clothing, as she fell into the moments of intimate pleasure. Something swam vigorously in her veins with eager joy. She found her lips producing noises that she'd forgotten it was possible to make without some sort of forethought. She writhed as her body spasmed, her back arched and the burning pleasure mounted.

"Doyle," she moaned between disjointed gasps. "I…"

As the evening progressed to this point, Doyle felt his fangs descend again instinctively, into the flesh of her neck. When the adrenaline from this bite flooded her system, Marcia let out a scream from the depths of her being as her body jerked forward, her own excitement pouring out of her body in a husky groan. She settled back down against the pillows with a soft gasp as the small shudders of aftershocks brought her back down and her eyes struggled to keep open. She felt Doyle's careful hands holding on to her . She smiled, curling into him and holding on tightly as she felt sleep washing over her post-coital state. Doyle briefly thought to himself on whether or not he'd share the events of the evening with anyone. He strongly suspected that he wouldn't. This wasn't something he'd ever tell Carson about. Of course, he wouldn't have to.

* * *

Norvita gripped her juice glass to herself as a phallic ally as her breasts arched when her mind became flooded with lurid thoughts. She twisted against the counter with an eager gasp, grinding into the barstool as a second wave of feelings hit her violently. Her eyes glanced up to the ceiling with a delight as she started to run towards the steps. Carson moved faster than her as he ran behind her. He grabbed her wrist and spun away. Norvita batted her long lashes at him with a sweet pout in the hopes that charm was going to work.

"I want to go see," she whined at him. "They're totes...."

"I know and Doyle ain't had that kind of fun in over hundred years. Let them be."

"But...But..." she frowned prettily at Carson's stern look. "I'm bored."

Carson let out a growl, gripping her wrist harder as he spun her roughly into a wall. She let out a surprised grunt when she fell into a helpless position under him as she stood back up. With his animal quickness, his hands gripped her neck with enough of a threat of choking out her life. Her dark eyes went wide as tears fell out on to her cheeks. Carson's fangs descended as he buried his nose into her neck breathing in her sweat and fight or flight pheramones.

231

"I have your scent," he growled in her ears. "You better run, little girl, before I do with you what I want."

He let go of her, letting her run away from him to hide. Carson eased back, checking the clock. He'd look for her eventually, but the longer he made her wait the more fun it was. There was never going to be a time when this game wasn't fun for both of them. She liked the game. Carson liked the chase and the five minutes he would have without his high maintenance girlfriend.

Carson had gotten had just gotten to the box scores when there was a demanding knock on the back door of the lair. He glanced up, deciding to ignore the knock. After the second, more aggressive knock he stormed towards the door.

"Fuck off," he yelled as he flung the door open. "We don't..."

Parked in the backyard was a blood red Cadillac. At his door was a dour-looking man in a dark red suit and matching top hat. Carson didn't like what this meant.

"Well, fuck me," he said.

"Carson O'Brian," stated the man. "It is time."

"Yea, I figured. I bet she wants Doyle too."

"You would be correct. It is time."

"Yea, I heard you the first time. I'll go get Doyle."

Carson left the door open as he walked up the steps towards Doyle's bedroom. It did not matter anymore if there was a girl in the bed next to him or not -- this was more important. They had been summoned and that meant he couldn't go alone. Carson knocked as respectfully as he could muster. There was a moment of swearing and stumbling as Doyle opened the door half-dressed.

"I'm busy."

"Yea, I know. Half the block knows. We got a visitor, Doyle."

"Do what you do to the Jehovahs and leave me alone."

"It ain't like that Doyle. It's the Valentine Carriage. It's time."

"Oh," Doyle said sadly. "Right, let me get my shoes."

Doyle shut the door to finish getting dressed. A small prayer left his lips as he did this. The Valentine Carriage was a bad sign and it was a bad omen of what could easily happen to them and he was terrified. He glanced back at Marcia who had rolled to her side, hugging a pillow as she slept. He knew he could make out of this night less alive than he was and that was okay. He had been with her and things would be okay. As last wishes go, there were worse things to do. He took a deep breath as he left.

XXX. The Green Fields of France

1948

At the end of the Second World War, Carson and Doyle found themselves in a unique position that they'd never experience again as long as they would be around. They were walking on foreign soil after saving their country from the brink of death. World War II had been interesting for the supernatural world. Hitler and, more importantly, Himmler's obsession with the occult had been something that many supernaturals had been aware of and very concerned about what this might lead to with mundane. Some parts of the community saw it as a way to assert a dominance that they didn't have before. They could rule once again. However, what couldn't be ignored was the authority that the S.S. would exert in any of these arrangements. The powerful tribe of werewolves in the Black Forest joined forces with Himmler. The Greifswald Clan agreed to help seek vengeance against the Carpathian Kingdoms, doing horrible things to the vampires they could catch. This barely scratched the surface of the Cabbalist magic that had once been protective throughout Europe, but had been all but lost at this time. It was then when Christoff Villaras, the Emperor of the Carpathians, along with others appealed to the elders of Europe. The Crone and the Great Wizard in Europe chose to remain neutral until Pearl Harbor. Then they even spoke to the elders of Europe. If the mundane went to war, then they had to go as well.

She had let them go too. It had seemed that it was perfectly fine with Her to have Her men out in the thick of the conflict. She Ĝwas smarter than most of the vampires or werewolves who aligned with the various world powers. She would have them do the work. She was still in the middle of a war with Prudence. She had no plans of losing that one. If her boys could kill some Nazis, then they could be feared when they got back and the sky would be the limit. She believed that She could go off to Europe, exploiting the war-ravaged areas and rule there as well. She would be queen of all.

It also made sense for Her immediate goals. If She could say that she was on the side of Crone and the Great Wizard, She could get the Department to support Her side in the war with Prudence. She was not going to fail.

Of course Her boys were eager. Doyle had become infatuated with his adopted land. He was proud to be in America and believed in the words of the soft spoken lawyer from Kentucky spoken so many years ago. The Union should remained enacted at all costs. If he'd had the chance he would have fought in the Union army, but that had never happened. Doyle patiently awaited the day that he could go off to war.

Carson had a more personal reason to go through this event. He had been too young to follow Francis off to the Great War. He'd wanted to go off and fight and now it was his chance. He thought he could go punch Hitler in the face like he saw in the comics. Even if he couldn't, he figured with his enhanced sense of smell he could hunt down the cunt who killed his brother.

Doyle and Carson joined the forces of the Department of the Arcane and went off to France.

Today was special for them. The fighting had stopped and they could walk outside quietly in the sunlight, which never happened. In an effort to gain an upper hand, the alchemists had found a way to allow them to walk during the daylight hours. This was wonderful for them as they still had the ability walk for a little bit before it wore off. It wasn't an easy spell to make and they knew it wouldn't last much longer, but for now, as they walked outside doing something they hadn't done for a long time, they were just enjoying their time. Or Doyle was. He walked with his sleeves rolled up and his service jacket flung over his shoulder, hit cap askew on his head, feeling clever.

Carson on the other hand, was working on his own mission. He almost trotted along the ground like a wolfhound trying to track the corpse of a man he knew was gone. Truthfully, Doyle didn't care. He was standing across from his homeland where he had been born in the sunlight. He truly didn't think that it would ever happen again and he wanted to revel in every moment. Carson snarled again as the poppies masked what he was looking for in the quiet white crosses of those who had fallen. Carson wasn't enjoying the sunlight. He was far too preoccupied searching for Francis's grave and he was finding nothing. That irritated Carson. The body simply couldn't be found.

In this place Doyle realized that he was different. The man he used to be was long gone and that part of his life was over. They walked along and he mourned for that Doyle Lanagan. He wished he could be more like Carson, who he had found that he liked. The separation from their mistress had let their personalities shine through and they found that they started getting along much better than they had before. Carson was pretty charming and jovial. He wasn't as stupid as Doyle had assumed. In fact, he began to think better of Carson after the night they'd just spent. He'd sat listening to the sounds of men enjoying a game of cards. It was the night that Doyle and Carson learned about each other. They had been living together without speaking for far too long. They could be a part of a family again and never knew it. Of course She wasn't there to be always whispering in their ears and playing them off each other for Her favor. They had their time to learn. Carson had told him about Francis. That's what prompted them to go on this hunt for Francis's grave. Doyle didn't want Carson to regret never saying goodbye.

"We don't want to have that," Doyle had said, wanting his new friend to have a luxury he couldn't afford himself. Doyle knew that he wouldn't ever find peace. Carson had a better chance of being happy in his afterlife if he got this grief resolved. So they walked out towards where the poppy grew after the gas and tanks had rolled out. Carson wasn't sure what to do. He wasn't sure he could find Francis, but he had to now otherwise Doyle would be regretting his unresolved issues and, even at this early stage of their relationship, Carson sensed that Doyle already had more than enough regrets for the both of them. Carson finally stopped walking down the rows of white crosses.

"Did you find him?" Doyle asked.

"Yea, I did," Carson said, drawing a cross into the ground. He stood up, wiping the French dirt from his hands. It smelled enough like him for him to believe he'd found Francis, but truly he didn't know for certain. "I can smell him over gas lamps and gin. What a fucking waste out here."

This was a lie and he knew it as he said it. Carson would never figure out if he lied to Doyle out of pride or guilt, but he'd always believe he was wrong for doing it. At the end of the day, finding a grave wasn't what was important. He still missed Francis and seeing him dead wasn't going to bring him back and not even getting to say goodbye in the right place was going to make things better. Carson was still too young then to appreciate fully what Doyle was trying to do, but when he was older, he would be grateful to have Doyle looking out for him like that. Doyle turned around to give Carson a little bit of privacy. Carson wiped his hands again before standing up.

"The history of War has a bad habit of sending poor young men off to die. A lot of them happen to be Irish."

"Thank you for this, Doyle," Carson finally said. "I figured we hated each other too much for you to do something this nice."

"Can't hate you really, in the twenty years we've been together, we've never spoken," Doyle said. "I'm jealous of you because she picked you, but you know when we're here, I can think maybe you aren't that bad."

"Is that why you're doing this?"

"One day She's going to be gone. I don't know if that day ever comes whether I'm going to be able to move away from Her and if I do, if I can then move past my life before now. You, I think can. It's why I think you need to be here. Maybe you can have peace where I don't."

"Believe it or not, Mistress is one of the best things that ever happened to me, Doyle. I didn't have much of a life before this. Shit, apart from occasionally running errands for St. Nick's I didn't do shit. Ain't hard to embrace a life with purpose when you didn't do dick in your old one."

"That's probably true. I guess that's why she chose you."

"Nah, it's because I could step toe to toe with you. You are a sad bastard, but see you're a sad Irish bastard. We put up one hell of a fight. At the end of the day, you aren't a complete waste of flesh as a vampire."

"You know what complete waste is?" Doyle mused. "This isn't even the last war we're going to fight. By the time we get back to the City, she'll declare the truce over and the war will start all over again."

Carson listened to those words and his face made a sharp-looking scowl. They'd supported their queen when She refused to turn over Gaiman Heights according to the treaty that had been agreed upon by the House of Burgesses. As far as they knew, they were a renegade state with the true queen being the protégé of Claudius Faustino. And that meant they were fighting a bloody war that had the same feeling of the partisan battles that they'd seen in Europe. They'd be ready for that kind of warfare, except for a small problem. Neither one of them exactly wanted go back to fight an unjustified war and the more they thought about that, the more it seemed it wasn't a bad idea to put Her out of power. They knew they didn't have any control of that situation though. Right now, they had free will. When they got back, they would be gone again. The She Wolf needed her hounds.

"Yea, ain't that some fucking bullshit," Carson finally said. "What we need when we get done over here is to go home and beat the fuck out of ourselves for her."

"Carson, you almost sound like you aren't terribly fond of Mistress."

"Are you?"

"I…well…"

"Doyle, I don't know what you've been dreaming about, but I know for the last fourteen months I've been thinking about stickin' it in some honey's warm apple pie and that ain't Mistress. We do better without her leash and you know it. I ain't fond of going back to the leash when I've been off of it for two years."

"We don't have a choice. We go home and….well you know."

"Yea and my plan has been not going home until last night," Carson replied. "The boys were talking about Claudius bein' over here. I figure he's old as fuck and might know how we can break her spell. Or at least give us some help on what we need to do to get rid of her."

"Do you really think that he's going to tell us that?"

"With his little shining star poised to take over, how could he not?"

When the Italians had sided with the Germans, a concern of loyalty was spread over a very old vampire. Claudius had never been a leader in the sense of being a king. He never wanted to be one. He was happier to live the life of a Captain. When that was no more, he became the educator of a ward that he'd collected. He'd remained adamant on the side of the established rule of North America during this war and when Mussolini rose to power, the world watched with baited breath to see which side he would come down on. Secretly, the Italian vampiric circles had hoped to use this leverage to reign again as the kings of Europe. Claudius knew what the dictators of Europe were and that their brothers in Italy would fail. He'd seen creatures like Commodious, Nero and Caligula rise to power. He also saw their hubris dashed on to the rubbish heap of history. He was not going to be on the wrong side of that debate. Claudius threw his support behind the allies to preserve what he knew was generations of old knowledge that could have been swept away.

Carson and Doyle tracked him down in Calais. He was also taking advantage of the alchemy-supplied immunity and enjoying the Southern French sun. He had a glass of red wine and a baguette before him that remained untouched. He sat with his eyes shut, taking in what it was like to sit outside with a soft smile on his marble cut features. Carson wasn't sure if he'd noticed them when they sat down at his table. Doyle knew better.

"Hibernians," he said slowly, in an accent that was so old it could have been cut in stone. "I do hope you are not here to end a truce when the mundane conflict has yet to even be resolved. A violation of an agreement will cause me to ruin my table manners and a very nice day."

"We're not here to break the truce," Doyle said softly, "but we do want to talk to you about the war at home."

"Ah, has the She Beast chosen to look for a deal? She will find no mercy."

"We ain't here on Mistress's behalf," said Carson. "She don't know what we're doing, but we ain't so keen to go back to the fight."

"We thought if someone might know how we can break a blood bond it would be you, wise elder."

Claudius cracked open his powerful old eyes and stared at the two of them. A sharp coldness went through them branching out on their spines as they were looked over like being chosen for a meal fit to be fed to Athena's owl.

"Betraying your pack," he finally said quietly. "I didn't think the Hibernians had it in them."

"Carson isn't fond of her control over him," Doyle stated.

"And you?" Claudius asked. "You wouldn't agree to this if you didn't feel some question of loyalty."

"I've seen men at their worst over here. Carson and I went into some of those camps and saw what they did. I've seen what they did to us. The thing they call the Striba? The half werewolf/half vampire: It's not holy. If we go back to Her war, it's only a matter of time She finds out what we know. I can't let that horror be brought back home. I'm tired of having Her blood on my hands."

"I understand your fears Hibernian, but I am not able to do anything about them. I am not active in your war. But what I will do is tell you that there was once a man named Gaius Claudius. He was a loyal captain in an army years ago. He had a wife, a young son, and the prestige of the world. One day, he was walking in the Totenberg Forest when he was struck down from behind. Gaius lost two days of his life. When he woke up, he found himself standing over his garrison where he had murdered all of them for their blood. Terrified of what that meant, Gaius went to his commanding officer and begged to be slaughtered because he'd become a monster. Unsure what to do, the commanding officer consulted with a local wise man. The Wise man told him that this was not necessary. If he helped the commander he wanted something in return. I do not know what the bargain was, but I know that they locked Gaius Claudius in a tomb and took him home to his wife and son. You find his grave, and you will find a tool to make us all happy."

It had taken them three days of hunting before they were able to dig up the grave of Gaius Claudius. Gaius had long flown the coop and instead of asking where he went, the two were more pleased to have the legendary tool. Doyle and Carson addressed the stone coffin to be sent to the Lewis Clan. Both of them agreed to save what they could of the day-walking potion for the day they would be able to get Her locked away. If they could help fight, they would, but both of them knew how difficult that would be once they returned home. Carson and Doyle knew they could be stronger.

XXXI. In The Hall of the Vampire Queen

Now

A blood red limousine turned down a street heading to the heart of Old Gaiman. It was called the Valentine Carriage by everyone who had ever known what its history might have been. The name came originally from its owner. On February 14, 1840, Prudence Goodchild became the Royal Burgess of New England. To commemorate her achievement her mentor, Claudius Faustino, gave her a blood red carriage as a gift. Every so often, Prudence put forth the effort to upgrade her carriage and it was always red and always did one thing: bring people to the Grand Palace.

The Palace wasn't a Palace in the traditional term of the word. None of the palaces in America were new palaces. The elite built their chateaus like that of the royal palaces across the ocean but the vampiric nobility were not the same. They had always attempted to keep their palaces most austere and mundane. The Palace of Gaiman Heights was large impressive home with a heavy basement. It had been the first palace built in the new world and had been crafted for George Trublood.

Prudence always felt like an orphan when she attempted to remember George Trublood. She could remember him coming late to her father's home and them speaking about salvation which he was all for. He could remember him standing over her and performing the last rites as she lay dying in his arms. He'd even asked her to forgive him for what he was about to do. Her memories were better of Claudius, who had raised her as one of his own brood and trained the young one to be a fighter and survive. Claudius had learned to stay alive even if she didn't know how old he truly was. By the time she came to power, Claudius had retired from politics, but was more than willing to offer counsel to his protégé from his quiet barracks up North.

Carson and Doyle entered the throne room of their old child queen sitting patiently on her throne. This was uncomfortable for both Carson and Doyle as the throne had been adorned with the dead-looking plastic and porcelain faces of dolls that eerily looked like the girl who collected them. Prudence waved a hand as she tilted her head back, giving the woman who stood behind her a chance to brush out her straight dark hair. It wasn't known how long Coraline had been in the service of Prudence, but if there was ever someone next to her it would be her associate Coraline. The grooming slowed as the two men took seats in front of the throne. There was something nerve-wrackingly embarrassing to be called to the Palace. This wasn't the first time they'd been called to Prudence's company before, but it was never good. Carson had never quite figured out how they hadn't been executed yet. Doyle knew. It was because, despite the questionable things they did, they were upstanding members of society. Whether they liked it or not, they were the de facto leaders of the South Gaiman Brood. If they did something out of line, Doyle had always had a rapport with Prudence that not many in Gaiman had. They were both what America had been built on: immigration.

Prudence gave them each a passive look as she sat forward in her large sofa chair.

"Gentleman, good evening." Prudence's archaic accent was always jarring for her and always seemed to be more pronounced in formal settings. She over-articulated, attempting to cover it up and couldn't. No one spoke like her anymore and that bothered her. The closest she'd ever heard was Jedidiah Gunden who led the Gundish Mennonites in Pennsylvania. She hated Mennonites. They reminded her of the communes and part of her always felt angry at them. Besides, who could ever agree with having dolls that had no faces? That was many shades of wrong.

"Thank you for coming on such short notice," she continued. "I shall be direct and to the point. I have requested your presence here because we must speak about your future in this city."

"We're going to get busted for our hunting activities?" Carson said, jumping to a conclusion.

"Carson, please," begged Doyle. "Don't make this any worse than it is already. Calm down."

"No, I ain't calming down," Carson said, standing up. "If this is my last moment, I ain't going down without calling this out as bullshit. Prudence, we did nothing wrong to nobody who don't deserve it. Those bastards made our neighborhood unsafe and put the broods in danger of being outed. Fuck, the pedo we took out was one of ours. You'da ordered that one if you knew."

Carson looked at the placid expression on Prudence's face. He felt his back arch as he quietly sat back down with a desperate bit of embarrassment. No one had ever really raised their voice to Prudence and not somehow gotten their asses handed to them in very short order. She was quiet for a long time as she considered Carson's outburst.²

"Did you collect his fangs?" she asked curtly. Carson nodded a yes. "Good, you will be surrendering them to me for my collection."

Carson leaned forward and handed Prudence a blue velour box. She opened the box with a quiet giggle that would have unnerved anyone. She handed the box to Coraline with a soft smile.

"They will make lovely earrings," she said, delighted. "As for your extra-curricular activities, I do have to say that I cannot condone your actions. It is not our place to judge what is good and evil and we must put our faith in the Department of Arcane and the Gaiman Heights Police Department to protect this city. Now if an employee of Trublood Manor had some sort of list that she compiled without my knowledge, it would be different. She isn't bound by agreements."

"I prepared a binder," Coraline said in a whisper. "It's at my desk. I'll give it to you later."

"I didn't realize that you knew about that already, Your Highness," Doyle said shamefacedly.

"There is very little that happens to my people and in my city that I do not already know about," Prudence replied calmly. "It is not the same reason we are speaking this eve, however. I am speaking to you with a concern about security. The House of Burgess has agreed that it is time. Appeals have run out. I need to be assured that when it happens, I will not have an uprising."

"I wouldn't dream of there being one, Your Highness," Doyle said quickly.

"Well, that's not surprising….Carson?"

Carson felt his arm hug himself as he leaned forward in the chair. He felt his each of his nails digging into his flesh as he thought. They were free of Her and yet he couldn't help but feel like he needed to save Her from this. In a moment he felt the need to murder Prudence in order to claim the throne for his Mistress. In that same moment he felt disgusted at himself for feeling that way. He knew that he couldn't be a part of this anymore.

"I ain't happy about it, but I ain't dumb," he said, after his internal struggle.

"That is most fortuitous for us both, Carson," Prudence said. "I would be most upset if I had to have you sunburned for treason to my crown along with her."

"We don't have to do it, do we?" Carson asked quickly.

"No, I suspect that it falls to me," Prudence said. "and I will give her all the mercy she has earned."

"That's it? Can we go now? This is all makes me kinda uncomfortable," Carson said.

"You are permitted to leave, but I need to have a word with Doyle. If you wish to not depart for your lair or where ever Ms. Patel is this evening, you may wait in the lobby."

"If it's about Her you can talk to me too. He don't need to be punished for me."

"It has nothing to do with you, Carson O'Brian. You are dismissed or I will dismiss you."

"Carson, it's all right," Doyle said. "Go have a smoke."

Carson gave Doyle a sneer as he was ushered out of the throne room. Prudence smiled, watching Doyle.

"I cannot tell if he is as protective of you as he is of Her. I believe you are quite important to him."

"Carson just gets upset when he's left out. He doesn't like being alone."

"He will have learn. Hounds can be trained. Doyle, I am concerned with what will happen after my death. The years of peace will go with me unless if I have someone in place."

"Then it is important for you. Why do you need to talk to me?"

"When I was wild, Claudius spent extra time on me because he saw my potential. Doyle, I see potential in you. If something happens to me, you will be my successor. The Lord of Gaiman."

"I can't do that."

"I'm not asking you to do this. This is my choice and your role in the event of my death. You are patient and command respect. I also know you are old and New World and you do it better than I."

"I have to decline."

"Is this about the woman?"

"You know about her too?"

"Dear cousin, I will always know about you. Romantic love is something of a mystery to me. It was not something I cared for and I haven't matured enough physically to want companionship in that way. What I do understand is we all need someone to walk with us. I have Coraline. I would think that Coraline would support me in my roles. If this woman does not do the same, she has no business being with you."

"There is no way I can get out of this, is there?"

"Not unless you want to be charged with a crime. I do expect you to tell Ms. Marquez I expect her here for tea."

"Yes, Your Highness. May I take my leave?"

"As Duke of Lafferty Street…yes.

Doyle walked out of the throne room and towards the waiting room. Carson had been poring over a well put together binder of everything they needed. He looked up at Doyle eagerly. Carson didn't need to know. Not yet; they had the notebook to go through when they got home anyway.

XXXII. **Stairway and Secrets**

Now

Marcia rolled over from her side to her back with a knowing smile. Her fingers lazily hunted for Doyle as she opened her eyes, only to find a cold empty indentation in the sheets. Marcia's nose scrunched in disbelief at being left by herself. Doyle hadn't seemed like the person who would ditch after sturdy catholic love-making. She stretched for a moment, when she heard someone rustling around in a closet. In the dark she sat up and eyed the dim figure seductively.

"It's lonely in here," she said in a honey-rich tone. "Why don't you join me?"

"I don't generally swing that way," answered a voice that was much too female to be Doyle's. "But I thought you'd never ask."

Within seconds there was someone beside Marcia who wasn't the person she'd entered the lair with. Not unless Doyle had the ability to grow breasts and change ethnicity. Marcia let out a startled scream when she realized Norvita was cuddling up against her.

"You are SO warm," Norvita said.

Marcia scrambled out of the bed quickly.

"Norvita! What the hell are you doing?!?" she yelled at the girl.

"You told me to join you in bed…whose fault is that?"

"I meant, in Doyle's room?"

"Oh, I've been like hiding for hours in Carson's bedroom and then they left in a red car, so I got bored. I've never been in Doyle's room, but I figured you were in here so it was cool."

"You aren't slightly worried about Doyle and Carson?"

"No. It's Prudence's carriage. She does this a lot more than you'd think."

"Prudence?"

"Vampire queen."

"That still doesn't make this not super creepy of you."

"It's not creepy. You were asleep."

"Norvita. I'm going to go ahead and ask, what the hell is wrong with you?"

"Many things, I have daddy issues and I feel entitled, so I can act like a child and no one ever stops me because my grandfather is a super powerful psychic and most people think I can turn their minds to jelly."

"Psychics aren't real."

"Says the woman who just spent two hours fucking a vampire."

"So noted. Find anything good?"

Norvita motioned for Marcia to join her on the bed as she sat up. Marcia slid back beside her, wrapping the sheet tighter around her body to cover up the parts that people normally paid $15.99 (USD, 20.00 in Canada) to see. Marcia turned on a lamp to inspect Norvita's findings.

"I don't know why you are hiding. Everyone in this house has seen you naked. I think most of this city has…except Karl, but that's because computers explode around him." Norvita handed Marcia a small jewelry box. "Here, Doyle's your boyfriend, so you get to open this."

Marcia looked at the small wooden box as she took it from Norvita. It was an unusual looking box. The blood-black of the finish in the soft lamplight contributed to the impression that it was radiating a feeling of foreboding. Her fingers touched the three hungry hounds chasing each other holding on to their tails with wide eyes. She felt a wave of apprehension flow through her. There was something that made her feel uncomfortable. There was something in that box that she did and didn't want to see.

"You should put this back where you found it." Marcia said quietly. "It's probably Doyle's keepsake box that he told me about. I don't want to pry in his box until he's ready to tell me about it."

"Oh please, you feel the anxiety around this thing too so we both know that isn't *that* box," Norvita rebuked. "You so want to see what's in the box too."

"So you really are psychic."

"Totes real."

"Don't ever read my thoughts again. Doyle tries to do it sometimes and it gives me a migraine."

"Sure. Open the box."

Marcia nodded, holding her breath as her fingers found the clasp. There was a soft click and the lid rose up. Marcia pulled the box up for a closer look, mentally reeling at the contents. Both of the girls sat there staring after a soft blink.

Do you think this is his fond memories of his mortal life?" Norvita asked sarcastically. "Or do you think he owned a man-sized dog?"

Marcia stared quietly at the contents in the box. Sitting in the middle of red velour lining was a thick black collar. It had been fitted for a person and was made of strong leather with heavy rivets. Her fingers touched a coarse black thread that sat in a spool with a needle that was sharp enough to piece flesh. Finally, her eyes settled on a large, ancient-looking silver key that sat in the center of the leather. Norvita vibrated eagerly as she was biting the inside of her mouth. She'd drawn a conclusion about Carson and Doyle long since and this confirmed it. Marcia ~~also~~ had that thought too, but she wasn't going to say it out loud.

"Oh, totally, explains a lot about Doyle now, doesn't it?" Norvita finally exclaimed.

"I really shouldn't be surprised," Marcia replied. "With all the repression he puts himself under, I figured he had some sort of outlet, but this comes as a little bit of a shock. I didn't have an idea about this level of..."

"Oh, I had an idea or two. Those two have been together way too long. Men get lonely."

"You've written erotic stories about them, haven't you?"

"Super totes. I'll bring you my journal sometime. What do you think the key is to?"

"I don't know. It's old, but not big enough to be a lock on something. It's like one of those old door keys. Maybe they have some sort of blood bag dungeon they aren't telling us about."

Norvita had always been suspicious of Carson's desires that she couldn't figure out. She lived a life of paranoia that he was going to replace her with someone younger and prettier. Vampires had groupies who would be craving their attention. They would sit in one of the back booth of Pitch's. In that moment, Norvita became determined to find out if this was true and god help that person who was moving in on her territory, Doyle or not. She shut her eyes and listened for someone else's thoughts. She didn't hear another sound. She took a deep breath and smiled.

"Nope," she said. "We're like Tiffany. I think we're alone now...get it?"

"Yes, I'm like, ten years older than you."

"Give me the key, I know where it goes to...I think?"

"Because you can read the energy off the key and get its history?"

"No, stupid. I think I saw a door in Doyle's closet while I was digging through it. So I'm totally guessing. Put your pants on because we are going on an adventure."

Marcia dressed quickly, ignoring Norvita who refused to leave the room because she had to find the door again. She squealed as she found a small knob and became excited. She fumbled a bit before she unlocked the door and looked back at Marcia. She had to take a moment and make sure she wasn't about to do something stupid. Whatever was in the basement might change Marcia and things would never be the same.

"You don't have to do this," she said. "You can leave."

"Too late now, Norvita. Open the door."

Norvita opened the door revealing a dark staircase descending down into the black. Norvita sighed.

"A spooky staircase with no lights at all, really?" Norita yelled, irritated at this turn of events. She had been in a similar situations before and she knew how it went. "You've got to be kidding me."

Marcia ran her hand along the wall before finding an irregular lump protruding from it. She flipped the lump, allowing a hard click. Norvita blinked as light cascaded down the stairs.

"Well, that's less like a murder shoot. Let's go crazy tits."

Norvita started down the stairs with Marcia following behind. They stopped at the bottom of the stairs and looked into a wide open space. The smell of neglect and dust settled in on them just at chest level. Marcia felt along the wall quietly again. She took a breath as the room filled with fluorescent light.

"Whoa," Norvita whispered.

The room was painted a slate-black that reflected horribly in the sick light. The windows had been painstakingly blacked out and barred with thick steel years ago. Marcia fidgeted as she looked around. The black-painted furniture was likely from a set of a Spanish language film about the Dark Ages. Marcia found herself gravitating to a large oak-finished wheel.

Norvita was more interested in the large throne that sat in the middle of the room. It had the same finish as the box that she found in Doyle's closet. She looked at the elaborate carving of a half-naked woman on a hill overlooking finely carved city. Her outstretched hand pointed to three hounds feasting on pieces of a corpse. Norvita's vision drifted to the matching chest that sat beside the throne.

"This is nothing that I expected," Norvita said quietly.

"So, the boys have a fetish room," said Marcia. "It does make my dirty pictures look pretty tame. Doesn't answer any questions. Oh, look, Norvita, another box. Do you wa..."

"I'm gonna!" Norvita yelled, diving towards the box.

Marcia leaned over her shoulder and watched as Norvita opened the heavy lid. They both blinked as they looked into the chest. There was a pair of stainless silver shears that sat a top of a soft blue dress adorned with bright beads. Norvita's eyes widened in jealousy at the beading on the bodice. It didn't sparkle like the costume jewelry that she'd seen. These were real gems. This was a dress fit for a queen. Norvita's hand brushed over a box with a violently snarling wolf on the face of the box.

"Maybe that's why they don't talk about this," Marcia mused. "I wonder which one them wears the dress."

"Neither, unless Carson is a size eight," Norvita replied, "and a b-cup. Doyle's hips are narrow enough and he's got the legs to pull off a princess cut, but his chest is too broad."

"Where are you getting that?"

"The bodice is hand stitched and tailored for a 34-b. Cross-dressers take in the underwire if they don't make the clothes themselves. You aren't going to buy something that doesn't fit.

This was made for a woman. Maybe Doyle bought this for his wife."

"After she was dead?"

"It's Doyle. Maybe he has some sort of weird Christian zombie thing."

"Christian…what?"

"Don't Christians believe that zombies will roam the earth when Jesus comes back or something?"

"Norvita, sweetie, when I have time I'm going to try to teach you the beliefs of Christians in a responsible adult way. This isn't that time."

"Fine, maybe they got bored and took up seamstressing. There's a lot of sewing stuff in here. Vampires have a…"

Norvita's voice trailed off. There was the distinct feeling of someone standing behind her. The jewelry box that she had been holding tumbled out of her hands and on to the dress as a cold shiver shook her body. Norvita stumbled back from the box and into a vision. Gone was the basement and she was in the middle of a night that was bright with orange dancing flames. Her eyes looked around as the city that she knew and loved was covered in fire and destruction. The air smelled of the spoiled ash that came only from swollen flesh being burned. She heard a soft roar of screams and suffering. Norvita knew what that meant. Those voices were the living and they were being murdered violently.

Norvita heard soft singing in the distance. She turned quietly towards the singing. Behind her, the throne sat on a hill looking down. In it was a pale woman with large green eyes that burned into her soul. Norvita found herself staring transfixed at the woman. The woman didn't seem to see her or care. Suddenly she looked down and grinned at Norvita showing her the wickedly sharp fangs in her mouth. She pointed a long finger at Norvita.

"Them," She ordered. "Kill."

There was a loud howl in the distance. There was the sound of giant paws pounding down on the earth. Norvita found herself falling backwards as her eyes were suddenly full of a large wolf hound's muzzle ripping at her face. She felt her chest felt crushed by massive paws. Norvita felt herself falling into blackness.

"Norvita! Wake up!"

Marcia shook Norvita, trying to bring her back the waking world. She glanced back, her eyes wide with panic. Norvita wasn't moving in any way, shape, or form. Marcia dug in her pocket for a phone. She let out a groan as she saw the unfriendly symbol telling her that she had no service. She couldn't leave Novita like this. That would be impossible. She was going to have to drag her up the stairs.

Before she could enact her plan, Marcia was pulled up by her shirt back. She let out a scream as she looked into the intense hazel eyes of Doyle as he scowled. She twisted loose as she felt her body shaking with terror. From the corner of her eye she watched Carson gently brush his fingers through Norvita's hair.

"I..I don't know what happened," Marcia tried to explain. "We came down and then she…"

She watched as Carson picked up Norvita without a single word and walked out of the basement. He gave Marcia a sharp glance before leaving. If he was upset, she didn't know. He seemed more concerned with the girl in his arms. Doyle let go of her and scowled down at her with disappointment. The last time Marcia had been on the receiving end of this look, it was her father, angry at her for stealing his cars. She smiled weakly.

"Doyle,"she said finally. "I didn't…"

"Marcie," Doyle cut her off coldly. "I'm very fond of you, but I need you to leave right now."

"Doyle."

"Get out before I do something we both regret."

She opened her mouth to protest. Then she looked at his cold expression. He wanted nothing more right now than to watch her suffer for her transgressions. Marcia left with tears rolling down her cheeks and stormed off into the streets. Doyle stood in the center of the room. He felt his knees buckle with the sudden sensation of hands on his shoulders. His head rolled to one side as he felt lips against his neck. Doyle shuddered, trying to throw it off the feelings. He vowed to break every piece in this basement and set things on fire.

XXXIII. **Fell In Love with a Girl**

Four Years Ago

Carson sat in a drawing room that was full of gold, orange and red. His eyes nervously stared at the elephant-headed deity who gently passed judgment on him. It didn't help that his understanding of Indian culture had been largely informed by Jules Verne novels and the <u>Temple of Doom</u>. When he walked into the penthouse home, he felt like he was walking into the den of a thuggee cult. He wouldn't say that out loud. Carson understood racism and appreciation for other people's culture and societies because he at least understood Doyle's problems. He had been in the marginalized minority when he first came to this country. There was something about that experience and then being turned into a vampire that made Doyle into something else. He knew that if he wanted to move beyond this point, he had to get away from the notion of being other or less than or more than people who were merely different from him. Carson was sitting in a real living room that belonged Vivek and Uttara Patel. Any racist notions would have to be cast into a pit of stupidity because Carson was sitting in the royal home of Gaiman Heights. Carson was sitting in the home of Swami Patel.

Swami Patel, as you should know by now, was the nation's leading psychic and had been since his arrival to North America in the last days of World War II. As such, he'd become a revered and respected man whose enlightened advice had afforded him grand prestige. His wife had been a genius to invest when she had in real estate in Gaiman Heights. Needless to say, they were both wealthy and powerful. Even in his retired years, The Swami was still a man of whom many sought council. This was not why Carson was here. Carson was here about a girl.

He fidgeted nervously on the sofa. This was not his natural environment. Sitting rooms and being civil in them was something that Doyle was better at. Doyle was the diplomat and Carson was the head smasher. He didn't do tea and sitting rooms. Maybe people thought he was dumb because of this, but he wasn't. Carson was just as smart as Doyle and had proved it by learning a thing or two from Doyle over the years. He just could play it up like Doyle. Doyle wore dapper little suits and did dapper things like teach an occasional class or consult when it came to antiques. Carson had just never liked the idea of being that guy. He was a tough mick who grew up at a time when he had to be tough and he was better at being a violent man. It's what he did for money, after all. Doyle consulted on things and Carson stepped into the ring.

Carson knew how to box and Saturday was the night that he would go into the local ring. He had figured out how to do it. He never wanted to go main stage because that meant questions would be asked that he wouldn't want to answer. Carson fought a series of fights, choosing the ones that he wanted to win and he'd throw the occasional fight right in the middle of a winning streak. Carson and Doyle would make their money on that. They'd bet all their money on a sure thing and then they would move on. Carson would be take a few months off and people would forget him and then he'd start all over again, sometimes in a different sport. They'd done well with the money, not to mention that Carson had made stars in MMA, boxing, and professional wrestling. This wasn't where he wanted to be forever maybe, but he had to calm himself down. He made a promise to his girl that he'd do this and be nice. He'd even promised that he wouldn't swear.

They had met just eight months before Carson was uncomfortably sitting on a coach. It had been a Saturday and a good one at that. Carson had gone six rounds with a kid who just needed a little more polish, but he was going to be a star in a cage. It was so good that even Doyle's generally dour mood had departed. He had gotten a sizeable purse from the bets that they had placed on Carson and it was going to be a good night. Doyle had been in such a good mood that he was chatting up some girl next to them who had wandered into Pitch's Carson watched him for a moment with a smile before glancing over at the bar.

Pitch's rarely had new people coming in to experience the world of their south Gaiman Hole. After all, Pitch's was Pitch's and those who came there were looking for a place to have a drink outside of the usual. This was their hometown bar and it was their community. It wasn't that they wouldn't be friendly to new people who came in. It was more about who they would never expect to see there. Tonight was different though. Tonight was fight night and that meant that Carson was representing their brood and being a hometown hero. That meant that there would be others coming in tonight. Carson had examined the new people who sat in the bar tonight. There was one guy who had been yelling at him from the bar. Carson pegged him for what he was: a tough guy who thought he was bigger when he drank. Pitch would have him escorted out by calling Weston Lewis and it would be okay. Then there was the girl who was also at the bar. That was what caught Carson's attention. There was nothing mundane about her.

Carson had spent his time trying to figure her out. She was wearing too much make up and in a way that only a teenager who had lived in a bubble would have known about from reading fashion magazines or watching celebrities on the E! Network. Her outfit even said "I'm a teenager who does not know what people four years older than me really look like". Carson didn't know much about fashion, but he knew off when he saw it, and had her pegged for what she was the second she walked in the door. He pegged her as a private school junior who'd just bought a fake I.D. She was clearly an upper class rich girl which was enough for Carson to want to mess with her a little bit. But there was something else about her that he wanted to explore. She smelled like nothing else he smelled in the bar. Carson knew what that meant. His private school junior was psychic.

This was a rare experience. Even in the world behind the veil, psychics were very rare because there were so few in existence. Most mundane creatures have the ability to be psychic. Few embraced that ability and even fewer believed that they could blossom into powerful beings. Sure there were the Silvia Browns and Jonathan Edwards but often those things are just people who have been lying about their ability to talk to the dead. A true psychic, like this girl, were very few and far between. He was pretty excited about this. The stories of innocent young psychics falling in love with a vampire is really completely fictional. Carson himself had been enamored with this idea. He had been waiting some time, secretly wanting a to fall into one of the erotic stories of vampires and psychics. Carson really wanted to put that notch in his belt.

A side note on this is that the vampire/psychic relationship is clichéd only because when a real psychic does find a vampire it really does happen more often than not. It is typically the first or second relationship for the girl to an older more experienced vampire, but rarely has anything to do with gender roles. Think of the older gentlemen or lady who has made their fortune and then chooses to have a second significant other that is half their age. It's almost a dream for many vampires to achieve that moment, but it is rarely built to last. Affairs of this nature can be taxing for both the vampire and the psychic, despite what other popular fiction writers may say.

She was too young for Doyle to be messing around with anyway. She might have known what she was doing but she couldn't have been too much older than sixteen, if that. She was on a very thin line that could have been dangerous for Carson to cross both legally and moral code wise. He might have been physically closer in age but he knew that it wouldn't matter to the mundane police or Prudence.

The edge of this line did not apparently apply to the man who was sitting beside her at the bar. He had been the heckler at the fight. Carson recognized the smell of him from the crowd and then he'd been over served at the bar. He'd yelled things at him and the kid he was fighting. Carson had made a promise to himself that if he ran across him out here that he would show him what they did in the south to people like him. He wouldn't do it in Pitch's though. Pitch ran an establishment that had one big rule: No violence. It was a neighborhood bar and he kept it quiet that way.

Pitch was running the taps and had started actively ignoring him as he sat there. That's when the girl started getting touched by the idiot sitting beside her. Pitch wasn't going to stop things before he needed to. Hell, Carson would have ignored her himself if she hadn't been more interesting than he thought she had any right to be. He watched her for a moment as she tried to avoid the thug as much as she could, but she finally gave him a look like she was about to mace him. Carson knew this would be a bad idea. This kind of guy would just get more pissed off by that. Carson wasn't sure that he could limit his reprimand to this asshole to a painful beating either. Carson really couldn't do that in good faith. He nudged Doyle lightly. Doyle was secretly thrilled. He couldn't exactly figure out where he was going with the girl he was chatting with, but it was a different direction than she wanted, so he welcomed the chance to extricate himself gracefully. Doyle feigned anger at Carson's insertion.

"Hey, Doyle, let me ask you something," Carson said casually, "See that girl at the bar?"

"Well, yea. It's not that hard," replied Doyle. "Is that your question?"

"Nah, that ain't it. How old do you think that girl is? I mean I know I ain't the best judge of age, but she can't be twenty one."

"Oh, I would say that she couldn't be more than seventeen, if that. Why? Were you planning on showing her a magic trick or some tine etchings?"

"I ain't plannin' on that, since you know that's some sort of Penthouse letter. I just think I should go over there and inform that dickhead how to treat a lady...you know?"

"Can I trust you to do something that isn't stupid or requires me to have to clean up after you?"

"Doyle, when have I ever made your life that hard?"

Before Doyle could give the exact list of times that Carson had made his life hard, Carson got up and left. Doyle found himself narrowing his eyes at Carson. Every time that Doyle thought Carson had grown up something like this would occur that would remind Doyle that he was the older one. No matter how old they got, Carson would always be the cocky twenty-something that thought he could best Doyle all those years ago. And that would never be more obvious than when it came to trying to save a pretty girl.

Carson knew that he had to do a thing or two in order to make things right. After all, this was his neighborhood and his bar and now someone was disrespecting a girl on his home turf. More importantly, that girl was one of their people. Maybe she wasn't a vampire, but she was one of the weirdos from the other side of the Veil and part of him thought humans with powers and vamps had to stick together somehow. Carson almost questioned his motives until the man grabbed her arm and pulled on her. There were a few things that he couldn't tolerate. A man harming a woman was one of them. No meant no and that was it and he needed to tell that to this man. He was lucky of course that Doyle hadn't seen it. Doyle's tolerance was less than his.

That man would be dead if Doyle got his hands on him.

Carson watched her smack his hand away one last time.

"Come on...you here in this bar," the man slurred at her. "Don't be a bitch."

"I said go away, you creeper," she said. "Like now."

"What are you, some kind of dyke?"

"No, just a standard slut who's not into you."

Carson found himself snatching the man's arm like a striking viper before his back-handed slap touched her face. He twisted the man's arm behind him, straining the bone and the muscles. Carson leaned down with a growl with his fangs drawn and his eyes burning.

"Easy man, I….." stammered the man with a tremor of terror in his voice.

"The lady said leave her alone," Carson growled at him with an aggressive snarl. "That means fuck off."

"I'll back off. Jeeze, or pay or whichever you want me to do with your slut."

The difference between Carson and Doyle is that before forcing the man's face into the bar to break his nose and eye socket, Doyle would have made a pithy remark. Carson had just proven that he was smarter than Doyle by smashing silently.He didn't want to lose the momentum of his actions.

Carson had placed his free hand over the man's hand and with a quick flick of the wrist, smacked his head off the bar. The man slid off the stool in the dazed stupor he'd been trying to drink himself into all night. Doyle let out an exasperated groan before getting up. He knew that he would be spending some time trying to clean up after Carson after all. Doyle gave Carson a pointed I-told-you-so look before he started dragging the man out of the bar. Carson snapped back to the girl.

She stood there quietly. Her large rich eyes stared at him in slack-jawed amazement. Things grew quiet as he listened to her excited heart rate.

"Did you kill him?"she asked.

"Nah, Doyle will tell him to forget what just happened. He's pretty fucking good at that."

She nodded.

"That was really awesome! I am totally buying you a drink."

"No, you're like sixteen. You're going home and finishing your algebra homework."

"I don't have algebra homework tonight and I'm so totally over 21," she said before hunting through her purse. In a flash she handed him her driver's license. "See?"

Carson looked down at the photo I.D.

"Yea, this says that you are over 21 and it also says that your name is Alexis Beaverhouse. You should get your money back on that fake name."

"No way! I paid good money for that name."

"Yea, you're not 21. I'm going to keep this until you're old enough to be here."

"Hey now. Not fair, you are totally the same age as me."

"I ain't...go home."

Norvita Patel never listened to Carson, not then and not now. She was determined to get her fake ID back. Never mind that she could have bought another one, that one *was hers.* Every night for eight months she stalked Carson. At first it was irritating to have his little dog yapping at him to get his attention. Or at least that was what Carson told Doyle. Doyle would roll his eyes and he knew that Carson was lying. Carson was secretly counting down until the day that she would be of legal age, because inner monster or no, kids were off limits. That eagerly anticipated day came, but alas, it came with a caveat. Carson had to go meet with her family. Out of all the things that Carson had faced in his life, this was the most terrifying. After all, this just wasn't something he did. You never held yourself to a point where you could be pulled down by a girl long enough to be introduced to her family. However, his interest in pursuing the relationship with Norvita meant that he would have to go through this one hoop. He would have been fine if he hadn't learned what her last name meant.

Patel, generally speaking, is a fairly common name. When literally billions of people have the same last name, it's hard to think of anything other than how nice of a last name it was. Of course, in Gaiman Heights the last name meant something else. If the added concern of meeting her family wasn't enough, he was now trying to bang a princess and that just meant things were somehow more terrible.

Carson sat in the middle of the elegant couch with his hands in his lap. He bit his fangs into his lip with a great deal of nervousness. He was trying very hard to tell himself to not say or do something that would be construed as stupid. He was also trying hard to choose his words so he didn't accidently say "fuck" to the high holy man. Swami Patel sat in the middle of the opposite couch, quietly looking at Carson with a soft placid smile. Carson couldn't figure out what the old man was thinking and that was upsetting to Carson.

He cleared his throat as Uttara set a fine silver-engraved tea tray on the coffee table. If Carson ate, he would have been tempted by the wide array of tea biscuits that stared up at them lovingly, waiting to be eaten. The spiced chai was just as tempting as tea had ever gotten for Carson, but that had never been his drink. Truthfully, Carson was too terrified to even move which meant he was even too scared to feed on something he did eat. He tried to give the lady of the house a polite smile. This was met with a cold gaze. She left the room quickly trailing a chain of heavy swears in a language that Carson didn't understand. Swami Patel chuckled quietly.

"She has sat by my side since we've been betrothed. This is only the second time I have told her to leave. She reacted as well as the last time I did. I do apologize for that, but it seems that actions and intentions towards daughters and granddaughters is not meant for Uttara."

"It's cool. You know how things are with dames."

"No, I do not believe I do. I come from another time and place that is different from yours. Speaking of which, may I offer you a biscuit and tea?"

"Oh, no thank you," Carson said too quickly. "Me and Doyle had a late dinner. We ain't fags or nothin'. He's my brother."

Swami Patel chuckled.

"When I was a boy my father was called late one night to a village. People had died pale and with no blood in their bodies, their throats slit open. After three days of hunting, he found a feral beast covered in blood. White and almost a corpse, it was living in the darkest parts of the jungle. I regret to say this, but your brothers in India were not as civilized as they are here."

"Oh, I ain't one of those…"

"We should not pretend at this point. You are a vampire. I know because I'm a psychic. We both know why you are sitting here in my drawing room. I find that my granddaughter fancies you. I assume you feel the same."

"She's seventeen."

"And almost eighteen. I know that better than you. I suspect that changes very little about your attachment."

"I already talked to her dad about this."

"I would be honored to have a daughter that would be married to Karl but I only had Prita. Karl is not my son-in-law. His fate lay on a less typical path."

"So, he's a f…"

"Marked Man," Swami Patel said, cutting off Carson. "Yes, we are not here to talk about Karl. We are here to talk about my granddaughter. I am told that you have a relationship with my granddaughter."

"I ain't touching her. I know she's seventeen. If you don't cut off my balls, then Prudence will."

"While your assurances to wait to defile my granddaughter until she's of age are pleasing, it is not my primary concern. I know your progenitor. I am not comfortable with my sole heir being placed in that position."

"See, Mistress ain't got that kind of pull on me. Norie is safe."

"And yet you still call her Mistress. Would you like me to tell you what I foresee? I foresee a time where my granddaughter's safety is your problem and you end up ruining her life."

"I ain't that serious with her."

"You are serious enough to not dissuade her from following you. You are serious enough to be in my home. I suspect you are lying about the level of your relationship."

"Just because my M...the She Wolf is evil don't make me evil."

"It makes you vulnerable. If you wish to continue your affair with my granddaughter, then you will grant me a vow against your blood.

"That's extreme. I ain't going to do that."

"Then you may leave. See her again and I will unleash the Marked Man on you."

Carson let out a sigh as he thought. This wasn't what he wanted to do at all, mainly because he knew what it meant and feared that the Swami's prophecy would come to pass. He leaned forward and sneered. He knew better than most that Norvita would be something he could hurt and frankly he was scared. He set a small cup in front of him as he reached for a purposely sharper knife than one would need for tea and biscuits. Carson made a small incision on his finger, allowing his blood to drip into the china. He took the cup and offered it to the old man who repeated his action before handing it back to Carson.

"I swear upon my name, Carson Faolan O'Brian, and on my blood that if I harm Norvita Kiran Patel that I will betray my bonds and be given in my death," he said as he drank the blood from the teacup.

XXXIV. **About Her**

Now

He was going to kick Doyle's ass for fucking up a relationship that was going so well for him just by being Doyle. That was the second thing he was going to do. The first thing he was going to do was get Marcia to start talking to Doyle again. Maybe if he was lucky, she'd do it for him. Maybe that's why Doyle liked her. She had some Carson-like qualities and you always want to fuck your best friend. If Norvita were a little like Doyle then, well, he'd have to punch her instead. He loved Doyle like a brother, but that didn't mean he wanted to have a girlfriend like him. Still, he had to get Marcia back into their lair to talk to Doyle. That meant that he had to talk to her first. He had to find her to talk to her, which wasn't that hard. She had a smell that he could easily track. He didn't think much of it either. She'd been rolling around in Doyle's bed and on top of and probably under Doyle. She probably smelled more like him than herself.

Even if he was mad at Doyle, this endeavor was somewhat fun for him because he got to spend time in his hound form. He trotted down the street as a hulking wolfhound with his head down towards the ground. His sense of smell was better when he was a hound and also there was something liberating for him about being a dog. Carson often wondered if he was some sort of kin to the wolves that he didn't know about. It wouldn't surprise him. He didn't know much about his old man except that he had been prolific in spreading the O'Brian seed and left his mother holding the bag until she died giving birth to him. It had all been before there were rules restricting supernatural mixing anyway. Maybe he was Conry. And he wondered how many people who turned into animals were conry or Morrcan ken. He suspected there were a lot. But he was by himself and it was nice to trot along a path towards Marcia. It was relaxing.

Getting in the middle of Doyle's relationship was not his first choice for an evening activity, but Norvita was lost in a vision. He'd learned a long time ago that there wasn't anything that could happen when she was in that dream state that he wouldn't know about. He was blood bonded to Norvita. That is to say, that if anything happened to Norvita, he would feel it. He also knew that he couldn't do much. He had to take care of Doyle, who had started sulking in his room. Carson knew this by the door being locked and a vinyl record loudly playing on a phonograph. This was the early stage of the funk and Carson had no desire to live through another one of Doyle Lanagan's temper tantrums. Not when he knew that he could just get Marcia to show up and tell him that he was an idiot. Sure, Carson was upset too. Their time with the She Wolf made him feel weak and helpless. He had been a puppy on a chain and Carson promised himself that he'd never be a puppy on a chain ever again. He never talked about those days because he knew if She ever got out, he could be that weak again and it scared him.

Carson found his human feet when he got to the front door of Marcia's building. For a moment he thought about coming in the way Doyle had at the start of this adventure, but that would end badly. He wasn't here to hurt Marcia. He was here to ask her a favor and that meant that he was going to do this right by pressing the button labeled M. Marquez.

"Go away, Doyle," Marcia's voice cracked over the intercom.

"Nah, it ain't Doyle," Carson replied a little too loudly. He wouldn't admit it, but pieces of technology confused him. "It's the other one. Carson."

"Carson? Why? What do you want?"

"I'm here to sell you Girl Scout cookies. Our troop is lookin' to set pants on fire in Yellowstone Park this fall."

"Really?"

"Fuck, no. What do you think I'm doing here? I'm here to talk to about that shit you found in the basement."

"And here I thought I was being shunned."

"Yea, Doyle's an asshole and my girlfriend is having a vision, which she don't do often. You weren't a priority. Can I come up or not?"

"Yea, sure."

Carson didn't wait for her to buzz him into the building. He entered the way he figured she was expecting him. Carson climbed up the side of the building much like Doyle had done in a previous chapter. When Marcia turned around from the door intercom, she found herself staring at Carson sitting casually on her couch. She instantly swung at him with a wooden object that she had kept next to her door as hard as she could. It didn't hurt Carson per say, but it did surprise him as he continued sitting on the couch looking at her as she kept swinging at him.

"Easy, Easy," Carson yelped at her, "It's only me."

"Carson?" She dropped the wooden object somewhat tired from her vigorous assault. "Why do vampires keep breaking into my apartment?"

"I didn't break into your apartment. You let me in."

"By buzzing the front door open like a normal person. Why are people coming in through windows?"

"It's a force of habit. What the hell are you hitting me with anyway; a lacrosse bat or somethin'?"

"It's a xistera, you use it when you play jai alai," she stopped when Carson gave her a confused look "I did a semester abroad in Barcelona. It's a very popular game there. Look, it's not really that important."

"Nah, just a weird thing to bring up. We need to talk anyway."

"Then talk."

"Sit down, will ya? I ain't never been comfortable with people standing over me."

Marcia grumbled before sitting in the adjacent chair. She folded her arms across her chest. Carson shook his head at her a little embarrassed. He and Doyle shared a preferred trait when it came to their women -- stunning when angry. Then again their girlfriends were also of the same build. Carson suspected that the only difference between them was Marcia was a little more mature. Then again Norvita was roughly ten years younger than Marcia. Carson suddenly realized that in a bizarre way, Doyle and Marica was some sort of horrible mirror version of him and Norvita and that was pretty scary for him. He had to help save their relationship now, as if it was his own... because it almost could be.

"If he sent you here to apologize, it's not going to work," Marcia said sharply, breaking into Carson's train of thought which was uncomfortably heading toward parallel universes. "I'm not about to accept it unless does it himself. He's a big boy."

"Don't get it twisted. He don't know I'm here. I ain't about to tell him that anyway. But I know you've seen my basement and that ain't something we talk about. Hell, we actively pretend we don't have one. I'm pissed he has a key."

"Well late night kinky smexy times is a wee bit embarrassing to everyone."

"Don't be a bitch. That basement ain't ours. We got that house as our play pen when She was queen. That's Her place for us. When we were good or bad or both. She never really distinguished."

"You don't own the house you live in or your basement?"

"It's our lair. We defended it and it's the only home we've ever known, but that's Her room down there."

"Who was She?"

"Doyle and me …we're brothers."

"Yea, I got the intro on your life. Skip to the part where Doyle owns a collar and there is a bondage dungeon in your house."

"We ain't supposed to be equals. We were Her pets. She liked my ability to hurt people and I don't know what she saw in Doyle. Maybe he was in so much pain that she got off on that. That's kind of her bag."

"Well, peachy keen; who was she?"

"You can call her what you want. You read the book, you know."

"She's the one who made you."

"Well, that's one way of putting it. I call her the two-faced bitch who murdered me and used my corpse as her kill puppet," Carson said with a spit behind his words. "When she had both of us, she built that room as sort of a pen to keep us in. We don't like talking about her because she fucked us up. Doyle especially. She took him out of what he thought was a good life and look at him. Me, I fucking love that bitch when I don't hate her. Maybe I'm as scared of her as Doyle. I don't want to be back under her claw any more than Doyle and I don't want to give her a reason to beat me when She does return."

"Did she have a name?"

"Not one she shared with us. She is simply Mistress."

Carson involuntarily growled at the word with his fangs dropping. He hated that word and how it rolled around in his mouth. Marcia curled back watching Carson with a feeling of pity she'd never felt. If Carson was having a hard time, she couldn't imagine what Doyle was feeling.

"Don't get me wrong. I don't hate her," Carson said finally. "We all love the person who made us and me and Doyle are Hers whether we want to belong to Her or not. It just pisses me off that

She still has that kind of sway over me. That bitch gets in your head and does things to you. I bet She did a number on Doyle."

"And so you guys don't talk about her and pretend she never happened because of your undying love?"

"Just because you're in love with someone don't mean they ain't bad for you. That bitch is in our heads and in our blood and that's more power than most. If I dwell on her too long I can feel her wanting me to do things. Maybe that's all right for some, but me I'm an independent modern guy."

"But she's not here…right?"

"Nope. I don't know where She is and I don't want to. She's someone who brought bad times and I can't wait for the time when people forget Her after She's dead. Doyle might mope around for a while but he'll get over his shit."

"I didn't know your kind could die."

"I fucking hope so. Immorality don't mean indestructible. We can be murdered. Hell, I've killed our kind before. It's not fun, well, not fun for them. I don't know if we can die of old age. I hope so. Who the fuck wants to live forever? Hell, maybe I'll go up on the block when I can't take this shit anymore."

"Block. She's going to be executed?"

"Yea, for whatever crimes they think She needs to be executed for. I ain't never seen the supreme rulers but I'm guessing if they want someone piked, then you get piked. We found out today that's what's going on, so you know Doyle is an emotional roller coaster running through a big trigger mine field of his own morose dumbassness."

"I picked the wrong day to listen to Norvita."

"Well, you learned what I knew years ago. Every day is a bad day to listen to Norvita. She's like that impulsive spark that tells you to make dumbass mistakes. Today just happened to be the worst day to do so. Doyle's got a lot goin' on and he ain't going to be Mr. Hearts and Flowers for a while. Shit, I might have to lock him in a root cellar away from me for a couple of days just to get a breather. Him hookin' up with you is the best thing he's ever done and it's going to keep me from wanting to end him. So I'm asking, as a favor, for you to be patient with him."

"So I shouldn't wait for him to apologize."

"Not unless you are planning to die alone. He already feels bad about it anyway, so that's enough. He's nothing but blood and guilt. If he had his way, he'd be in that box with her going half mad with hunger or she'd already have eaten him."

"Wow, Carson I wouldn't have expected you to be this understanding of psychology or this articulate."

"I ain't as dumb as I talk. Just don't tell too many people. I got a reputation to protect."

"I won't tell anyone. Think I should go back?"

"And get him to stop playing that weird suicide song? Yes. I'll walk you back."

By the time that they returned to the lair, Doyle was standing on the stairs in utter confusion and loneliness. People had fled and no one bothered to tell him where they were going. He opened his mouth as Marcia ascended the stairs attempting to form the proper words. She stopped and looked at him before taking his hand and leading him back towards his bedroom. Carson thought to himself that it might be overrated to have parents. If they were anything like these two, He'd rather just have himself.

XXXV. **This Fire Burns**

Now

Norvita found her eyes opening painfully slowly as she became aware of where she was. She screamed as she felt something hit her shoulders with fear and looming disaster. That is what convinced her to turn around. She had been overcome by fire and flames and the smell of burning. She felt herself gagging on the sweet horrible smell of burning flesh. In that moment she had to convince herself that it was a vision but this argument was overwhelmed by heat and ash. The ground she was standing on had suddenly become very soft, causing her to fall. She choked again as she sat on the ground. Sweat rolled off her and her throat seized up. She bent down and stepped forward into the flames. She watched a figure flee the inferno only to be reduced to ash. She fell to her knees searching for cool air. Through the roar of the fire she heard someone sing to her,

"Oh, my time has come

To sing the song of the world undone

Close your eyes, sweet child, and lay in your bed

I will sing to thee until you're dead."

It was as sweetly ominous as every horror movie trailer soundtrack and put Norvita ill at ease. Her eyes searched again in the flames. In the center was a white wolf who didn't belong and seemed terrified. It shook its head and walked indignantly through the flames.

"The night shall overcome,

The craft will be done,

The earth will burn and the seas will rise.

I shall watch thy demise."

The flames parted like a curtain for the wolf, who quickly disappeared through the night. Norvita crawled forward on her hands and knees trying to follow the wolf. She stopped at the grand marble steps of a large porch.

"Lay your head down, oh Child of Man,

Swallow the mouthfuls of ash and sand,

Sleep now in your forever bed.

I will see you dead."

Norvita cast her gaze upward to the porch. She stared at a pair of black boots through the haze of a hot breeze. The hem of the black duster that swept around his feet whipped in the wind like a war flag. She tried to look up at the man standing before her. Between the flames and shadow and his own personal expression, she couldn't see him. The shadow chuckled lightly as he looked down at Norvita. She cringed as his laughter crackled through her skull.

"I was wondering when you and I would cross paths. You've grown, little one."

"Do I know you?" she asked bitterly.

"No, not yet, but I know you. I knew you before you were born, little one."

"You did this, didn't you?" she asked, attempting to make sense of her vision. His intense scrutiny made her shake uncomfortably and she couldn't stand it. "But why?"

"Little one, I bring chaos with my steps," the shadow laughed again. "But this is not my doing. You will know when I do it."

"Then...who?"

Suddenly the ground shook with an aftershock of violence softening the hot sod. Underscoring it was an inhuman growl that caused the fire to dance around her. Norvita turned back to her path. She watched as gnarled hands gripped the flames and tore them apart like ripping apart tissue paper. A hunched figure stalked forward with its knuckles scraping the ground. Its shoulder blades rose up and down as it walked. Blood dripped off its protruding horns as the beast emerged from the shadows. Their eyes locked and Norvita felt her body shake with sudden sadness. She recognized the face of the beast and it broke her heart.

"Karl," she whispered. "Oh, no."

"You can't save him from his fate," said the shadow. "You can't save anyone."

Norvita found herself pushing forward with a scream. She covered her mouth and looked around for a moment with a soft blink. Carson hadn't heard her and that was okay. Her head spun as she tried to regain her footing in the real word. This was Carson's bedroom. She'd seen two terrifying visions together which was not something she'd experienced before. She'd had dreams about the future before but none were this violent. The world was changing and that bothered her somehow. She felt cold reality envelope her body.

Norvita knew that it had to do with Asher. The world was changing now that he knew who he was and what he was capable of. It meant everyone was changing. She hadn't quite gotten used to prophecy. It was like getting her period all over again. It was exciting to be growing up and doing things like her mother did. But like getting her period, it was inconvenient, painful, and often made her unusually horny. She wasn't horny this time. Truthfully, she was scared.

It was the shadow that scared her. Karl was going to Fall. She knew that. The nature of the Marked was to one day become a demon because the soul becomes far too corrupted by the possession. Her ability to save him was not even possible. But it was the shadow following her that bothered her. The fact that there was someone claiming to be the driving force in her life made Norvita very uncomfortable. Her only hope was that when she figured out who the shadow was she would be able to stop him from creating more mayhem.

There was more pressing issues at hand for Norvita. She knew what she'd seen in the basement. There was some sort of force that was coming immediately and whether or not it was related to the shadow wasn't important. What was important was that there was a spirit trying to exorcise herself from her cage and Karl was going to be in the middle of it. She couldn't save Karl from his ultimate fate, but she could try to help him to avoid the one that was waiting for him in Tennessee. She had to do this. After all, Karl was not only her partner, but he was her best friend. There were even days she pretended that he was her father.

She scooted to the end of the bed and dug through her handbag before she found her sleek, tricked-out phone. Quickly she dialed the number that she had known by heart for years. There was a sudden soul-numbing click.

"Norvita," said a familiar voice. "What's on fire?"

In case you were wondering, Karl was fine. He was at the other end of a decades-old Nokia that was built like a tank. It was rude to answer a call during dinner, but having known Novita for most of her life, he also knew that if he didn't pick up then there would be more frantic calls. She smiled into her phone, relieved that Karl was okay.

"Norvita? Hello?"

"You," she said quickly. "Are you on fire?"

"What?"

"Are you on fire?" she asked a little slower.

"Literally or figuratively? Because if I'm literally on fire that bodes poorly for the rest of my evening and I'm not confident I would have answered the phone."

"What about figuratively?"

"Well, I think I'm going to be able to convince Henry to play a couple rounds of Uno with me before I retire, which might be trouble, but I'm fine." Karl paused. "Are you on fire?"

"No, why?"

"Because you sounded upset and you don't call unless something is about to happen. What's going on? Did you have a premonition or something?"

"No," Norvita lied. She found herself lying to Karl to avoid telling him the very reason she had called and that was very confusing to her. In that moment, she couldn't bear to be the one tell Karl. And maybe, just maybe, it was only a dream. "I miss you. They won't let me take Asher out when you aren't here. The Desk work is super boring."

Karl chuckled which made Norvita feel more guilty. He had believed her lie.

"I'll be back on Monday," he said. "Late. The Crowes are doing something on Sunday so I'll get the flight and..."

There was a loud crack of static through the line. Norvita realized instantly that she should have told him what she'd seen in her dreams. She held her breath for a moment.

"Karl?" she asked meekly.

"Norvita, sorry, I've got to go," he said before hanging up.

XXXVI. **The Lonesome Death of Virgil Blackmore**

1842

On the day that he died, Virgil Blackmore sat down at his desk. He watched the wispy gray clouds pass hurriedly by a half-spent moon. His mind was racing with the stories told to him by his staff and now the thoughts that were in his head. He'd found himself walking the halls the other night with an axe in hand, preparing to chop up his wife and children. He could no longer handle this madness and it was time to save everyone else. Before he took the final steps to do so, he sat down to write the words that he would leave behind.

My dearest Charlotte,

Lord forgive me for what I am about to do to you and our children. It wasn't my intention to abandon you. I fear, however that if I stay with you like this any longer, then harm shall come to our family. I hear a black voice of a woman who tells me that I will murder our children and you. I regret to say that I love her more than I could ever love you and I know that her commands are what will be done by me if I am not careful. I cannot permit myself to do that. The concept of harming our family has kept me awake at nights and her visits are more regular then. I am shamed, but I have betrayed your love and trust with this woman and her voice and I know that it is time for me to not be a liar anymore but I cannot shake off what my father called the Vile Cajun woman.

I know that we have always ridiculed the people back in the woods who tell us that there are strange spirits here that we cannot begin to comprehend, but the longer I walk the more I believe it to be true. Mr. Carter says that there is a curse on my family and now I fear it this is indeed so. When my father died, my grandfather would go off into the woods with a young hog. I had never understood that until now. He was keeping her away from the house, but now she has come back. I cannot stop her from coming for you after I am gone. I can only hope to do something about her.

I will be going off to the woods to do what I must. I am going to offer myself to Her. Please leave when you can take our children and never ever come back to this place. You are better off that way. If the things I am imagining are correct, I will be dead by the time you read this.

I love each and every one of you.

Forgive me,

Virgil

He made a trip to his master bedroom where his wife slept. He gazed at the woman with whom he'd fallen in love and for a moment, saw her as she'd looked before they were married and had children. She rolled to one side in a heavy slumber. He wasn't proud of himself for drugging his bride or children into deep sleep but he knew what he had to do and he could not afford to have them following him off into the woods. He could not say these words to them while they were awake. The words good-bye could not be uttered to their faces. He was doing this for them and he knew that and right now his actions would seem evil and hollow. With his last turn out of the study, Virgil Blackmore took a rifle and walked away from his estate never to see it again alive.

It was late at night by the time he made it all the way into the hollow where he chose to end it all. The moon passed behind thick clouds making the night blacker than was comfortable. Virgil Blackmore found a place to settle down among the trees. It was the place where he had first seen Her work. The smell of blood and ash still hung in the air in a way that he knew would never leave this place. He sat himself down and waited as night passed with a cold chill. Virgil took the time to make a fire as he prepared to end of his life. Next to the fire he set his shoes and socks and took off whatever else he thought were too expensive to ruin. He placed the barrel of the rifle under his chin and started to pull the trigger. Before he could voices started singing to him. Virgil Blackmore put down his gun.

He felt his body get very cold very fast. Elegant hands slid from behind him and rested on his shoulders. He sat up as breasts heaved into his back before she pivoted around and sat down on his lap. She kissed him with an eager breath. He couldn't resist her any more and his body slowly gave in to its physiological reactions. He looked back at her with a soft gasp, leaning into her kiss passionately as they pushed down on to the forest floor. He pushed down again as she tried to pull the clothes off her body. He sighed as he looked down and officially gave up. This was going to be his life. He was devoted to Her.

"Oh, you finally have decided to join me and eagerly," she said in a thick, sultry accent that ended any remaining resistance to her seduction. "Why are you willing to do so without any issues?"

"I know what you did to my father. I don't have much choice now, do I? You claimed me."

"Well, that is obedient. You are mine now."

"All I ask now that I'm yours is that you leave my family alone."

"Oh, I won't be the one that hurts them."

He should have reflected on the words which left her mouth in that moment, but the passion of the Ritual and a loss of rational thought passed over him. The hours sped by faster as he fell into the blackness of sleep from which many never wake. It should have ended there for him as he intended, but it did not. She knew the cost of loyalties that were not to her. She'd suffered it once before and she would not suffer it ever again. Her plan was vengeance against the men who had imprisoned her. She laid him gently in what would be his tomb. Carefully she placed a stone over the cold dampness of rock and clay and uttered a small prayer she'd learned centuries ago from a man in black. It would keep him locked down until it was time. He'd wake up hungry, but it wouldn't be enough. When the time was right she'd unleash him with fury. She stretched her long arms and then started up the hill towards the Estate. She smiled, smelling the lives that bustled there. The children would be last.

"Mine," she whispered. "All mine."

XXXVII.Rattle and Hum

Now

A violent wind rattled the frame of the house as the ground shook with an unnatural force that made Karl drop his phone. Believe it or not, the shifting tectonic plates do affect the Appalachian Mountains, however an earthquake of any magnitude in the heart of the mountains generally meant that there was something wrong. When his eyes gazed up to see an explosion of dark light and a slowly cascading red shadow over the moon he knew there was nothing else to draw. Evil was awake. He grabbed his sidearm and ran down the hill towards the cemetery. Part of him leapt with joy and that scared him. It was a side that he had never known existed and now he was terrified. That side felt black. Someone was using black magic and the parts of him that were demonic were excitedly joyful.

It made sense, of course. There weren't many ways someone could stop the protective pixies that guard against evil in graveyards without resorting to human sacrifice. Spirit Pixies were hard to kill and could only be stopped by the blackest of magic. It was why Karl had made sure that he grabbed his 9mm Beretta. It wasn't a typical weapon. Karl's sidearm had been etched with powerful runes that made it a useful tool. Of course, it was the last thing that Karl had ever wanted to use. He was still a cop whether he wanted to admit to it or not. The last thing he wanted to do was draw his weapon on a suspect. That didn't matter. People had to keep on going.

Karl made it down the path towards the cemetery. Once he got there things were about what he expected as he raised his weapon and walked forward in the silence. He walked down the path towards the crypt. He saw a bloodied man tied to a large gravestone. He glanced down at him with a cold look.

"*S'il vu plait,*" begged the man. "*a Dieu, mon.*"

Karl was a good cop in his old life. It was his possession that had caused him to lose his position but he was a good cop. That didn't mean he was naive about life in this world. He'd seen the horrors that men could visit on each other. Nothing prepared him for the scene that lay at the wrought iron mouth of the cave. Behind him were the pleas for life from the man tied to the tombstone to a god that was far too busy. Before him in a circle painted with blood and lined with the flickering corpses of the graveyard pixies stood a young man with his back turned. He saw a body in pieces on the concrete. Karl cringed when he realized the younger man had his hands in the chest of the corpse, fishing out pieces of what remained of the heart and was shoving it into his mouth.

"Federal Agent," Karl yelled loudly as he raised his weapon. "This is an unauthorized blood ritual and act of Necromancy. I need you to cease your actions at once and step away from the altar."

The young man turned to Karl with a passive look. He wasn't possessed. Not in the sense that Karl would have known. He was quietly enjoying every moment of this interaction. He laughed at Karl.

"You don't belong here, Marked Man," he said. "This is my Mistress's house now."

He'd given a warning and that worked for Karl. He was left with no choice but to fire on a suspect. He knew how well that had worked for him last time. It was firing on a suspect that had cost Karl his badge. When he'd shot a suspect in the West Hills, he'd become possessed by the demon. He couldn't wait any longer. He pulled the trigger, firing at the man. He was able to get at least one off into the boy's chest and torso before he collapsed. Karl wondered for a moment if it counted as further human sacrifice and had created another layer to this ritual. Karl walked forward slowly before he was blown back by an unholy blast of flame. The man stood up and stared at the gate of the crypt cave.

"Speak to me, Keeper of the Riddle Box," the man said. "What is your name?"

"Pandora," the box hissed at him.

With another heavy blast of bright pink flame, the gate to the crypt blew open and out. Karl found himself lunging towards the man only to be battled away violently. Karl landed none too softly with his head resting against the tombstone where the other man was tied. He struggled to focus as a sudden blur exploded out of the grave and seemed to shake towards the bound man. He let out a scream as the shaking blur stopped. Karl heard the clicking sound as something leaned forward covering them both in a cloud of black hair.

"*S'il vous plait, jui de la famille,*" the man begged.

"*Mon aussi,*" growled the owner of the black cloud of hair in response.

Karl saw the glint of fangs before she sank down on to exposed flesh. There was never a sound that he hated more than hungry drinking late at night. The man let out a cry of pain before being swiftly taken from this life. That's when the creature stood, rising like a small fox stretching itself as she brushed back her matted hair. For a moment Karl caught a glint of her green eyes. She sauntered over to him before she sneering as she caught the faint smell of brimstone that hung on his person.

"Marked Man," she hissed. "Why on earth, Jacob, would you bring me a Marked Man?"

"I didn't, my Mistress," Jacob said, hurriedly clinging to her side. "He came down here when I liberated you. He's a guest of Virgil Blackmore."

She shook her head in disapproval.

"Why do all my pets bite the hand that feeds them?"

"My name is Karl Spangler," Karl said in a desperate attempt to gain an upper hand. "I'm with the Department of the Arcane."

"And he's aligned with the Magi," she clucked her tongue in a disapproving pout. "Virgil has grown soft. Jacob sweetie, show Mistress what you've learned. Don't kill him -- I need him alive, but not necessarily awake."

Jacob nodded obediently before he flung himself on Karl's downed frame. As he attempted to struggle to get the boy off of him, a fist came down on his face, quickly breaking the skin with rapid blows. He hit Karl again with increasing force -- force someone his size shouldn't have. Blood rituals. This boy has been doing blood rituals for weeks, Karl assumed from the increased impact of each hit and punch. Slowly his face swelled with bruises and blood. She watched from a position on top of the grave marked for "Vera Blackmore". Her legs parted as she straddled the rounded top. With each rhythmic blow, Karl could hear her let out a warm moan of pleasure as she rode the gravestone for her own amusement. That just encouraged Jacob to break further pieces of Karl's face with his fist until Karl finally felt hands around his throat. Jacob squeezed as hard as he could as she rode her excitement to the end. Just as Karl lost consciousness, she arrived at a climax.

XXXVIII.   The Beast

The night felt manic as Virgil Blackmore ran through the farm. The blood pumped a loud banging rhythm in his ears. He let out a growl that felt startlingly inhuman as he found himself covered in the sweet-tasting liquid. He wasn't fully aware of where he was until he dropped the house slave as he marched into his home. There was the sound of screaming and the heavy scent of blood and that made him hungry. He ran into a room and sank his newly-formed fangs into the flesh of the first person there. He had just realized what he was doing when he heard a small voice beg him, "Daddy, please stop. You're hurting me!"

Virgil ran through the rooms in the estate with a growing horror. He might have gotten to the farm, but when he woke up he was in his home and each and every child of his life had been slaughtered. He shook in terrified shame as tears threatened to stream down his face. With deliberate care he cleaned up his children and prepared them in their Sunday best. He left them beside each other arranged neatly on the porch. He stopped and blinked for a moment.

His mother and wife were missing.

He was frantic before he heard his beloved Charlotte scream from the base of the Farm. Virgil ran down the road in a panic. The sight he was greeted by was nothing but pure horror.

Along the homes of his slaves were the bodies of every man, woman, and child he'd owned. Their faces were twisted and contorted into masks of horror. They hung along the dirt road like trophies of pleasure and joy. In the middle of this, tied to each other by what he hoped were someone else's intestines, were his mother and wife. Virgil rocked anxiously before attempting to figure out what he was to do. That's when he heard familiar giggling behind him.

Her hands brushed through his hair as he knees buckled. He looked up as She stood beside him with a soft smile. She looked down with appreciation at the pleasing sight that she'd been working on. He grinned.

"I told you I wouldn't hurt them," She said finally. "Of course I did help."

"I murdered them all," he said in final realization. "My children are dead because of me."

"Yes, and now I have a present for you. Which one do you want to be your first? Mommy or Wifey?"

"I don't.....I'd rather spare them this...."

"Now, Virgil. Before I make the choice for you..."

He'd never regretted taking his wife into this life. He loved his mother, but an eternity together would have been terrible for him and her. Of course, in that moment as he came back to the estate from their meeting with the Prince, he started thinking that perhaps it would have been okay if this was his mother. He wouldn't have felt any guilt over poisoning his mother with hemlock to paralyze her and then watching her burn in the back seat of their town car. She had been complicit in his father's crimes and deserved the murder that would have come. It's why he took his wife into this life instead. However, now it did not matter. They were both dead by his hand either way. It was better this way. Charlotte had been a better substitute, but now that she was free, he could go back to Her side. No matter how old he would get, Mistress would come first.

Virgil Blackmore walked away from the burning wreckage of his car towards the great home with joy. He had only thought he was wrong when he felt a pang of liberation when she came back, but now as he drew closer, he could feel her sweet song moving through his body. She was so close that it was almost painful to be this happy. All the anger he'd felt over the years for the things that she had done to him melted away and he was only extremely joyous to be returning. He stopped on the great porch that he knew all too well. Henry had been waiting for him at the door. His face was almost as joyful as his masters.

"Her Grace the Queen is willing to see you now," he said quietly.

Virgil Blackmore nodded as he walked towards the study. He allowed the door to creak fully open before he dropped to his hands and knees and crawled forward. She was sitting in the middle of the study on the elegant chaise lounge that had been brought from his bride's home in Georgia. She sat stretched out with a leg dangling over the edge. Crouched at her feet was a boy who was drinking from her inner thigh. She grunted excitedly and then leaned back with a heavy moan as her breasts pushed up in a giddy arch. She rolled her head to one side and looked over at Virgil with a soft smile. He wasn't sure, but he suspected that the boy had his fingers were somewhere under her skirts. For a moment, a flash of jealousy filled him. How dare a boy take the spot where he was supposed to be kneeling? He made a great effort to not growl at him loudly. She clucked her tongue and then beckoned him closer. She loosened her top, exposing her breast to him.

"He was shot by the Marked Man that was on your property," She informed him as he nuzzled his face against her breasts. She felt his fangs rake her skin hesitantly. She watched him as his suit jacket slid off. "I didn't want his frailty take over. I have plans for him."

Virgil listened intently, waiting for each and every unspoken command as he loosened the buttons from his dress shirt. There was a moment of pleased satisfaction as she saw the stitching that was still emblazoning the word *Mine* on his chest. For a moment she felt fierce vindication. He'd let the magi on his land. He'd let something with filth in his veins walk, but he was still loyal to her cause. She brushed her hands through his hair before gripping it by the follicles and pulling his head away as she let out a snarl and glared into his eyes.

"You still have betrayed me, Virgil," She growled. "I cannot permit you on my flesh while I know you've sinned."

"I...I was weak without you, Mistress," he pleaded. "I cannot...."

"You will have to pay. The Marked Man is awaiting punishment. Deliver such and then take him back to his kind in my city. Then I will allow you back in."

"Yes, My Mistress."

"Good Boy, now get out of my sight before I choose to take something else from you instead."

Virgil left as hurriedly as he could from his Mistress's presence. He glanced back as the boy crawled on top of her as she invited him into herself. He growled for a moment as he heard her pleasured grunts brought by what he could only assume were novice acts of love-making. That had been his position, but he knew he had to repent. He would kill the Marked Man and take his head to the Magi and once he was in Gaiman Heights he'd murder the boy and his brothers. There was only room for one in his Mistress's heart and that would be for him.

291

XXXIX. **The Cold Part**

Now

There were three sounds that made Marcia jump out of her skin in this particular instant. First was the sound of a very old piece of china hitting the floor and shattering into a million pieces. The second was the soft thunk of the warm grilled cheese sandwich that Doyle had offered to make her as a peace offering landing on the million tiny china shards being rendered inedible. The third was Doyle letting out an animalistic scream that she'd never heard before. She hesitated to ask if he was okay as the muscles in his body stiffened, popping forward veins and breaking off a piece of the Formica countertop as his back arched angrily. He threw something across the room as he let his fangs drop. She'd seen this expression once before on a neighbor's dog who had reached the end of his leash unexpectedly and was furious about it.

"Doyle?" she asked as she carefully stepped closer to him. "Are you okay?"

Doyle said nothing in return as he pushed her away from him. She stumbled into the refrigerator, concerned about this sudden change in his demeanor. Before she could yell at him for being rude, he was out of the kitchen. She followed Doyle cautiously. There had been many moods of Doyle Lanagan, none of them had been rabid. She stopped as she watched Carson enter the living room with Doyle. Carson looked, somehow worse, than Doyle. He seemed to be stuck between both animal and human. He'd grown a long snout dotted with white fangs as tufts of red fur ripped through his shirt. She could see the same stitching on his chest as was on Doyle's. The two of them circled in a panicked step.

"You felt her too," said Doyle.

"Yea, and I was fucking hoping it meant that someone finally put her head on a stick, but I know we ain't that fucking lucky."

Doyle nodded as he made his way to the window. The streets looked quiet as of now. He glanced up at the moon which shone a cold pale yellow. Then he heard a loud trill of Arcadian French start in the North. A sick feeling went through Doyle in that moment. When She was still in town the queen had created her own special group to maintain her law. She'd brought them from Nova Scotia as they were the best or maybe the only ones left after the great flight or so went the story. Doyle knew that stories were just that in his city. Everyone made up their own legend and She was no different. That meant nothing. He could hear them call out to deliver the news to those who would be more than pleased to hear that She was back. The screams told the city that their queen walked among the living again. Doyle knew that it would only be a matter of time before they would all be in Execution Square before her troops moved out. They wouldn't move without Her, but how long did they have? He looked at Carson with a grave look. Carson knew they were in a tight spot.

"You're hearing something I don't want to know about," said Carson.

"The Frog Patrol is up and moving," Doyle said. "She isn't dead, but someone let her out of the Box."

"Your Mistress?"

Marcia had thought she didn't say that out loud until both of them snapped their heads around to stare at her. She felt her throat go dry as they both started towards her with aggressively cold looks that would have ripped any sane person apart within seconds. She felt words crowd to leave her mouth in embarrassment as she took a step back. There was nothing more nerve-wracking than having two very, very upset vampires staring daggers at you. She smiled sheepishly at the two of them as she backed out of the living room.

"Doyle broke a plate," she finally blurted nervously. "I should go clean it up before Norvita hurts herself."

Without another word, Marcia ran out of the room. The two vampires looked back at each other.

"She's going to try to overthrow Prudence," Carson said. "Think she'll succeed this time?"

"She'd have to have a trump card and the magi have the Nexus. They'll take care of it unless She has something no one's ever heard of, but She's definitely going to be coming after us so…"

"I hear ya."

"I know where Marcie is, do you even know where Norvita is?"

Carson gave Doyle a stupid, blank look before he took a step back. Within seconds, he pulled Norvita from the living room closet. She giggled as she threw her arms around his neck.

"I hid my panties somewhere to throw you off, but you found me!" She bent backwards and furrowed her brow as her head twisted sideways to take in their audience. "Is Doyle joining us? I mean sure, but the deal breaker is Marcie….."

"No, sorry, Norvie, no Vampires of Gor tonight," said Carson. "What I need you to do is go to that place for me and take Marcie with you. Think you can do it for me?"

"I guess but…."

She held out her hand as Carson fished out his wallet from his back pants (Carson would like it pointed out that he had "Bad Motherfucker" on his wallet long before it was in Pulp Fiction. This might also be a lie). Norvita grinned as he counted out each bill and placed it in her hand. She embraced him with a flurry of passionate kisses.

"I'll call you when it's safe," Carson said to her.

"I'll be good."

"I don't believe you. Just be quiet."

There had been very little discussion between Doyle and Marcia as she was forced from the lair. She had been shocked when he picked her up and even more so when he carried her out of the kitchen and set her on the street. Now that the shock had worn off, she was very upset. He had effectively dumped her on the street like yesterday's trash. Marcia started to pound heavily on the door with a loud wail. When her cries were not answered, she found herself sinking to her knees as her hands throbbed with vibrating pain. She placed her head on the door, exhausted from the recent emotional rollercoaster. Then she heard the shuffling of money. She glanced up, watching Norvita stop counting her cash and shove a neatly folded wad into her bra cup for safety. She wasn't sure, but it certainly seemed that giving her a disapproving look was the thing to do.

"There's probably a red shadow on the moon," Norvita said. "It's a bad omen or something for them. Carson always flips the fuck out and tells me to leave town."

"Do you?"

"No. I have school and work. I usually just pocket the money and catch up on reality TV."

"You know they're keeping something from us."

"Duh, I know -- that's why I'm going to break into their lair to find out what's going on."

"Oh, can I come with you?"

"Duh, I assumed you were. Come on, I'll show you what we need."

Marcia wasn't quite sure what she had expected when she walked into Norvita's apartment. She was expecting, perhaps, some sort of dorm room with candy pink furniture and posters of pop groups. It wasn't an elegant home furnished in saffron and red oak. She definitely didn't expect a large gold statue of a friendly looking Ganesh staring at her when she walked through the door. She wandered slowly through the large penthouse as Norvita flew from point to point- ~~be concerned as she left the kitchen~~. She stopped and looked at Marcia.

"What?"

"This is your place?" she asked quietly. "This is your home?"

"Oh," Norita looked around. "Yea, kinda. Nana and Nani own the building and do the super work. I get to stay at the apartment while they're in Florida at a reduced rate. I'm sorry about this, but I need to find Mischief.

"What is Mischief?"

"He's my cat. I can't find him. I'm a little worried because I left the window open."

"Does he run away a lot?"

"No, but he floats out when he can't control where he goes."

Before Marcia could utter the word "float," a cat with more fur than body entered the room. It was an odd looking animal with varying degrees of blue covering his body. The cat floated approximately four feet off the ground, exposing his blue belly to Marcia. Marcia let out a soft cringe as she heard the stoned meow as the cat-like creature batted lazily at the air. Marcia looked at Norvita in a state of perplexed panic. Norvita plucked the cat from the air and placed him in an opulent cage. She was relieved that he hadn't left. Before Marcia could say anything, Norvita marched into the back bedroom, dragging Marcia behind her.

"Norvita, what the hell is going on?" Marcia finally asked.

"I probably have another pixie infestation either in my bathroom or in my kitchen." She said as she walked into the large closet in what Marcia assumed was Norvita's bedroom. A theory that was confirmed by a picture of a small Norvita and a younger looking policeman at a graduation. Norvita dragged a large tool box out of the closet. "I'll have to get Amaya to look at it. She's amazing at catching pixies."

"Pixies aren't real."

"Okay, really? Are you going to say that to everything I say? If you are, then we're going to have a long night."

"Pixies."

"I get it, you live in a stupid mundane world where this shit doesn't happen, but hey guess what, it does and a lot more. Are you going to help me or not because I'm not going in unprepared."

Marcia nodded before she scooted over next to Norvita. They sat down on the carpet as Norvita opened her tool box. For a moment she dug around before she found a plastic bag labeled "vampires". Norvita carefully put an aerosol can of hairspray, a flashlight and lighter down on the floor. She picked up the bag. She furrowed her brow.

"Did Karl help you build this kit?" Marcia asked.

"Yea, he told me that I needed to be ready. The vampire part came when I started dating Carson. Hairspray works as a projectile when it comes with fire. It won't kill them but it does a hell of a lot of damage on them. Silver doesn't really work and Christian icons only work on Christian vampires."

"You don't think it's weird that Karl taught you all of this?"

"No. My parents died when I was baby. I was raised by my grandparents and Karl's always been there. He's been my father for a long time," she said. "But the weird thing is whatever's going on with them. We're going to find out. So we need to rest up."

* * * *

Marcia had gone home as quickly as she could. Sleep didn't come quickly but she had to get some rest. If she'd had the book still, she might be able to figure out what else to do, but right now all she could do was pray. They were going to need all the help they could get.

XL.   Meanwhile, Rick James

Now

Asher blinked the fatigue from his eyes as he stood in front of what he could have described as the world's oldest vending machine. The florescent lights hummed obnoxiously as he stood, causing his head to pulse painfully like he was listening to dubstep. This was awful. Asher was fighting off sleep as he walked around the surprisingly mundane center for the control of magic in this world. However, training was starting to take a toll on him. It had been similar when he worked for the Stop and Shop while he was in college. That was before he got on the addictions, but he was past that now. He had Natalie who made sure he stayed sober. He loved his doctor fiancé and she loved him which is why he kept clean. It was just so draining to be in this place watching the training videos. He never thought he'd say this even to himself, but he missed Karl. At least when Karl was in town they would do on the job training. He was starting to like learning everything about the world behind him that he had never seen. Here, he was watching videos and doing paper work. He was very, very bored. Maybe he could convince his mother to do another exercise with the witchcraft. He wasn't sure, but Asher was becoming very confident that he wasn't just a mage. Anything to get him through the next six hours. Training videos had to be the most mind-numbing thing he'd ever experienced. Even for the Department, these were boring training videos.

This was why Asher was standing in front of the vending machine. He wasn't exactly sure what he was expecting. Something had to be different on the other side of the glass and yet there was nothing. In fact, the most exotic choices were what he would have seen somewhere like the convenience store down below his apartment. He should have been upset, but somehow this actually made him feel safe. Life was already very weird in Gaiman Heights -- some feeling of familiarity made things more comfortable.

Asher sighed as he fed quarters into the machine. The sounds of change hitting change made him smile because it was familiar. And it made him hungrier. Quickly Asher pressed the buttons that corresponded with a caramel chocolate treat that he'd been dreaming about for the last 30 minutes. He could feel his tongue dance excitedly as he watched the candy be pushed forward by whirring metal springs. It inched closer to freedom. Then, the whirring stopped.

Asher put his hands on the glass and stared forlornly at the betrayal. His treat hung in an odd position just at the end of the row, swaying tantalizingly. Asher heaved an exasperated sigh as he nudged the machine, trying to dislodge the candy. He then pushed a little harder, going so far as putting his shoulder into it.

You know, you don't have to get frustrated. We could just get it.

"What? How?"

You know how.

"Magic?"

Yes.

"It seems like overkill for a candy bar…wait…is this a test?"

No, I'm just as hungry as you are. So are you gonna do it?

"No."

You are no fun at all, Asher.

XLI. Temptation

Now

Karl felt a heavy pop as his knees finally gave way. He let out an internal scream as an ancient injury became aggravated by the pop. His jaw clenched shut however, as blood poured into his mouth. His feet kicked, attempting to regain a hold on anything. He was aware, but he couldn't wake up. He couldn't get himself get to a point where he could function and get to safety. He was only half-awake as he swung limply from his wrists. His throat was dry and tasted of blood, which he knew lined both his lips and mouth. There was a broken ocular bone that pulsed painfully. What had attempted to bring Karl back from his black dreamless stage was the feeling of his arms burning. With his full weight bearing down, his arms burned with tension and at least one shoulder had been popped out of socket. He knew which one it was. It was the same one that he'd wrenched out of place during his exorcism. He swung and his ankles twisted sharply as he attempted to find his footing. He couldn't. All he could do was hold on to what was left of his human side. He could feel something else poking through and God help everyone if that made it to the surface.

Karl hung in swelling pain that was slowly pushing him back to consciousness. He was only half aware of the ringing sound in his ears until he felt a hot wind roll around him. Then there was the sound of a low and sweet song.

"Oh, my time has come," sang a voice. "To do the deeds for a time unsung...."

Karl's body stiffened as that blackness worked through him. He could only hope for relief, but this wasn't it, yet it was a comfortable feeling that Karl had felt before. The warmth of a malevolent truth looked at his open wounds and stung sharply. Even long-healed wounds from his life before his possession burned aggressively in the back of his mind. Something inside Karl wanted to be let out to play and he tried hard to repress it. Karl both feared it and wanted it to be free more with every passing moment, but something held him back.

The sound of black boots shuffled along the concrete floor as a figure walked around him. Karl felt something kiss his skin like a cold vapor. With what was left of his rational mind, he searched his encyclopedic knowledge of the supernatural and the occult to figure out what was touching him. Something had to be a reference. As his rational mind knew well, there was nothing good that could come from this, but his baser side knew that this was a friend here to help. On some level, he could call this thing brother.

"Oh, what a shame that you fight this. You are such a marvelous creature," said a voice that was so cold and calm that each word was over-annunciated. "Even in this frail form, your strength is just magnificent. Most people would have succumbed to pain and died and yet here you are. Trying to fight through it and wake up. I can see why you are a rare Marked Man. Not many live long enough to become what you are and what you'll become. What do we call you?"

"K…k…." he sputtered.

"No, Karl is what you were called. That doesn't fit such an astounding beast that you are now. No? Hmm. That's all right, you are new to all of this. We'll work on it. It's not that important."

The smell of charcoal shuffled over flames wafted into the barn, mixing with the sickly metallic scent of blood. Then there was the slow sound of the barn door creaking open, backed by the distant sound of muttering. Karl tried to find the strength to pick his head up and see what noise was behind him. He found himself dropping back into a dreamlike state. He couldn't draw himself out of his slumber. Not even a grunt could pass his lips. Karl was in a state of paralysis.

"Sssh," said the voice. "Being awake now serves you no good. Enjoy this moment of rest and odd fugue state. Not many could be here. It'll be better this way. Less suffering."

Then there was the shuffling of feet. Karl felt panic as someone pushed his feet back under him and he was still unable to bring himself out of his current state. That person picked his head up to examine his mangled face. As his eye was pried open he attempted to catch a glimpse but it was all in vain. Suddenly there were a pair of fingers placed at his neck.

"Well," an impatient Lord Blackmore angrily asked, "Is he dead?"

"No, not yet," replied Henry. "Though that boy has done a number on him. You will be able to get a few good licks in before he dies."

"Well, sadly we can't eat him. I imagine that his blood does contain something powerful, but I can smell the sulfur from here. Are we prepared?"

"The irons are heating, my lord. Should I wake Mr. Spangler up?"

"No, Henry. Karl might be the enemy, but he's too honorable a man to hear the screams of death from. I would like to spare him his dignity. You know what we used to do. An honorable man like Karl shouldn't have to be awake when we do this. You may start when you are ready."

Henry stepped back from Karl for only a second. Then the sound of scissors surgically cutting away fabric slid past the ringing in Karl's ears. Karl found himself laboring to breathe at that moment. Henry's assertion was right; if something didn't change, he was going to be dead soon. Each moment passed as the mountain air beckoned to him like the grace.

"I do wish this wasn't how things ended for us, Mr. Spangler," said Lord Blackmore loudly. "But this is a day that I have awaited for and feared for longer than I've known you. My Mistress will return to her throne. She will wage war until the city is hers finally and I'm afraid that she'll have the troops to march over your people. It seems cruel, yes, but it's truly a blessing. You get to die before she murders you and I will be kinder. I'll let you keep your head."

"My lord, I believe they are heated now."

Karl felt a long pause as there was the sound of metal clanging against metal. Awake or not, he was going to start hurting all over again. He had to make a plan to get out of this position and soon.

"Did you know that East Tennessee was a Union stronghold during the War of Northern Aggression? It was a rarity, and yet I remained with my land. Of course, that doesn't mean that there weren't sympathizers who thought they could do something to my land. We don't talk about it much, but those Crowe boys tried to take my land over during that time. They found out what I did when they came here. Now you don't have fur on you, so that smell won't be a problem, but human flesh smells terrible anyway. Do us a favor, don't wake up."

Karl felt his body sway gently. If he were awake, he'd be jerking to liberate himself. Instead, he hung limp. Then there was a cracking hit to Karl's rib cage, followed with the sizzling of burning flesh. Karl felt a scream move to leap from his lungs and be trapped still behind his teeth. He rocked back at a second hit. His screams came out as a gurgled murmurs.

"Karl," said the voice. "I know you are strong and very lovely, but this is the time to keep yourself alive. If you die, they will use your corpse as a banner to rally the troops."

Karl felt the final crackling sizzle on his bloody skin. This was his back breaking sharply. The chains on his wrist jangled as his legs went out from under him. If both his shoulders hadn't been pulled out of place before, they were now as Karl's legs stopped working for him.

"Are you going to let a blood sucker murder you for his Mistress?" said the voice, more urgently. "You are too perfect to be his victim. You have a glorious purpose."

There was another moment of silence as metal clacked again. This was going to be a second and more terrible round. Feet paced behind Karl feverishly. The voice was nervous.

"Your purpose isn't glory is it?" said the voice. "Fine, ask yourself about this noble death. Do you think they will stop with you? You have children."

Karl felt his heart beats slow as the thought went through his head. He thought about Norvita who he'd known since she was far too young to care for herself. He couldn't leave her behind. Then there were his daughters. Karl had been the father of two very young little girls whom he cared for more than his own life. He might have been taken out of their lives after the divorce. No one would hurt any of Karl's daughters...not while he had a fighting breath in him. He felt his heart beat faster as the blackness started to take him over. His fingers curled around the chains as his shoulders popped the joints back into place with a slow sickening click. The voice felt it.

"They will murder your children if you are lucky. God damn you to hell if you let them carry out what they want to do."

Karl envisioned the unspeakable acts that his twisting mind could conjure against his ex-wife and his daughters. The savage violation of Norvita by a crowd of fang drawn beasts. As twisting metal penetrated his torso flesh.

"Are you going to let these parasites who serve a false goddess to take your life? Defile your daughters and Norvita? You could crush them with your hands. You can keep your city and family safe. You have the strength. Wake up Karl, and rise to your destiny."

In a report he would file about the event, Karl wouldn't remember waking up. He wouldn't remember his eyes opening, dancing with an orange flame as he let out a violent growl. He'd vaguely remember bringing down the barn like Samson at the temple on the heads of his torturers. The sounds of chains clanking as he chased the vampire who was never quite fast enough as Karl tore out his heart and lungs to feast on whatever insides he could find. He would remember choking Henry to death with the chains as the fire spread through the Farm towards the antebellum mansion. He let out a howl that was not anywhere near human or even wolf. He hunkered down on all fours and ran towards Gaiman Heights.

XLII. Dracula Moon

Now

For someone who came off as Daphne, Norvita had proven herself to be a Velma when it came to being an investigator. She walked softly, guided only by the light of a police grade flashlight as she watched vigilantly where they were going in the dusk-filled lair. She was on a mission with Marcia in tow for more crucial information. Her main goal was to acquire this information while avoiding going back down to the basement. There was something black about it and she would had rather not go through that again. It was the last thing she wanted to do. Of course if she had to she would go on and do what needed to be done, but that was currently marked as the last resort in her mental list of options for the evening. Norvita stopped for a moment and furrowed her brow. She glanced back at Marcia quietly. Marcia glanced back before looking at Norvita. She didn't see anything. Neither did Norvita. She felt something else though.

It was a cold breeze that hit her like it was gusting down a mountain. Darkness descended on her vision more so than the physical lack of light that was registered by her eyes. She felt a shiver convulse through her body. An outside wind shook the lair. For an instant, but just an instant, she saw a flash of pillars of flames. The inside of her mouth went dry as she felt tears start coming down her cheeks.

"Karl...." she whispered, "no."

Marcia looked at Norvita, waiting for an explanation that she would never ever get. Her line of thought and the question on her lips was interrupted by two shrill screams coming through the lair from the upstairs rooms. Norvita grabbed Marcia and pulled her hard into the living room closet. Marcia gave Norvita an angry look at they sank beside a vacuum cleaner and she pulled down jackets over their heads in an attempt to mask their odor. Novita climbed onto Marcia and watched from the slits in the door.

"Norvita," Marcia finally ventured, "What in the glorious fuck…?"

"Hush," said Norvita through her teeth.

Marcia had never seen Norvita really serious and instantly was quiet. Norvita leaned forward watching. She couldn't get saliva down her throat to ease the tension. She could only hope that this was just her nerves overreacting but she knew better. Black was coming.

The cold wind blew the front door open finally as a shadow crept over the door and something whispered in a sinister tone. Norvita scooted back as her instincts made her feel even more afraid in this situation. She then heard the song that made it all make sense to her on some level. It was a low, sweet song that she knew she'd heard before. Norvita's body began to shake.

"Oh, my time has come, to commit the deeds from time unsung."

Norvita felt her body try to wrench out of the blackness that she felt seeping through her subconscious and into her limbs. She knew what that song meant and it made her blood run cold. She found herself clinging to Marcia for strength, which was something that Marcia seemed to be made of. This was an extremely bad turn of events.

"She's here," Norvita mouthed so softly you could barely even qualify the sound as a whisper. "We need to be very careful."

Marcia nodded as she sat otherwise motionless on the floor under a layer of clothes. For a second, she tried to recall what she had read in the book by Carter Lewis. After all, the most part of his work was on the interactions with the She Wolf. However she wasn't able to recall a single act. The longer things went and the more panic she felt, the harder it became to recall a single word of this book. She clung to Norvita and they huddled together as footsteps had sounded louder towards their hiding place. For these slow passing moments, Marcia found herself becoming more and more religious. Prayers that she hadn't thought about since leaving the Catholic Church passed through her mind, begging for protection from whomever might be there to save her. Suddenly the steps stopped in front of the closet. They could imagine that they felt a pair of bright green eyes bore through the door at them, examining each and every moment. At the moment their silent terror was pitched highest, someone let out a low, chocolaty laugh at their fear. Then there was a sudden loud high-pitched whistle that went through the lair.

The next sound they heard was heavy, rhythmic footsteps like a dog heading towards its returning master thunder from upstairs and down to the ground floor. They stopped just before the closet as well. Norvita's heart broke as she heard knees hit the hardwood floor. She knew it was Carson because she desperately wanted to stop him but knew she couldn't be out there with him. Carson wasn't her boyfriend right now. He was pushing his face into Her thigh in a friendly nuzzle. Norvita knew all too well that the She Wolf was there.

"*Bonjour mon petit chiot,*" sang a soft French voice. "Did someone miss their Mistress?"

Carson let out a pathetic whine that would only be used by a begging, scolded dog. Norvita found herself stiffing a sob as she heard this noise, burying her face into Marcia's shoulder. Marcia knew that this development was terrible for Norvita. It was one thing to see the basement and cope with that past horror, but to be confronted with her lover's metamorphosis in this adrenaline-charged moment had to be a strain on the sanity. She hugged Norvita while feeling sick herself. If this was how Carson was going to act, what could they possibly do for Doyle? He'd been with Her even longer than Carson had. They had to get out of this place.

"Where's the other one?" asked the She Wolf.

They weren't sure what Carson said but there was respectful bark to her which elicited another giggle. The feet shuffled again away from the closet. Norvita pulled her head off Marcia's shoulder while wiping off the tears shed for Carson. She knew that they had to get out. This was a fucking awful turn of events and she needed to report it to the Department before things got completely out of hand. She leaned close to Marcia with a plan that only Karl would have been proud of.

"When I open the door," she instructed, "Run and don't look back."

Marcia nodded quietly in the hopes that no one would hear their communication.

But someone did.

Doyle had used all of the remaining restraint he had to keep from running at her call and he knew that it wouldn't last too much longer. The She Wolf's pull on him was far too strong. He also knew that he had Norvita and Marcia in a closet downstairs and with each passing second he knew that he wanted to hand them both over to Her more and more. Doyle had decided that he liked Marcia too much to give her to the She Wolf though, and if anyone was going to get her out safely, it would be Norvita. He hadn't planned on killing his Mistress as he broke off a piece of wood from his rocking chair. He was merely planning on keeping her busy while people he cared for got out.

Time moved slower than he would have liked as he turned around to face Her. She smiled lovingly at him in the split second before he lunged at Her. The She Wolf had expected this from him, however, and snarled at Doyle as he charged her, before batting him down effortlessly. The thump of his body echoed through the lair before she pounced, snake-like, and sat on his chest. She grabbed his hair, pulling his head up with a full-fanged yell. He looked back at her as the fight left his body on taking in her look of utter disappointment.

"Insolent and ungrateful boy," she growled at him as she spit in his face. "I was going to not keep my promise but just for that, I am going to take my time and muzzle you. Jacob! Bring Mistress her sewing kit."

Norvita watched through her crack as feet walked away from the closet up the stairs. Things were getting worse and they had to move soon if they were going to. She stood up slowly with Marcia behind her ready to sprint at a moment's notice. If Norvita timed it right, they could get out quickly and be safe, but only if she moved now.

"Carson," she whispered. "I'm super sorry about this."

It was the sound of the door being kicked open that reverberated next and the smell of burning flesh that triggered Marcia to sprint like a prized three-year-old at the opening gates of the Kentucky Derby. Carson let out a pained whine as aerosol-propelled flame drenched his face, causing him to flinch away from them as Norvita ran out the door. Novita could have kept up with Marcia if it hadn't been for the pity she felt as she heard Carson swear angrily at her as he declared vengeance against her. She backed out quickly, keeping her arms raised before Carson got to his feet. Ragged breath pushed out of his body as his fangs drew down. She wasn't sure what he was waiting for, but she was terrified.

She was at the door when the She Wolf looked down at her. Norvita looked up with her arms raised ready to fight. She wouldn't win if she had to and she knew it. The kicking Doyle that the She Wolf gripped like a child holding a doll was tossed to one side as she walked down the stairs. Norvita didn't hesitate anymore before bolting out.

She grinned for a moment.

"Jacob? How many are there?" She asked.

"Two, Mistress," he said. "That one is a psychic."

"Good. Carson, Jacob, sic 'em."

The two them leapt from the lair after their prey. She walked back towards Doyle as he started to crawled away from her. She cleared her throat loudly. Instantly Doyle stopped and glanced back. He found himself settling on his knees with a soft rocking motion as he waited. She walked towards the closet to head down the stairs. She turned back and she patted her leg. Like the shamed dog he was, Doyle followed her down to his destiny.

XLIII. **Out on the Ridge**

Now

Jodee squatted down on an old stump in the clearing on top of a hill. He spat out black-laced saliva along with an expired wad of tobacco. He clucked his tongue and set the rifle down beside him as he reached for an ancient thermos. He grimaced as he poured the thick red liquid into the lid of his thermos. It was the downside, as he saw it, to chewing tobacco. No matter how well you did at getting it out of your mouth, the next thing you tasted was going have the flavor of Red Man. Marlene had made him and the boy her famous tomato and basil bisque and he'd been dreaming about that for almost a week. She made the best bisque in the county. If there was one thing that everyone agreed on, it was that Marlene Crowe could cook up a storm. It was the best part of being out on a night like this.

Jodee had spent his life in the woods hunting. It was what he was raised to do. Running on the occasional Saturday night was fine for those city clans who had their day jobs and their Starbucks, but you couldn't do that out here. There was always going to be something out in the hollows waiting to do some harm to the good folks. It was easier to be a hunter out here anyway. He knew everyone and vice versa. Something new showed up, you knew that it was there to do you harm. Not that there weren't people around he thought were also there to do harm. He'd always privately thought those Crowe boys needed a good pruning, but they also had Marlene to set them straight. Had she not been in that family, then those boys might be the ones that Jodee would be hunting. Nothing scares a mountain man more than a mountain woman.

The ridge, however, had gotten quieter since Marlene had married Paul Crowe and they'd had Jodell. It hadn't changed much, even when Jodell went to the Department's field office.

Jodee figured that's why she was recruited -- to get those boys under the Department's control. They listened better to one of their own than to those who were assigned to come out to handle all those hillbillies up there on the Ridge and he liked both Arils and Ed.

Arils Thursday was a good old boy. He'd been raised as a hunter who found himself suddenly out of a job. It was a shame because he was one of the best that Jodee'd ever seen. Arils fit right in on the hollow because he might as well have been from the hollow. Jodee figured that southern boys were really the same whether they were from East Tennessee or South Texas. He was fairly sure that no one cared if Arils was gay. That was the thing about it out here. People knew stuff about you and if you were half decent then they wouldn't care if you were gay. Politics and religion had nothing to do with it and that was fine by Jodee. Arils was nice and good enough to keep himself out of trouble and be useful when things got out of hand. Jodee had only hoped it could have also been thought of regarding his partner at the Department.

Jodee hadn't liked Edmund Trumper at first. He was was a pressed and starched human being who lacked any sort of humor to himself. Maybe it was because he was too clean or maybe it was the British accent, but he came off as someone who thought his shit didn't stink. And in Jodee's defense, when Ed had first arrived, it was obvious he was here to straighten out those dumb hillbillies. Then Jodee learned why Ed Trumper had really chosen to settle here. Ed had joined forces with Lila Zmeya of House Grendel when the abyssal Hordes had risen to take over the 1980s. In an effort to fight back what was simply referred to as Typhon from finding her rookery, she'd lain down her life. He would have been destroyed if Typhon knew where the hatchlings had gone. Ed was the only person who knew where Lila Zmeya's offspring were and he had no intention of sharing that information with anyone. Ed was an honorable man protecting dragon royalty. Jodee could understand that. He himself had sworn to protect his people out here and that meant everyone. He'd found similar loyalty in George and they were teaching that to their son Rusty.

He took that first sip with a grimace as he watched the dancing tree line. He could see flames flickering over the mountain. Something was down there, but it wasn't about him in his life. It was about the boy.

Jodee hadn't been in favor of having Rusty at first. He wasn't quite sure if he was meant to be a father and the backward notions of two men raising a son and him not be confused did plague his mind. Maybe religion and politics did play a little into it. Marlene was the one who had convinced them it was going to be okay. Hell, she even served as the boy's mother. That had made Jodee a little more uncomfortable. It wasn't fair to deny Rusty the interaction with his biological mother and that meant the Crowe Boys. Since then, they had learned it was okay -- Rusty was understanding the community and what he needed to do as a hunter better than either Jodee or George could. As such, Rusty was becoming a very good hunter during the short period of time that they'd gone on these hunts. He'd inherited the natural skill that Jodee and George had both learned (they'd decided they never wanted to know who the biological father was). Rusty just needed a little polish. George had spent time teaching the boy basic spells and rituals. Jodee was doing the rest. Rusty lay on his belly with a pair of binoculars watching the tree line and the valley. Despite his lack of desire to go forward, Jodee was happy to have Rusty as his son. He was very lucky to have him.

"See anything Russell?" Jodee asked.

"It's just Russ, now, Dad," Rusty corrected him. "But no sir, I don't see nothing."

"You're doin' a fine job, Russ. We'll give it another hour before we pack it in."

Rusty gave his father a nod while never once diverting from his task at hand. Jodee felt a smirk cross his lips as he sat back to bask in the pride of the boy that he was raising. Not many his age would want to take on this sacred task, but Rusty was different. This was his legacy and he was aiming to do right by his parents and family. Jodee kept his eye on the smoke in the distance. Suddenly an inhuman scream came from that smoke as it belched forth a flame of blue. Instantly, Jodee dove down next to his son, rifle in hand, discarding his tomato bisque to the ground and looking forward, his keenly-trained eye watching the shaking leaves of each tree. Rusty sat up, but never announced seeing anything until he was sure.

"Dad, I seen something," he said. "It's coming from the vamp's house."

The boy was right; something was coming from the north. The trees shook with whatever was running through the woods, heading out towards the main road.

"There was a blue fire. You saw that...right?" Rusty nodded at his father's explanation. "That generally means that a vampire was burned alive. Now, I don't know what the scream was. Do you see a vampire?"

"No, sir. It ain't no Crowe neither," replied Rusty. "I ain't sure it's human."

Dutifully, Rusty handed his father their binoculars. Jodee stared down into the valley. Rusty was right again. It wasn't human. The thing that was down on all fours had started turning from pink flesh to a mottled black gray. Horns were starting to grow out of its forehead. Black blood dripped out of its mouth.

"Rusty, load my gun. That thing is going to go nuts."

Rusty grabbed the shotgun while shoving two bullets into it. Within seconds, Jodee was crawling down the hill with the rifle gripped in his hands. He watched as the creature stopped and turned. It bounded towards Jodee violently. Without thinking, he fired at the beast. It let out a scream and recoiled. For a moment, Jodee saw its human face before it flickered back into the night. That was before it embers of eyes sparked again with anger and pain. A fiery paw pushed out and onto Jodee's face. He scrambled to reach his feet before the beast grabbed the older man by the collar. Pressure pushed down on Jodee's chest as bones started to make a popping sound. Then there was ear-splitting crack of a shotgun that had been loaded for bear. Jodee found himself being thrown off into a tree and sliding down it with his back. The thing turned away and stumbled off. Jodee felt his eyes close quietly. He was damn lucky to have Rusty. Damn lucky indeed.

XLIV. **Run Like Hell**

Now

Marcia had seen enough horror films to know not to look behind her as she ran out of the lair and into the street. That was just inviting something to impede her escape. The last thing she needed now was to trip over an unexpected object on the sidewalk or to run into someone. Things were bad behind her; this was established and she sure didn't need to see it to know that. There was Doyle who had been captured and Norvita wasn't with her anymore, so who knew what had happened to her. She couldn't worry about them. It sounded terrible, but logically she had to keep going. The priority in this matter was her safety. The second priority was helping those who were left behind which she couldn't do if she was captured or killed and she was dead certain that one of those would be the outcome of going back now. She had to get off the street. The sustained panicked running was made the streets all look the same from turn to turn. She was going into a state of shock. She had to find a place to calm down and find someone to call. If she could hide, she could maybe figure out who she needed to call. Who do you call about this? The police? Who would believe her?

The only person she could think of was Karl.

It hadn't dawned on her before, but Karl seemed to know what was going on with the world. If anyone knew who could save her, it would be him. Where was Karl? At this time she wasn't sure, but she knew where to find out. Karl had given her what she believed was his number. If there was a problem with Doyle, he'd said she could call. She would be safe. She searched her memory as she ran thinking hard as she gasped for breath. Where did she leave that number? It was on the ink blotter at her desk at the library. That made sense as a safety spot. Her mind was made up to head to Goodchild Memorial Library. It was safe enough to get free from her attackers or would-be attackers. She turned down an alley and started in the direction of Goodchild Library. She stumbled to a stop as she made her way towards the front of the library.

Never in her life would she have expected to see the kind of scene that was before the library. There was a circle of men of similar height and hair color. There was a man who was bigger than them standing on a burned out vehicle. She watched as a group of men marched out the last of the late night patrons of Goodchild. The man called out loudly in a language loudly. Marica didn't recognize the language, but it sounded terrible. The crowd responded enthusiastically. The leader reached for a bottle with a cloth sticking out of it. She watched the man light the cloth before the bottle arched up towards the sky. It crashed into a window and started to burn on the second story of the library. Flames danced up towards the sky as a fire spread through the library. Marcia covered her mouth as she fought back a sob. All that important knowledge was gone. She took a step back. The crowd rushed upon the hostages, devouring their blood and flesh. She felt her stomach turn. This was what she'd brought to her city. It was only a matter of time before Doyle would do the same to her. She crept back shaking. She needed help and now it was hopeless.

She felt a hand dropped over her mouth as she was pulled into an alley. Marcia let out a squeal as she felt other hands push over her body, feeling her curves. A nose pushed down against her neck breathing her scent. She twisted for a moment as teeth bit down on her neck. She was grateful there were no fangs. She should run, but she was too tired. Part of her fell into his grip, almost succumbing to her fate.

"Ssssh," he said, breathing into her neck before biting her again. "I'm not here to hurt you. I'm here to save you. You see, that's the Arcadian Guard and they are here to serve their queen. She will sit on her throne again and then everyone will be pulled into war. People like us will be first."

"I'm not like you," she said coldly.

"Oh but you are. Not like the other one or like me, but you have something unique about you. That's why I asked if I could have you. She agreed."

"I'm not hers to give to you."

"You let her least favorite touch you so…yes, you are," he said. "Now, we have a choice. You could fight or just come with me."

"I could run."

"And the guard will smell you and you will be ripped apart. Come with me. You're mine."

We always tell ourselves that if we are there in that situation, we would do what was the right thing. We wouldn't sell ourselves out and we'd never give up. It was the hypothetical situation on which many movie plots are based. Sadly, for Marcia, this was real life and there was no luxury of what ifs. She would never regret the choice that she made. For a moment she knew that the movie choice meant immediate, horrible death. Surrender was a human choice. She went with him back to the basement.

He led Marcia back into the basement that had been the center of Her torture. The mix of damp walls and old blood twisted in her nose, making her feel sick. The dim light made Her bright eyes dance out of in the yellow light. Marcia was pushed down forward on her hands and knees before the throne. Her face fell into warm blood, stale blood. She tried to hold back soft gags of a dry heave while trying to push herself up. There was a chocolaty laugh as Marcia struggled to maintain some semblance of sanity. She placed Her foot under Marcia's chin and pushed her head up. Marcia looked up at the She Wolf. She stared back at the green eyes as they cut through her soul. She looked away from Marcia and then looked at the bloody piece of flesh the She Wolf turned over in her hand. She leaned forward and licked the chunk of carnage before putting her heeled shoe on Marcia's face and kicking her back as she started to chew on the flesh. Marcia coughed as her cheek swelled and laid on her side as Jacob slid over beside the She Wolf. He knelt as she rested beside him.

Marcia furrowed her brow. The smell of blood was stronger as she lay there; there was a bloody mess beside her. Marcia twisted as she looked at the body beside her. There was blood that looked sick and black. Lines of purposely sloppy stitching stood out along his throat, chest, and mouth. Marcia looked back at the eyes that looked at her begging her to forgive him. Marcia knew she couldn't be afraid. Not in front of Doyle and not for someone who looked like she was enjoying the spectacle of terror.

"Where is the other one?" the She Wolf asked, almost irritated.

"I don't know. I didn't see the dog or the mongrel," Jacob replied. "They must be out in the city still. This one was found near the library. Your soldiers have let the usurper know you are here. They burned her books and murdered her followers."

"Well, she is interesting and I suppose smarter than the other redbone," the She Wolf m conceded. She turned her attention to Marcia. "Who do you belong to?"

Marcia ran her fingers over Doyle's neatly stitched lips. He shut his eyes and turned away from her as if this was a terrible embarrassment. She gave him a soft smile, trying hard to not choke out a cry before she shuddered.

"Doyle," she whispered.

"Oh good," said the She Wolf. "You at least got the one that you wanted."

Marcia had made a promise to herself that she would be a no man's woman. She was not to be bought, sold, trophied, or traded. That was the only way you could do some of the fetish work that she did. You belonged to no one and definitely not to any man. She knew what the She Wolf was and that made her angry. Marcia wasn't going just to let things happen to herself without trying to maintain control. She sat up on her knees, looking back at the She Wolf while holding her jaw.

"Oh, I'm sorry. I was talking to him. I don't belong to Doyle," Marcia said coldly. "I don't get into that petty domme game of whose subbie is who. I fuck Doyle on a regular basis, but I belong to no one."

Marcia felt her face crushed as a sharp heel kicked it in. She tried to pull herself up. She felt her head yanked back with the sound of pain echoing in her ears as hair was ripped out of the follicles. She struggled for a moment as the She Wolf flashed white fangs at her while they looked back at each other. Not the time to be afraid she told herself. A bully is a bully no matter how you dress it up.

"You worthless little pachuco," She growled. "Do you know who I am?"

"Some people call you queen, some call you Mistress. I think you are some sort of racist street walker who is demanding attention from someone who couldn't care less. Honey, you aren't the first Domme to not realize I'm Puerto Rican or to think you can intimidate me with the shear power of your daddy issues."

Marcia saw her feet as she flew from her knees and hit something heavy and wooden with such force that her spine vibrated with pain. A surprised gasp pushed out as she felt someone hold her throat. The She Wolf rolled her fangs over exposed skin drawing small amounts of blood. The She Wolf licked with a soft grin as she pushed her body against Marcia eagerly. She should be scared of the She Wolf being aroused by her. Someone was going to start hurting. Marcia's thighs were forced apart. She felt the She Wolf's knee grind into her as Jacob walked behind her. He handed Her something that Marcia knew was cold and sharp.

"Oh, I can see why Doyle likes you so much," She said, running the cold blade over Marcia's cheek leaving a fine cut along her cheek bone. "You have such a sharp tongue. You'll have to show me what else you can do with that, apart from throwing barbs."

"Aw, that's cute," said Marcia. "You think that your words are super intimidating to me. I told you once. I'm not scared and this is a typical Saturday night for me. So either you need to start hurting me or making me wet, because frankly, this is boring and at least one of us should get off."

For the first time, Marcia let out a scream. There was not much else she was able to do as the bladed edge of a pair of scissors went down into the superficial flesh of her collar bone. Marcia finally slumped into the fingers of the She Wolf when, suddenly, there were lips on her wound sucking the blood away. The She Wolf pulled her head back and licked the blood off of the scissors while looking viciously at Marcia.

"Oh, I really see why he likes you. You are so very tasty," said the She Wolf. "I think I'm going to keep you around so I can bathe in your blood."

Marcia was never very clear about the next moments. She found herself being pushed against a wall. She blinked slowly as her head felt sore and heavy from another hit. She felt her body pulled back as something was forced around her neck. She watched the She Wolf who paced gently. This was contemplation and for a moment she was safe but that wouldn't last long. She hazily remembered Jacob's hands running through her hair before he suddenly stopped. Jacob stood up and stared off at nothing. His fingers left Marcia's body as he became rigid.

"Elizabet LaVouve!" Jacob yelled at her in a voice that wasn't his. It was oddly Dutch-English. "You will speak to me this instant!"

"Oh dear little sister," the She Wolf said softly. "What took you so very long?"

"Elizabet LaVouve!" Jacob yelled again. "You will speak to me this instant!"

"I heard you the first time," She yelled at the phantom of her sister. "It is time I suppose, for you and I to finish our rivalry. Where shall we speak?"

"You know exactly where."

The She Wolf snarled for a moment before stroking Jacob's cheek. She smiled at him as he blinked, looking back at his Mistress. He smiled at her.

"Jacob, sweetheart," She said softly. "You can play with her now. Make sure you put your toys up when you are done."

Marcia felt Jacob put his body on top of her. She struggled for a moment as he pushed her down while tearing off her clothing like a boy on Christmas opening a toy. She screamed at the violating pressure as he pushed her wounded body on to the ground. She struggled under his hands, looking around for Doyle while cursing herself for her first thought being for her man to rescue her. If he was there, he wasn't in the small illuminated circle she could see in the blackness. She was somehow pleased to know Doyle wasn't seeing this. Now, all she could do was pray for the whole thing to end quickly.

XLV. Love Will Tear Us Apart

Now

Norvita had never been so happy to have listened to Karl than in that moment. He had insisted that she needed to run a little faster. They went for speed training four days a week at the track up at the high school. She had thought that Karl was overreacting and super-paranoid, but that thought was forever purged from her mind as she ran away from Carson. She knew to wear comfortable shoes during stakeouts. That was smarter than she would give herself credit for being. Despite this choice, the muscles in the back of her thighs were starting to throb and sting with fatigue. Her blind running wasn't yielding a resolution to her problems. It was time to start thinking in a super adult way, without her usual ditzy pretense. She had to ask herself one question.

What would Karl do?

Karl would avoid Montgomery Avenue because the sidewalk was uneven. She wasn't going out like a bimbo in a bad horror film by tripping. That was the worst way to go. *Ha! Smart decision made!* She needed to jaywalk when it came to Baylor Road. It was the busiest street in South Gaiman and the smell of excessive car exhaust would buy her time when it came to her scent. She had to cover her scent, which was why she was running down a storm drain. The Ditch ran behind Byrne Jr. High and that would run to the Midtown Water treatment plant and that could confuse his sense of smell long enough for her to put some distance between her and Carson. All of this was temporary, of course, Carson had her scent like no one else's. It was only a matter of time before he was on her. Then she would be dragged off to a fate worse than death.

Norvita pushed that thought out of her head as she climbed into the drainage pipe. This wasn't the time to worry about what could be if she got caught. She had to focus on where she needed to go for safety. Her apartment was just on the edge of Old Gaiman. She couldn't run there. Same thing when it came to the Spire. It was too far to run and not in the condition that she was in. Norvita coughed out the foul smell that filled her lungs. She couldn't panic at this point. This was the time that she had to think clearly. She was at Byrne Jr. High in the north east. If anything, that gave her a buffer when it came to Carson. He wouldn't hunt on the North Brood land. She took the moment to catch her breath as she dug out her phone. If she could get a message either to Karl or Weston Lewis then she might be able to get away. This was not to be the case, however.

Norvita let out a scream as the phone was knocked from her hands and into the mud underneath her as she was yanked from the drain pipe. She let out another scream as she fell on to the hard ground. She tried to pick her head up to get her bearings. It had to be the parking lot of the junior high. She found herself being forced to her knees as she looked up. She didn't know those faces but they were vampires. She looked up into the perfectly symmetrical faces of Northern vampires that she had no desire to ever see. Norita was going to be Norvita.

"Well drat," said the one who'd pulled her up by her hair. "This is a terrible gift to bring to her Ladyship. I don't think she'll want a coolie."

"Oh, we could drink her like a purple slurpee," said the other one as he got into Norvita's face. "I bet her cunt tastes like mango chutney."

"Excuse me, my name is Norvita Patel; I'm with the Department of the Arcane. My pussy tastes like maraschino cherries and right now you need to let go of me or be in violation of your terms in this city."

"That's cute, sand mouse, but didn't you hear? The Queen is back in town and we're not going to listen to the magi." The other vampire grinned, leaning in and breathing in her scent. "I'm going to chew on your cherry all day if I want."

What Norvita saw next wasn't really too surprising to her. It was a large Irish wolfhound leaping over her head and onto the back of the vampire who was holding her up. His claws went into her back as he leapt away from her and the other vampire. Norvita fell to the ground, curling defensively as the wolf ripped the vampire into tiny pieces as easily as if he were made of tissue paper. Norvita knew this was the proper time to get out. She got to her feet and ran. She got roughly five feet before she hit asphalt again. Fangs stung, ripping a hole in her shoulder to take her down like a beast who had downed his prey. Norvita clawed at the blacktop, attempting to liberate herself.

"Get off of her," growled a canine voice. "That slut is mine."

Norvita let out a ragged scream as she tumbled forward from a sudden impact and rolled for a moment. Her shoulder burned as a piece of it was ripped out along with the second Northie vampire. She laid on her back and watched Carson carefully rip off the man's limbs like he was a younger sister's Barbie doll. She sat up dizzily as she felt blood cover her face. She shook gently as she got to her feet. Carson turned his head to one side with a low desperate growl.

"You better run before I tear you apart," he warned her.

"I…I can't anymore," she said. "Please."

"Run or I'll eat you alive, Norvita!"

It was awful to start running again, which it turned out she could sort of do -- adrenaline is pretty cool. Her legs throbbed with pain as she limped along in her slower run. This was where things were going to start to turn bad for her and she knew it. She couldn't possibly outrun Carson or any of the other vampires who were going to be roaming the streets. There was no way that the Department was going to get involved in enough time to save her. Norvita stood at the edge of an overpass that connected North with Old Gaiman. This was it. She could still run and struggle until she was offered as a gift to the She Wolf. Then what would she be? She would be tortured and played with like a toy before she died. She knew what her mother had gone through in her death. She wasn't going to let herself be tortured to death. She was going to go out on her own terms. Norvita watched as the bright shine of headlights cascaded over the bridge. This was a sign. She had to be brave.

She wasn't going to be murdered.

She took a deep breath in as she shut her eyes. Slowly she allowed her stiff muscles to rock her body forward as she waited for the feeling of a metal frame to come crashing into her. The car stopped just inches away from her though. She furrowed her brow as she felt hands on her shoulders. She looked back at the man who had found her with sudden recognition.

"Norvita?" said Weston Lewis. She was quite relieved to see him. She smiled quietly. "What the…"

"Crossbow," she said quickly. "I need your crossbow."

What should be amazing about this wasn't that Norvita knew that Weston Lewis was carrying a crossbow in his civilian vehicle, but the fact that it had become an effortless question like asking for a wrench. These are the lives of Gaiman Heights. There was no need to question; when a Department Agent asked, you gave them your crossbow.

"Back seat," he said.

"Hemlock-tipped bolts?" she asked as she dove into the back of the Volkswagen. She stayed on her stomach as her shaky fingers loaded the rounds into the crossbow.

"I'm hunting vampires; of course I'm carrying hemlock -- it's like shooting them with an elephant dart," he said. "Did Car…"

When Norvita looked up to see what had stopped Weston Lewis from talking all of a sudden, all she saw was a pair of shoes.

Carson had found her really quickly and that took her by surprise. Norvita scanned the area, finding Weston Lewis sprawled out on concrete with Carson on top of him, his hands up for a strike. He was hesitating that was for certain, which meant Norvita only had a few minutes to fire off a shot. Norvita raised the crossbow with only mild hesitation herself. It was Carson and she had some trepidation about shooting her boyfriend. Of course, one thing was sure: if she waited any longer Weston Lewis would be dead. Norvita had to do something.

Using the backseat as cover, she stood up with high elf grace and without another moment wasted on useless thought, she fired a bolt into Carson's shoulder. As he crumbled she aimed at him again, her body twitching with the effort of holding the weapon steady and with the emotion of shooting her lover.

She'd heard from Karl what it was like shooting a man. He had prepared her for that moment by telling her how there was a feeling of your heart working overtime as everything started to slow down. You would remember every part of what happened in that moment. Norvita would always remember the sound of the bolt as it whistled through the air and flew into Carson's throat. She could remember the smell of old blood pouring out of Carson's mouth as he went over backwards and the color of the hemlock as it worked through his veins with a killing blackness. She watched for a moment as Weston Lewis pulled himself up from the prone position and looked at her. Norvita looked down at Carson as she limped around the trunk, her body burning with crashing waves of fatigue.

"Holy shit, Norvie," Carson rasped. "I didn't feel dick. That's a good fucking shot. I didn't even think…"

"Oh hush baby," she said, looking down at him. "You haven't even seen me crazy yet."

Without another word, she fired another bolt into Carson, expertly going through his cheek. His eyes went wide as he finally lay motionless. She hadn't killed him, though at this point, that was becoming quite the temptation. Deep down she knew she couldn't do something like that. She watched as Weston Lewis dragged Carson's body towards the car.

"Really?" she asked.

"If we leave him here, the Northies are either going to rip him apart," Weston said, "or get him to a point where he's manic. My trunk is sunlight-proof and rune marked. He's safer there. Now let's get the hell out of here before they come looking for us."

It was a quiet few seconds on their car ride away from one place and off to another before either one of them even moved to make a sound. Then it was Norvita playing with the radio. She stopped when she found a very cheery pop station. Weston Lewis gave her a look.

"Before you ask," she said without provocation, "No, I'm not fine. I just hate silence."

"I don't expect you to be fine right now Norvita. You shot your boyfriend in what I'm guessing has been a night of unusual vampire violence. It's hard enough when it's someone you don't know, let alone a loved one."

"You ever shoot anyone?"

"No, not yet. Karl taught me how to shoot when I got on the force. He always said to shoot to kill. It's what he did in West Hills with that possessed guy. He did everything right then. He'd be proud of you for handling yourself with Carson like that."

"If he's still alive," she said. "I had nightmare about Karl. He wasn't Karl, he was something else. I called him to tell him and I couldn't and now...I can't feel him. It's like he's gone. Something black is coming in Weston and it's not just the She Wolf. Something is riding in on her train and it's not good."

"Let's handle one crisis at a time, Norvita," was Weston's sensible answer. "We'll take care of the vampires and then we'll go find Karl. What do we need to do, head to the Spire?"

"I could use a drink and maybe some first aid. But I'm not going back to the office. Department won't be on the street until it starts spilling into the mundane. If it's just in South Gaiman they aren't going to move too fast. Besides, I want to put a bolt in that bitch's heart."

"For what she did to Carson?"

"And that her goons ruined my favorite bra and panty set by ripping out my shoulder." She stopped. "Weston, I'm sorry that I made you fall in love with me for my own amusement."

"What?"

"I know it sounds like a dying confession, but you saved my life back there by just showing up randomly and I feel the need to say it. I'm sorry for using you like I have."

"I don't know what to say."

"Nothing. Just say nothing."

XLVI. **Too High**

Marcia laid on her side as her stomach folded in on itself in a sick, aching reaction to the damp basement floor. The smell of must and stale blood choked on the inside of her mouth and there was a thin layer of dew on her skin. She brought her legs up to her hips as her shaking arms held her torso, trying to generate heat and modesty in a futile effort. Human decency wasn't hers anymore. The last two hours had been spent ripping that away from her by the man she suspected was called Jacob.

She quietly blinked back tears as she lay motionless on the floor. He'd relented from his assault and now she felt devoid of anything. There was no anger or fear in that moment. It was all just the assentation of what she expected which was going to be pain and suffering and then there was nothing at all. It was as if all the air in her rage balloon had been let out, leaving her deflated and feeling nothing.

Her fingers touched a heavy leather collar that he had put snugly around her neck. She slid a finger in to make sure there was that sustainable gap as she grasped at something that was more than familiar, hoping for a grounding wire back to reality. That familiarity made her stomach sink into a horrible place and had filled her with the first feelings of hate. Marcia had always been fond of what she did for a living before her librarian days. The notion of being able to let go of a part of her into that lifestyle had been, she found, liberating for her as woman. Now there was a sadist who used the fear that people thought was the real way of dealing with the lifestyle. If anything, this made her upset and even made her question whether or not she wanted to continue in her life. She squared her shoulders. She couldn't begin to think of life down the road yet when she still had to get out of her present situation. She'd known this choice would suck, and hell yes it did, but she was still alive and mostly sort of unhurt, wasn't she? Marcia had to formulate a plan to get out of the basement if for no other reason than she had to find Karl. If anyone could help her it would be him. Of course she had thought maybe Norvita had gotten away and was getting help, but as time pushed forward that thought seemed less and less true. With each second she was losing her hold on her own sanity.

They wouldn't kill her. Not at first anyway. Jacob had spent his time assuring her of that. If she complied with what he asked her to do, then he would keep her alive. He could almost assure that. After all it had been his plan since he went on his hunting trips for his Mistress. He'd proven his ability to hunt and to do what he had to for her. Therefore when he found what he wanted, she would let him keep it. He would have gotten her sooner and their time would have been longer if Doyle hadn't ruined it. He'd make her love him one way or another. They would have a family and be protected when this city went up in flames under their queen's control. They wouldn't be a part of the herd that would survive; their family would rule over the humans in glory of their Mistress.

"Why me?" she had asked finally.

"Because you have a fate to be the mother of monsters," he'd told her. "I can see it."

In that moment, she had come to hate her supposed betrothed. It wasn't because of his inept attempts to be forceful. She couldn't be angry at someone who was pressured into playing a role that he was never meant to play -- it was his sincerity towards her. If he had been a decent human being before the She Wolf had gotten her claws into him, it came out when he tried to assure her that they were meant to be. He wanted her to be comfortable in his presence and that made her hate him more. She hated everything about him; his fingers on her skin leaving prints on her body, his decaying breath on her neck when he spoke to her. She froze for a moment as she felt his wiry frame pushed against her. He was excitable to say the least and he touched her with every violating touch when he woke up enough to feel it. He had done this six times at least since the She Wolf had left and it was now burned in her memory. She just wished that he would shut up.

"Mistress has been teaching me how to use my skills better," he told her. "I'm special because I can read auras, but now I can read thoughts and it's pretty amazing. I can hear secrets. See, I know your secrets now and I still love you despite them."

He told her about her first sexual encounter. It had been the second semester of her freshman year. She'd been fooling around with a guy since the start of the semester and he hadn't been like the guys she knew back home. It was hard for her to find someone to date with all her brothers that had been around. It was spring when it had happened. It had been a cold day that hung on from the winter blowing in from Canada. He'd sat on her chest as she lay on the floor of her dorm room, forcibly pushing her mouth open. The whole relationship had felt wrong and this was the pinnacle of it. She didn't protest, despite things feeling so uncomfortable and somehow it had always been something she had never quite come to terms with in her own life. The feeling of shame had always haunted her and it was always a problem for her. She had never really forgiven herself and maybe never would. Her problem wasn't with him, but always with herself. It had been easy when he dumped her over the summer, which had helped her move and just bottle up the unresolved anger.

"You are stronger than you think though," Jacob said to her. "You accepted things pretty easily then and this is something that you will also accept."

He told her that he was looking forward to having a family with her and to her being a mother which she would be excellent at and he felt that he needed to tell her that, because he knew about her miscarriage. How the guilt that she felt over her first real relationship had driven her to a party lifestyle. How she'd ultimately lost her virginity to a nice guy that she wasn't seeing anymore and that had been better for everyone involved. She hadn't know she was pregnant at the time. She had found out when her period started early in September. This wasn't uncommon since her body had gotten unusual after contracting mono the year before, so it was ignored. The night before she left town though she'd woken up in extreme pain swelling through her abdomen. She hadn't been able to move or breathe. What she should have done was go to the hospital at that point but she didn't. It was being prideful about being a woman and hoping it was nothing more than stomach cramps. Why would she even think about getting up and seeing a doctor about that? Instead, she took a sleeping pill and went back to sleep. It was when she fell asleep at a rest stop that someone had made her go see a doctor. She'd lied to her mother about it, who kept her tucked in at their home and accepted what she told her as truth although her mother always knew better than that.

If there was anything she felt the most guilt about, it was a lie she'd kept from her mother, even as she'd been on her deathbed.

The last year had been hard for Marcia and her family. From her mother's diagnosis and valiant fight over the years to the fading and painful end. She had been close to her mother -- or as close as a daughter could be to her mother in those days. That's what had made life more difficult after she'd died. Marcia should have gone home, but instead she stayed in Gaiman Heights, a world away from the grief that was the Marquez household. The deep-seated guilt that Marcia still felt over her mother was the fact that when she was gone from her hometown and family life she could pretend that her mother never existed. That meant she had never been in pain. It only seldom worked because at the end of the day, she missed her mother. Now it was a deadly poison in her mind because Jacob now knew she missed her mother.

"Eventually you'll see that this is your family now. You'll forget the pain of losing your mother in time."

In that moment, Marcia vowed to see both Jacob and the She Wolf dead even if it killed her.

That goal meant she had to get out. Jacob's stamina had not matched his frail human frame and he had fallen into a deep slumber. She found herself working her way out of his lazy grip in absolute quiet. She crawled away as fast she could on her shaking hands and knees and then she stopped. A large wooden object stood between her and freedom. Her hands went along the piece of furniture until she felt something cold and metal in her hands. A smile crossed her face as she realized that she had put her hand on a weapon. If nothing else, she could get what she wanted. She would have freedom at any cost.

She rose to her feet steadily. If she could find the stairs, she could get out through Doyle's bedroom and then out on to the street. Then she would have to work things out from there, but the first thing to do was get out of the basement. She gripped the blade as she shuffled along the wall, trying to feel her way out. Her foot pressed against Jacob's back. Marcia looked down and felt her body shake with triumph. Her current fear had been having to choose between freedom or revenge and now she didn't have to. She could take her vengeance right away. She raised the sharp object over her head and brought it down as quickly as she could. It would have slammed home if it hadn't been for a force pulling her away in a sudden iron grip. She felt her body draw breath to scream out before a hand was placed over her mouth. With the other it guided her fingers to coarse stitching. Marcia felt her face contort with dark comfort.

"Doyle?" she whispered.

It was the nod that made her heart break into a million pieces. Doyle not only was still in a state of what she could only imagine was physical pain but now he'd seen her at her weakest and heard every word spoken to her by Jacob. This was not something he needed to be a part of and now he was fully entrenched in her heartache. Hot tears streamed down her face as she felt herself tumble into his arms. This was all very tiring.

"I want to go home," she sobbed. "Let me go home."

She felt him pick her up in his arms. She clung to his neck as he walked her out of the basement without any further fanfare. He didn't have to carry her out and maybe it was old fashioned and clichéd but honestly, Marcia wasn't sure her legs could have worked to get out. The two of them stood in the middle of his bedroom quietly. Doyle quickly threw one of his dress shirts over her before he shoved an old cigar box into her hands. She looked up at him, clutching the box to her chest. She sighed as he leaned and pressed his stitched lips to hers. She shook her head and looked at him. Carefully she cut the threads loose on each stitch, opening his tongue-less mouth. She watched as his fangs swelled with hunger. Quietly she stepped back, looking at him.

"Go," she said coldly. "Get vengeance for us both and heal."

Doyle turned sharply as he sprinted down the stairs towards the basement. She found herself quietly shutting the door behind her as she walked out of the bedroom. There was an inhuman howl of pain. She wanted to smile at this suffering, but she couldn't quite do that. She looked down at the box. She opened it to find what she had expected: a picture of a young man and his bride who would bear him children only to die from starvation, another photo of the children who'd lived long enough to be photographed, and an old green rosary. She pushed the pictures into the breast pocket of the shirt and slipped the rosary around her neck and then walked out of the lair logically and with purpose. Doyle would come for her next so she needed to find a place where he wouldn't go. A place he wouldn't even think of, since the She Wolf could compel him to tell her.

XLVII. And Then

Asher Stone sat blinking his blurry eyes as he followed the figures that were dressed in fashions that were roughly out of date when this masterpiece was filmed, if they were ever in style then. He lazily drew small stick figures on the back of a piece of paper that informed him of the retirement benefits that he could take advantage of in thirty years. The draconian stack of paperwork had told Asher to not worry. This job might have been dangerous and supernatural, but it was also like every other job on the planet, which took him somewhat by surprise. Of course, what was he expecting? The Department of the Arcane was a government agency and that meant double the paperwork and some of the most uninspiring training videos on the planet.

Asher blinked away tiredness as he picked up the empty coffee mug and then became transfixed on the screen again. He had to at least be happy for the actors who had found work making this video. Or at least he hoped they were actors who had gotten paid well. He wondered if this was what they had hoped for themselves when they'd gotten their drama degrees. That they were going to be actors in boring corporate videos or did their lives take a turn somewhere and this wasn't where they were supposed to end up? This wasn't where he had expected to be either. Then again he wasn't sure where else he would have been in life. Maybe that's why he accepted this new life so easily. No expectations means being a part of an agency that regulated magic wasn't that hard to accept, let alone being something they cannot understand as magical.

Then again, maybe he was so brain dead from the orientation that things in general were just very easy to accept.

Asher set his empty cup down while letting out a slow breath of boredom. Slowly, he found himself leaning forward with a soft yawn as sleep overtook his eyelids. Another yawn slipped out of his mouth as he drifted into a dreamless sleep. This wouldn't be a problem normally, but today wasn't normal. The nexus had discovered boredom today. This was new for the nexus and it wasn't planning to plumb the depths of boredom. How did one fight boredom, she wondered? She looked down at the mug. Humans seemed to fight boredom by drinking coffee. She could do that, but she wasn't going to drink the coffee from the break room as that clearly didn't do the job very well. She knew where she could find better coffee. She took a deep breath as she transported herself as well as Asher.

XLVIII. Carter Lewis's Last Stand

Now

Carter Lewis sat with his back to the door as the music from half a century ago pulsed over the slowly filling bar, making it feel as best as it could that Annette and Frankie would be hopping around the corner as Elvis conquered the big Kahuna. He watched as the flashing lights lazily danced over the feet of the people who made up the dance floor. All the regulars were there tonight. Irina was forcing Tom to keep up with her elaborate steps while she danced her soul out the same way she had done before the fall of Communism. Irina was a ballerina who'd defected from Lithuania in hopes of becoming a star on Broadway. When she met Tom he was making student films at NYU and was going to be the next big thing. The world was going to be theirs and then Irina got pregnant and Tom had to find a real job. He worked as a local news producer in Gaiman and still did work on channel five. Irina had given up being a star and tried to create new ones at their studio. Most of her students were young girls or old men trying to learn how to mambo. She felt the most alive when Tom took her out on the dance floor, even if he wasn't much of a dancer. He was happy as long as his Irina was happy.

Stavros was there too with the newest model of girlfriends. He was twice widowed. The legend is that he killed his first wife before coming to the states because she found out about the other woman who was with child. Others say that in her grief and fear of leaving her homeland she'd thrown herself on the rocks. Either way, his Stella's death prompted him to marry Melora who had been working as the family's nanny for a long time. She had died several years ago from what could have been best described as old age. Since then Stavros had gotten himself a string of girlfriends to replace his now dead wife. Of course, there was also a chance that he was doing this long before she had even passed. Every so often they would be upgraded. He suspected that they enjoyed the ride. Stavros had made his fortune ages ago in the shipping industry and now with his business being taken care of by his sons, he had time to wear flashy and unusual suits with bad toupees and take out young girls as pleased as it was possible be. Carter wondered when Stavros would find someone who could keep up with him on the dance floor. The only person in this room who could would be Irina. They still could do so. After all, the night felt young and the band hadn't even started playing yet. Anything could happen. If he got a couple more glasses of wine into Margaret he could get her on the floor. Somewhere in the past that thought hit home terribly.

Carter Lewis took a hearty swig of his bourbon and soda to push down the wave of sadness that threatened to break through his stoic face. When he was a younger man, Carter Lewis had fought with Alistair DeWitt for the love of one of the students of St. Hubert's School for Girls. In the end, he'd made Margaret Hauge fall in love with him. He missed her more than anything. Margaret was one of the most radical hunters that he'd ever met and had been just a pleasure to know. She'd been an exceptional student and had finished her studies early from the School. Instead of returning home to her clan, as women were supposed to do in those days, she hadn't. She joined what became known as the Sisters in Saffron. Like many radical movements, the Sisters were a group of girls who found that it was time to move forward and hunt like men. Maybe they'd always been around and no one knew, but it was certain that they were going to continue to be around and do as well as the men. The Patriarchal nature of the clan mentality meant that women were meant to learn healing work and rear the sons for another generation. They were too weak to be in battle. He challenged anyone to say that his Margaret was weak. And that's what he fell in love with. Margaret never backed down from a fight. It's why he chose to wear her Saint Key around her neck. It was powerful hunter's charm that not many ever claimed and somehow he'd hoped that her energy could stay with her. He touched the carefully crafted key as it swung around his neck. It's what he had left, but she wasn't there anymore.

Carter Lewis tried actively to ignore the empty seat next to him that he'd reflexively look over at every so often. If she had been there, she would have been sitting in the chair next to him. She'd be watching the crowd with wide and pretty eyes. And then she'd start dancing and singing along with the music. That's why he would be there. She loved music more than her children and him. He missed his warrior woman. He only wished that she could have fought off what had killed her. There was nothing she couldn't hunt, but the abnormal cells that set up in her bile ducts and took over her liver had been an entirely different monster. She then fought. The kids came back and they made the most of what they could, but eventually the cells won. She still fought as long as she could. They said that her heart rate was at 112 when she died. He knew that it took a full minute when they pulled her off the life support for her body to die. They said it was like she'd been running a marathon. Carter Lewis knew better. Always brave even until the end. Margaret Sue Hauge never backed away from a fight.

Carter Lewis swallowed his sadness with another drink of his bourbon. Men of his generation didn't talk about sorrow or loss. Instead they held on to it and let it eat them up. This wasn't the life that he wanted to live. He was supposed to be retired with her by his side. They would be doing the traveling more than did when they were both hunting. He'd stopped hunting partly because he couldn't find the drive to move on with his life. He had his wife in a box on his desk and nothing else to do with his time. He still dreamed about her and even more so than when she had been alive. They weren't bad dreams; in fact, they were pleasant. He hated those dreams. He would get so wrapped up in these dreams that he'd forget that they were dreams and she was gone. Then he'd wake up in his bed alone with her cold as the grave. Carter Lewis did most of his crying in the morning.

He decided that it meant one thing: she was still with him. He often felt like her specter hung on his shoulder and that was great. She was still with him. If he was lucky enough to go on, then he knew God would reunite them at the end. It had made him accept his death a little more than he should. All Carter Lewis wanted was to see her again.

He wouldn't tell Prudence but he was thrilled to hear about Dagmar's prophecy and what it said about him. It was enough to tell him that it was time to get ready and he was excited about it. Every person had their time and eventually he was going to die. Maybe he should have fought harder to stay with Prudence, but she was a big girl -- she would have to deal on her own. He turned as the door opened. He knew that face.

The Arcadian Guard had long served the She Wolf as her personal guard. They weren't anything new, but they were certainly the most aggressive. They would march in the street and round up those who dared to question their queen and their authority. Their leader was something that had made the DeWitts more upset. It was something they didn't talk about. Carter Lewis had lost one of his brothers to being turned and it was at the hand of Heller DeWitt. Heller had become the captain of the guard. And now he stood in the doorway of the bar. He knew that there would be more outside. In that moment, Carter Lewis knew that men like him didn't retire. They die bloody deaths in the trenches.

In the end this is what he chose. He could have died at home in his study or watching the game. It's where he spent his days now, but he went out into the streets now in his nights. He wasn't going to wait. Men shouldn't wait for death; they should march off to death. He wasn't going to die like that.

Carter Lewis looked at Heller DeWitt for a moment before he finished his drink. If that wasn't enough proof that the world wasn't something he didn't want to live in. He was drinking a mixed cocktail out of a plastic cup like a freshman at a kegger. He knew this wasn't something he wanted to be a part of and never again would be in a world where they served drinks in plastic cups in bars. They'd started doing that almost a year ago. The easy thing would have been to find a new bar, but he was stubborn. This was his bar; he wasn't going anywhere.

His resolve came stronger when he could hear the marching feet settle outside the bar. He knew that if he didn't go with them then there would be death and above all he had to protect the mundane. It was time.

"Margaret, I'm sorry," he whispered. "I'll see you soon."

Carter Lewis stood up, taking his necklace off and placing it with his wallet on the table. He left it between the folds next to a picture that had been taken during a Christmas a long time ago. He liked that picture because it was the time that he felt like they were really a family and they got a portrait made. The little girl in their family insisted that Winnie the Pooh was a member of the family too. He walked out quietly as he stared at Heller DeWitt. Heller smiled at him viciously as he walked away from the table. He looked down at his hands as he walked out. The Acadian Guard screamed in delight as Heller DeWitt threw a hood over his head. They then marched off eagerly.

XLIX. **Homecoming**

Now

The She Wolf had tried to forget everything about Trublood Manor and how much she hated it. She hated him more, which is why she hated his home. He was so much more than what he became in the end and he had forgotten that he was a powerful creature when he was still alive. He used to be a great man.

When she met him he'd been Siegfried Von Jaeger. He'd been the count of his own little fiefdom on the edge of the woods with black trees. It was the custom in their day. Many of the lords of old Europe were vampires themselves and had set up their kingdoms according to tradition. A fractured Prussia was the easiest place for them to live since many could have their own kingdoms with no significant troubles. She had become his after being kidnapped off the street. Her mother had been a whore and so was she. It was almost a family tradition to be taken off the street. She was taken as a part of his herd. When he'd bought her she was a worthless girl with a worthless name to be used and discarded like one of Bluebeard's brides. She was his food and then he'd have been done with her. What he hadn't realized was that when he brought her in, he didn't have a sheep. No, he had a wolf among his flock.

She had been a predator from day one. She was thief by trade but it was never enough for her. The sinful pleasures of sex and robbery were her true loves. When she hurt a john for the first time she found pleasure. Something about suffering pleased her greatly. With those skills she got more out of her work than anything an honest job could have given her. She was terrifying. How had a woman like that become a part of his harem? It was her own fault. Money had dried up due to her condition and she knew that she had to disappear. If it hadn't been for the screaming bastard she'd drowned and the fear that its father would have her hanged, she wouldn't have needed to vanish. Her plan had always been to find a count to use. She just hadn't counted on him being a vampire.

Death had hung over the human herd. Not a day would pass that there wouldn't be someone who disappeared and was eventually replaced. She knew that her time would be short if she didn't do what she had always done. She had survived by falling back on the sadistic skills she had developed. Her sisters in the herd had hated her. If one had tried to run, she would find them and drag them back. After a while, they began praying for death at the hands of the Count of Jager instead of their master's bitch. She made an impression on her lord and master and started to rise through the ranks. She loved him and it would be the only relationship of its kind in her life.

Her conversion was a momentous event for both of them. Her awakening came with the kill and then a baptism. In a font of blood she washed away her cheap human life. There was no more an Isebelle who was a common French whore. She was now Elizabet La Vouve. They were happy in their life of torture and mayhem. That had been before they met Dagmar.

It began after they'd killed the son of a cousin of a high ranking authority that they went to hide out in Bavaria. They could outlive the peasants, but for the time it was time to be quiet. She had found a castle for them to live in and it was here. She'd been pleased to find a secluded abbey where they would be able to eat. One day they would return to glory. It wouldn't be soon, but they were safe. What She hadn't counted on was finding the exact place where Dagmar had chosen to spend her so called Twilight Years.

Dagmar was a quiet woman who had made it through her life as long as she could be a nun and away from prying eyes. Dagmar was blind and taking refuge in the Abbey of the Blessed Vision because she had blessed vision. Dagmar had written down everything that she had seen in a book and part of the problem with being prophetic was that she knew that one day that she would have to give her visions to a man who would kill her, but she was okay with that. She knew this was the thing she had to do. She had been waiting for Siegfried when he walked into her room. She smiled at him.

"Come in, young man. It's time we talk," she'd said to him.

It had stopped Siegfried from eating her that night and he became concerned. He sat down and listened to what the old sage wanted to say to him. She told him about her visions and that the world was going to be an interesting place in the future. She told him about the conversion that he would experience in the chapel of that Abbey. She also told him that he would die to bring forth a powerful being almost eagerly.

"Why would I do something so foolish, old woman?" he'd asked.

"Love."

She told him about the love of Christ that he would feel for a child and that they would change the world together. On that day, Siegfried became a friend of Dagmar and they spent many nights talking about Christ and Salvation. This naturally made the She Wolf hate the old woman. She watched as Siegfried became weaker and weaker and she couldn't continue this. She had to kill Dagmar or better yet, he had to kill her.

She had him locked up for almost a week in a cellar before she let him out into the abbey. She knew that no one would survive a half-starved vampire and that was exactly what happened. She had hoped that it would bring things back to where they needed to be. However, he hadn't come back to her. Instead he'd come back troubled and believing that God had spoken to him. She couldn't be with him anymore. They parted ways. Siegfried left for North America. She would eventually find her way to following him. She came up through New Orleans, brought over by the casket girls who populated the towns. It was how her kind had made it so freely to the New World. Pay a girl from France to bring them over in caskets. She'd spent her time there until she had been kicked out of the colony. She made her way north and met Gerald

Crowe who'd blocked her into that damnable cave until her liberation by Cyrus Blackmore. Mortals blended together in her demented mind and she took her vengeance on Virgil instead of the Crowes. It was easier to harm one mundane family than a pack of werewolves so perhaps her mental lapse wasn't entirely inadvertent -- She wasn't stupid, after all. She kept going north looking for her Siegfried. When she found where he had died, he was no longer Siegfried or alive. She found a sister in his place who had been shaped out of his weakness. Above everything she hated, or ever had hated, she hated Prudence.

This was why she was angry about the call. Yes, she had used Jacob, the She Wolf's own tool, which was irritating enough, but the true indignity was being brought to her palace by the little sister that she had always loathed and resented. She was queen; no one talked to her like that. This was the time that she would take care of her little sister.

Her feet stepped on the stone finish of what was once Execution Square. She had made it a point to hold trials there. They had to know they needed to live in fear of her. She didn't know what Prudence did here these days, but she didn't care. She was here to take things back. She walked into the grand hallway with a snarl and stalked quietly towards the throne room. She sniffed the air, searching for Prudence.

"Do you really think that you can hide from me?" She said in a sing-song voice. "Dear sister, this was my home."

"Well, it's mine now," Prudence's voice echoed through the rooms. "Don't think I cannot hide forever here."

"Of course, I thought we would speak instead of you being a wretched coward. Come and face me."

"You will forgive me if I decline. I have a few things to tell you and I do not wish to be torn apart....just yet anyway."

"Then speak, I'm bored."

"You are quite impatient, dear sister. Did Father know about that?"

The She Wolf let out another snarl.

"Oh, I forgot you are not fond when I call him Father. Perhaps I should call him by his Christian name…George, or does that hurt more?"

"Little Sister, you are trying my patience. I am very close to ripping out your tongue."

"You would have to find me and as I am smaller than you, I can hide forever…you cannot. However, I agree this banter has become rather silly. I think you should know that I've been reading the works of Dagmar. She speaks of both of us. I regret to inform you that this is where we end. Your reign and mine. I am unsure if it means death or if it something else, but I feel like I need to tell you that your death is soon. It is a shame, but it must happen."

"Now, you are trying to intimidate me."

"Just stating fact. Maybe it was true that she hated you. I don't know."

"Then, bring my death."

"Very well."

Prudence was nothing if not fast and the She Wolf knew it well. She bounded towards what looked like a blur in the middle of the hallway with a violent growl. Fangs were drawn and flesh tore at flesh. She should have expected this. Prudence wasn't going to go down without a fight. She saw Prudence's claws coming at her and ducked just in time for her to miss eyes. Fingers moved into the She Wolf's mouth. She snapped her jaw down tight taking three fingers off. Prudence's scream throbbed through Trublood Manor. The She Wolf dropped Prudence to the ground and looked down with an aggressive snarl. She found broken glass pieces that she shoved into the Puritan girl's body. Prudence jerked for a moment before being stopped by blood loss. She stood for a moment amused. It wouldn't keep Prudence down permanently, but it would be enough to move forward. She looked up as she heard her troops chanting for justice. They'd caught someone. It was going to be a good night being home.

L.   A Church is Burning

Now

The sound of the heavy wooden door slamming shut on the sanctuary is what woke him up from the state he was in. He had dozed off in the confessional because it had been a surprisingly quiet night. When the door slammed, it shook him into reality and caused him to run out in a PTSD haze. He stopped and stared for a moment at a young woman who looked like she was breaking apart something in an aisle. He watched for a moment as she gave up on what she was doing and headed towards the altar in a traumatized stagger. Her toes curled awkwardly to compensate for the bruises and cuts on the bottom of her bare feet. He knew that gaunt, haunted expression was from something that she had seen and it was horror. She glanced at him through a sheet of dirty hair. For a moment he wasn't sure if the she was real or not. He felt like he was standing on a dirt street looking at a woman who'd had the same exact expression during what he guessed had to be the same situation. She never cried, she just look very tired.

"My name is Marcia," she said finally, confirming that she was real. "My boyfriend Doyle went crazy."

"Did Doyle do this to you?"

"No, not yet."

Father McCreely opened his mouth and then stopped. He heard something out in the street which he knew all too well. He still wasn't sure if what he was experiencing was real or not. That sounded like the chants of rebel forces in the night. He felt panic go through his body and that meant he was terrified, because he really wasn't ready to fight again.

"Marcia," he said calmly and quietly. "If you can tell me, then I need to know what's going on out there."

"In the streets. I'm not sure you'd believe me if I told you."

"I'm a Catholic Priest in Gaiman Heights. Try me."

"There's a vampire back in town called the She Wolf. I don't remember much of it, but a guy named Carter Lewis wrote about her. She was their queen before she was overthrown. I'm guessing that her loyal supporters are looking for homecoming gifts."

"And they'll be attacking people they feed on. Then we don't have much time. Sunrise is hours from now. Are we safe in here?"

"No."

"That's what I thought," the priest nodded. "Okay then, tell me what you know can hurt them?"

"Fire," Marcia thought out loud quickly. "They really hate fire."

"Are they going to come after us?"

"I…" Marcia's voice trailed into a sob. "I don't know."

"Okay, now listen to me," the priest said firmly, sounding more like a solider. "I have every intention of getting us out of here alive. I can't promise that we will get out safely, but we have advantages. What we have is a building I know better than most and that works in our favor."

He was interrupted by a woman's scream that seeped into the church and echoed with a high pitch of alarms. The doors buckled under a forced entry. He knew they would be okay for a moment more. Those doors could keep out the collective army of Genghis Khan. Of course he wasn't sure if Genghis Khan had had vampires in his ranks. There was then the sound of old French and the chanting and banging stopped. Marcia shook as she stared at the door. They both knew that the vampires would be back. Father McCleery thought for a moment in prayer and then his eyes gazed upward to a stained glass saint. The saint looked back at him with a passive glance under his medieval armor and red and white banner of England. St. George had his foot firmly planted on the dragon's throat and in that moment he knew what he was going to do. Father McCreely stood up quietly.

"They can smell me. I know they can smell me," Marcia said in the first moment of real panic of her day. "They won't stop now. We're going to die because they can smell me."

"No we aren't. We have a weapon they don't."

"The love of God and the blessing of Jesus?"

"No, fuck that. We have a fifty-year-old furnace and a stove that operates on gas in the fellowship hall. We'll let them in and set the tank on fire."

"Well, okay, that wasn't the answer I was expecting."

"Really, I don't think we have much of a choice. I don't think we have time to craft weapons and they hate fire."

"How many of them do you think we can kill?"

"I don't want to think about it like that. After all, this is an unusual situation and it's not supposed to be adversarial."

"Yea, but how many?"

"As many as we can. They come through those doors, they aren't here to confess."

"Good, what do you need me to do?"

They grabbed what they could from the church. He couldn't let the venerated relics that the church had safeguarded for years go up in smoke. Logic told him that they weren't all real and they definitely couldn't be, but as a good Catholic he simply couldn't abandon religious relics to the flames. Fortunately for them, some of the forbearers of this church had figured things may come to this ages ago and chosen to prepare for it. They found a place in the wooded area on the church grounds that seemed made for stashing relics where they would be safe from fire damage.

Next, he and Marcia spent their time making Molotov cocktails as they sat behind the altar. She took a moment to grieve for a man who had done so much for international politics and yet all he would be remembered for was the improvised explosives that bore his name. Father McCreely let out a sigh as he finished ripping up what was left of the altar cloth and shoving the strips down into the half empty bottles of ceremonial wine that he and Marcia had been making less full. It was at least a relaxant for her as she tried to fight off tears. Her eyes glanced up at the priest who was giving her a sympathetic smile.

"So," she said finally. "This something they teach you guys at the seminary?"

"If by seminary you mean two tours ~~on~~ in Barsa and some other awful little village outside Kandahar, then sure. How are you holding up in all of this?"

"I feel sick. Like there is a layer of filth on me that won't ever wash off. Nothing is going to be good again."

"I can't even imagine. Trauma does that to people. I won't bore you with war stories because I can't even begin to understand what you are going through right now. I just know that there are people out there to help. The only thing I can do is ask you a huge favor. I don't know how Doyle is involved, but I know he is. I've known him a very long time. Don't hold this against him; he's a good guy."

"I don't plan to, but what if he holds things against me?"

"Did you do something to him?"

"I asked him to do something in all of this that I know was wrong."

"This is a dangerous time and I can't even begin to understand what you were going through before this. I know that in times like this, we all do things that don't always reflect us as the best people we can be. Doyle will forgive you because I don't think he doesn't do anything at the end of the day that he doesn't ultimately want to do. I hope he forgives because he's a better man with you in his life. Are you ready to do this?"

Marcia nodded.

He walked around opening the vents throughout the church and turned on the stove. The priest looked around and sighed for a moment in deep prayer. He asked for forgiveness and then for hope that it would work. He stood in the back of the church next to the tank putting a long sheet in the fuel spigot and he waited.

Marcia shook as she tried to regain her resolve. This was her plan and her way of striking back. Not just for her but for Doyle who had been tortured, for Carson who was probably now insane under Her thumb and even if she hated him, for Jacob whose soul had been fine until he crossed paths with the She Wolf. She had to strike hard enough to get Her attention if for no other reason than she had to in order to be tactically effective. Marcia took a sharp breath as she gripped the pair of scissors she'd stolen from the vampire queen and forcibly carved into her arm letting a thin line of red form and drop. She felt the silence as she took a step back. Then there was the sound of a heavy thunk against the door and then another. She didn't want to see them bust through -- she ran as fast as she could through the church with snapping jaws behind her. She couldn't outrun the jaws. She knew she couldn't. This was what had to be done.

"Now!" she screamed at the priest.

She felt the overwhelming heat of orange flames push her away from the blast as hard as it could. Suddenly burning pain tore through her as she fell forward, her back being licked by explosive fire. She could hear inhuman screams as the flames blasted blue with human ash. She could have gotten up, but at that point any strength had left her body. The fight was over. At least she was taking some of them down with her and she could die in peace. Marcia shut her eyes waiting to be consumed.

She waited for what felt a very long time. The ground below her shook as something broke through the floorboards in its bright red and gold. It streaked through the fire and picked up what it could describe as something it wanted. Father McCreely stood and watched as the creature and Marcia flew off into the night sky.

LI.   Red is the Color of Angry Men

Now

Light passed in shades of amber and blue as vehicles that had what could only be described as a government looking paint job passed into the streets of Old Gaiman. The sirens announced that there was some sort of law enforcement moving into the streets. The Department could maybe get North and South taken care of, but it would be Trublood Manor that would be overlooked. They could not in good faith take on the capitol without threatening the autonomy of the vampire nations. It would fall to Prudence as it had before to regain control over her people as she had before. If Prudence could get the crowds under control then things would be fine. He knew that the PD wouldn't be involved; neither would the Fire Department. This had become a supernatural problem and protocol said they had nothing to do with this kind of containment.

How fortuitous, he told himself, that he was able to find Norvita before it all got nasty. He knew better though. At this point in his life, there was no such thing as random happenstances. He was fated to find her and be in this moment. He almost expected that his father had set this up. Despite his insistence that he should start seeing Kelsey DeWitt, it was his father who had left the house unexpectedly tonight. Since the death of his mother last year, Weston Lewis knew that his father was not one to go out quietly. He was a private man who spent his time being private and drinking away his pain. Tonight he'd gone out which made Weston very concerned about life in general. Weston Lewis, being the policeman that he was, had tracked his father. He went to Benny's Beach Bar which was a place that his father and mother had frequented regularly. The waitress gave him Carter Lewis' wallet and the Hubert Key. These were things that his father would never leave unless there was something wrong. Carefully, Weston Lewis deduced that the only people who would do harm to his father would have been the vampires now running amok. So he was out on the street looking for him with his armed crossbow when he'd found Norvita.

"Damn it."

Weston Lewis turned his attention back to Norvita as they took a short break in the convenience store parking lot. Norvita looked rough. Her hands were shaking uncontrollably as she brought the energy drink to her lips. He cringed as he watched her spill the drink over her breasts and her shirt that was going immediately into the building's incinerator when she got home. She let out a series of swears as she fumbled with the bottle, managing to set it down in the cup holder before picking up the crossbow to check it for the nineteenth time. This made Weston Lewis more than nervous about it. The open wound on her shoulder had to be affecting her body. He knew this not from the black flakes around the exposed wound but the grimace on her face which was already weak from a long and tired fight. The several times she had nearly drifted off, she'd pull her arm up and press the open wound together. The sting would have been enough to wake her up. He hated himself for this since he made a vow to stop mooning over her, but he could not help but admire Norvita. It wasn't the same as the romantic notions that he'd had before, he tried to tell himself, but it was more like riding into war with a general. You had to admire the fact that Norvita was tired, sick and hurt but she wanted to go back into the fray. For a moment he wondered if this was the experience that his father had being on hunts with his mother. You go out with someone who you trust and you like. He wouldn't admit it, but Weston Lewis was starting to fall in love with Norvita Patel all over again.

She cut him a cold glance when she saw him staring at her.

"Sorry," he said finally. "I need to get you the Department offices. We are…"

"They'll have their hands full if both broods are up in arms and that doesn't stop the She Wolf before it's too late. That's what we need to do."

"Norvita, you're missing a piece of your arm."

"Yea, I'm not worried about it bleeding out. I'm worried about the fact that people are going to die in this city if we don't do anything."

Weston Lewis chuckled at her.

"What?"

"Nothing. Sorry. I forgot you were half hunter."

Norvita narrowed her eyes at Weston Lewis. His body seized up under an icy wave of anger that invaded his body and threatened to stop his heart. The flames of vengeance danced eagerly in her rich brown eyes, just waiting to be let out.

"Whoa," said Weston Lewis. "I didn't mean it like that. You are just really good at hunting and I didn't expect that."

"Karl taught me to hunt for my own safety, not the DeWitts," she replied sharply. "I could care less about them and what they do."

"Karl should be proud of you. You are more than just a psychic. You should hunt more."

"Oh, like you should cop less."

"Touché. I get it. You have the Department and they handle most things. What is there left to hunt anymore?"

"Tonight? Bitch."

Weston Lewis started the vehicle. If their speculations were right they had to be off to Trublood Manor. In addition to it being the grand palace for the vampires it was a meeting place. Where else would someone make their grand entrance? This was it for him; the start of a war he'd never been interested in being a part of. There was nothing noble or romantic about what they were about to do. He wasn't going to be a hero in all of this. This was a bad idea. Norvita was normally too much of a child to be useful, but had proven when it came down she was a valuable fighter. If Karl had trained her then she had his qualities along with natural talent when it came to aiming and shooting. That would be fine and all, but she was hurt and already fraying at the edges with exhaustion. It would only be a matter of time before the adrenaline she was running on quit flowing through her body and she'd crumble like a small paper doll. He wasn't much better. Weston knew that any natural talent he had hadn't been honed and shaped since he joined the force. He wasn't proud of it, but his conditioning had fallen by the wayside since his patrolman days began. Needless to say, he wasn't in fighting shape. A wounded psychic and an out of shape cop were off to fight a vampire queen. This wasn't a war. This was suicide.

"Should we pull over to say something to Carson?" Weston Lewis asked.

"He'll be in recovering sleep.," she replied. "It'll be impossible for him to take."

"Norvita.'

"I'll talk to him later…when everything is done."

Nothing else needed to be said as they parked in an alley one city block in front of Trublood Manor. The pair climbed to the condemned steps of a long abandoned apartment building. Among the rats and dust, they found a vantage point overlooking Execution Square. They watched as the Acadian guard formed a line around the square as who she assumed was their leader and Weston Lewis knew was Heller DeWitt led a hooded figure to the center of the square and dropped him to his knees. This was good for them. The grandstanding of a trial meant they could take out both Heller DeWitt and the She Wolf, which meant that central authority would be down. Cutting the head off the snake, so to speak.

"Weston, I need you to be my eyes," Norvita said finally. "I'm good but we only have this one chance to do any damage before the Guard figures it out. I don't want to waste any bolts on mistakes."

Yes, he was definitely in love with Norvita Patel. He nodded silently as he crouched beside her, watching the crowd carefully. She practiced lining up shots and if she did it right they could take out maybe Heller DeWitt which would take care of the Acadian Guards and then she could hope that she could take down the She Wolf. She would be there for them to hit. That was all Norvita hoped for.

The roaring crowd quieted as the doors to Trublood Manor opened, revealing a regal looking woman in an ornate dress. The light of the street lamps made her dress sparkle with shining stars. Norvita raised her crossbow, aiming at the She Wolf while watching carefully. The She Wolf dropped the limp body of Prudence next to the man in the hood. Norvita hesitated as she saw the hooded figure drop a wrist down next to Prudence. Prudence bared her fangs stealthily to feed on his blood.

"I have defeated the usurper queen," called out the She Wolf loudly. "If you wish to challenge my rule, do it now or I will take anything you do hereafter as treason."

The crowd was silent.

"That's what I thought. My children, I have returned to lead you to glory. First, we must return to our uncontested power and show the world we are not afraid. My fall was only because I was betrayed by my own blood. I was turned over to hunters and the magi for imprisonment and we cannot allow that to happen again. I will send my loyal who shall go forth and find those who betrayed me. Now we have two. Tonight we seek vengeance for a generation of violence that has happened against our people."

An ancient execution block was rolled out before the hooded figure as the She Wolf read off a long list of charges, none of which were in English. Norvita assumed that they were charges because she heard the crowd call back with what sounded like "guilty" after each one was read. This wasn't good. She knew that justice never came from a mob and definitely would not come from this one. She watched as Heller DeWitt picked up what looked like a large axe as two others pushed the hooded man's head down on the block. The She Wolf smiled, knowing that the crowd had made their call. Heller DeWitt removed the hood.

"That's my dad," Weston Lewis whispered. "Norvita, take the shot."

Carter Lewis looked up as best he could. He locked eyes with Norvita for a moment, but it was long enough for a thought to go through his head that he needed her to understand. He had a plan and he needed her to help him with it. Norvita had to listen to him and learn very quickly what he wanted. Hit Heller DeWitt with a headshot. It wouldn't kill him but it would get him out. He'd create a diversion to get Prudence out of this situation. Then take a shot at the She Wolf. Vampires are pack animals so without Heller and the She Wolf they wouldn't be able to attack unless Prudence tells them. Hopefully, someone will take this chance to usurp power from both of them. By then the Department should show up and things will be okay. They can't kill the She Wolf, but we can be in a safer position.

"You can't save me, so don't waste energy trying," he told her. "No one can."

"But," she protested out loud.

"Norvita! Take the goddamn shot!" Weston Lewis yelled at her.

Norvita did what she was told by both men. As Heller DeWitt raised the axe, she fired two bolts rapidly into his skull. She watched him fall like a ton of bricks to the ground. At that same moment, Carter Lewis sprung up futilely towards the She Wolf armed with nothing but vengeance. Norvita only took her eyes off him for a second to see the blur that was Prudence crawl through the crowd and up into the building next to Weston Lewis. When she fired at the She Wolf, it was when she raised her arm in triumph showing a mass of organs that she'd pulled out of the aging hunter. Weston Lewis attempted to let out an anguished scream before Prudence put her hands over the man's mouth to keep him as quiet as possible. Norvita quickly fired into the She Wolf's chest and watched her expression change as she fell back.

The She Wolf's skin turned corpse gray as she started to collapse. Norvita aimed again waiting for her to tumble over next to Heller. But that didn't happen.

As she fell amidst the shocked chaos, a lone figure dragging a body behind him caught her easily as she fell, before running inside with the She Wolf in his arms. The mass of onlookers dissipated quickly from the square, knowing full well that it was only a matter of time before they would be eradicated by the magi save for the Acadian Guard. Those stood loyally in a tight circle around the entrance to Trublood Manor. Norvita aimed again looking for a second shot at the She Wolf as she was taken inside. Before she could fire again, hands pulled on Norvita's pant leg.

"Do not shoot," said Prudence.

"I have a clean shot."

"And Doyle Lanagan has your nexus."

LII.   Table Turned

Now

Here is what happened with Asher and Doyle. I will start with Asher since he is only a little more important. After the nexus got bored and chose to leave, it found a coffee place that had better coffee than the break room somewhere in South Gaiman, which was conveniently open at this late hour. Of course it was South Gaiman and we've talked about the vampires there. The Nexus had enjoyed the coffee until Asher came around. Asher woke up only slightly concerned. He had become somewhat used to this at one time. Of course, those times Asher was using a large amount of drugs and now he wasn't and this was a bit concerning. This meant that the only place he could think the memory lapse came from was the nexus and that irritated him. He hadn't realized that she was becoming more willing and able to take over. He and Doug were going to have to have a word. He wasn't going to trade one bad influence for another one. Then Asher looked down at the table. Before him was a piece of apple pie that was drizzled with caramel and a melting scoop of vanilla bean ice cream. Asher sighed happily.

"Doug, you are too good to me sometimes."

What happened next is a shame because the pie at this place is quite good. Asher would only know this, because when his face hit hard on the plate he tasted a bit of the pie before he fell into unconsciousness.

Doyle, like Carter Lewis, had a plan. Of course this plan was much dumber than Carter Lewis' plan but he knew that he couldn't kill Her himself. After everything She'd done, She was still his maker and he couldn't do that to her, but if he didn't do *something* then she would always be around and the supernatural world would be unbalanced, not to mention his own personal miserable enslavement to her bloody, sadistic whims. What he did know was that if he fed his Mistress an edible bomb, then he could get away with it technically. He also knew that he wouldn't have his resolve for much longer and he certainly didn't have time to fight with Asher, who seemed like someone who would fight. After he knocked out Asher with a rather impressive sneak attack, he marched off to Trublood Manor.

When they arrived, the crowds were already getting rabid with their manic chanting. Doyle kept his head down as he heard the whistle and thunk of a bolt going through Heller DeWitt's skull. This was it. Someone had already begun taking measures to end this fight and he could have been pleased, but that only lasted until he saw his Mistress fall. Doyle couldn't have that. Vampire ties are wired hard. He ran ~~as~~ quickly to catch her and ran with her in his arms with the terror of Her being shot again. They took off to the safety of the throne room.

He set her in Prudence's high throne. The She Wolf screamed as she pulled the hemlock-tipped bolts from her body. Dolls were thrown and shattered as they were repelled away from her. He watched her body swell and bloat with each passing second. She was getting sicker with each passing second as black passed into her vein. For a moment Doyle furrowed his brow and thought to himself. Her powerful grip loosened on him. He looked at her and realized that the years of punishment made him sick to death of Her. She looked up at him contentiously. The murder of her new favorite was on the cuffs of his clothing. The dogs were gone and now she had to wait for her salvation ~~had~~ to come from her biggest mistake.

"You traitor," She spat at him. "You betrayed me one to those filthy hunters before and I bet you've done it again. Why shouldn't I just rip you apart?"

Doyle laid Asher in her lap. She blinked as she looked down at the angel. She dabbed a finger on his oozing head wound and licked quietly. She let out an elegant purr as life started to return to her body. Doyle struggled with his hatred, but if she took things slowly then he knew he was going to lose himself in her bloodlust and strength of command. He knew this was true as he dropped to his knees, secretly pleased with himself. She had forgiven his transgressions.

"Oh, Doyle, how I have misjudged you," She squealed. "What is he?"

"The reason your master came to this city," answered Doyle. "And he is yours to consume."

"Good."

Doyle stripped Asher of his shirt and propped him up in the throne. She straddled Asher in a custom that Doyle had become all too familiar with. He watched as she groaned against the tattooed mage. Her fingers traced the ink-scarred skin entranced with the workmanship. Despite her travels, she hadn't seen anything like this. Had he been some sort of savage like the ones she'd read about? If he was then he had to be powerful and that pleased her. She had a powerful and brave man in her clutches. And he also tasted and smelled amazing.

Doyle was growing concerned as he struggled to keep his head about him. She had been publically shot by a hunter's arrow. So had Heller DeWitt. The crowds may have come to their wits and maybe they could all move on with their lives. That wasn't what he worried about. He had the Department's golden boy. If they stormed the Palace to get him back there would be a world of trouble. People would die. Doyle prayed for him to wake up and get his magic on.

After what seemed like an eternity, Asher drifted back to reality. Panic worked through him until he locked eyes with Her. That fear worked out of his body quickly as he leaned into her fingers. His will power slipped away as she saw her smile. She was suddenly everything that he wanted. In an instant he stopped caring about Natalie, his mother, and even the Department. This was his new life. If the nexus knew he was in danger she wasn't saying anything or trying to take over. She couldn't. Asher's will had always been stronger than her and he was busy being Hers. He smiled sheepishly as her cold lips brushed against his.

"I like how you smell, brave boy," She said. "You are very handsome."

"Can I put my mouth on you?" he asked.

"Soon, you and I are going to be together for a very long time," She said. "Now, brave boy, I need your help. Your Mistress is sick. I bet you can make me well."

"Anything you ask."

"Show me where I can drink from you where I won't ruin your pretty pictures."

Asher looked down along his torso. His fingers traced along as they searched for a clean spot. Doyle watched her frantic hunt excitedly. He wanted something but it wasn't Her. In this moment he saw her for what she was. She was an angry, desperate woman who had used him for the last few centuries for her own ego. Doyle felt ill as he thought about it and then he thought about himself. He ran the South Gaiman Brood pretty well. He was the heir to Prudence and next in line to be king. He'd sort of civilized Carson which he thought made him in line to be a saint. And in the last two years he'd found a girl who was smart and sexy. She loved him despite the fact that he was Doyle and that made him love her more. Doyle looked at the She Wolf and realized that he didn't need her anymore. He was just much better than that.

She found a spot under Asher's navel. Her tongue lapped at his skin bringing forth several purple veins. Asher let out a groan of pleasure as she sank her fangs into the largest vein. Doyle watched her with baited breath as she greedily drank.

First, her wounds oozed out the poison of the hemlock that stained the cushions. The deathly pallor of her complexion dissipated, leaving her skin glowing with a bright radiance. She then felt a cold light dance off her skin. She broke off her feeding, leaving Asher to slump like a rag doll. She grinned at her new power that danced within her. She flew out of the throne room and back to Execution Square. She let out a loud call that echoed joyously through the city. They loved her as their queen, they would adore her as their God. She watched as the crowd returned to watch her come into her glory. Even the Department had sent containment vehicles at this point and they couldn't stop her. She now had a grand audience for her glorious coronation. That's when the pain started.

It was in the pit of her stomach at first. It then it started to expand painfully out to her hips and stomach. Then her hands and fingers joined in the swelling. Her skin started to rip apart, letting out light and boiling blood. Her body because rounder as she started to swell. She turned back to the Palace in anger. She'd been betrayed again. Sure enough, Doyle stood in the doorway with with a small amount of sadistic pleasure.

"You ungrateful bastard," She hissed as her hair curled and smelled of fire. "What did you do to me?"

"Just doing what you could never do," Doyle said. "Let go."

"Who the hell do you think you are?"

She lunged at Doyle. Doyle quickly found his boot on her chest. On a good day, the She Wolf would have broken off his foot and beaten him unconscious with it, but at this point she was far from a good day. She stumbled back hitting her knees on the block. With the sway of his arm she was in the correct position on the block. She was far too bloated with incompatible power at this point to get up. Doyle watched as she floundered with an ounce of pity. That moment passed as he picked up the axe. With all his strength, he brought the head down on her neck.

Doyle found himself questioning his better judgment as he was flung backwards in the resulting explosion. The ground shook, cracking the foundations of the surrounding buildings. A line of ash went out from her neck stump and the execution block.

A scream tore out of Doyle's mouth as her body fell, severing the blood tie. He climbed to his feet. His hands kept a white-knuckled grip on the axe. He looked at the crowd with a wild-eyed expression and fangs drawn. He glanced up to the abandoned building. He saw the face of Prudence Goodchild. She nodded, approving as his action. Who said he wouldn't be a great king?

"I defeated your queen," he yelled loudly. "I'm Lord now. You have ten minutes to challenge me or keep your bloody mouth shut. Otherwise get off my palace land or I will take your fucking head."

Doyle watched the crowds disperse quickly. He looked up.

"Oi, Lewis!" he yelled. "I'll trade you the nexus for my brother. Think about it. I'll be easy to find."

Doyle walked back into Trublood Manor. It was over, he told himself. For the first time in life he had nothing hanging over his head. He'd see if Carson was all right. He was pretty certain from the blood tie feedback that he was in terrible pain. But it was the best for both of them. They'd be fine from this point forward. Then he'd go out and find Marcia. He had to tell her he loved her. They had to move forward.

Doyle stopped as he saw a figure lunging at him. Doyle would have been more concerned if his attacker wasn't missing at least a pint of blood. He watched Asher fall flat on his face. Doyle crouched down beside him.

"Have you never given blood before?" he asked Asher. "Blood loss like that causes you to be a little faint, especially when making sudden movements. You should rest until you get your strength back up. Maybe drink some fluids."

"You badly-written 90s stereotype," Asher yelled from face down on the floor. "I WILL murder you."

"Course you will. Want me to get you some juice and cookies?"

"Y-yes."

* * * *

Elsewhere.

It was the television that woke her up. It was the distinct sound of brightly colored puppies that were singing about friendship on the TV. She rolled her head to the side and blinked weakly. The last thing she could remember was the church and the fire. She should be dead and maybe she was. No, this was her apartment and that was always a sign of things being sort of normal. Had she gotten a look at what pulled her out? No, she didn't but that didn't help the fact that her back hurt.

She looked up and recognized the posters with her speckled ceiling. She was home. That was her couch and her living room. She sat up holding the blanket to her breasts as she looked over. She felt her body shake at the residual image of the fire. That's when she saw her.

The little girl she saw was sitting on her knees and was very small. In the television light she saw a petite girl with curly black hair. Marcia watched the little girl roll up the sleeves of Norvita's band T-shirt. She shook at an incorrect assumption. Her hands covered her stomach terrified.

"How?" She whispered as tears rolled down her cheeks. The little girl turned and smiled, letting her deep amber eyes dance in the dark. Marcia knew that this was her savior. It didn't change the question.

"I just learned how to do that," said the little girl proudly. "Are you proud of me, mummy?"

"M-mommy?" Marcia panicked. "I'm not…"

"I saw you when I hatched so I assumed you are my mother. I know we aren't exactly the same species, but I don't know anything else. So, mommy."

"Why does everyone insist on making me a mother?"

"Because at thirty-three and after one miscarriage you are starting to question if you'll ever have kids."

She stopped herself with a hand across her mouth and climbed on to the couch and sat beside Marcia. "But you are stronger than most mundane people and that's really nice. I don't have a real mommy I guess, but you are nice and strong and you were willing to sacrifice yourself for a stranger. I want you to be my mommy."

Marcia found herself clinging to the little girl as she finally started crying. Maybe it was being exhausted from everything or maybe she'd finally reached a breaking point, but all she could do was hug the little girl who just hugged her right back.

LIII.   The Place of Dead Roads

I

Jodee looked at the two men who sat across from him. His jaw hurt from his encounter but this wasn't the time to complain or to bitch about it. They looked at him with as clear and concise a look as the man in the neatly pressed suit looked at him. If he didn't like Ed Trumper before, he definitely didn't like him now. How was he supposed to know that the man he took a shot at was a part of the Department. He wasn't a man when he'd looked at him. He was something else and it was something terrible. However, it wasn't something he'd seen before and they needed to know whether or not it was one of theirs. Besides, Arlis Thursday paced behind him and that meant at least he wasn't in too much trouble.

"And you shot it?" asked Edmund Trumper in a crisp English accent.

"As I said, it had an aura of evil and I did what I thought we needed to do. Bullet didn't take it down too much and I couldn't get it in a binding circle," explained Jodee. "I don't know if it's your missing fella or not, but if it was he ain't human no more."

"Spangler is a Marked man. Perhaps what you saw was demonic?"

"Marked man or not, I know a demon when I see one. He wasn't a demon. I just know that something happened to your man and I don't know what it was. By now he could be somewhere far, far away."

II

A man in a long black coat leaned over his table as he watched the front door before taking the cup of coffee he was nursing to his lips and then stopped. He paused for a moment taking in the smell and feel of this small diner on highway 11. If things had stayed the same, this place would have been buzzing with life and people in it. Highway 11 connected New Orleans to the North and was the major road. That was long before Eisenhower and the highway system. Since then, the major roads came in and this place had barely changed since then. There had been small upgrades here and there. For example, the TV where the fat man was talking about the weather had been upgraded to a slick thin TV as opposed to some sort of Rabbit eared thing. It didn't drown out the old boys who were trying to figure out the world's problems while they were drinking coffee. They didn't notice him in the corner.

Few did.

He was hard to look at for too long. It wasn't that he was unattractive. In fact, he was a solidly averagely handsome man. There was something about him that made him hard to look at. Maybe he was too average, but he made people very, very uncomfortable. That was fine; he'd rather not interact unless he had to. Today he needed interaction though. The man looked at his watch with his brow furrowed.

Just as he'd predicted, Karl Spangler staggered into the diner, only gaining the briefest attention of the brain trust, but more importantly the lady behind the counter. He wasn't too surprised by that. Karl was beaten and mangled looking and that meant that he had to go on to be ignored. The waitress didn't ignore him. She quickly poured Karl a cup of coffee as he sat at the counter with a blink and shake of his head to clear his mind.

"Still serving breakfast?" he asked, not slowly, but carefully, as if he were remembering how to talk.

"Up until 11:00 and not a minute later," said the waitress.

"Good. I would like the Denver omelet, hash browns, grits, two stacks of hotcakes, toast with jam, sausage gravy and biscuits, and bacon."

"Anything else, darling?"

"Can I use your phone?"

The waitress nodded as she walked back to the kitchen. The man in the long black coat made a note in a journal he was carrying and looked up.

"Hungry?" he yelled at Karl.

"Famished," Karl said between sips of coffee. "It's been a hell of a night."

"And it's not even done yet, Karl."

Karl sat up and found himself turning to eyeball the man in the long black coat. All Karl did see was an empty table.

III.

Weston Lewis sat at a table with his hands folded as Prudence had tea poured into his cup. He watched Prudence as she sat across from him. She gave him a pleasant smile. He looked tired but that had to be the case with these mortals. Burying a parent was never easy. She would know. Prudence had been permitted to live in Trublood manor as she'd had nowhere else to go. Doyle had no real problem with this since this was an unusual situation -- deposing one queen, while another was still in residence -- but he was quite all right with things. Despite everything, Prudence was rather happy with what had happened. She had invited Weston Lewis to the Manor. He was angry and she knew that. Carter Lewis was angry when his family died in the war and now it was Weston's turn.

She looked up at him with her placid expression.

"I am truly sorry for Carter. He was a good friend and he was an amazing man," she said. "Can I assume you wouldn't be following your father's wishes?"

"I don't know. He arranged a marriage between me and a DeWitt but it all seems like it's… fate."

"Weston, before your father died, I shared with him the works of Dagmar of Bavaria. She knew that things were heading towards us in violence. I think what we need to know is that things are starting towards a new world. I think that we need to start thinking about the world we are heading towards."

"What does that mean?"

"It means that maybe you are better off taking your father's advice and hanging out with the DeWitt girl. Patel is an island that you'll crash your ship on."

"What will you do now?"

"I don't know yet. I thought I'd be dead at the end of this. Perhaps I shall find myself a playmate."

IV

When Carter Lewis pushed open the door he was dumbfounded. Before him was a large cathedral that stretched out forever. Sunlit illuminated the stain glassed windows lined with holly. Was this his eternal fate? Trapped in the limbo of advent in a sparsely attended church? He shouldn't complain. There were worse hells that he could be in, but not by much.

"Carter, over here." a familiar voice called. "You made it."

Carter Lewis' heart leapt when he heard her voice. Before he knew it, he sat in a pew clutching the hand of the only one who mattered. Hell or Heaven or something else, it mattered not. Carter Lewis finally knew peace.

V.

"Will you hold still?"

Marcia gave Doyle a serious scowl as she stood over him with a pair of scissors. He tried to hold still as she sat down on his lap again with an apologetic smile. Her fingers played over the stitching on his chest as she brought it up to a place where she could clip the strings off. He steadied his hands against her hips as she looked down at him.

"You're cheating, Uncle Carson!" yelled a little voice outside the room. "Stop cheating!"

"No I ain't. You just don't know how to play yet."

He heard Marcia let out a sigh as she tried to not roll her eyes. Doyle could find himself chuckling quietly at the sounds of unusual domestic bliss. He didn't have to think of the child as his. He didn't have to stick with Marcia. She'd given him an out. That was stupid. Doyle had been hoping for something like this in his after life and now he'd gotten it. The person who was having a better time was Carson. Something about being an uncle made Carson exceedingly happy.

He had the whole family with him in the Penthouse that had been given to him as his residence. He would use Trublood Manor as the center of business, but he wasn't going to live there. Prudence would remain there and more likely serve as the Burgesses. He glanced out a widow as neon lights danced in the sundown. He watched for a moment as she finally cut the stitching loosening the skin with a sting. She let out a frown as she looked at her handiwork. She wasn't happy about it, but things would be okay. They would be okay. It wouldn't be yet, but they were moving forward.

"I could have done better," she said with a frown. It looks like I stabbed you all over again."

"My wounds will heal," he told her. "Thank you."

She smiled at him, looking down from his lap. They would work at it. After everything, to throw it away in a rage was not worth it. They could move forward together.

"Still going out?"

"Heller DeWitt isn't dead and that means he could raise his forces," Doyle said. "If they don't fear me, then that puts you and Scarlett in danger."

"Well, I need to get that one down for sleep anyway. Shall I wait for you in the resting chamber, my king?"

"I'm not king, I'm the Taoiseach. Sounds more honest."

"I was hitting on you, Doyle. Learn to pick up signals."

"Oh?" Then a thought crossed his mind. "Oh! Yes."

She smiled at him as she slipped off his lap with a relieved kiss. They would be all right. She knew that they would be all right. Doyle wasn't completely healed, but he'd get there and so would she. She was stronger than she looked. He pulled down his shirt as he walked out of the study. He nodded at Carson as he picked up his gold club. It was a hunting night and they would have to find something good.

The End...for Now.

www.ingramcontent.com/pod-product-compliance
Lightning Source LLC
Chambersburg PA
CBHW070753280626
47162CB00016B/210